INTERVIEW
WITH THE DEVIL

A Christian Journalist
A Muslim Extremist
A FORMULA FOR TERROR

By
CLAY JACOBSEN

*A MAN IS APPOINTED ONCE TO DIE,
THEN JUDGEMENT.*

PROMISE PRESS
An Imprint of Barbour Publishing

Acquisitions & Editorial Director: Mike Nappa
Editorial Consultant: Jody Brolsma
Art Director: Robyn Martins

Scripture quotations are taken from either the Holy Bible, King James Version or from the HOLY BIBLE, NEW INTERNATIONAL VERSION®. NIV®. Copyright © 1973, 1978, 1984 by International Bible Society. Used by permission of Zondervan Publishing House. All Rights Reserved.

Published by Promise Press, an imprint of Barbour Publishing, Inc., P.O. Box 719, Uhrichsville, Ohio 44683, www.promisepress.com

Member of the
Evangelical Christian
Publishers Association

Printed in the United States of America.

DEDICATION

While researching this story, I grew to have an incredible respect for the journalists who put their lives on the line daily in war-torn areas throughout the globe. Their dedication and self-sacrifice in order to bring us the news about world events is inspiring.

As I was nearing the completion of this manuscript, Daniel Pearl, the reporter from the *Wall Street Journal,* was kidnapped. His disappearance and subsequent torturous murder affected me greatly and serves as an example of the enormous dangers journalists face when covering the volatile Middle East. In honor of his tragic death, I wish to dedicate this novel to the memory of Daniel Pearl—and also to the innocent lives that have been tragically lost at the hands of Islamic extremists, from 9/11 and other acts of terror around the world. I pray that God will comfort their families with His presence. My hope is that the world will be at peace, yet I know that will only truly come from the Prince of Peace, Jesus Christ.

PROLOGUE

The North Syrian Desert
Mid-January

At first there was nothing, a void to be embraced.

Then flashes of green light darted across Mark Taylor's vision, appearing like fireflies dancing in the blackness of a moonless Tennessee night. Next came the pain. . .terrifying waves of agony. He fought desperately to keep hold of the darkness.

Through the mental fog, his first thought took shape. . .not about himself, where he was, or how many bones might be broken, but a hazy impression of his wife, Tracy. The image lured him toward consciousness. His eyes blinked open, the light immediately piercing through his head. He winced and shut them in a vain attempt to block out the pain.

After a moment he tried again, slowly this time. Before he could orient himself, he heard footsteps. Holding the image of the stark room and dirt floor around him in his mind, Mark gently closed his eyes and lay still.

There were voices now, but he couldn't make out the words. Arabic? It sounded like it. The noises combined with the pain began to clear his head.

He remembered where he was—somewhere in the Middle East—Turkey, possibly Syria. And as the thought took shape, so did the realization that he was in desperate trouble.

Lying on his side, Mark was curled up in a fetal position on the hard surface. There was no way to tell how long he'd been unconscious. As the voices approached, he remained motionless, taking in short, shallow breaths.

Suddenly a shower of foul-smelling liquid drenched him. His

attempt to feign unconsciousness shattered as he gagged and coughed. The pain throughout his body was nearly unbearable.

"I trust you've had a pleasant nap," a voice spoke above him in near-perfect English.

Spitting away the putrid water and wiping at his eyes, Mark looked up. Surrounded by three men brandishing AK-47s stood Ahmad Hani Sa'id, the infamous leader of the Jihad al Sharia terrorist network.

"Now, Mr. Taylor," Sa'id continued calmly, "I think it's time you and I had another little chat."

Chapter 1

She sat on the edge of the tub, watching—waiting, looking at her watch, then glancing back at the strip on the counter. Fidgeting with her hands, Tracy Taylor mindlessly pushed back the cuticles of two fingernails before taking note of the time once again.

A faint glow was just beginning to appear in the eastern sky. Tracy had lain awake most of the night. The deep breathing of her husband had soothed her, at times enough to catch a few restless moments of sleep. Then she'd wake up again, wondering. She was over three weeks late—something not that uncommon with her, but this time it felt, well. . .different.

On the way home from class the day before, she'd stopped at the drugstore and picked up the pregnancy test. She was too nervous to take it then and had placed it in her closet, hidden under her sweaters until a few minutes ago when the curiosity finally overcame her.

She stood up, glancing at herself in the mirror, then turned sideways, lifting the fabric of her nightgown away from her body as if her stomach were the size of a basketball. She smiled, moving her right hand slowly over her imaginary belly. How would her small frame handle the transformation if she were pregnant? She puffed out her cheeks, giggling at the image facing her in the mirror.

She tiptoed across the bathroom and glanced through the

crack in the doorway out to the bedroom beyond. Mark was curled up under a heap of covers, his unruly brown hair sticking up in all directions, his breathing even but heavy. Her stomach tingled deep inside. How would he handle it? They hadn't even been married a year. She knew he wanted children. . .someday.

His alarm would ring in the next few minutes. She looked down at her watch anxiously. It was time!

DAMASCUS, SYRIA
5:07 P.M.

Josh Mclintock walked along the busy street, glancing nervously over his shoulder every few steps. The avenue, Souk as-Sarouja, was crowded with shoppers lining the narrow road, buying the latest fashions and jewelry from the vine-covered old homes. The shop-keepers fought for his attention, waving their goods at him as he passed, but he had no interest in haggling.

He walked toward the Thawra Bridge just as he'd been in-structed on the phone one hour ago, waiting for Mustafa to con-tact him.

Josh raised his shoulders and tucked his head slightly into his black overcoat as a gust of wind sent a chill down his neck. *Anytime, Mustafa,* he thought nervously as he continued to walk.

Josh Mclintock was the Middle East deputy chief for National Network's cable news division, and their lead on-air reporter. All aspects of the War on Terror from this part of the world were under his control. He'd been living in Syria for the past six months as America's focus had shifted to this part of the Middle East.

With the overthrow of the Taliban and the al-Qaida terrorist network based in Afghanistan nearly two years before, Americans had begun to settle back into their pre-9/11 sense of security when a series of new attacks once again plunged the nation into a massive state of fear and uncertainty. The first wave was the Sunday Massacre, when four school buses exploded within minutes of each other inside National Football League stadiums in Chicago, Dallas, New Orleans, and Washington, D.C., killing over twelve thousand people and injuring tens of thousands more. The suicide terrorists had approached the entrances to the stadiums during halftime, driving school buses marked from cities that had been invited to appear in the special activities. All but one was allowed to pull up into the loading areas just before the bombs went off. Thanks to an alert security guard in Chicago, one bus didn't get under the stadium. Thousands of lives had been saved.

Next came the bombings of the American embassies three weeks ago on Christmas morning in Saudi Arabia, Kuwait, and Egypt, again timed within minutes of each other. Nine hundred more lives tragically ended. It was reminiscent of the type of planning attributed to Osama bin Laden. . .and had America in another tailspin.

As evidence was collected from the various law enforcement and security agencies, all information pointed to one place: the Jihad al Sharia network. Its leader, Ahmad Hani Sa'id, was an enigma to the Western intelligence coalition. Their file on him was paper thin, only a brief history of his childhood years in Saudi Arabia as the son of an oil sheik before he disappeared at the age of eighteen. He had resurfaced within the past five years as head of the terrorist network believed to be based in the northern desert of Syria. . .undoubtedly the next target for American cruise missiles and laser-guided bombs.

The relationship Mclintock had with Mustafa wasn't official. Any of his dealings with the Arab were kept secret and never reported to his superiors back in New York. To do so would be to cut off any further source of information from inside the terrorist organization, useful tidbits that had kept National News a step ahead of the competition in the Middle East. Of course, the other reason Mclintock had to keep any dealings with Mustafa secret was to protect his own skin. Mustafa had made that very clear the first time Mclintock was contacted.

"Good to see you again, Josh," the heavily accented voice echoed from behind him, freezing Josh in place. He turned slowly, seeing the shape of a robed figure in the shadows of an alley to his left. Josh glanced down the street quickly, then stepped into the darkness behind the as-Saada Hotel.

"I hope this is important." The newsman tried to keep an edge of irritation in his voice to mask the fear he always felt in the presence of Mustafa. Josh knew he was connected somewhere at the top of the terrorists' hierarchy. Every tip he'd received was dead-on, usually resulting in Josh looking like a genius for being in the right place at the right time.

Mustafa placed a bitter-smelling Arab cigarette up to his lips and took a long drag before responding. "I think you'll find your trip worthwhile."

Josh didn't respond, having learned it was not wise to engage in unnecessary conversation.

"Sa'id wishes to grant your network an interview."

Josh was shocked. Was this some kind of joke? He studied the face of the terrorist, looking for any hint of deception under the black turban—there was none, just the dark, lifeless eyes.

"Ahmad Hani Sa'id? I find that hard to believe." Josh laughed cynically. "He's never been interviewed or even photographed since he was eighteen."

"It is time," Mustafa answered matter-of-factly.

Josh angled his head, juggling the possibilities. If Mustafa was for real, this would be the scoop of a lifetime—his ticket out of cable news and straight to a major network.

"An interview with Sa'id? How would I even know it's him?"

Mustafa grunted through his long beard. "There will be proof, but this interview is not for you."

"What do you mean not for me?" Josh spit back angrily. "I've been stuck in this hellhole for over three years covering this blasted war. I've earned the right. . . ."

"No!" Mustafa's hand lashed out and grabbed Josh's face, his fingers sinking into the flesh of his cheeks. "You have no rights! Sa'id does not care that you have suffered so terribly living in this 'hellhole,' as you call it!"

Josh pulled away, breaking the hold of the terrorist as the precariousness of his situation became crystal clear. He stretched his jaw, then rubbed at his bruised cheeks.

"The interview will take place in three days. On that day, he will talk to only one man from your network in *America.*" Mustafa spoke the last word with seething hatred.

"And that man is Mark Taylor."

STUDIO CITY, CALIFORNIA
7:10 A.M.

"Another day of sunshine here in the Southland," the disembodied voice filled the bedroom as the clock radio broke the early morning silence. Mark groggily slapped the button on top of the clock radio, then rolled over on his side, his left arm reaching out to take Tracy and engulf her in their morning ritual of cuddling through the first snooze period. When he grabbed nothing but sheets and a pillow, his eyes opened in surprise.

"Tracy?" he called. She wasn't a morning person, usually staying in bed through Mark's shower.

She came out of the bathroom with a leap, landing on top of Mark and pinning him under the covers.

"You called?" She laughed directly over him.

"Yes, I did," Mark answered with a smile, never growing tired

11

of her beautiful face, outlined exquisitely by her long dark hair. He stretched his neck up to kiss her warmly on the lips. She responded eagerly as she leaned forward, allowing him to lay his head back on the pillow. The kiss lingered.

"My, aren't we cheerful this morning?" Mark said when she finally pulled back.

Tracy blushed, rolling off beside Mark. "Why not? It's a beautiful day, and just looking at you lying there, well. . ."

Mark laughed; he knew his hair would be a mess, not to mention the stubble on his face and the morning breath. But if Tracy found that desirable. . .who was he to argue?

He made a move toward her as the radio blared back to life. At the same instant he was pressed deeper into the bed as Shandy, their sheltie, jumped up onto the bed between them. Mark looked into the passion evident in Tracy's emerald green eyes and groaned as he reached over and gave the dog a quick scratch around the ears. The digital display on the clock radio read 7:15 A.M. He shook his head and shut the alarm off.

"I need to get moving. Staff meeting today."

Tracy met his gaze as she reached up and caressed his rough cheek. "I know."

Then her eyes twinkled and a fiendish grin spread over her face. She jumped off the bed, heading back to the bathroom as she yelled over Shandy's barking, "Race you to the shower."

"What time do you think you'll get home tonight?" Tracy asked thirty-seven minutes later as Mark was settling into the black leather seat of his silver Lexus.

"It shouldn't be too late, maybe around six, six-thirty." Now clean-shaven and ready for work, Mark's hair only managed to flare out in a few spots. Tracy found it charming.

"Good." She smiled. "How about I have dinner ready for us here?"

Mark leaned toward the window with raised eyebrows. "Don't you have to study tonight?"

Tracy leaned in and gave him a quick kiss. "Nothing that can't wait. Let's make tonight special."

He grinned as he started the car. "That sounds good to me. I'll see you tonight, honey."

Tracy watched Mark back out of the driveway, then waved as he spun off down the street. They had met several years ago when Mark, an investigative television journalist, was working on a story about public opinion polling. He'd chosen her grandfather's firm to do his research, and since Tracy was the press liaison for the company, she had shown Mark how the business worked. There was an immediate attraction between the two that quickly blossomed into a romance, complicated greatly by Mark's investigation proving to be the downfall of her grandfather and his media empire.

If she were pregnant, how would she tell Mark? The plan for dinner had just spilled out, but the more she thought about it, the more she liked the idea. There were a couple of steaks in the freezer. . .or maybe she should make something Italian, reminiscent of their first meal together. Mark would come home to a lovely romantic dinner, soft music playing lightly in the background, candles flickering on the table. Tracy giggled as she wondered how far into the evening she could get before blurting out the news.

But first she had to be sure. The home test had turned out positive, but they weren't 100 percent accurate. This was going to change their lives. . .ready or not! She'd recently enrolled in law school at UCLA. She could complete this school year without any complications from the pregnancy, but she'd still be a year away from graduating. How would she finish her degree with a newborn around the house? She smiled, gently touching her belly. *We'll just have to figure that out, won't we?*

She walked back into the house, heading toward the bedroom.

Her early class would have to do without her today. She decided to be the first appointment at her doctor's office instead.

CIA Headquarters, Langley, Virginia
11:32 a.m.

While most people on the East Coast were entertaining ideas of where they might go to lunch at the halfway point of the workday, Wendy Hamilton had already been at her desk for over six hours. As a CIA analyst for Middle Eastern covert surveillance, she couldn't find enough hours in the day without starting before the sun rose.

She had begun her intelligence career in January of 2002. She was one of thousands who had applied to the agency after the hijacked airliners had crashed into the World Trade Center and the Pentagon. They were called the 9/11 class.

Wendy had a lot going for her: a double major in psychology and sociology from Dartmouth, and she spoke three foreign languages fluently—French, Farsi, and Arabic. At five feet three inches, she had an athletically trim body and brunette hair accented by natural blond streaks. She had accelerated her schooling so that she had enough credits for graduation a semester early. Then, to the surprise of her parents, who had wished a more normal life for her, she applied to the CIA.

Wendy had made her way through only half of the reports stacked in front of her this day when Phillip Nest entered the cubicle they shared, carrying an armful of reports accented with large colored banners and the words TOP SECRET.

"Just what we need, more field reports," he muttered, setting them down on her desk. Wendy and Phillip were just two of the thirty employees who shared the huge space separated by half-walled cubicles on the lower floor of the Old Building. Phillip had been with the agency for over three years and was amazed at how quickly Wendy had picked up the spy trade. She had poured herself into the job, having an uncanny knack at spotting associations and picking out patterns in what seemed to be unrelated people and events.

Wendy glanced up. "Anything important?"

"Don't know," Phillip responded. "Haven't looked through it."

Wendy sighed and picked up the top part of the stack, flipping through the reports as she gave each a quick glance. Too often, it felt like her job whittled down to pushing papers around her desk or staring at her computer screen for hours on end. It was frustrating when all she wanted was to get definitive intelligence on the Jihad al Sharia terrorist network.

Her analysis of the reports was interrupted by a *beep* from her computer. Something had triggered one of the many alarms she kept activated. She put the papers aside and reached for the mouse as her eyes scanned the dialogue box on the screen.

"What have you got?" Phillip asked from behind her.

"Another NSA report that mentions Sa'id," Wendy answered calmly. She received a hundred of these alerts per day, but it was worth it to make sure nothing of importance slipped past her desk. She clicked on the "open" button and waited the few seconds until her screen was filled with the document that had triggered the alarm. That's when her eyes widened and her heartbeat increased dramatically as she read the words on the screen in front of her.

NATIONAL STUDIOS, HOLLYWOOD, CALIFORNIA
8:51 A.M.

Mark parked his Lexus behind three other cars waiting at the front gate of National Studios. It was the same routine every morning since the attacks at the football stadiums in November. Once he reached the guard shack underneath the archway with the huge studio logo, he popped the trunk for one guard to search inside while another one checked his ID. They both knew him well, having played this routine over and over five days a week. They'd had similar procedures after the 9/11 attacks, but those had slowly fizzled out as time passed. Now they were back in full swing.

To Mark it served as a daily reminder of the terrorists' war on America and inspired him to spend the minutes driving into the studio to pray for his country and her leadership. The freedoms he'd taken for granted so many years seemed a little more precious each day.

He made it to the production office a few minutes before the scheduled meeting, allowing him time to put his briefcase in his cubicle before heading into the conference room.

Their show was called *Across the Nation,* a newsmagazine broadcast similar to *60 Minutes* or *Dateline NBC.* The National Network had not achieved the status of the big four networks, but they were gaining. Through local affiliates and their access on cable and satellite, they now covered over 90 percent of American households, and in some markets their coverage of the War on Terror on the cable news division was rating higher than CNN and Fox News. *Across the Nation* was in its third season, airing twice a week on Sunday and Thursday nights.

Mark walked into the bustling room full of people and settled into the chair next to his producer, Ross Berman. At six feet-four inches, Ross made Mark feel short at five-ten. Compared to Mark's casual dress of a pair of Levi's and denim shirt, Ross looked like a GQ model with his jet-black hair and trim physique displayed in pressed charcoal gray slacks and sport coat over a silky, knit black shirt. He had joined the show at the start of this season, a recent graduate of Princeton University in broadcast journalism. He still had a lot to learn, but Mark didn't want to tell him that.

"I got the interview lined up with Senator Boxer," Ross whispered to him.

"When?" Mark was impressed. He had been unable to get her office to commit to a story they were doing on an upcoming bill before the Senate that Boxer was cosponsoring.

"Tomorrow afternoon before the show, she'll be in town for a fund-raiser."

Mark nodded his head. That would be perfect.

"Mark, Ross. . .Frank wants to see you in his office right away," Heather Franklin, the assistant to the executive producer, called out from the conference room doorway.

Mark flashed an inquisitive glance over to Ross before getting up from his chair. "I wonder what we've done now?"

Frank Russell was sitting behind his desk looking outside the window at the huge stage across the alley. Mark had great respect for his boss, a former NBC news reporter some twenty-plus years ago. Russell clung to the principles of classic journalism and spent most of his time fighting with either the network's top brass or their legal department. He'd mentored Mark, teaching him that the heart of reporting was the story. . .to never let the ever-present Ivy League executives and the pushy bean counters stop him from getting to the truth.

"Come in, boys; take a seat," Russell ordered without turning from the window.

They quietly obeyed. A moment passed before Russell turned around in his squeaky executive chair. Although the same gruff exterior confronted Mark, he sensed something was up. Russell's bald head shone from the reflection of the light above the desk as he tilted his head down to be able to see them above his reading glasses. His eyes! That was it. They were sharper, more alive than his normal tired-of-fighting-the-network-executives look.

"I just received a call from Steve Thompson, the head of our cable news network in New York." He pulled his glasses off and looked directly at Mark as the corners of his mouth raised ever so slightly. "It seems that you've been invited to interview Ahmad Hani Sa'id."

Mark blinked, attempting to comprehend what he'd just heard. Russell waited patiently for his response.

It was Ross who spoke first, swearing excitedly.

"Are you s–serious?" Mark finally stammered.

"Dead serious, pardon the expression."

"But that's impossible," Mark exclaimed. *Where? When?* There were so many questions running through his mind, but mainly, "How?"

"He's never agreed to an interview before," Ross blurted. "Why now? And why Mark?"

"I asked Steve those very questions," Russell explained. "Look, all we know is this—Josh Mclintock was approached by a Jihad al Sharia contact today in Damascus. He made it very clear that Sa'id was ready to do an interview and that Mark Taylor was to be there in three days to do it. We don't know why, just when and where to make contact."

"It doesn't make any sense," Mark muttered, more to himself than to the others. "We have correspondents throughout the Middle East, news reporters for both the network and the news channel. I'm sure Mclintock is frothing at the mouth to do this himself. Why me?"

"I can't answer that," Russell responded with a full-blown smile. "But opportunity has knocked, my boy; all you've got to do is open the door and let her in."

"So we're going to do the interview?" Mark asked.

"You bet we are. . . ." Russell paused, then looked intently at his young reporter with a slight tilt to his head. "Why wouldn't we?"

"I don't know," Mark said, trying to pull his thoughts together. "It just seems that with all that's happened over the past couple of months, do we really want to be the ones used to get his propaganda out?"

"Oh, come on, Mark, we're journalists. . .that's what we do." Russell laughed until he saw the stern expression on Mark's face.

"But we're also Americans." Mark stood up, walking over to the window and looking outside, taking a quick moment to pray for guidance. "Right now, if I knew where he was, the first thing I'd want to do is have our Air Force bomb him straight to hell." He turned back to Russell. "Frank, he's responsible for more deaths than bin Laden."

"You're serious about this, aren't you?" Russell asked.

"What could he possibly have to say that the world would want to hear except his confession in front of a firing squad?"

"Mark," Ross cut in, "think about the potential for your career, for this show."

Mark grunted, walking back toward his seat while shaking his head. "This is so much bigger than my career or this show's ratings, Ross."

As Russell leaned back in his chair, another squeak filled the room. "Ross, why don't you let me talk with Mark alone for a second?"

"Okay, Frank." Ross got up and headed toward the door. "Anything you say."

CIA HEADQUARTERS, LANGLEY, VIRGINIA
12:12 P.M.

"Can I see you for a minute?" Wendy asked after a sharp rap on the open door.

"Sure, come on in," Jack Murphy replied, pulling away from his computer.

He was the assistant director of Central Intelligence for the Middle East, the head of Wendy's division that had been pulling unbearable hours since the latest wave of attacks. He looked the part: His suit coat was draped over the back of his chair, his sleeves were rolled up, and his tie was lying somewhere around the cluttered office. Although only forty-five, the last few years in the intelligence agency had worn on him. His once-thick hair was now thinning and receding, and a defining gray highlighted the area just above his ears. Jack hadn't seen his home in two days.

"This must be interesting, Wendy," Jack responded as he studied her determined face. She turned and closed the door behind her, then walked up to his desk and handed him a piece of paper. "What've you got?"

She took the seat opposite him. "NSA intercepted a conversation last night between Josh Mclintock—National Network cable news station chief in Syria—and Steve Thompson, head of the network in New York."

Jack raised his eyebrows as he scanned the paper. It was always touchy when conversations were recorded from the news organizations of their own country. Whatever information they received had to be handled very carefully.

"What's the gist of it?"

"Basically, it looks like they've got an interview lined up with Sa'id." Wendy waited for her boss's eyes to look up and meet hers. "In three days."

Jack shot up from his chair, uttering a phrase mixed generously with both the religious and the profane. Then collecting himself, he asked, "Any idea why now?"

"None, but to me this proves what I've suspected all along. Mclintock is connected to the Jihad al Sharia."

"I agree." Jack rubbed his chin, looking over the document at the exact wording of the phone conversation. He then looked up at Wendy, a smile spreading over his unshaven face.

"You know what this means, Wendy?"

"Yes." She returned the smile, an overwhelming excitement enveloping her. "We've got Sa'id!"

CHAPTER 2

"All right, Mark," Russell said, closing his office door. "I don't get it. This is a reporter's dream. What gives?"

"I don't know, Frank," Mark answered truthfully. His strong reaction to interviewing Sa'id had come as a surprise to himself. Mark waited for Russell to cross the room and sit in the chair vacated by Ross before he continued. "Giving Sa'id any of our airtime to propagate his sick, twisted jihad makes me want to. . ."

"We covered that when Ross was in here," Russell cut in to avoid whatever visual Mark was about to imagine. "Look, you've been after me for months to let you do a piece on the dangers of fundamentalist Muslims. . .now here's your chance!" Russell paused, studying his reporter's reaction. "There's more going on here, isn't there?"

Mark took in a deep breath and let it out slowly. "Yeah, it has a lot to do with how our profession has covered this whole War on Terror. When our networks aired that first bin Laden tape—live, right off the Al-Jazeera feed—with no concern for what it might contain or that there could have been some kind of hidden code to initiate more attacks. It was incredibly stupid, and National Cable went right along with it. Then there was that whole flap about journalists needing to stay impartial, concerned that we'd be used as propaganda for the White House. Impartial, Frank? Propaganda for the White House? We're at war with a bunch of nuts that want this country destroyed, and those of us in the media wear our proud badge of neutrality as if we were covering some skirmish between Iraq and Iran. It's ludicrous."

Russell sighed. They'd had this discussion several times over the past couple of years.

"I'm sorry, Frank. I got carried away. It's just that we've got another freak over there sending his goons across the ocean to kill themselves and as many Americans as they can. . . ."

"I understand," Russell acknowledged, "but everything you've just said makes me believe more than ever that you are the one to do this interview."

Mark had been looking straight ahead, staring at Russell's wall of pictures with his palms pressed together in front of his lips. The words caught him off guard. He turned back toward his boss with raised eyebrows. "Come again?"

"Well, think about it," Russell said, standing and walking to the other side of his desk. "The legwork's already done; you've spent the better part of two years researching Islam since 9/11 occurred."

Mark nodded slightly.

"So I think you'll be able to put the right perspective on Sa'id. If you're concerned the interview would be propaganda for his cause or that our press has been neutral to the point of treason. . . then what better newsman is there to go into the snake pit than you?" He emphasized the last few words by leaning over the desk and putting his face right in front of Mark's.

Mark's brow furrowed in response.

"Mark, there's a degree of separation journalists have to possess to be impartial, and right now it's probably the toughest part about covering this war. But we do it. We must. . .because it serves this country well. Our job is to lay out the truth. . .whatever that may be, from Sa'id's point of view as well as our government's. Then democracy takes over, our system weeds through the lies, and we arrive at some sort of consensus."

"I understand all that in theory, Frank, but this situation

ought to be the exception."

"There are no exceptions," Frank said sternly, then softened his approach. "But look at it this way. You can make the story whatever you want it to be, Mark. Paint him as the wicked terrorist, the evil Satan himself if you want to," Russell said, falling back into his creaky chair with a heavy laugh. "And use his own words to do it!"

VAN NUYS, CALIFORNIA
9:21 A.M.

Tracy checked in with the receptionist at the front counter, then took a seat in the lobby. She nervously scanned the room, shuffled through the magazines on the coffee table in front of her, and eventually decided on the current issue of *Time*. *People* and *Us* didn't seem to hold her interest since the last wave of terrorism.

After a few moments, she took her eyes off the magazine's pages and glanced at the women around her, all in different stages of pregnancy. Funny, she could have sat here a few days ago and not noticed how many were pregnant, much less how far along they might be. She found the apprehension about being pregnant slowly fading. . .being replaced by a growing excitement.

"Mrs. Taylor?" A young nurse appeared at the doorway leading to the back room.

Tracy got up and followed her down the hallway. She went through the normal weigh-in, urine sample, temperature and blood pressure checks, then answered all the pertinent health questions before once again being left alone.

It gave her a moment to collect her thoughts. What a wonderful miracle, carrying Mark's child. . .if she really were pregnant. She glanced around at the posters on the wall, showing the various stages of fetal development. She marveled at what could be happening inside her and the changes that would be taking place.

Her gaze stopped at the last poster showing a baby emerging through the birth canal—her eyes bulged. *Wow! That's gotta hurt!* Suddenly reality began to kick in. . .her dreams of completing law school, of passing the bar. . .how would she accomplish those with a baby at her side?

Her thoughts were interrupted by two quick knocks on the door, followed by its opening.

"I hope you're ready for some good news," the doctor said with a large grin.

NATIONAL STUDIOS
9:30 A.M.

"So I'm pleased to announce that Ahmad Hani Sa'id's first interview ever will be broadcast on our network. . .on this very show, Sunday night." Frank Russell had the attention of the entire staff, who were crammed into the conference room. "By our very own Mark Taylor."

It took just a second for the momentous words to sink in; then a spontaneous burst of applause filled the room, accompanied by various "attaboys" directed toward Mark.

He smiled and nodded to the group, trying hard not to show the conflicting emotions bottled up inside him. Scanning the faces, Mark felt a great sense of unity coming from the rest of the staff until his eyes met those of Tad Forrest, one of the other on-air reporters. His smile was forced, pursed at the edges of his lips. Mark interpreted the look as saying, *It should have been me.* Mark wasn't so sure he didn't agree with Tad.

"Speech, speech," someone was yelling from near the doorway.

As the room quieted down, Russell turned his attention to Mark.

"I'm not sure what to say," Mark began. "I have no idea why I've been given this assignment. But I have, so I guess I'm off to the Middle East. If it were up to me, though, I'd do the interview, then leave him with a nice American-made hand grenade stuffed underneath his turban."

Laughter filled the room, followed by round of shouts and cheers.

"Nice." Russell finally regained control with a smile. "Mark and Ross are flying out tonight, and we're not sure when they'll be coming back. So that means the rest of us are going to have to step it up a notch and fill the void."

Russell continued, assigning another reporter to handle Senator Boxer's interview and lining out the rundown for Thursday night's show. The other stories Mark and Ross had been working on were placed on indefinite hold until they returned. Russell planned for Mark to record his lead-in and wrap-up to the interview while out in the field. Then the whole thing could be sent via satellite back to Los Angeles, edited and ready for air on Sunday.

VAN NUYS, CALIFORNIA
10:14 A.M.

"Have you been nauseous in the mornings?" Dr. Alice Hoyt asked Tracy, who was sitting perfectly still on top of the examination table so that the sanitary paper wouldn't rustle.

"No, I've felt tired, though."

"That's normal," Dr. Hoyt said with a smile. She pulled a circular card out of her pocket and began spinning it around. "From the date of your last period, the wheel chart says you're six weeks pregnant, which would put the little bundle of joy popping out. . . September eighth."

Tracy didn't respond as she looked at the pattern on the floor under her feet. Her mind was mulling over the fact that some eight months from now, she'd be taking home a baby to care for.

"Does your husband know yet?"

"No." Tracy looked up. "I wanted to be sure."

"Well, I'm sure. You're going to be a mother."

"It seems so unreal." Tracy shook her head from side to side.

"I'd like to do an ultrasound. It'll give us a more accurate picture of your timetable and the due date. We have one in the office; we could bring it in right now."

"Now?" Tracy gasped.

"Well, no. Not if you're not ready." The doctor paused, then stepped over and sat on the examination table, placing her hand over Tracy's. "Are you all right with this?"

"What?" Tracy cocked her head. "Oh, sure. I mean, it's shocking and all, but, yeah, I'm excited. It's something I've always wanted, and Mark will be such a terrific father." Then a huge smile broke out over her face as her arguments took hold. "Yeah, I'm all right with this."

"Good, then what do you say about that ultrasound?"

"Actually, Dr. Hoyt, would it be all right if I wait until Mark is with me? I'd like to share that experience with him."

She smiled. "Of course, that's a wonderful idea. Whenever it's convenient, just call and make an appointment."

"Would tomorrow be okay?" Tracy asked.

Dr. Hoyt laughed. "I'm sure we can fit you in. Now lift up that gown; let's see if we can hear a heartbeat."

Tracy's eyes widened. "She already has a heartbeat?"

"She?" Dr. Hoyt laughed.

"I guess I've always thought I'd have a girl."

The doctor turned behind her and grabbed a small gray object no larger than a pack of playing cards with a wire sticking out of it. When she ran the transducer at the end of the wire over Tracy's belly, a squishing sound filled the room. The doctor moved it around for a moment, then looked up at Tracy, smiling.

"Do you hear it?"

Tracy strained to listen, trying to filter out the embryonic noise. There it was, so faint, yet so real—the steady rhythm of her child's beating heart. Their child. . .possibly her daughter. Tracy closed her eyes as a tear escaped and slid down her right cheek.

NATIONAL STUDIOS
10:32 A.M

Mark and Ross had taken over the conference room, poring over a bundle of magazines and newspapers spread the length of the table that they had gathered on the latest terrorist attacks. Very little of it shed any light on the Jihad al Sharia or its mysterious leader.

"You know what we need," Mark thought out loud, "is to get briefed by someone in the news division."

"That's a good idea. We can look over all this stuff on the plane." Ross got up from the table, heading to the door. "I'll set it up."

Russell crossed paths with Ross at the doorway. "How's it going?"

"Slow," Mark confessed. "There's nothing on Sa'id. He just disappeared when he was eighteen, then resurfaced five years ago when he combined more than a dozen terrorist groups under the banner of the Jihad al Sharia. Ross went off to set up a meeting with the news division."

"If you need me to make a call to someone over there, let me know." Russell dropped an envelope on the conference table. "Your tickets. We've got you booked on a red-eye tonight to New York. You'll connect from there to Paris and spend the night."

Mark noticed the white envelope with the words "Air France Concorde" in bold blue letters across the top. He looked up at the grin on Russell's face. "We're on the Concorde?"

Russell nodded.

"Wow, the network's really pulling out all the stops."

"It helps when the brass is drooling over the ratings potential, but don't get used to it. It was the only way to give you enough time for a night's sleep in Paris."

Mark opened the envelope and searched through the flight

schedule, seeing the overnight layover in Paris. Then he saw the next day's itinerary, a flight from Paris to Istanbul.

"Turkey?"

"Yeah," Russell confirmed with a nod. "We've been instructed to get you to Diyarbakir—it's in the southeastern part of Turkey, roughly sixty miles from Syria."

"I thought Mclintock was stationed in Damascus."

"He is, and it would have been a lot easier to fly you straight there. But we're following the instructions from the guy who contacted him. That's to get you to the Dedeman Diyarbakir Hotel. Mclintock will meet you at the airport."

"What about the crew?"

"Mclintock's handling that. You'll arrive Friday night at eight-thirty—just within their timetable. Then it's up to the Jihad al Sharia to contact you."

"It sounds a little spooky, Frank," Mark admitted.

"I know, but your marine training should be an asset. Think of this as a mission. Are you having second thoughts?"

"I don't think I'm done with my first thoughts yet. . . ."

Russell took the seat next to Mark. "I know you have to be thinking about Daniel Pearl."

Mark studied his boss's face. The lines of age were marked with concern. Mark nodded once. Daniel Pearl had been kidnapped in Pakistan shortly after the fall of the Taliban in Afghanistan. He'd been held for ransom, then executed—beheaded—gruesomely captured on videotape.

"Your situation is different." Russell tried to quell the images running through Mark's brain. "Sa'id himself has invited you. They'll treat you like royalty."

Mark smiled, appreciative of Russell's concern. "I hope you're right."

Russell grinned, letting the moment linger before continuing. "There's one more thing we need to discuss—another journalist to go in with you."

"I don't understand. I thought Ross was going?"

"That's not what I'm talking about. You need a corroborating witness to verify the interview. Usually a television person will take somebody from print or radio, but it has to be somebody outside of our network. Anybody come to mind?"

Mark thought for a second. "Not off the top of my head."

Russell placed a torn-out page from a notebook on the table. "Here are some names of people who are already in the Middle East. Look it over and we'll talk."

Mark scooped up the paper as Russell stood to leave. "Frank, are you sure Ross is up to this? I can't picture him running through the desert in the middle of the night meeting with terrorists."

Russell looked over his shoulder to make sure Ross hadn't returned. "I've thought the same thing. . .but I think this trip will be good for him. I know he's green and has led a pampered life, but this could be his great reality check if you're up to taking him along."

"That's his decision," Mark said evenly. "I don't plan to baby-sit."

"I'll talk to him, make sure he knows what he's getting into. Is there somebody else on the staff you'd rather have go with you?"

"Besides you?" Mark grinned. "No."

Russell returned the smile. "Oh, that I were young again. I'd be on that plane in a heartbeat."

Mark paused, his expression serious. "Why don't you come?"

"No, I've had my time behind enemy lines; it's best left to the young at heart. You go—just be careful. This could be the memory of a lifetime."

"I've had my share of experiences in the Gulf War. I'm not sure I need to be making any more memories. . .except for the ones I want to have with Tracy."

"Have you spoken to her yet?"

Mark shook his head, looking at his watch. "No. She's in class right now. Besides, I don't exactly know how to tell her."

Russell laughed. "There's probably no good way to approach her on this one."

CIA HEADQUARTERS, LANGLEY, VIRGINIA
1:37 P.M.

"This had better be good, Jack. I'm speaking with the national security advisor in twenty minutes," George Tenet, the director of Central Intelligence, said as Jack walked into his spacious office in the New Building.

Jack got right to the point. "We have gotten a lead on Ahmad Hani Sa'id."

"Take a seat," Tenet responded, immediately looking up from his paperwork. "Let's have it."

"We intercepted a phone call out of Damascus—the National Cable News station chief reporting to his network in New York. It seems National has an interview set up with Sa'id and some reporter on the West Coast. . .a Mark Taylor."

"I'm not familiar with him."

"He's on *Across the Nation.*"

"When's the interview to take place?"

"In three days."

The director's eyes hardened. "Three days?"

Jack nodded.

"That's interesting. We're receiving alerts from the FBI about possible Jihad al Sharia action this weekend here in the States. I'm putting out a red flag on all Middle Eastern surveillance to see if there's anything to corroborate the threat."

"You think the interview could be a diversion?" Jack wondered.

"Anything's possible with Sa'id. But we've got to treat it as legitimate while still trying to clamp down on this recent threat."

Jack licked his lips. "I'd like permission to approach Taylor."

Tenet eyed his assistant director closely. "You want to what?"

"I want to recruit him. See if he'll help us get to Sa'id."

The director thought over his options carefully. "What do we know about him? Is he approachable?"

"We're checking now, sir." Jack looked down at a brief biography Wendy had handed him for this meeting. "Originally from Tennessee, he's been on the show for three years now; before that he was in journalism school at California State University, Northridge, on a GI scholarship after serving in the Gulf War."

Tenet nodded, encouraged by the news. "What branch of the service?"

"Marines, special ops."

"That's interesting. . . ."

"If we're going to approach him, we need to get somebody on the West Coast to talk to him right away."

"Not so fast," the director warned. "Let's take this one step at a time. We're not in the habit of recruiting members of the press." Tenet leaned back in his chair, contemplating alternatives. "I'm going to get the White House involved with this before we do anything. If we do, we'll have to coordinate with the FBI and Homeland Security. In the meantime, I want you to prepare a team to have Taylor in constant surveillance when he leaves the country, whether we approach him or not. Whatever you need is at your disposal. I want you on top of this, Jack—use our best people."

"Yes, sir," Jack returned with a smile.

NATIONAL STUDIOS
10:41 A.M.

"Hi, this is Tracy. I'm either on the phone or in class. Leave a message and I'll call you back!" *Beep!*

For the first time that Mark could remember, he was glad she hadn't answered. "Hi, honey, it's me. Just checking in. I've got some interesting news for you; give me a call when you can. I'll talk to you later. Love ya."

Ross stuck his head into the conference room doorway. "It's all set up."

"Who did you get?" Mark said, hanging up the phone.

"We're meeting with the station's Middle East expert. Come on."

Mark grabbed his keys and cell phone and followed Ross to his car. They had to drive a few minutes across town to get to National's television station. The studio that housed *Across the Nation's* offices was the production facility for all the entertainment television shows and films that were in production. National also owned KNNT, channel 6 in the Los Angeles market.

As Ross drove his BMW outside the studio gate and onto Sunset Boulevard heading east, Mark looked over at him. "Did you talk with Frank?"

"Yeah, he kind of gave me a reality check," Ross answered, then glanced over at Mark. "Was that your idea? You think I can't handle this?"

"No, it wasn't my idea. And, no, not necessarily," Mark returned with a smile. "It's just going to be a lot different than Princeton. There's nothing in your past that will have prepared you for this. That's all."

Mark paused, hoping Ross would understand, but he could tell by the pained expression on his face that he hadn't.

"I'm not trying to upset you." Mark attempted to soften his comment. "You're about to enter a whole new world, a lot different than the one you grew up in. I just want to make sure you know what you're getting into."

Ross grunted. "I suppose since you were in the Gulf War, you've seen it all."

"Don't turn this into my past versus yours. You won't win," Mark stated.

"Look." Ross made a right turn onto Gower, passing the Starbucks in Gower Gulch. "I'm a journalist too. Just because I'm not on-camera doesn't mean my heart isn't behind our stories."

"I know that, Ross."

"Maybe we don't see issues eye-to-eye. You're a right-wing religious fanatic; I'm a liberal heathen. . . ."

Mark smiled, relieved at Ross's attempt at humor.

"But that's what makes us a great team," Ross continued. "We see both sides, and frankly, I think it makes you a better reporter. I'm excited about this trip. I think as you put it, it'll open up a whole new world for me."

"I'm glad you're looking at it that way." Mark grinned.

"Good." Ross drove past the stages of Paramount Studios and turned left onto Melrose. "This is all happening so fast—what about visas and inoculations?"

"Neither country requires them, although in Turkey we might run into typhoid or yellow fever, and Syria has hepatitis A and B. If you haven't had a tetanus shot in awhile, you might want to run to your doctor this afternoon. We can get our visas for Turkey on entry. I don't think we'll be needing any for Syria. . . ."

Mark's comment hung in the air as Ross pulled into the entrance to Channel 6. "You think we'll be crossing the border illegally?"

"Let's put it this way, Ross: They have us set up sixty miles from the Syrian border out in the middle of nowhere. I don't think Sa'id is planning a trip into Turkey."

"Oh, brother." Ross sighed as he rolled down the window to give his name to the guard. Mark glanced out the window to his right, trying to hide his amusement.

33

CHAPTER 3

"You wanted to see me?" Wendy asked, popping her head into Jack's office.

"Yeah, come on in." Jack grinned as she entered. "The director is approaching the White House as we speak. I think we'll get the green light, so I want to be ready."

Wendy nodded.

"He's put me in charge of keeping tabs on Taylor all the way through this thing."

"That's great, Jack."

"The important thing is for us to get the drop on Sa'id. Any further intelligence arrive from Syria?"

"Not on this."

"Keep a sharp eye out. The FBI is putting out an alert—potential domestic threats this weekend."

Wendy looked concerned. "Any hint as to what kind?"

"No, not yet. I'll keep you posted. Now, until we can get surveillance going on Taylor, we need to find out where and when this interview is to take place."

"We're trying, sir. Mclintock said he'd call back with the details as soon as he was contacted again. Either that call hasn't been made or the NSA missed it."

"We need to get the FBI on this immediately. We should have had all of Taylor's phones tapped by now," Jack muttered, looking at his watch.

"If Taylor is to hold the interview in three days, they need to get him out tonight. . .early tomorrow at the latest. I'll start checking flight manifests and see if his name pops up."

"Do it," Jack said, then paused. "No, have somebody else get on that. I want you to keep looking into Taylor's past. I want to know what his political leanings are and any potential weaknesses we can use. I want to know how we can run him."

"I've been working on it, sir. I should have it completed in another hour or two."

"I'm going to be assembling our team in the situation room within the hour; have it ready by then. As of right now, we're on twenty-four-hour alert. Now get to work."

"Yes, sir," Wendy acknowledged as she got up to leave. Just as she reached the door, Jack stopped her.

"And, Wendy. . ."

"Yes?"

"We just may get this sucker."

"I certainly hope so."

CHANNEL 6, HOLLYWOOD, CALIFORNIA
11:10 A.M.

After checking in at the receptionist's desk, Mark and Ross were led back to a conference room near the news studio. The news director met them briefly before turning them over to their Middle Eastern expert, Hashim Basayav, a young man dressed in khaki pants and a red KNNT sport shirt.

"How can I be of service?" Hashim asked with a thick accent once the news director had left the room.

"Actually," Mark said, "before we get into details about the Jihad al Sharia, I'd love to hear about your own background."

Hashim smiled shyly. "I was born in Iran twenty-four years ago. My father is a surgeon. We visited this country many times when I was growing up. I have always had a fascination with your entertainment industry. I came here on a student visa, USC premed."

"Following in the family business?" Ross asked.

"You might say that, but being a doctor was not for me." Hashim glanced at Mark. "I switched to a film major with a minor in journalism. I interned here my senior year. After 9/11, I was asked a lot of questions about the Middle East and Islam; eventually, they offered me a full-time job."

"You're Muslim then," Mark stated.

"Yes."

"It sounds as if you're just what we're looking for." Mark grinned.

"I'll be as helpful as I can." Hashim smiled warmly.

"Good, let's start with Ahmad Hani Sa'id. . .what can you tell us about him?"

Hashim opened up a folder in front of him and took out two pages he'd prepared and handed one to each of them. "When I heard you were interested in the Jihad al Sharia, I took it upon myself to prepare this."

Mark's eyes quickly scanned the page. It was divided into two sections. The heading at the top read AHMAD HANI SA'ID and had a small section detailing his early childhood through the age of eighteen, then a second section, slightly larger, detailing the past five years after his creation of the Jihad al Sharia. Right below that was a bullet point list of details known about the terrorist organization.

"As you can see," Hashim explained, "there is very little information available on Sa'id himself. He was born in 1960 in Saudi Arabia—Riyadh, to be exact. He was the first son of Faud Kareem Sa'id's third wife. His family was tied in very close with the royal family. . .in a way very similar to the bin Laden family; only the Sa'id wealth was not in construction, but oil."

Mark kept his eyes glued to Hashim, only occasionally glancing down at the page in front of him. He found himself analyzing the manner in which Hashim spoke. . .he sensed a respect, almost a reverence, as he talked.

"Faud was a religious man, but he wasn't what you'd call a zealot. In fact, he supported the royal family allowing American troops on Saudi soil, and he continues to do so today. As far as anyone has been able to research, Ahmad had a normal Saudi upbringing."

"I'm not sure how normal it would be when your father is worth millions," Ross interjected.

Hashim smiled. "That may be true. In any event, he attended the Saudi schools and was being trained in his father's business. But as you can see, when he turned eighteen, no one seems to know what happened to him."

Mark shook his head. "That's what I find incredible. It's as if he disappears from the age of eighteen to. . .what is he now?"

"Forty-three, but he was thirty-eight when he resurfaced," Hashim answered.

"Are there any theories as to the missing years?" Ross asked.

"The common belief is that he assumed another identity and went off to a university somewhere. No one has been able to come up with the name he used or where he studied. But upon his return to Saudi Arabia he seemed to have gained an incredible amount of knowledge about financial matters, computers, weapons, politics, business—he had mastered them all, including his knowledge of the Koran."

There it was again. Hashim was speaking of Sa'id as one man in awe of another.

"The belief in some Muslim circles," Hashim continued, leaning closer to the table as if telling Mark and Ross a deep secret, "is that the missing years are a sign of his being a prophet, like Jesus, peace be upon Him, where little was known about him from the time he was twelve until he was thirty."

Mark looked intently into Hashim's eyes. "You're telling me that there are Muslims who equate Sa'id with Jesus?"

Hashim answered with a slight lowering of his head. "In some circles the two are compared, yes."

CIA HEADQUARTERS, LANGLEY, VIRGINIA
2:12 P.M.

Wendy Hamilton worked at her desk, compiling the report on Mark Taylor. His service record from the marines now sat in front of her along with transcripts from the California State University, Northridge, and Smyrna High School in Tennessee. She had also downloaded transcripts from the National Network from several of Mark's on-air reports. She felt as if she was getting a handle on just who Mark Taylor was when her phone rang.

"Hamilton," she answered.

"Wendy, we've got him." Stuart Woods was on the line. Wendy had asked him to check the flight manifests. "He's flying out of LAX tonight, ten o'clock to Kennedy, connecting to Paris on the Concorde tomorrow morning. He spends a night there, then flies to Istanbul, eventually winding up in Diyarbakir, Turkey."

"Good work. E-mail me the itinerary right away, and start looking for hotel reservations in Paris and Diyarbakir."

She hung up the phone, then looked above her desktop to a map of the Middle East pinned to a corkboard. It took her just a few seconds to spot Diyarbakir in the southeastern part of Turkey, just above the Syrian border. She grabbed her phone and punched in Jack's extension.

"Murphy," she heard.

"Jack, Taylor's leaving tonight. He's flying to Turkey, but I think the meeting's going to happen in northern Syria."

UCLA, WESTWOOD, CALIFORNIA
11:15 A.M.

Corporate litigation in hostile takeovers didn't hold Tracy's interest on a normal day, much less this one as she attempted to take notes from the monotonous speaker lecturing before the fifteen hundred law students. Her mind kept drifting, thinking of what the future held. . .imagining the wonder that would appear in Mark's eyes when she told him the news over dinner. She looked at her watch—forty-five more minutes to go; then she could fold up her iBook, head to the market, and pick up what she needed.

Her mind flashed back to the message he had left for her. She hadn't taken the cell phone into the doctor's office, so she missed his call. What news did he have? He sounded guarded on the phone, so her imagination had run wild. Was it bad news? Something to do with his job? Or did it involve not being able to make it home for dinner? *God, please,* she thought, *let nothing stand in the way of tonight.*

She'd try to call him when the class was over. Right now, she had to focus her attention on her professor. This course was hard enough. She didn't need to make it more difficult by having incoherent notes.

HOLLYWOOD, CALIFORNIA
11:22 A.M.

Mark and Ross sat through the continued briefing from Hashim Basayav at Channel 6. After disappearing at the age of eighteen, Sa'id briefly resurfaced in Saudi Arabia in 1998, reconnecting with his family and setting up various businesses, not only in his home country, but also in Syria, Lebanon, Iraq, and a few other Arab nations. He did so much of it behind the scenes, it wasn't until he disappeared again that his business activities were even noticed. By that time, he was deeply respected—even revered in various terrorist organizations as he supplied them with money, resources, and brilliant advice. Through his influence, a coalition was established between over a dozen terrorist organizations, creating a network that was well financed and highly organized, the Jihad al Sharia—the Holy War of Islamic Law. Their mission: to clear the Holy Places in Saudi Arabia and Jerusalem of the infidels. . . and in the process unite all Islam.

"There is no proof," Hashim continued the briefing, "that Sa'id had any dealings with Osama bin Laden, but personally I have to believe they knew each other. . .perhaps even planned operations together. The events of the past couple of months mirror bin Laden's strategy of coordinated attacks at several different locations simultaneously. The question is, did Sa'id learn from Osama, or was it the other way around?"

The room was silent as Hashim closed his folder. Mark sighed. His hatred for this. . .terrorist—he couldn't bring himself to refer to Sa'id as a man—was so impassioned. Such a great loss of innocent life, all at the hands of a rich, spoiled Arab, seeking revenge on a culture he knew nothing about. *Why me?* The question reverberated in his mind. Of all the journalists covering this war, both here and overseas, why was he the one manipulated into interviewing this vile snake? Mark had no answers, but his mind was shocked when a passing thought crossed his mind.

Love your enemy. . .the words of Jesus. He'd have to think about that later. . .right now that seemed impossible.

"Hashim," Mark broke the silence. "May I ask you a personal question?"

"Yes, I will do my best to answer."

"I want to try and understand the Muslim mind. What are your feelings about Sa'id, from a religious viewpoint?"

Hashim lowered his head for a brief moment, then looked up at Mark. "You must take into account that Sa'id was raised in a totally different world, Mr. Taylor. In Saudi Arabia, the children are taught in the *madrasahs,* their schools, that Christians and Jews are infidels to be despised. Although his father might have been a moderate Muslim, Sa'id became a zealot. There is nothing more important to him than fulfilling the will of Allah."

"And you respect that. . . ," Mark chided.

"Yes. But don't get me wrong; I condemn acts of terrorism, and I will condemn Sa'id if it is proven that he is behind the attacks. The killing of innocent lives is forbidden by the Koran."

"Then explain to me," Mark fought to keep his voice under control, "how this self-proclaimed prophet can justify killing thousands of innocent lives as the will of Allah?"

"I cannot." Hashim looked down. "And it is a travesty to the peaceful tenet of Islam if it is proven that a Muslim committed these acts. I'm just trying to help you understand where Sa'id is coming from."

Ross jumped in. "And we appreciate that, Hashim."

"If you want more background on Sa'id," Hashim offered, "there are contacts I could give you in London and Paris. . .charities that raise funds for the organization."

At the mention of Paris, Mark's interest piqued. "That could be very helpful."

Hashim pulled out a piece of paper and copied down the names and phone numbers of the two people across the Atlantic from his notebook and handed it across the table.

"Thank you," Mark said. "I'm sorry for getting emotional about this, Hashim. I just have a very hard time when people try to justify atrocities like what this man has done in the name of God."

"My apologies; I was not trying to justify his actions. But I do respect a person who can sacrifice so much for what he believes. Is there not somebody in your religion, Mr. Taylor, whose values you respect, but you might disagree with his actions?"

Mark sat back chuckling; the tension in the room dissipated. "You make an interesting point, Hashim."

CHAPTER 4

The meeting had just begun as Wendy stepped into the Middle East situation room at CIA headquarters. Unlike any conference room in the nation, this one more closely resembled a high-tech studio control room. The walls were lined with a black sound-reducing fabric around three sides of the room. The fourth wall was filled with different-sized plasma monitors, slim flat-screened panels that portrayed video images in high-definition clarity. In the middle sat a highly polished, dark green and black marble table in the shape of a semicircle that could seat a dozen people on one side facing the video sources. A low glow spread around the table from recessed lamps in the dark ceiling. Each station had its own protracting light that could be placed over the desktop while not interfering with the video screens on the other side of the room.

Wendy quietly made her way around the table, placing a copy of the report she'd compiled on Mark Taylor in front of each person.

Jack Murphy stood by the flat side of the table, flanked on his right by Kristen Robertson—his personal assistant; Dean Hatchet—special assistant to the Homeland Security director; and Brad Faxon—the CIA's leading expert on electronic surveillance. On Murphy's left sat the FBI's assistant director over counterterrorism, Seth Maxwell. At the rest of the table were various members of Jack's staff and other high-level personnel he had brought in from other departments within the CIA.

43

"What you've just received," Jack explained as Wendy completed her task and took the empty seat next to the FBI representative, "is what we have on Mark Taylor. Has the FBI tapped his phones yet?"

Seth nodded. "As soon as we got the green light from the White House and the judge's signature. We're now monitoring his home and office, plus the cell phones of Taylor and his wife."

"I guess that'll do." Jack smiled. He turned to Wendy. "Fill us in on Taylor, Miss Hamilton."

Wendy nervously cleared her throat, then addressed the group. "Mark Taylor was born in Smyrna, Tennessee, 1969." While she spoke, images of him began filling the plasma screens on the wall. "He went into the marines right after high school graduation. . . ended up in a special operations unit and distinguished himself in the Gulf War—awarded the Silver Star and a Purple Heart."

Wendy noticed a few heads nodding their appreciation. The wall was now filled with different photographs of Mark, from high school shots of football and baseball to photos taken of him in uniform during boot camp.

"After the war ended, Taylor was discharged from the marines and moved to southern California, where he managed to land a job as a production assistant at National Studios. He went to night school at CSU Northridge, eventually earning his degree in journalism. Three years ago he got his break and was hired as a reporter on the show *Across the Nation.*"

The largest screen in the middle of the wall came to life, showing a clip from one of Mark's shows. The smaller plasma to the right of it switched to a photo taken from a newspaper showing a bride and groom. "He's recently married. . .no kids or former marriage, pays his taxes and goes to church. He seems to be a model citizen."

"What are his politics?" Seth asked.

"Conservative." Wendy glanced at her notes. "There was a controversy around him a few years back that you might recall. Mark took the position that the media was liberally biased in a report he did on abortion. It put him on the talk-show circuit for awhile, but things quickly died down after a few weeks."

Wendy glanced at the reaction around the room; evidently they didn't remember. "But where he really made his mark was when his investigation led to the downfall of the media mogul that owned his network—Jason Reynolds—and his clandestine group that had manipulated the public approval ratings."

Now the group reacted, most of them having some recollection of the scandal. "I've included a full report that was classified Circle of Seven for each of you, as well as the transcripts of a few of his more thought-provoking stories."

"If I remember correctly," Jack thought out loud, "wasn't that kept under the radar?"

"Yes, sir," Wendy answered. "Taylor was asked to keep a lid on his findings until the Justice Department could complete their investigation. Plus the network didn't want the bad publicity."

"Will he work with us?" Dean Hatchet asked from across the table.

"Unknown," Jack spoke up before Wendy could answer.

Seth leaned forward with his elbows resting on the conference table, hands folded under his chin. "Do we know why he was chosen to do this interview?"

"That's still a mystery. Only Sa'id knows the answer to that one," Jack commented.

"Any hint of Middle Eastern sympathies in Taylor's past?" Seth asked, looking up at Jack.

"Nothing. Clean record, exemplary service in the Gulf," Jack answered. "The other possibility we're looking into is whether or not this could be a diversion while the Jihad al Sharia plans some sort of attack this weekend."

HOLLYWOOD, CALIFORNIA
12:08 P.M.

"You were kind of getting intense in there, Mark," Ross prodded as he drove off the Channel 6 lot.

Mark stared out the window for a moment, then turned to Ross. "Didn't you hear the. . ." He searched for the right words. "The admiration in his voice?"

"Yeah, so?"

"He's talking about a man that's responsible for the murder of thousands of Americans, and all you can say is, 'So?' "

"Look, I hate Sa'id just as much as any American," Ross answered as he swerved slightly to avoid a man who had stepped off the curb holding a "will-work-for-food" sign. "But Hashim condemned the attacks."

"Only after I pressed him on it, and did you hear his qualification? 'If it's proven that Sa'id did it.' " Mark shook his head. "Whenever I hear Muslims condemn terrorism, it's always followed by a 'but,' like there is some kind of justification for it because of our foreign policy. . .or like with our friend Hashim back there. There's an unexplainable admiration for the man behind the evil."

"Do I detect some prejudice here?" Ross said with a smile. "I thought Christians were supposed to love everybody."

"We are. . ." Mark responded sharply but was interrupted by his cell phone.

"Hold that thought," he said as he answered the call.

"Hi, honey, it's me," Tracy's voice came over the line.

"Hey, Trace." Mark's attention was swiftly diverted from the conversation with Ross. "How was your class?"

"It was okay. . .boring, really. So what's the news?"

"Ahhh." Mark paused, not knowing what to say. "I'll tell you when I get home."

"Okay," she responded. "I've got some news for you too."

"Tell me." He smiled, intrigued.

"You'll just have to wait until tonight," she teased.

"Cute."

"Are you going to be late?"

"No, actually, I need to get home early." Mark caught himself before he said too much. "I'll explain later. Ross and I have some things to wrap up back at the office; then I'll head home. Do you want to go out?"

Tracy's answer was garbled in a bunch of static and a weird echo.

"Say that again, honey," Mark said. "You're breaking up."

"I said, let's eat at home; I've already got something planned."

"Great." Mark thought that'd give him a jump on packing. "I'll see you as quick as I can."

"Okay, honey. Love you."

"Love you too."

Mark hit the end button as he put the phone down. "That was weird. There was this strange echo."

"Must be the area of town," Ross offered.

"Maybe, but I've never heard my cell phone sound like that."

"So you haven't told her we're leaving town yet, huh?"

"No," Mark admitted. "I think I'll wait until tonight when we're together. She's not going to like this assignment."

"No kidding." Ross smiled.

CIA HEADQUARTERS, LANGLEY, VIRGINIA
3:09 P.M.

The government employees assembled in the CIA's situation room had discussed the life of Mark Taylor from every conceivable angle. Everyone agreed it was a gamble to approach a member of the media. . .but the situation with Sa'id was critical to national security.

"We have to approach him," Dean Hatchet said, looking intently at Wendy's report on Taylor. "Whether it's a diversion or not, this could be our only shot at getting Sa'id without risking a full invasion of Syria."

"I agree," Seth Maxwell added.

"The question is, how and when do we approach him?" Dean asked.

"And with whom?" Seth added.

"FBI," Jack answered. "The president wants them to approach him first. If Taylor is cooperative, they will turn the operation over to us."

"And if he doesn't want to play along?" Seth questioned.

"Then it's a covert operation, combining all of our departments. We try to follow him in and get Sa'id without his help," Jack answered matter-of-factly. "Seth, do you have somebody in L.A. that can reach him tonight?"

"Yes, of course," Seth said. "Michael Weston—assistant special agent in charge of counterterrorism at our L.A. bureau is standing by. He's a good man."

"Good. Taylor's got a ten o'clock flight out of LAX. Weston will have to catch him before that. Wendy, take Agent Maxwell to a secure phone where he can make contact."

The two stood up to leave.

"And, Seth." Jack stopped them just short of the door. "I'd recommend letting Wendy talk to Weston. She knows Taylor better than any of us at this point."

"Understood."

As the door closed behind Wendy and Seth, Jack glared over the people assembled before him. "All right, let's start making plans for every contingency. I want him covered each step of the way from his front door all the way to Syria, whether he's with us or not."

Ross turned onto Sunset heading west. "You're not getting off the hook that easily just because Tracy called. Now explain to me this attitude you have toward Muslims when a Christian is supposed to love his enemies."

Mark grinned. "Are you sure you want to do this?" Since the two had been assigned together, Ross had always steered clear of any in-depth discussions on Mark's beliefs.

"Yeah, maybe it's time." Ross nodded. "Let me have it."

"Okay," Mark said, adjusting in the seat so that he could better see his partner. "First of all, loving a Muslim doesn't mean that we shouldn't analyze the belief system that is used to encourage young followers to sacrifice themselves in the act of murdering innocent men, women, and children."

"I'll accept that," Ross said. "But aren't you generalizing a bit about Muslims? I'm sure they all don't feel that way."

Mark thought for a second. "Granted, but hear me out. Muslims have a word—*ummah*—which means community. It underlies the fundamental Muslim belief that all people are intended to be a single *ummah* under God. That transcends nations and boundaries. Early Islam divided the world into two parts, *dār-al Islām*—the abode of peace, or the present world under Islamic rule, and *dār-al ḥarb*—the abode of warfare, or the rest of the world that soon will be under Islam."

"You sound paranoid, Taylor." Ross chuckled. "Like they're planning to take over the world or something."

Mark laughed, trying to keep his intensity down. Since 9/11, he had read everything he could get his hands on about the Islamic faith, including the entire Koran.

"That's what Muhammad envisioned. You see, there is no separation between the religious and the secular; to a Muslim all is sacred. Islam means *peace* or *submission* depending on whom you talk to, entering into a condition of peace through submission to Allah. For the Muslim, to do the will of Allah is to restore the intention of God's creation by creating a single human community, or *ummah,* unified under Islam."

"You're saying all Muslims believe this?"

"To one degree or another, yes. To the moderate Muslim, I don't think they'd give it much thought. If there was to be a unified *ummah,* I hope they'd want it to be brought about peacefully. But to a Muslim fundamentalist, it's an entirely different matter. I think it really gets dangerous when you mix classic Islamic belief with a highly charged political conflict, especially in the Middle East. . . then you have the recipe for suicide bombers in Israel and people willing to die as they blow up football stadiums and World Trade Centers.

"Saudi Arabia has invested millions in building mosques and madrasahs in the U.S., and it's not to further the cause of a peaceful religion. Do you know that in those schools, you won't find a map with Israel on it?"

Ross looked at Mark. "You're kidding?"

"No, I wish I were."

"What do they have against the Jews anyway?"

Mark sighed. "It goes back a long, long time. Actually, both the Jews and the Arabs trace their ancestry to the same man."

"Abraham," Ross jumped in.

"Right. The Jews, descendants of his son, Isaac, and the Arabs from Ishmael," Mark said.

"So you'd think they'd get along."

Mark chuckled. "I wish. Do you know how the division came about?"

Ross admitted that he didn't. Mark told him the story of God's promise to Abraham to make his descendants into a great nation and that all the people of the earth would be blessed through him.

But his wife, Sarah, was unable to have children, so she gave her Egyptian maidservant Hagar to Abraham as his wife to bear a child. She conceived and Ishmael was born. Fourteen years later, God's promise was fulfilled through Sarah when she miraculously gave birth to Isaac when she was ninety-nine years old.

"But there was great jealousy between Hagar and Sarah, so Sarah asked Abraham to get rid of Hagar and Ishmael. Although it distressed Abraham, he did as Sarah requested and they left the land.

"As I've studied Islam," Mark continued, "it's fascinating to go back and look through the Bible at what was prophesied over Ishmael. Even though God said His promise to Abraham would be fulfilled through Isaac. . .and it was in Jesus, God also promised Hagar that Ishmael's descendants would be a great nation, but they would not live in peace. Genesis 16:12 said that Ishmael would be like a wild donkey of a man and his hand would be against everyone—he would live in hostility toward all his brothers."

Ross's eyes widened. He'd never heard the complete story. "Wow, that's what we're seeing today, isn't it?"

"It is. First in the Middle East, and now it's spreading into our country. And Islam is at the heart of it. We've painted Ahmad Hani Sa'id as a radical Muslim, a fanatic, comparable to the likes of our own Jim Jones or David Koresh. But the reality is, Sa'id is a fundamentalist. He reads the Koran like Billy Graham reads the Bible."

Ross took his eyes off the road, glaring at Mark. "What?"

Mark grinned. "I thought that would get your attention. What I mean is that the same way Billy Graham believes in the ultimate authority of the Bible as the inspired Word of God, Sa'id believes the Koran is the word of Allah. Sa'id is more comparable in our history to a Martin Luther, a reformer. . .called to purify Islam. That makes him a fundamentalist. His mission is to bring the world under the religious system of the Koran and the *Ḥadīth,* the sayings and traditions of Muhammad, hoping to take the world back to seventh-century Arabia.

"That's what got me going with our friend Hashim back there. Sure, he condemns the attacks with his words, but while he's talking, there's an awe. . .a respect for the man who perpetrated this enormous evil. Hashim may not agree with Sa'id's methods, but there seems to be an allegiance with his goals."

Ross smirked. "It's religion. He's just following what it says in their holy book. Allah or God, it's no different than what some of your Bible-thumping friends have done."

"I don't believe that." Mark fought to keep his tone conversational. "It's totally different from what Christians believe. Jesus taught about the kingdom of God being inside of us, a change of heart that's not political. It was Jesus who said, give to Caesar what is Caesar's and give to God what is God's."

"Okay," Ross argued. "But your Bible also says if a man sleeps with another man's wife, they are to be put to death. Children were stoned for not honoring their parents. Several times your God told the Jews to kill entire nations—women and children included."

"That's Old Testament," Mark interrupted. "And I know you can make the point that there are similarities between that and the Koran. But what separates Christianity from any other religion on earth is the life and message of Jesus."

"Oh, boy, here we go." Ross rolled his eyes before making the next turn.

"You asked for it," Mark quipped. "I'll admit there are harsh punishments in the Old Testament, stuff that, to be honest with you, I don't understand. But it was part of God's plan to bring a path of salvation to the world. The laws and strict punishment in the Old Testament were overridden by the grace of the New Testament. When you look at the whole story, it shows the mercy of God, not the anger."

"What do you mean?"

"The Bible states clearly that the result of sin is death—that's the penalty. We can never be good enough to be in relationship with God by our own merits. The examples you brought up point that out. But Jesus paid that price with His life, and with that He told us to love our enemies, as you so eloquently stated earlier."

"All right, Mr. Hotshot," Ross chided. "Then why weren't you loving Hashim?"

Mark sighed. "I'll admit I'm not perfect, Ross. Loving a person —any man—is no easy task. When you complicate it with a religious viewpoint like Islam that I find downright dangerous, that makes it all that much harder. But let me say this: Just because I'm disturbed by Hashim's misguided sense of respect doesn't mean I can't or don't love him. Actually, the more I study Islam, the more I'm concerned for Muslims like Hashim and their eternal future, as I am for yours."

Ross laughed. "I'm very happy without having to follow some ancient rules of do's and don'ts, thank you very much."

Mark smiled. "That's a great description of Islam, Ross. After death, at the judgment day, a Muslim has to hope he has accomplished more do's than don'ts or he doesn't get into paradise."

"Doesn't sound like a fun way to live."

"I agree. What's missing from the Koran is the New Testament."

Ross took his eyes off the road and gave Mark a questioning stare.

"Let me give you an interesting comparison between Muhammad and Jesus. Both had historical examples of having a woman brought to them who was caught in adultery. Muhammad told his men to take the woman away until the baby was born, which they did. When they brought her back, he told them to allow her to nurse the child until it was two years old. When she was brought back before him after that time, his final instructions to his men were to take the baby from the woman and kill her."

Ross's eyebrows rose.

"Jesus offered a radically different way. The religious leaders of His day brought an adulterous woman before Him, claiming the law commanded that she be stoned to death, as you pointed out earlier. Jesus stopped them from doing so by declaring to them that whoever was without sin should cast the first stone. One by one, the people in the crowd lowered their heads and walked away until only Jesus and the woman were left. He then told her He didn't condemn her but that she should go and leave her life of sin."

Mark glanced at Ross. "Which person would you choose to follow?" ? ? ?

Ross smiled. "You put it that way, and it's pretty obvious."

"Jesus' whole life was about loving and bringing people into a relationship with God; then His death took our place. It's not about a set of laws but freeing us from them."

Mark paused to see if Ross had any comments, but he kept his eyes glued to the traffic light, pulling forward as the arrow turned green.

"Islam traps its followers into a system of laws and rules—in an attempt to be accepted by Allah. Their language of infidel and jihad is left unchecked by the simple message Jesus left us to love one another, even our enemies. You won't find that verse or anything like it in the Koran."

Ross didn't respond as he pulled up to National's main gate. He popped his trunk, and the two presented their National IDs to the guard.

"You talk about loving your enemies," Ross spoke after he was waved through. "Do you have any relationships with Muslims?"

Mark thought for a moment. "I know a couple of guys on the crew, and I've interviewed a few Muslim scholars as I've researched. . . ."

"That's it? I wonder if you'd feel the same way about Muslims if you had a deeper relationship with one."

"Interesting point," Mark had to confess. Would his conclusions about Islam change if he had a close Muslim friend? Then a face appeared in his mind, and Mark grinned. "There was one guy; his name was Abu Zaqi Ressam. I first met him during the

Gulf War when he saved my bacon on a mission into Iraq. He came out here on a student visa after the war and we got pretty tight. We'd spend hours talking about Islam and Christianity."

"And you two remained friends through all that?"

"Yes, very good ones, actually, but we kind of lost touch when he went back to Saudi Arabia. . . ." Mark's voice trailed off; he hadn't thought about Abu in a long time.

Ross pulled into the structure, parking his car on the first floor where his name was neatly painted on the wall. He shut the engine off, then glanced over at Mark with his eyebrows raised. "Well, it looks like you're going to get your chance to confront the evil side of Islam face-to-face."

Mark sighed as he opened his door. "Yeah, I guess I am."

Chapter 5

"Mike, I've got you on speakerphone." Seth Maxwell raised his normal speaking voice a notch. "CIA analyst Wendy Hamilton is with me."

"Good afternoon, Agent Weston," Wendy acknowledged.

"Please call me Mike." The voice over the telephone's speaker filled the small conference room.

"All right, Mike it is," Wendy said.

"You on a secure line, Mike?" Seth asked.

"Yes, I am."

"Okay, here's the plan," Seth instructed. "You are cleared to make contact with Taylor. . .the sooner the better. His flight's at ten this evening, so you'll have to catch him before that."

"Understood. We've intercepted one phone call so far, from Taylor's cell. He's having dinner at home with his wife this evening. It will probably be best to meet him there."

"Agreed. We don't want to approach him at the studio," Seth added. "Wendy's got the most intel on him, so I wanted her to brief you. I'll fax over her full report when we're done."

Wendy brought Mike up to date.

"Do you think he'll work with us?" Mike asked.

"We're hopeful," Wendy answered. "He served his country once as a marine. Let him know we need him again."

"Has anybody thought about having his former CO approach

him?" Mike asked.

Wendy glanced over to Seth. His eyebrows raised and his head tilted slightly. "That's interesting," he acknowledged. "We'll check into that from here and get back to you."

NATIONAL STUDIOS
12:31 P.M.

"Ross, I need to see Frank for a second," Mark said as they made their way back into the production office. "See if you can run down that contact in Paris. . .I think we should set up a meeting during our layover."

Ross nodded. "I'll get right on it."

Mark dropped off his briefcase in his cubicle, then headed over to Russell's corner office. His assistant sent him right in.

"Get any good stuff?" Russell asked as Mark walked into his office.

"Some. Not what we were looking for, though," Mark admitted. "To make this story more than just Sa'id's comments, I think we need to fill in the holes. We need a name, and the complete history of those years between nineteen and thirty-eight. . .then we've got a story."

"Ahh, the missing years." Russell sighed as he leaned back in his chair.

"One thing we did learn: There are those in the Muslim world that take those years as a sign that he's a prophet. . .equating him to Jesus."

Russell looked up at the expression on his young reporter's face. "That must have burned you, didn't it?"

"I didn't like the comparison, no," Mark said with a smile. "But I think I kept my cool."

"That's good; I wouldn't want to be getting any phone calls

from their station manager."

"One thing is bothering me, though."

Russell pulled off his reading glasses. "I'm all ears."

Mark turned and shut the door behind him, then moved slowly back to Russell, searching for the words. "Are we doing the right thing here, Frank?"

"You mean the interview?" Russell questioned. "We already talked about that."

"No, it's not the interview." Mark shook his head. "There's another aspect of this whole thing we haven't covered." He walked over to the window, looking at the sound stage across the street for a second.

Frank followed him with his eyes but remained silent, waiting for his reporter to continue.

"We've got a chance," Mark began, still looking out the window—not willing to make eye contact with his boss and mentor. . . someone whom Mark held the utmost respect for, "to do much more than interview Sa'id."

Mark let the comment hang in the room as he kept gazing outside the window.

It took several seconds before Frank responded. "Are you speaking as a journalist, Mark, or as a former marine?"

Mark turned, taking the few steps toward Russell, then leaned forward and placed his hands on the desk. He looked intently at his boss. "I'm speaking as an American, Frank."

Russell locked on to Mark's heavy stare, communicating much more than words ever could.

"Sit down, Mark," he said firmly.

Russell waited patiently without blinking until Mark sat down.

"Okay. Let's hear what's on your mind."

"Hypothetically," Mark stated, "let's say you're a French reporter in 1939 and you've got an invitation to Berlin to interview Adolf Hitler. . ."

"Mark," Russell interrupted. "This question has been asked by moralists for decades. If you had the chance to kill Hitler before the Holocaust, saving millions of innocent lives. . .what would you do?"

"Exactly!" Mark accentuated his point by slapping his palm on the desk. "Sa'id is already responsible for killing thousands of Americans and who knows how many Israelis. How many more will die over the next five or even ten years? Or how many innocent lives will be lost in Syria when our military starts leveling the country like it did to Afghanistan, until we pull Sa'id out from under his rock? It's been three weeks since the embassies were hit, Frank. You know the president has to be about ready to start bombing."

Russell shook his head. "Mark, you've got to. . ."

Mark interrupted, "We. . .or at least I. . .have a chance to do something."

"Yeah, get yourself killed," Russell grunted.

"Have you even considered the idea of letting the government know what's going on?"

Russell nodded. "I've thought about it but never seriously considered it. You wouldn't make it home, and you'd put every member of your profession in extreme danger. How many more Daniel Pearls do you think there would be if just one journalist is discovered working as a spy?"

The weight of Russell's words pressed Mark deeper into his chair.

"The Arabs have an interesting culture when it comes to hospitality, Mark. If you are their invited guests, they will protect you with their lives. If anything should happen to you, not only will the people who did it pay with their lives, but your hosts who were obligated to protect you will also pay. So you just go out there, get the story of your career, and then you can walk away with their blessing and stay very much alive."

Russell's eyes flared with passion. "But if you go out there, son, with the slightest hint of suspicion, with some electronic thingama-jig hidden in your bag, then that protection is gone—immediately—and they'll have your neck slit so fast you won't even have time to cry out to your Maker. You'll never see this studio or the likes of my ugly mug again. But worst of all, you'd be making Tracy a very young widow. Is that what you want?"

Mark lowered his head, shaking inside. Frank rose from his chair and crossed over to Mark's side of the desk and sat next to him.

"But beyond the personal risks, you'd be letting down every person in that next room and every journalist across the world. There's a code of ethics in our profession, Mark. We aren't com-batants—we're neutral. The minute one of us breaks that rule, all the rest of us are under suspicion."

Frank put his hand on Mark's shoulder. "Look, Mark, I know you're a decorated Gulf War vet. I don't doubt for a second that you could take Sa'id out with your bare hands. And like all of America, I'll cheer from the rooftops when he's dead. But at what cost? Your life? No, thank you."

"I'm not saying I want to go in there and kill him personally, although the thought had crossed my mind," Mark said with a gentle smile. "All I'm saying is that we should consider letting the Feds know what's going on. They might have methods that we couldn't even dream about to get to him after the interview. . . ."

Russell shook his head. "You can't, Mark. It's too dangerous. Sa'id and his henchmen started this, and they're calling the shots. Involving any government agency only puts your life at risk. . . and, believe me, the Feds won't think twice about sacrificing your life to get to Sa'id. I think the best way for you to serve your coun-try is to get this interview. When it's over, you can be debriefed by the CIA, even before you return if that's what you want. Your observations from the inside may be all they need to get to him."

Mark released a long sigh. "I hear what you're saying, Frank, but I can't see myself doing this interview without trying to do something. This evil has to be stopped."

"Then let me put it another way, Mark." Russell's voice took on a cutting edge. "I'm ordering you to let it go. Do not involve the CIA, the FBI, the NSA, or any other group that can be identified with initials. Get the interview and get yourself home safely. You owe it to me and to Tracy. . .you served your country in the Gulf War, but you're not a marine anymore."

"What if one of those organizations approaches me?"

Russell grunted. "That's impossible. There's no way they know what's going on. Just come home safely, okay?"

STUDIO CITY, CALIFORNIA
5:24 P.M.

Mark had stopped at a wholesale floral shop just off Freeway 101 on Barham before driving over the hill into the valley. As he pulled his car into the garage, he reached over to the passenger seat and picked up the dozen long-stemmed red rosebuds intermixed with baby's breath and wrapped in green tissue paper. He took a deep breath and held it for a few seconds. He still had no idea how to approach Tracy with the news. He prayed the words would come to him.

He stepped into the house, met at the garage door by Shandy, yelping her pleasure at his return. He bent down and petted her briefly, leaving his briefcase in the laundry room.

"Tracy," he called, "I'm home."

No response.

With his right hand, Mark hid the flowers behind his back as he stepped into the hallway and headed toward the kitchen. The house was dark, which surprised him.

"Tracy? Are you home?" *Maybe she got hung up at school,* he thought. Then a smile broke out as he noticed flickering light

61

coming from the dining room and the aroma of Italian cooking in the air.

He rounded the corner and was met by a sight he couldn't quite fathom. Tracy was seated at their dining room table, which was decorated elegantly with their best china, red cloth napkins wrapped in thick gold bands, and a dozen candles adding the defining touch of warmth.

She was wearing the long black evening dress Mark hadn't seen since the previous year's Emmy Awards, accented by the diamond heart necklace and earrings he'd bought her for Christmas. Her hair was pulled up, leaving her ivory skin bare around the neckline where the diamonds shimmered as they reflected the glimmering candlelight.

Her eyes looked up, the sparkle in them more magnificent than the diamonds. He gulped, shaking his head slowly.

"You look beautiful," he managed to say. Then he brought the roses from behind his back and presented them to her.

Tracy rose as a smile brightened her already glowing face. "Oh, Mark, how sweet. What are these for?" she asked.

"For you," Mark responded.

She took them in one hand, then reached around his head with the other and gave him a tender, lingering kiss. Then she pulled away. "They're beautiful. Thank you."

Mark smiled. "And what's all this for? Did you talk with Russell today?"

Tracy shook her head, confused. "No, why?"

"Never mind." He deflected the question. For a moment, he thought she'd talked with his boss and already knew about the trip, but that didn't make sense. Her reaction would have been quite different.

"Why the candles, the romantic dinner. . . ?" His eyes moved from the table, slowly taking in the image before him. "The dress?"

Tracy grinned. "I just wanted this evening to be special."

"I think you've succeeded." Mark sighed, taking in a deep breath. "It smells wonderful."

"Fettuccini Michelangelo."

"Our first meal together."

"You remembered." Tracy smiled, holding Mark's gaze.

A moment later they spoke in unison, "So what's the news?"

Mark laughed while Tracy giggled nervously. She turned from the table and opened the china cabinet.

"You go first," Mark offered.

Tracy reached in and pulled out a vase, then turned toward the kitchen. "No, you go first. I want to hear what happened at work."

Mark followed her into the kitchen, the smell of the fettuccini making his stomach rumble. While Tracy filled the vase with water, Mark opened up their utility drawer and pulled out a pair of scissors to buy more time. He unwrapped the roses and began cutting off a small portion of each stem.

"Well, come on. . . ," Tracy pleaded. "What's going on?"

Before Mark could answer, the phone rang. They looked at each other to see who was going to answer it. Tracy was closest to the kitchen phone, so she turned to grab it.

"Just let the machine get it," Mark suggested.

"It might be important," Tracy said.

"Mrs. Taylor, this is Chris at Dr. Hoyt's office," Tracy heard on the other end of the line. She forced herself not to look back at Mark—sure that her facial expression would give away her shock.

"Yes," Tracy answered cautiously, relieved that Mark hadn't answered the call.

"The doctor wanted me to check and see if you and your husband were going to come in for the ultrasound tomorrow?"

She couldn't stop herself—the mention of Mark brought her eyes over to him standing by the counter, cutting the ends off the roses. He glanced up at her with a questioning shrug, wondering whom she was talking to.

"I'll have to call you back on that." Tracy turned away from Mark.

"Okay, but we're about to close the office, and Dr. Hoyt has a pretty full schedule tomorrow. If we don't hear from you first thing in the morning, it may have to wait until next week."

"I understand," Tracy answered. "I'll call you tomorrow."

She hung up the phone, turning back to Mark.

"Who was that?"

Tracy cringed inside while stepping back to the sink and pulling out the vase. She hated to lie, but, "That was Veronica. . .from school. She wanted to go over some notes, but it can wait until tomorrow."

She picked up the roses that Mark had cut and brought them to her face, breathing in the wonderful aroma. She looked up at Mark, and a grin spread over her face as her eyes sparkled. "They're lovely."

Mark smiled, the phone call quickly forgotten.

"So tell me your big news?" Tracy asked as she began setting the trimmed roses into the vase.

"It's kind of one of those good news/bad news kind of things," Mark answered, suddenly nervous again.

"Well, let's have the good news first."

"The good news is," Mark continued as he snipped at the remaining roses, "I've been assigned a story that will definitely be the scoop of a lifetime."

"That's great, Mark!" Tracy responded with a quick hug, stretching up to kiss his cheek before asking, "What is it?"

"That's where the bad news comes in," Mark answered carefully, then put down the scissors and took Tracy's hands. "I'm going to interview Ahmad Hani Sa'id."

Tracy gasped, the hope and expectation in her eyes doused by a rain of unbelief. "No, how is that possible?"

"To be honest with you, we're not sure." Mark left the rest of the flowers on the counter and pulled her toward a chair at the kitchen table. He sat next to her, all the while never letting go of her hands.

"Frank called me into his office today," he explained. "It seems that Sa'id has agreed to do an interview with our network, but only if I do it."

"I don't understand." Tracy shook her head, the confusion in her eyes giving way to fear. "How would Sa'id even know you?"

"We don't know." Mark went on to explain how the show had been approached through their cable news division in the Middle East.

"I don't like it, Mark," she responded. Her expression had grown cold.

"It'll be okay," he tried to console her. "Frank thinks I'll be treated safely as their invited guest, like royalty, is how he put it," Mark rambled, trying to convince himself as much as Tracy. "For whatever reason, Sa'id is ready to talk and he's chosen me."

Tracy glanced down, then back up with her eyes tearing up. "What about that guy from the *Wall Street Journal*? The one they executed."

"This isn't the same group. . . ," Mark tried to explain softly. "Sa'id won't be out to hurt me. He'll want to make sure I get his message back here and on the air. I'll be in and out in no time."

Tracy wasn't convinced. "Where's the interview?"

"We think Syria. We're flying into southern Turkey near the Syrian border."

"When?" Her eyes pleaded for him not to go.

Mark lowered his head. "Tonight, ten o'clock."

Tracy took her hands away from Mark's, then stood and walked back to the counter. She picked up the remaining roses and began setting them into the vase. Mark followed her, placing his arms gently around her.

"Everything will be fine," he said quietly. "God will protect me."

"Mark," Tracy stepped out of his embrace, moving to hide the tears pooling in her eyes. "Our troops are building up along the Turkish border. They could invade Syria at any time. . .or start a massive bombing campaign like we did in Afghanistan. What if you're in Syria at the time. . .why you?"

"I don't know, Tracy." Mark was out of words.

"What am I supposed to do?" Tracy's voice took on a hard edge as she turned back to face Mark, her eyes slanted. "Just say okay, praise the Lord, and sit here calmly while you run off and meet with the devil halfway around the world? A man who could kill you just because you're American? I'm not sure I have that kind of faith, Mark."

"Tracy, honey," he pleaded. "I didn't ask for this assignment."

"Well, did you even consider not taking it?"

The force of her statement made Mark's eyes widen; then he looked down. No, he hadn't.

"I didn't think so." Tracy looked away as well, willing herself not to cry. "What about me, Mark. . .what about us?"

Mark struggled, trying to come up with something to say, but nothing came before Tracy turned and ran from the room.

She couldn't stay and risk blurting out the next question. . . . *What about our baby?*

CHAPTER 6

CIA HEADQUARTERS, LANGLEY, VIRGINIA
8:39 P.M.

Wendy took her eyes off the computer screen for a moment, rubbing them with her right thumb and forefinger. She leaned back in her chair, glancing at the digital time display on her telephone. She'd been at it for nearly fifteen hours, but she couldn't go home until she heard how it had gone with Taylor. The outcome of that meeting would determine the direction of the CIA's task force. Taylor had better cooperate. Getting Sa'id had become the rallying cry around the agency for the past few months, but for Wendy it was much more than that.

As focused and intense as Wendy had been on her job due to the 9/11 tragedy, it had all changed last November. Her brother had been at the football game between the Redskins and the Eagles, one of the targeted stadiums for the Sunday Massacre. Unfortunate enough to have been sitting in the section behind the southern end zone, he was right above the tunnel where the terrorist had stopped his school bus and set off the explosives, leaving behind a young widow and three children forever without their dad, all under the age of seven.

The events of 9/11 had been enough to get Wendy to devote her career to the CIA; the Sunday Massacre had made it personal.

She called up the CIA's facial identity program on her computer, showing several possibilities for how Ahmad Hani Sa'id would look today, extrapolated from pictures of him when he was eighteen.

Hatred burned within her as she studied the photographs.

Her reflective moment was interrupted by a presence behind her. She turned to see Jack Murphy standing outside her cubicle.

"We'll get him, Wendy," he said gently.

"I'm counting on that."

"Don't you think you should go home and get some sleep? We're going to be at it pretty hard when Taylor leaves the country."

"No." Wendy shook her head. "I want to hear how the meeting goes in L.A. Besides, I'm still running some research on Taylor. . . ."

"Wendy, go home," Murphy ordered. "I'll call you myself when they've talked with Taylor. We'll be at it twenty-four/seven as soon as his plane leaves our airspace. I'll need you sharp. . .get out of here."

"I will, Jack, soon."

Jack smiled as he shook his head. "It's an order, Wendy."

"Okay." Wendy smiled. "I just need to initiate one last search."

Jack left without further argument and Wendy turned back to her computer. She had run every search she could think of on Mark Taylor, trying to make sure there was nothing in his past that she'd overlooked. Now she prepared a massive search for every known terrorist in the CIA database against any possible connections to Taylor, known associates, workplace—anything that would put him in the same place at the same time with a terrorist. It would take several hours to run anyway, so she thought she'd start it, then head home for a few hours sleep.

STUDIO CITY, CALIFORNIA
5:41 P.M.

Mark walked sheepishly into the bedroom, approaching Tracy as she sat on their bed in the darkness holding Shandy, her head tilted toward the floor.

"Look, Trace," he muttered, sitting down next to her on the bed. "I know this is a shock. . .it was to me too."

Tracy didn't move as she continued to stare aimlessly at the bedroom carpet. All her plans of the intimate dinner, sharing with her husband the greatest news of their young married life. . .ruined. Mark continued to talk, but the words just filled the room with noise. When she blinked, a tear slid slowly down her right cheek. Mark reached up and gently wiped it away.

"How can you just go?" Tracy pushed his hand away, her voice shaking. "There are reporters all over the stinking desert that would die for this interview. Let one of them have it."

"I said the same thing to Frank, but it isn't an option," Mark argued. "Sa'id's contact made it very clear. . .it's me or nobody."

"I find that hard to believe." Tracy was surprised at the sarcasm rising in her voice. "What do they think, that you're the Barbara Walters of international television?"

Mark suppressed a biting comeback, trying to keep his voice under control. "Look, Tracy, I don't know why this has been dropped in my lap. I—" The ring of their doorbell interrupted his response. Shandy jumped off the bed, barking and running to the front door. Mark looked out to the family room, then back to Tracy, aching to get his point across.

"Trace, please understand. . . ."

"Go get the door," she said coldly.

Mark reluctantly got up and left the bedroom. The doorbell chimed again as he walked through the living room switching on the lights, destroying the romantic mood of the flickering candles. *What a time to be interrupted by some door-to-door salesman.* Whoever it was, Mark was going to get rid of him quickly and get back to Tracy. She was responding worse than he had imagined. It wasn't like her.

"Shandy, quiet," Mark ordered.

He opened the door and his jaw dropped. Standing before

him were two men. One was a black-haired man of medium height and build wearing a black suit with a white shirt and black tie. If he wasn't a federal agent, he could certainly land the part at any Hollywood studio. The second of the two was an African-American, a good head taller than the first, built like a brick wall with short-cropped hair and dressed in a marine uniform.

"It's been a long time, Mark," said Griff Baxter, the lieutenant who had led Mark's special operations squad of marines in Desert Storm. Mark fought the urge to salute. Ten years out of the service and the impulse was still there. Had it been any other time in Mark's life, he would have been thrilled to see his former platoon commander. But the timing was too suspect.

"I hope we're not interrupting anything. . . ," Griff continued as Mark struggled with his thoughts.

"No, sir." Mark smiled tentatively as he noticed the gold oak leaves on his shirt collar. "Major. . ."

Griff returned the smile. "Yeah, you stay in long enough, they have to promote you."

"Please, come in," Mark offered, opening the door fully and standing back. Shandy growled softly, scrutinizing the two men.

"Is it safe?" Griff asked.

"You're a marine," Mark joked. "Can't handle a vicious attack dog?"

The two men entered as Griff introduced the man with him. "Mark, this is Mike Weston; he's FBI, with the Counterterrorism Unit."

The reason for the visit suddenly became crystal clear.

"It's nice to meet you, Mr. Taylor," he offered along with his outstretched hand.

"Please, call me Mark," Mark said as they shook. "Have a seat."

Griff and Weston took opposite sides of Mark's couch.

"It looks like the marines are treating you well, Griff," Mark said as he made his way to the La-Z-Boy chair next to Griff.

"And it looks like you've done all right for yourself too." Griff paused, looking around the house, seeing the lit candles on the dining room table and the china set in place. He motioned down the hallway with his head. "We're sorry for the interruption. Are we able to talk freely?"

Mark nodded, appreciating Griff's offer to speak privately. But stepping outside at this point would only serve to increase Tracy's anger.

"As Major Baxter pointed out," Weston jumped in, "I'm with the FBI. Mr. Taylor, we know about your planned trip to Turkey."

"Uh-huh," Mark answered blandly, refusing to commit.

"We also know about the interview with Ahmad Sa'id," Weston pressed, waiting for Mark's reaction.

"Uh-huh."

Weston let the moment linger, then looked intently into Mark's eyes. "We'd like to enlist your help in locating him."

Mark held the man's gaze for a moment, then sighed and looked up at the ceiling. There was no point in denying it; part of him was thrilled that they'd somehow been alerted to the interview. This is what Mark had wanted from the beginning, to lead his government right to Sa'id's doorstep. But the words of Frank Russell reverberated in his head: *You go out there with the slightest hint of suspicion, and they'll have your neck slit so fast you won't even have time to cry out to your Maker.*

"How did you find out?" Mark finally asked.

Weston took his eyes off Mark and glanced at Griff.

"Tell him," Griff ordered.

"Intercepted communication between Josh Mclintock and the network in New York," Weston acknowledged.

Mark's eyebrows rose. "You're wiretapping my network?"

"We're at war, Mark; they're on foreign soil," Griff cut in sharply.

Mark's mind flashed back to his cellular call with Tracy earlier in the day and the strange echo he'd heard. "Do you have my phone bugged? Is that how you knew I'd be home. . .you heard the conversation I had with Tracy?"

The stoic expression on Weston's face remained unchanged. Mark looked over at his former officer, his friend.

"Griff?"

Griff's expression hardened, reminiscent of the look Mark would get when his answer was on a need-to-know basis.

"We are at a critical time in this country, Mark." Weston sat up on the edge of the couch. "In the past three months, nearly thirteen thousand American citizens have been slaughtered at the hands of this man. We'll do whatever it takes to find him. If there's a possibility that we can take him out without invading Syria, we're going to take it. Thousands of Americans' lives could be saved."

"And don't think that from the moment I was assigned this interview I haven't been agonizing over that possibility," Mark returned with a cold stare.

Tracy breathed as lightly as she could in the back bedroom, straining to hear every word. The growing knot in the pit of her stomach had nothing to do with the pregnancy. Mark was caught up in something she couldn't fathom. The anger that had flashed through earlier was slowly draining away as an overwhelming fear replaced it. She turned away from the door and quietly stepped toward her closet.

Mark glanced over to Griff. "When were you brought in, Major?"

"This afternoon," Griff said. "I didn't know what was going on until Agent Weston met me at Point Mugu when I landed."

"Where are you stationed?"

"Quantico."

Mark looked confused; Quantico was in Virginia, three thousand miles away.

"They put me in the backseat of an F-14 Tomcat," Griff explained. "Things move a lot faster since 9/11."

"I guess so." Mark grinned, then turned back to Weston. "Did you consider, Agent Weston, that I could be under surveillance from the Jihad al Sharia? That arriving at my doorstep in your Man in Black outfit alongside a Marine Corps major could have already compromised the situation?"

"Yes, we did," Weston answered. "We checked the street before approaching. Nobody's watching."

Mark wasn't convinced. "Who else knows about this?"

"The president and the vice president, the national security advisor, the directors of Homeland Security, FBI, CIA, Seth Maxwell—my boss in D.C.—the two of us, and a handful of officers at Langley," Weston answered.

With each name, the pressure on Mark grew, like weights on a barbell that he would never be able to press. He felt so alone.

Before Mark could respond, he sensed Tracy's presence behind him. Griff and Weston politely stood as she sat on the armrest of his chair, placing her arm around him. The black dress was gone, replaced by blue slacks and a white sweatshirt boldly declaring National Studios in blue across the front. Her touch warmed him.

"This is my wife, Tracy." Mark took her hand in his. "Tracy, this is Major Griff Baxter—I served under him in the Gulf War—and this is Agent Weston with the FBI."

"It's a pleasure, Mrs. Taylor," Griff said. "We apologize for the intrusion."

"It's nice to finally meet you, Major." Tracy smiled warmly. "I've heard so much about you." Then she turned and nodded to Weston as her eyes darkened suspiciously. "Agent Weston."

"Mrs. Taylor," Weston returned the acknowledgment, then continued as he returned to the couch. "We are sorry for the inconvenience. But time was of the essence."

"Evidently so," Tracy said.

The three sat in silence for a moment, no one sure how to deal with the presence of Tracy in the room. Mark felt Tracy's hand move slightly in his, her fingers pressing lightly on his thumb, then each of his fingers one at a time. It was their way of silently communicating the five words "I love you very much," one word for each finger. The faint lines beside Mark's eyes deepened as he looked up at her, and a smile creased his lips. He repeated the motion across Tracy's fingers, once again feeling the bond with his wife that had been broken earlier. Weston's voice brought Mark's attention back to the discussion.

"Do you have any idea why they've chosen you, Mr. Taylor?"

Mark shook his head. "No, it shocked all of us at the show."

"It does seem strange. You're not an internationally known journalist. . . ," Weston argued.

"I know. There's no reason Sa'id would even know my name. I'm frankly baffled why this has happened to me."

Weston stared intently at him, calling on years of FBI fieldwork to discern the truthfulness of Mark's statements. He couldn't spot anything in his body language that conflicted with his words.

"What are you proposing?" Mark asked in the silence.

Weston's eyes went from Mark to Tracy and back. "Are you sure you want to continue this discussion with your wife present?"

The condescending tone was just about all Tracy could stand of Agent Weston. She was about to jump in when Mark responded.

"Whatever you have to say to me can be said in front of Tracy," he stated firmly. "Because any decision that involves this trip. . ." Mark turned toward Tracy, ". . .will be decided together."

Griff put his hand up to his mouth in an attempt to cover up his smile. Agent Weston wasn't amused.

"All right, have it your way." He softened his tone, realizing his mistake. "I apologize, Mrs. Taylor; this is just highly sensitive and classified. No offense intended."

Tracy only nodded once, her lips pressed together. She gently squeezed Mark's hand.

"We're hoping," Weston continued, his voice seeming to echo

in the quiet room, "that we can place a CIA operative with your team, and let you lead us to Sa'id."

Across the street, the curtain parted as Ishmael Basra's eyes stared intently at the entrance to Mark's house. He'd seen the two men enter moments ago; one man had obviously been a federal agent. The other had surprised him. A military officer hadn't been expected.

Ishmael stepped away from the front window, walking past the dead bodies of Mr. and Mrs. Frost. He'd overpowered the retired couple earlier that afternoon, killing them to make sure he could never be identified. Then he'd sat and waited patiently for Taylor to return home.

He reached inside his black canvas bag and pulled out a digital camera. He wanted to capture the faces of the two men as they came out. He would transfer the images to his computer and add them to the report he'd be e-mailing shortly. Ishmael knew nothing of why he was watching Taylor's house, but it had been an assignment he readily accepted. It seemed whatever interest the Jihad al Sharia had with Mark Taylor was certainly warranted.

CHAPTER 7

The room was silent. For Mark, what had been churning beneath the surface since Russell first brought up the interview now confronted him head-on. Here was the chance to act on the passions within his heart and help bring Sa'id down—but at the risk of his career, and quite possibly his life.

He prayed silently for wisdom.

Tracy's struggle was much more intense. She had fully supported the military action against terrorism, bravely denouncing the evil acts. But that was a different war, one that had not involved her personally. Now she faced her worst fear. . .losing Mark. What had been easy to endorse then now seemed to cost her too much. She silently prayed that Mark would somehow find the courage not to go.

"What do you think, Mark?" Griff asked.

"You don't know what you're asking of me," Mark said quietly.

"Yes, we do. . . ," Weston began.

"No, you don't," Mark lashed out, startling Tracy.

"I know we're crossing over every boundary that exists between the free press and a government covert action," Weston acknowledged. "But life and the way things are normally done have changed since 9/11 and have become further complicated since the Sunday Massacre. We want your help in stopping this man before he has a chance to take more innocent lives."

"And I can't think of anything I would rather do than to help bring this monster down, but it's not that simple. There's much more at stake here than just helping you."

"We understand that," Weston replied. "But it doesn't take away from the fact that your country is asking for your help."

Mark sat silently, holding on to Tracy's hand. "I can't answer you right now. . .we're going to have to talk about this."

"There's not a lot of time, Mark," Weston interjected.

"I realize that, but you rush this. . ." Mark backed his point with piercing eyes; ". . .you lose me."

Weston nodded quietly.

Mark looked over at Tracy, trying to read what she was thinking. . .her eyes pleaded with him. He nodded understanding but turned back to Weston. "What are you hoping to do. . .use the interview to pinpoint his location for later assault or take him down right then and there?"

Weston answered carefully, not wanting to inflame the look he was getting from Tracy. "We don't want to put you in a compromising position, Mark. You're a civilian now, and we respect that and are greatly concerned for your safety. Our best-case scenario is to play this out. . .let you do the interview and get you safely out of the area. Then before Sa'id can move, we'll strike—and take Sa'id out."

Mark wondered how plausible that was. . .and how quickly his career would disappear when word got out of his complicity with the government.

He turned to his former platoon leader. "What are your thoughts, Griff?"

Griff sighed. "Fate is a funny lady sometimes. There isn't one journalist in this nation, Mark—probably in the world—that has the military capabilities and talent that you do. When Weston told me what was going down, my first thought was that Sa'id has no idea who he's dealing with. In my opinion, you're the perfect man for this assignment."

"But. . ." Mark picked up on the hesitation in Griff's voice.

"Well, I want Sa'id's head on a platter as much as anyone, but not at the expense of your life." Griff paused, glancing at Tracy for a quick moment before continuing. "I saw you serve your country bravely and with honor, Mark. You don't owe her a suicide mission."

Griff ignored the look of contempt shot at him by Weston. "If you agree to this. . .make sure you have mission approval."

Mark smiled warmly. The advice went far deeper than Griff's words. He was reinforcing the fact that Mark wasn't in the military any longer where he would have followed Griff's orders instantly without question. He was now a civilian. He was telling Mark he didn't owe Agent Weston, the FBI, or Homeland Security any kind of blind trust.

Mark turned back to Weston. "Is there anything else?"

"No," Weston answered. "Not until we know your decision."

"Okay." Mark patted Tracy's hand and looked at her. "Then we need to talk."

Griff stood, but Weston remained seated as if he expected Mark and Tracy to trot off down the hall and return minutes later with his answer. Mark caught his attention with his eyes. . .then Weston reluctantly stood with Griff.

"How do I make contact?" Mark asked.

Weston reached into his pocket and pulled out a card and wrote something on the back of it. "Here's my cell number. Call me as soon as you decide." Weston hated leaving without his answer. "The more time we have, the better we can plan."

"I realize that," Mark said, then turned to Griff. "I wish this had been under different circumstances."

"Me too, Mark," Griff said as the two men embraced.

"If you need any advice," Griff handed Mark his cell phone number, "call me."

Mark watched the two men head down the sidewalk, all of them oblivious to the digital pictures being taken by Ishmael from across the street. Mark noticed Weston already grabbing for his cell phone as Mark closed the door, turning to face Tracy. She held her ground by the chair, looking down at the carpet. As Mark stepped toward her, she slowly raised her head.

"What are you going to do?"

"I don't know," Mark replied, coming up behind her and wrapping his arms around her waist. "What are you feeling?"

"Don't go," she whispered.

Mark's stomach dropped. He wanted to talk this through with her; be analytical; weigh the pros and cons. She went right to the heart of the matter, and her obvious pain tore into him.

He came around the chair and knelt before her, speaking softly, "Tracy, that's like asking a firefighter to not go on a three-alarm fire, or a police officer to not go out on patrol. . .a pilot not to fly. It's my job; I have to go." He paused. "I'll be back, I promise."

"You can't promise that."

Mark pursed his lips, not knowing how to respond.

"Our lives are just beginning." Tracy struggled to keep from breaking down altogether. "We haven't even been married a year. It's not fair to do this to us. You don't know what you're doing to me. You don't know. . ." She caught herself, then looked directly through Mark. "Why you? Of all the people in the world, why you?"

"I don't know. God must have a plan. . . ."

"Or Satan's got one and that's to get you killed."

"Trace, I've been struggling with this all day. The minute Frank told me about it, I've wondered what to do. . .should we let the government in on it or not? I even went to him this afternoon to discuss it."

"What did he say?"

Mark sighed. "To leave it alone. He thinks the safest plan is to brief them once it's all over."

"You don't see the wisdom in that?"

Mark nodded. "Yes, if I'm only concerned about my own skin. But what about the thousands of lives that could be saved if Sa'id is stopped now, not ten or twenty years from now?"

"Is that your responsibility?" Tracy asked, her voice rising.

"In this case," Mark nearly whispered, "what if it is?"

Silence. Tracy's head hung down. . .she knew she couldn't win with logic.

"I can't stand the thought of losing you, Mark," she blurted out, surprised at her honesty.

He reached under her chin and gently pulled her face up so their eyes could meet. "And I couldn't stand the thought of losing you either."

She slid off the armrest and wrapped her arms around him, comforted slightly with his closeness, disturbed greatly by the path they were being forced to walk.

Mark held her tightly. Tracy was shaking, fighting to hold back the tears. The image burned in her mind—their child, born without ever knowing her dad. It wouldn't go away.

The two held each other for what seemed like forever. In the stillness, Mark's voice quietly broke through.

"Father," he prayed, "this is one of those times where I just don't have the words."

Tracy listened, gently closing her eyes, releasing the built-up tears.

"We need to hear from You, Lord; show us what is right. Do I go or do I stay? I want to be Your servant, but this is a path I don't want to walk unless You're in it. Am I part of Your plan to bring justice to this evil one. . .or am I only to go and fulfill my assignment? And, God, please comfort Tracy; bring peace where turmoil reigns right now. We know that You work all things together for good for those who love You. You alone are God. We need Your wisdom."

Tracy sucked in a couple of quick breaths, reaching up and wiping at her nose with the sleeve of her sweatshirt. Mark gently wiped the tears off each of her cheeks, then leaned in, bringing his lips to hers. She kissed back, gently. He pulled away, smiling.

"What happened to the dress?"

"It didn't seem appropriate anymore under the circumstances."

"Do you think dinner's ruined?"

Her eyes opened in shock. "How can you think about eating?"

"That smell has been driving me crazy ever since I got home."

"What about that prayer? What did God say?"

"To eat," Mark said with a laugh.

"No, seriously, Mark; what are you feeling?"

"I am serious; I'm hungry." Mark chuckled as he headed for the kitchen, pulling her along. "I don't know what God is saying yet. So let's try and recapture the moment. This might be my last home-cooked meal for awhile."

Tracy shook her head. . .sometimes he was just impossible.

WEST McLEAN, VIRGINIA
10:10 P.M.

It was one of those nights when Wendy couldn't decide if it was worth it to take off her clothes and climb into bed or just fall asleep on top of the covers. She'd stopped for a Subway sandwich on the way home and eaten it in the car, and she was ready to grab whatever sleep she could before waking up at four and starting the marathon of covering Mark's trip.

Her head had just hit the pillow when the phone rang. She groaned and reached for the receiver.

"Wendy, it's Jack." Her drowsiness was instantly shattered by the sound of her boss's voice.

"What have you heard?"

"The meeting took place. . . ." Jack spoke in general terms, knowing Wendy's home phone wouldn't be secure. "Went well, but no decision yet. Target thinking it over."

Wendy sighed, disappointed by the news. "I'm surprised. Any

idea when we'll know?"

"No, we're sitting tight."

"Okay, let me know."

"You got it." Jack disconnected.

Wendy slammed the phone down into its cradle harder than she intended. What was keeping Taylor from committing? She shook her head, trying to hold her frayed emotions in check. Not everyone in the country had her determination to see Sa'id pay. *If it has to be done the hard way, so be it!* They'd get him without Taylor's help if they had to.

STUDIO CITY, CALIFORNIA
7:13 P.M.

The candles had burned down to stubs; wax was dripping all over their bronze holders and onto the centerpiece of the table, but it went unnoticed. Tracy and Mark sat on stools at the kitchen counter eating out of the pans. It wasn't the most romantic setting, but it was the perfect way to get Tracy to open up and talk.

They began to discuss various options. Tracy soon realized that as a journalist, Mark had to make the trip. Once they had reached a consensus on that, the conversation turned to whether or not he should cooperate with the government. That wasn't as easy a decision to make. Mark was very conscious of Tracy's fear for his safe return, lightly touching on any of the inherent dangers. He felt like she was holding something back, but he couldn't figure out what.

"I think it boils down to what Griff said," Mark thought out loud after he'd swallowed his last bite of fettuccini Michelangelo. "Man, that was good."

Tracy smiled. "Glad you liked it."

"By the way," Mark suddenly remembered, "what gives with the great meal, the candles, the dress I wish you had kept on? You said there was some news. . . ."

Tracy blinked, making her decision in an instant. "Oh, nothing compared to yours. I got the top score in my class on the wills and bequests exam. I thought it'd be fun to celebrate. Let's get back to the topic at hand. What did Griff say?"

Mark continued gazing into Tracy's eyes, knowing she wasn't telling the truth. He contemplated challenging her on it but decided to let it go. If there was something she wanted to tell him, it'd come out when she was ready.

"Remember Griff said to make sure I had mission approval?"

Tracy nodded, relieved he hadn't forced the issue. "Yeah, and that means. . ."

"Look, I don't think we can make the right decision until we know exactly what their plan is. For me to say no without seeing what the Feds think they can pull off is just as bad as saying yes to a plan I've never seen before."

"I guess that makes sense."

"Here's what I'm thinking, and see if you agree. Let's tell them I'm interested, but I won't commit until I see a full, detailed plan."

Tracy thought for a few seconds. "How is that something we can discuss together? By the time they get you the plan, you'll be halfway around the world."

"True, but I won't agree to anything until we talk it through. I'll demand to brief you fully, or no deal."

Tracy looked intently at the man she loved. "Is this what you feel like God is saying?"

Mark paused, carefully weighing his words. "Yes, honey. I do."

"I'm not so sure I'm there yet," she admitted quietly.

"I know you're not."

She reached out and caressed his cheek with her fingers before whispering, "Come back to me."

He put his hand on hers as he embraced her with his eyes. "I will."

CHAPTER 8

LLOYD'S COFFEE SHOP, STUDIO CITY
7:20 P.M.

"I'm not sure I helped you too much in there," Griff mentioned as he poured some creamer into his coffee. Weston sat across the booth from him, two bites into his apple pie in a coffee shop near Mark's neighborhood.

"That's an understatement," Weston responded bitterly. "What was with that suicide mission garbage?"

"Just calling it as I see it." Griff smiled before he leaned toward Weston and got deadly serious. "Look, Mike, if he agrees to go along with you, remember this: He's a trained marine, ran a dozen special ops missions into enemy territory. Don't treat him like a civilian. If he agrees to work with you, he can be a tremendous asset."

"You have a lot of faith in somebody that's been out of the service for over ten years," Weston grunted. "It won't be up to me anyway. It'll be a CIA op all the way."

Weston lifted his fork up with another load of pie when his cell phone rang. He stuffed the fork into his mouth, then reached for the phone, mumbling, "Weston."

He chewed while listening, until a grin appeared. "That sounds fair." Weston responded to Griff's upraised eyebrows by nodding. Griff smiled, expecting nothing less from Mark.

Weston listened a bit longer, then said, "Okay. We'll be right there."

"We're heading back?" Griff asked.

Weston stuffed a couple of quick bites of the apple pie in his mouth before pushing the plate away and looking directly into Griff's eyes. "He wants to see you."

"What time do we have to leave for the airport?" Tracy asked as she brought Mark his favorite afghan sweater.

Mark was stacking a week's worth of underwear into the suitcase he had sitting on their bed. "We need to leave pretty soon. I'm not sure how hard it will be to get through security this time of night."

"Why all the clothes? I thought this interview was on Saturday?"

"It is, but by the time we fly there and get back, it could easily be five or six days."

He stopped packing, put his arms around her, and pulled her into a tight embrace.

"I kept thinking in terms of three days." Tracy's voice was soft, almost as if she were talking to herself. "I don't know if I can hang on for a week."

"The interview's in three days. . .when that's over, I'll be back in safe territory, heading straight back to you." Mark kissed her lightly on top of her head, taking in the fragrance of her hair with a deep breath. They stood in silence a moment, before Tracy walked to their nightstand. She picked up Mark's Bible and brought it to him.

"Don't forget this," she said.

Mark took it and placed it into his briefcase. "How about First John this time?"

Whenever Mark would go away on a trip, the two had kept up a ritual of reading through a book of the Bible together. It had proved to be a wonderful spiritual link while they were apart.

"First John it is," Tracy agreed.

Mark put the rest of his clothes into the suitcase and zipped it up as the doorbell rang.

"That must be Griff and Weston. You know what to do?"

"Go ahead," Tracy said. "I'll be out in a minute." Mark walked down the hallway, praying they weren't making a big mistake. "Come on in," Mark offered upon opening the door.

"I think you're doing the right thing," Weston said as he stepped through.

"I haven't agreed to anything yet," Mark returned. "Let's go in here."

Mark led them into the kitchen to sit around the dinette table. "I don't have much time; my plane leaves in a few hours," Mark stated. "I want to make sure you understand that when I hear the plan in Paris, nothing is agreed to until I talk it over with my wife."

"That can be approved on one condition," Weston said.

"What's that?"

"In Paris, we'll get you to a secure phone. Your wife will have to come to our office to receive the call. Nothing about your cooperation gets mentioned on a cell phone or any landline telephone, only on a secure line."

"The studio gave us satellite phones. What about those?"

"No. Too risky."

"Understood," Mark agreed. "Now what about my producer? Do we let him in on this?"

"No," Weston replied quickly. "The more people that know, the more your life will be in danger."

Mark assumed that for Frank Russell as well. It seemed that if he went through with this, he'd be alone. "How will I be contacted in Paris?"

"We'll have somebody with you at all times, although you won't see them. Do nothing out of the ordinary. We'll approach you at the right time. Whoever does will use the code name 'Dumbo Drop' to let you know he's with us."

Mark couldn't believe what he'd just heard. "He'll use what?"

"Don't look at me," Weston pleaded. "I don't name these things."

Mark smiled. "There was a movie by that name, wasn't there?"

"I think so. . .could be why they're using it."

"You know it's not bad now that I think of it, referring to Sa'id as Dumbo—kind of ironic."

Weston cleared his throat. "Actually, Dumbo is your handle."

"Great." Mark rolled his eyes.

"I bet it's a reflection of how the CIA views you boys in the press," Griff chuckled.

Mark grimaced. "We won't look suspicious at all talking about elephants outside de Gaulle Airport."

"Welcome back, gentlemen," Tracy said as she walked into the kitchen. "Sorry about the mess."

"Not a problem, Mrs. Taylor," Weston said. "We apologize again for the intrusion."

Tracy stopped by Weston's chair. "Could I speak with you alone for a second?"

"Sure," he replied, somewhat taken aback.

As he followed her out of the kitchen, Tracy said, "I assume you'll be staying here in L.A. and other agents will be handling Mark. Is that correct?"

"Yes, ma'am," Weston replied.

Tracy continued all the way into the family room. "I want to make one thing absolutely clear here, Mr. Weston. I want nothing held back from me."

"I understand."

"I also want access to you twenty-four/seven. If I call, you answer. . . ."

Mark had kept quiet until Tracy's voice could barely be heard in the kitchen. Then he whispered to Griff, "We don't have much time. I want you to do me a favor."

"Name it."

"I'm willing to go along with them on this, up to a point. But I want some backup."

"What do you mean?"

"I want somebody with me that I know I can trust. Somebody like you."

"Me! You've got to be kidding," Griff exclaimed.

"Keep your voice down," Mark said.

"Sorry," Griff answered, looking back toward the family room. "I can't go with you."

"Why not?"

"Forty-nine reasons, all of them having to do with age. I wouldn't be any good in the field anymore. . . ." Griff paused as a thought jumped into his head. "But I know someone who would."

Mark looked toward the other room and made sure Weston and Tracy were still talking, then anxiously turned back to Griff. "Who?"

"Chuck Fleming."

Mark knew immediately Griff was onto something. Chuck had been one of the top men in their unit—the best when it came to being inside enemy territory.

"Chuck would be perfect. Is he still in the marines?"

"Technically, no," Griff said. "But he's on the payroll as an outside contractor to plan counterterrorist scenarios for our embassies in danger zones. I think I can reach him, but he'd need a cover story."

Mark had already thought of that. "My boss told me this afternoon that I need to bring along another journalist. . .standard procedure to corroborate the interview. Chuck could pose as that journalist."

"That could work, but there's not much time." They could hear Tracy coming back with Weston. Griff shrugged his head in their direction. "They'd have to agree to it, and he's going to have to have legitimate documentation to get past Sa'id's men."

Mark hesitated an instant. . .he would have liked to get Chuck in without the CIA's knowledge, but Griff had a point. He nodded quietly as Weston rounded the corner into the kitchen.

"I appreciate your help, Agent Weston." Tracy flashed Mark a quick smile and slid into the chair next to her husband.

Mark glanced over to Weston as he took the seat next to Griff. "Here's the deal, Weston. If I approve of a CIA guy going along for the ride, I want something in return. I want someone else there."

Weston looked from Mark to Griff, wondering what he'd missed while he was in the other room. "And that man would be. . ."

"An ex-marine, Chuck Fleming," Mark said.

"He was with our unit in Desert Storm," Griff filled in. "He was one of the best soldiers when it came to crunch time behind enemy lines."

Mark and Griff briefed Weston on Chuck's history and his current assignment, including their plan and the possible cover story for bringing Chuck along.

"I'll pass your request on," was all Weston would say when they'd finished.

"No, Agent Weston," Mark corrected. "You'll pass on my demand. If Chuck's willing to sign onto the mission, he's part of it, or we won't have a deal."

CIA HEADQUARTERS, LANGLEY, VIRGINIA
10:29 P.M.

Five men sat in the CIA's second-floor conference room, checking and rechecking every detail of Operation Dumbo Drop. Jack had brought in Vince Ruzio, one of their top field officers who had just returned from the Middle East. Vince, being a dark-skinned Italian, had passed himself off as an Arab in numerous undercover assignments. The group had created two detailed plans. . .one that involved Mark's cooperation and one that didn't. All five desperately hoped they would implement the one that did.

"So, any problem getting all assets in place by Friday?" Jack asked the group.

"None," Ryan Drake, the agency's logistics officer, replied. "We've already been pouring resources into Turkey in advance of the Syrian offensive. Most of the pieces we need are already there."

"Good." Jack tapped his pencil on the conference table. There wasn't much else to do but wait for word from the West Coast.

"Why don't we take a break?" Jack said, glancing at his watch. "Everyone back here in half an hour."

Jack stood up and stretched. . .wishing he'd had the sense to spend at least one of the previous nights home in his own bed. It looked like another night of catching whatever sleep he could on the couch in his office.

As the room emptied, Vince hung around, leaning back casually in his chair. "You need some sleep, Murphy."

"I know." Jack rubbed at his forehead, then spread his fingers and ran them through the top of his thinning hair. "When this op is over, I'm taking a break."

Vince laughed. "Like the one I'm on now?"

Jack smiled. "Yeah, my apologies. Do you want me to get somebody else for this mission?"

"No!" he objected. "I wouldn't miss this trip for anything. I'm just making the point that until we get Sa'id there won't be a break."

"Yeah, you're probably right." Jack sighed, rolling his head from side to side and stretching his arms out in an attempt to loosen his tight muscles. "What do you think of the odds?"

"The chances of waiting for Taylor to do his interview, then try and get Sa'id with an air strike. . ." Vince shook his head. "Not good. They'll have Sa'id out of the area instantly and probably hold onto Taylor for a while. I still say our best shot is just to treat this as a black op."

One aspect Jack and Vince had talked about privately, granting that Taylor cooperated, would be for Vince to have the authority to assassinate Sa'id on the spot—a tactic known as a black operation. In 1976, President Ford had issued an executive order banning the

CIA from such practices. After 9/11, President Bush had revoked that order.

The only problem with a black op being sanctioned in this case was that with Sa'id heavily guarded, it would be very unlikely that either Vince or Taylor would return alive.

"I'm operating under the assumption we'll have a green light," Jack stated flatly.

Vince sighed, looking past Jack to seemingly nothing, and nodded slightly.

STUDIO CITY, CALIFORNIA
7:34 P.M.

Weston had spent the last five minutes trying to give Mark a crash course in espionage. The more he talked, the more Tracy's face showed her concern. Mark had heard enough. He glanced at his watch as a pretext.

"We're going to have to get going to the airport," Mark interrupted.

"Yeah." Weston paused. "I guess you're right. Now remember everything I told you. Do nothing out of the ordinary until somebody mentions Operation Dumbo Drop."

Mark nodded, finding it difficult to keep a straight face. Suddenly he felt like he was cast in a B-grade spy movie.

"I'll remember," he said, then turned to Griff. "Will I see you again?"

"Probably not until you return." Griff stood along with Weston. "I'm going to try and contact Chuck."

"I'll take the major to my office, and we'll attempt to reach your man on a secure line. Don't hold your hopes up, Mark. It's a long shot to make the connections to join up with you in time. We'll get word to you in Paris."

"I want to know by the time we hit New York," Mark demanded. "My boss is already working on another journalist. I don't want two people showing up in Turkey."

"You're not making this easy," Weston argued.

"I know," Mark answered, knowing that God would have to work a miracle.

"We'll find him, Mark," Griff assured him.

Mark reached out and grasped Griff's hand. "I would love to see you when this is over."

"Me too." Griff smiled.

Weston reached out his hand. "I wish you luck, Mr. Taylor."

"Thank you," Mark said, feeling the agent's firm grip. "I do appreciate your service to our country."

"Mrs. Taylor." Weston nodded toward Tracy. "We'll be in touch."

Tracy smiled thinly.

Moments later, Tracy and Mark were alone. He stepped away from the door and approached her, knowing they needed to get to the airport—yet also knowing she needed him now more than ever. Mark stepped behind her, wrapping her in his arms while reaching down and nuzzling her neck.

"Oh, Mark," she sighed. "I'm not going to like this."

"I believe God has His hand in this. . . ."

"I know you do. I just wish I did."

Mark turned her around and gently placed his hands on each of her cheeks. "Have faith. This is the right thing to do."

A tear escaped Tracy's left eye, trickling down her cheek slowly. Mark kissed it away. They brought their lips together, touching lightly. The kiss lingered, then became passionate. They were lost in each other. . .for a moment there was no terrorist threat, no trip to Syria, no television shows or law school. Just each other.

As Mark's lips moved to lightly kiss her neck, Tracy had a fleeting thought of telling him she was pregnant. But she repressed it once again, not willing to add to Mark's burden for the next three days. She prayed it was the right decision.

"I want you so. . . ," Mark whispered the words Tracy loved to hear. Then he backed away, looking longingly into her eyes. "Unfortunately, we've got to get going."

Reality. Sometimes it stinks.

CHAPTER 9

Mark counted the seven cars in front of him with one hand grasping his steering wheel and the other intertwined tightly in Tracy's fingers. The security at Los Angeles International Airport was on maximum alert since the Sunday Massacre. No cars were allowed to drive close to the terminal. All passengers had to take a shuttle bus.

Mark hadn't anticipated having to wait in line just to be dropped off, much less to get on the shuttle. Then he'd have to get through security, sure to be another long delay followed by the possibility of being pulled out of line at the gate for yet another search—the new cost of travel for a freedom-loving society. Mark quickly calculated the amount of time it would all take, and added it to the digital display on the dashboard of his Lexus. He was cutting it close to get on that plane by ten o'clock.

"I hope Ross left early enough." Mark looked over at Tracy.

"Maybe you'll miss the flight?" she asked hopefully.

He smiled warmly. "You wish."

Mark pulled up one car length as Tracy continued, "We could just keep driving, head to San Diego. . .nobody would miss us."

"I wish it were that easy." Mark looked straight ahead, his left foot tapping on the floorboard.

"Relax, honey, you've got plenty of time."

They filled the time saying good-byes and praying once more together. It was a most difficult departure, and Mark's fear of missing

94

the flight didn't help.

He finally pulled up to the curb. Putting the car in park, he hit the switch that popped the trunk and proceeded to head toward the back of the car. Tracy met him there as he pulled out his suitcase and briefcase. He set them on the curb before pulling her into a tight hug.

"I'll be praying for you," he whispered into her ear.

"As I will be for you," she returned. "I love you."

"Love you too." He hesitated, pulling back to kiss her good-bye, letting the embrace linger. He was holding back his emotions, trying to make this appear like any other drop-off at the airport, but in his heart he couldn't help but wonder if this could be their last good-bye. He opened his eyes wide and blinked a couple of times, trying to hold back the tears gathering before one of them escaped. He pulled back slightly to bend down and kiss Tracy, nearly losing it as he saw the tears in her eyes.

They kissed gently, finding more warmth in the embrace. Mark held the back of her head as he tucked it into his chest.

"I'll miss you," Tracy said as she clung to him, shuddering slightly in his arms.

"Miss you too." He let the moment stretch a few seconds longer, then he had to pull away. "I'll see you in a few days."

Tracy watched him pick up his bags. "Call me every chance you get."

"I will." After one more quick kiss, he turned and headed away from the car. Tracy watched him for a second until a horn blared behind her. She wiped at her cheeks, closed the trunk, and walked around to the front of the car. Getting in, she kept her eyes on Mark as she put the car in drive but still held her foot firmly on the brakes, imprinting every facet of his image in her mind as he walked toward the shuttle bus.

He turned, waving and giving her one last smile. She waved back, blew him a kiss, then pulled away from the curb. She fought back the tears, knowing she'd have all night to cry when she got home.

Ross looked nervously up and down the concourse, glancing at his watch every few moments. The plane was scheduled to depart in fifteen minutes and still no sign of Mark.

"American Airlines flight ten with service to New York, JFK, has been delayed. The new departure time will be ten forty-five," the announcement came over the public address system.

Ross pulled out his cell phone; Mark should have been here by now. Where. . .wait, there he was. The producer rushed over and met Mark at the line in front of the counter. "Where have you been?"

"I got pulled out at the metal detector," Mark huffed, sweat beading on his forehead. "Went through my bag. I thought they were going to strip-search me."

"Well, you were sure cutting it close, but now the flight's delayed."

"Yeah, I just heard."

"Russell wanted to talk to you before we boarded."

"Next. . . ," a young blond ticket agent wearing the blue jacket of American Airlines called.

"Just let me check in, and we'll call him."

Mark went through the final check-in procedure, once again showing his ID and answering the necessary questions. The ticket agent seemed satisfied and finally handed Mark a boarding pass.

"Have a nice flight, Mr. Taylor," she said.

"Thank you," Mark acknowledged and stepped away from the counter. Ross handed him a cell phone.

"Here, it's Russell."

Mark glared at him, then took the phone. "Yeah, Frank."

"You never got back to me on a corroborating journalist. I've got Peter Baker from the *London Times* standing by."

Mark's mind raced. "That's fine, Frank, but hold off on sending him to Turkey. I've got one lead that might be in the area."

"Who's that?"

Mark fidgeted, moving Ross's phone from one ear to the other. "I'll let you know if it works out. I'll have word before we get to Paris. There'll still be time to bring in Peter if we need to."

"Okay, I'll give you until Paris. You all set for this?"

"Yeah." Mark wanted to get off the phone. It was too uncomfortable talking with Russell.

"Okay, have a good flight."

Mark blew out a breath of air as he hung up, then handed Ross his phone. "Did you get the satellite phones?"

"Yeah, they said they're all charged up."

"Good." Mark looked down the concourse at the gift shop across the way. "We've got some time now. Come on, I want to grab a snack."

Before Ross could argue, Mark already had a three-step lead on him.

THE CARLTON HOTEL, TEL AVIV, ISRAEL
8:18 A.M.

Chuck Fleming had started out the night before on Hayarkon Street along the beautiful Mediterranean Sea. He'd planned to avoid his room at the Carlton until well after daybreak, unless he was lucky enough to find somebody to bring back with him. Coming off three days of intense scrutiny and training of the marines stationed at the U.S. embassy in Tel Aviv, he felt he deserved to blow off some steam.

Tel Aviv reminded him of Las Vegas—the Mediterranean city that never slept. Not a bad assignment for a change. It sure beat the nightlife offered in Manama, Bahrain, the week before.

The pressure to secure all embassies in what the State Department considered the "hot zones" had kept Chuck either planning, briefing, training, or on a plane for the past three weeks straight. Today was his first day off since the three coordinated bombings of U.S. embassies on Christmas Day. He'd been successful in blowing off steam, coming back to his room after seven in the morning. He didn't often let himself go like that, but the stress was getting to him. . .further fueled by his desire for revenge. He wished he'd stayed in the marines. Then maybe he could be part of the counterattack against the Jihad al Sharia.

He'd thoughtfully put the DO NOT DISTURB sign over his door before crashing to the bed in a combination of stress-filled exhaustion and alcohol stupor.

An hour later, the hotel phone was screaming into his brain, as painful as a sledgehammer on a migraine. He groaned and stuffed the extra pillow over his head—until the next ring sent spikes of pain down his spine. He reached up and grabbed the phone, letting off a string of curses as he brought the receiver under the pillow with him.

"This better be an emergency!" he managed to scream in spite of his cotton mouth.

"Is that any way to talk with your superior?" Griff answered coldly.

The fog cleared somewhat, but Chuck couldn't quite make it out of his mental pea soup. "Who is this?"

"Wake up, Fleming! It's Griff Baxter."

One eye opened, then the pillow pushed off him as he sat up on one elbow, and he growled, "Griff! How did you find me?"

"It wasn't easy. We need to talk."

"I'm all ears. . . ."

"Not here. Get to the embassy. I'll call you back in fifteen minutes."

"Wait," Chuck responded into a dead phone. He tossed the receiver toward the nightstand, missing the cradle by two feet. Fifteen minutes! He forced himself to pull his feet off the bed and hit the carpeted floor as the room spun around him and his head pounded. He couldn't imagine why Griff would be calling.

American Airlines Flight 10, Los Angeles International Airport
10:29 p.m.

Mark settled in by the window, placing his briefcase under the seat in front of him, and Ross took the aisle seat in the front section of the Boeing 767. Traveling first class was great when it wasn't his money.

He glanced out the window, looking back at the gate area they'd just come from. Tracy would be home by now, alone. He closed his eyes, concentrating on her for a second as he prayed that God would bring her comfort. He knew it was going to be tougher on her the next three days than on him. . .he prayed she'd be all right.

Mark's concentration was interrupted by Ross nudging his arm. He looked over and saw Ross nod his head toward the front of the aircraft. Boarding just as the flight attendants were about to close the door were two Middle Eastern men, one dressed in normal American clothing with a clean-shaven face, the other in loose-fitting slacks and a white long-sleeved shirt that hung down to his knees, accented by a white turban and long beard.

The cabin suddenly became very quiet as all conversations stopped and most eyes discreetly followed the pair. The clean-shaven Arab stopped in first class, sitting two rows in front of Mark and Ross. The other man slowly walked down the aisle and disappeared into the next cabin.

"Make you nervous, Ross?" Mark asked quietly.

"Yeah, I guess it does," Ross confessed.

"And you accused me of being prejudiced."

Mark smiled thinly. His mind was scrambling on how to handle the next two days. Traveling with Ross while trying to keep his dealings with the CIA a secret was going to be difficult, to say the least. He quietly reflected on how many times he might be forced to lie. . .not a pleasant thought, but necessary under the circumstances. He thought back to the midwives of Moses' day who had deceived Pharaoh when he had instructed them to kill the male Hebrew children. They had feared God and He had blessed them. Mark prayed that whatever deception he'd have to be part of would be blessed by God as well. Or at least understood.

Ross remained quiet, settling in and securing his seat belt over his lap. He pulled the magazine from the seat pocket in front of him and flipped through a couple of pages.

"Why do you think they do it?" he said at last. Ross seemed to be speaking to the magazine.

Mark turned toward him, wondering whether to respond or not. His curiosity finally got to him. "Do what?"

"The hijackers." Ross brought his hand up with his thumb and pinkie spread out like wings and slowly flew his hand into the seat back in front of them. "Fly a plane into a building, or strap a bomb to themselves and set it off. I just don't get it."

Mark shrugged. "I don't either, but a pastor I was talking to about Islam a few months ago shed some light on it for me."

"Really." Ross inclined his head. "What'd he say?"

"You're really interested?"

Ross nodded. "You sparked my curiosity this afternoon in the car. Since we're heading off to the Middle East, I may as well try and get a handle on this religious stuff."

"It'll do you good." Mark smiled, then leaned closer to Ross, lowering his voice slightly. "It has to do with their understanding of God. In Islam, there are no consistent attributes of Allah. You can't define him. . .give him eternal characteristics, not even as a spirit. To do so is to limit him and is considered blasphemy. He is beyond anything we can comprehend, and his will is all there is. So he can arbitrarily change his mind. A Muslim can follow all the dictates of his religion to the best of his abilities, but when he dies, he waits in his tomb until judgment day. At that time Allah can still refuse him entry into paradise, just because he's Allah."

"You're kidding."

"No. There is only one way a Muslim can be assured of heaven."

"And that would be?" Ross asked.

"Martyrdom," Mark answered. "To die in jihad, while fighting the enemy of Islam, in which case he goes directly to paradise. . . no waiting for judgment day; do not pass go—they go straight to heaven. In Muslim countries, when a person dies as a martyr, there's a different burial procedure. His body isn't cleaned and put in nice clothes but buried as is. His injuries and blood are a witness for him in front of Allah—a sign of honor."

Ross shook his head, finding Mark's words hard to accept. "But those hijackers supposedly went to strip clubs before 9/11. That doesn't sound like a religious zealot to me."

"Think about it, though," Mark argued. "They thought they had a free ride to paradise—they wouldn't even have to wait in the grave. So what's to stop them from indulging in a little sinful play-time? It wouldn't count against them if their ticket's already punched."

"So they live it up the night before—guaranteed to wake up in paradise when they die."

"Well, that's one guarantee I don't think was honored."

"I hope not," Ross said. "Still doesn't sound too religious to me."

"You know, Ross, there's a big difference between what Christians believe heaven will be and the paradise of a Muslim."

That surprised Ross. "Like what?"

"Well, paradise is supposed to be a beautiful place, has a wonderful climate, lots of flowing rivers of water, milk, honey, wine. . . which in itself is ironic since alcohol is condemned in the Koran, but supposedly it doesn't affect you like earthly wine. Anyway, I digress. Paradise is supposed to have the tastiest foods that you can dream of and thousands of servants at your beck and call. Oh—and virgins—lots of virgins are mentioned with dark eyes and full breasts, to grant you your most sensual desires."

Ross was leaning back in his chair, smiling as he pictured the scene Mark painted in his mind's eye.

"There are mentions of young boys to serve you as well," Mark said, watching for Ross's reaction.

He wasn't disappointed as Ross brought his head up quickly. "What?"

"Well, there are different interpretations of what those young boys are there for. Muslim scholars say they're servants, but there are those who interpret their role as you just did."

"Well, it sounded pretty good up until that point."

"But think about it. That vision I just described for you feeds into man's hedonistic desires—sexy virgins, food and wine aplenty. . .it's like a celestial orgy."

"Yeah, sounds heavenly to me."

Mark nudged him with his elbow. "You don't get it. Why would a religion make great demands on chastity and modesty in an attempt to keep the sensual aspect of human nature under control, then promise a reward in the afterlife that indulges in it? It doesn't make sense."

"No, but I'll bet it sounds attractive to the Muslim men," Ross joked. "What's the difference then in your version of heaven?"

"The Bible refers to it as a very beautiful place—but the most important element is something far deeper than anything that has to do with sensual pleasure. It's more like the end of a wonderfully romantic story about a couple who have been separated by thousands of miles and carried on their courtship with letters while not being able to touch and feel their true love. Heaven is like the day they finally are reunited. That's the promise we all hope for—to be face-to-face with God, the Creator of all things and the Savior of mankind. To fulfill what was intended from the beginning of creation, to live in relationship with God. Jesus described it as a wedding feast when He returns to claim His bride, the Church.

"There is no mention in Scripture of the type of hedonistic version of paradise that's in the Koran. As a matter of fact, the Bible says there is no marriage or giving in marriage in heaven. It's not a place to fulfill our sensual desires. . .those won't matter compared to living in eternity with our heavenly Father."

Ross lifted an eyebrow. "Oh, I'm not too sure I wouldn't rather spend a few months in paradise first."

Mark shook his head. "You're impossible."

Ross grinned, loving to get under Mark's skin. "If Islam's version of paradise is what you say, what's in it for a Muslim woman?"

Mark laughed. "That's been debated for ages, and there's no easy answer. Some Islamic scholars say that women will be rewarded just as men for their faithfulness, that the descriptions of paradise are symbolic in nature, and women will be fulfilled equally. But there are really no Sūrahs that spell that out—it has to be inferred. Since I've been studying Islam, I've been unable to comprehend what's in it for a woman—not just paradise, but the whole thing. Muhammad was quoted in one ḥadīth as saying, 'A cheap rug is more valuable in a man's home than a woman.' "

"This is unbelievable. Is there anything good about it?" Ross asked.

Mark paused to think. "In a spiritual sense, I'd have to say no. Although it strongly promotes a monotheistic belief, I don't believe that Allah is the God of the Bible. On a social level, I can see how it brought unity and order to ancient Arabia, but that has to be offset by the atrocious civil rights record toward women that continues in

Islamic countries today. The best thing I can say about it is that the fourth pillar of Islam is about giving a portion of one's wealth to the poor."

"Well, I will say one thing about you, Mark Taylor." Ross smiled at his partner. "You certainly have done your homework, but I'm not sure how this will relate to Sa'id's interview."

"Are you kidding?" Mark was incensed. "This is the heart of what's going on in the world. There is a direct tie-in between terrorism and Islam, and our report should bring that out. There are many other religions in the world, but I've never seen a Christian suicide bomber, or a Hindu one, or a Baháí, or a Buddhist. Part of this report has to bring out the dangers that lie in the volatile combination of political upheaval and radical Islamic extremism. You mix the two together, and we've seen the greatest surge of terrorism in the history of the world. To me, *that* is the story. I want to know what's behind a movement that would send their children to their deaths on a mission to murder the innocent."

Two rows ahead of Mark and Ross, sitting quietly by the opposite window, the Arab man listened intently. . .straining to pick up bits of the conversation going on behind him. He'd heard the word Islam a couple of times, but there was too much noise in the first-class cabin to make any sense of it. Frustrated that he hadn't been seated closer, he resigned to sit quietly and bide his time.

CHAPTER 10

Chuck Fleming glanced quickly at his watch as he ran down Hayarkon Street toward the American embassy. He was out of time. He'd never make it through the marines at the front gate within Griff's deadline, much less inside the embassy.

What would normally be a beautiful walk alongside the Mediterranean Sea was totally lost on Chuck as he sprinted, trying to hold back the nausea hitting him in waves. After he'd jumped out of the bed, staggering slightly as he headed into the bathroom, he'd taken the time to splash some water over his face and brush his teeth, hoping to get the awful taste out of his mouth. It hadn't worked.

He was staying at the Carlton, just one kilometer from the embassy, which was convenient but not close enough. At least the brisk breeze blowing in from the Mediterranean revitalized him somewhat.

The cobblestone walkway smacked at the balls of his feet through his tennis shoes as he approached the guards at the front gate.

"Let me in," Chuck yelled while still several feet away.

Screaming as he ran up to the gate of an American embassy that was on high alert wasn't exactly the best approach to have the gates swing invitingly open.

"Halt!" one of the marines ordered.

Fortunately for Chuck, the second marine—who had an M-16 rifle aimed directly at him—recognized who he was. "What are you

105

doing, Mr. Fleming? Is this some kind of a test?"

Chuck held his hands up passively, breathing hard. "It's okay."

He looked horrible. Hair tousled from one hour's sleep, still wearing last night's clothes, he looked more like a drunk than the antiterrorist consultant the marines had spent the last two days training under.

"There's a secure call coming in for me from the States in. . ." Chuck looked down at his watch. "Now! I need to get in."

"All right, let's see some ID," the first marine asked.

Chuck started to protest but thought better of it. He'd been the one pushing them to follow procedure yesterday—he couldn't expect them to break from it now. From their point of view this had to look like a test.

The phone at the guard's station rang. The second marine picked it up, listened for a beat, said "Okay," and replaced the receiver.

"It seems you do have a call." He smiled, opening the gate and letting Fleming through.

Chuck was ushered into a private office on the second floor of the embassy. He picked up the phone, apologizing, "Sorry, Griff. I got delayed."

"Losing a step in your old age?" Griff chuckled.

"No, sir," Chuck responded out of habit. "I just. . .it's a long story."

"From the sound of your voice, you're either sick or you spent last night doing elbow bends at the bar, maybe both."

Chuck decided not to respond.

"You secure there?" Griff asked.

"Yeah, what's going on?"

"What's your schedule, Chuck?"

"I'm supposed to fly to London tomorrow. Why?"

"A fellow recon member needs you in Paris tonight."

Tracy kicked off her slippers and climbed into bed, feeling more alone than she had in a very long time. There had been nights since they'd gotten married when Mark had been away—but it had never felt like this. Mark would be off the ground by now, flying across the country for the rest of the night. She sighed. *This is probably the safest part of his journey.*

She propped a couple of pillows behind her, then pulled the covers up to her waist. She smiled as she heard the jingle of Shandy's collar as she came down the hallway. Before Tracy knew it, with a jump, Shandy was on the bed with her. She made her way next to Tracy, then lay down with her back cuddled up against Tracy's side.

Tracy leaned over, rubbing behind the dog's ears, enjoying how the soft fur felt to her fingers before gently kissing her on top of the head. It was comforting. . .but didn't fill the void felt by Mark's absence. Shandy responded by licking Tracy's hand.

"So, you think you can get away with sleeping on the bed while Mark's away, do you?"

Shandy rolled on her back, legs sticking straight up in the air, and let out a soft moan. Tracy scratched gently at her belly for a moment before Shandy got up and moved to the corner of the bed.

"I guess you do." Tracy grinned. She reached toward the nightstand and picked up her Bible, a New International Version leatherbound edition with her name printed in gold on the front. It had been a present from Mark after she'd become a Christian. She cherished it.

She flipped through the pages until she landed on First John and began to read. Knowing that Mark would be studying this at some point on his flight warmed her. She started reading chapter one, pausing briefly at the end of verse five.

"God is light; in him there is no darkness at all."

She knew the words should be encouraging—which made her feeling of doom and despair that much more depressing. There seemed to be so much evil in the world, and Mark was heading right into the heart of it. Where was God? Would He let her husband be taken away from her this way? Leave her alone to raise this child? So many questions. . .and she felt the emptiness envelop her.

AMERICAN AIRLINES FLIGHT 10
11:12 P.M.

Mark quickly lost sight of the lights of the Los Angeles basin as the American Airlines jet passed through the marine layer fog settling over the coast. He punched the button on his armrest and leaned back in the reclining leather seat. He mentally prepared himself for the first five hours of the journey. They'd be landing in New York sometime after six in the morning. The supersonic flight to Paris would take them less time than this trip from L.A. to New York. Which reminded him. . .

"Did you get ahold of Sa'id's contact in Paris?" Mark asked.

Ross was reading a paperback by John Grisham. He dog-eared the page and closed the book before turning to Mark.

"Yeah. He said he had to check with those above him, but I think he'll meet us."

"What's his name?"

"Abdul Khaliq. He runs some organization called United Islamic Aid. It's supposedly a humanitarian relief group for orphans and the starving in Islamic countries."

"I'll bet. I wonder why the Bush administration hasn't frozen the company's assets?"

"Because the French government hasn't cooperated."

The politics of terrorism, Mark thought. He rubbed the side of his face, his five-o'clock shadow feeling like a light-grade sandpaper. "When will you know about the meeting?"

"He's supposed to contact Russell while we're en route. We may not know for sure until we're in France."

Mark sighed. It seemed like there was so much out of his control. He didn't know if Chuck Fleming was on board or not. The CIA's strategy wouldn't be revealed until Paris. The terrorists' plans wouldn't come until he was in Turkey, and now the meeting with Sa'id's alleged fund-raiser might happen in Paris. What topped it all off, though, was how unsure Mark was of his own plan. Could he offer to help the government, then sit idly by and watch what happened, or would the situation dictate greater involvement on his part? He couldn't be sure.

Ross opened up his novel and began reading once again. Mark reached down and grabbed his briefcase, pulling out the Bible Tracy had handed him and his copy of the Koran.

"Ladies and gentlemen, the captain has turned off the seat-belt sign, should you need to get up from your seat. . . ." The flight attendant's voice cut through the cabin.

Ross's eyes left his page for a second and caught sight of Mark's reading material. "The Bible I can understand, but what's with the Koran?"

"Research," Mark answered.

"That's a good idea."

"I'll have to say, though," Mark smiled, pointing toward Ross's novel, "it's not a page-turner like that book."

"You like Grisham?"

Mark nodded. "Yeah, a lot."

"Read me something," Ross said.

"From the Koran?"

Ross leaned back in the seat, closing his eyes. "Give me a taste of Islam."

With a grin, Mark looked through a notepad he kept with the

Koran. He looked quickly through it, then opened the book to *Sūrah* five:

> *Infidels now are they who say, "God is the Messiah, Son of Mary," for the Messiah said, "O children of Israel! worship God, my Lord and your Lord." Whoever shall join other gods with God, God shall forbid him the Garden, and his abode shall be the Fire; and the wicked shall have no helpers. They surely are Infidels who say, "God is the third of three" for there is no God but one God; and if they refrain not from what they say, a grievous chastisement shall light on such of them as are Infidels.*

"I'm no expert on theology," Ross opened his eyes and commented, "but isn't that saying Christians are infidels?"

"Especially when it mentions 'God is the third of three.' That's an obvious reference to the Trinity."

Ross angled his head at that, evidently confused.

"Christians believe that God is one in purpose, comprised of three distinct Beings," Mark explained. "God the Father, God the Son, and God the Holy Spirit. It's hard to describe, but we believe that Jesus was the Son of God, but also God Incarnate, the Second Person of the Trinity. He was fully human and fully God. In Islam, that concept is blasphemy, what they call *shirk*—the most offensive thing a person can do."

Mark referred to his notes. "Now let's look at what the Koran says is to be done with infidels in Sūrah eight. 'I will cast a dread into the hearts of the infidels. Strike off their heads then, and strike off from them every fingertip. This, because they have opposed God and his apostle; And whoso shall oppose God and his apostle. . . Verily, God will be severe in punishment.' "

"Wow," Ross exclaimed, his interest growing. "I never heard that before."

Mark's eyes caught sight of the Arab gentleman who was seated two rows up moving toward them. Ross looked up to see what had stopped Mark. The man walked slowly down the aisle, seeming to pause right beside Ross. His eyes glanced down, noticing the Koran in Mark's hand. The dark eyes remained hard, unreadable. He looked back down the airplane and continued moving slowly, finally passing into the business-class cabin.

Ross took a quick glance behind him. "Is he gone?"

"Yeah."

"That was weird. I wonder if he heard what we were talking about?"

"I don't know, but he definitely noticed the Koran."

"He makes me nervous," Ross said, squirming in his seat. "And that stuff you're reading doesn't help."

Mark smiled. "There's more, Ross. There are a lot of passages that make me question Islam being a tolerant, peace-loving religion. Sūrah four orders Muslims not to take infidels as friends until they have fled their homes for the cause of God. Sūrah five gets even more precise, saying not to take Jews or Christians as friends.

"But what we're hearing from the Islamic world are different quotations," Mark said, flipping the pages of the Koran to another section. "In Sūrah two there is one sentence they use all the time to say their faith is peaceful: 'Let there be no compulsion in religion.'"

"I've heard that one a lot," Ross interjected, taking another quick look behind him.

"It seems to be the most quoted Sūrah since 9/11." Mark chuckled. "The moderates will also bring up the passages that mention the *Ahl al-Kitab,* the People of the Book."

Ross brought his focus back to Mark. "What does that mean?"

"That phrase refers to Jews and Christians. Those who have followed the Torah and those who have followed the Gospels. According to some Sūrahs, they are to be granted respect and left alone. Sūrah two states, 'Verily, they who believe, the Muslims, and

111

they who follow the Jewish religion, and the Christians, and the Sabeites—whoever of these believeth in God and the last day, and doeth that which is right, shall have their reward with their lord: fear shall not come upon them, neither shall they be grieved.' "

"That sounds a lot better," Ross quipped.

"Yeah, but if you understand the chronology of Muhammad's revelations, you realize those verses have been overridden." Mark had Ross's full attention as he continued. "Muhammad was in Mecca when Islam first began. The recitations were more peaceful as his movement was weak and he was attempting to convince the Arab world to this new belief system. But his tribe rejected him and Muhammad fled to Medina. It was there that he was able to build up an army, and it was there that the revelations became less accommodating and more militant. Most of the Koran was revealed after Muhammad left Mecca."

Mark shifted in his seat, smiling slightly as he came to his point. "When there was a conflict in the Koran, Islamic scholars had to determine which verse to follow. They came up with the principle of *nasikh,* where the new revelations override previous revelations. If a verse is *nasikh,* it is as if the verse doesn't even exist."

Holding the Koran out for Ross to see Sūrah 9:5, Mark said, "This one overrides the Sūrah about no compulsion in religion. 'And when the sacred months are passed, kill those who join other gods with God wherever ye shall find them; and seize them, besiege them, and lay wait for them with every kind of ambush: but if they shall convert, and observe prayer, and pay the obligatory alms, then let them go their way, for God is Gracious, Merciful.' "

Mark closed the Koran and held it up. "Sixty percent of the Koranic verses talk about jihad."

"Why aren't we hearing any of this from our government?"

"Because we don't want to declare war on one billion people around the world who call themselves Muslim," Mark answered. "And I can understand that. But we have to realistically look at what Islam teaches, as well as its roots. It has been violent from its very inception. Muhammad spread Islam with the sword and used his revelations to condone it. Three of the first four caliphs who succeeded him were assassinated by different factions of Muslims."

Mark paused to look at his notes. "Omar Abdel Rahman, the blind sheik who's sitting in federal prison for masterminding the first bomb attack on the World Trade Center in 1993, came to this country and was received openly by the Muslim community. He taught at Al-Salaam Mosque in Jersey City after being freed from an Egyptian court when he defended his involvement in the assassination of Anwar Sadat by using the Koran. Listen to his quote: 'There is a whole Sūrah called "Spoils of War." There is no Sūrah called "Peace." Jihad and killing are the head of Islam. If you take them out, you cut off the head of Islam.' With a history like that, I find it hard to seriously take Islam as a peaceful religion."

"Yeah," Ross argued, "but he's one of the radicals. You can't quote him for all Muslims."

"He has a doctorate of philosophy in interpretation of the Koran and Islamic law," Mark returned. "He was a professor at Al-Azhar University in Cairo, Egypt, the oldest and most prestigious Islamic university in the world. It serves as the spiritual authority for Islam worldwide."

"Wow, now I know why I don't follow any religion." Ross shook his head. "This just gets more complicated."

"I'm with you on that." Mark surprised Ross by agreeing with him. "But don't confuse religion with a relationship with Jesus."

Ross blinked as he smiled. "I see where this is going. I'm going to take a walk."

"You worried about that guy?"

"Not worried; I just want to see where he went." Ross unbuckled his seat belt and headed toward the back of the plane.

Mark watched him separate the curtain and disappear from sight. After working nearly half a season with Ross and having every attempt at a serious discussion on faith flatly refused, Mark was amazed. He was finally beginning to see a crack in Ross's armor.

Mark put the Koran into the seat-back pocket in front of him, bringing the Bible to his lap. He flipped through the pages, ending up at First John, where a folded piece of paper awaited him. He smiled warmly, opening up a note written by Tracy. He could almost hear her voice in his head as he read.

You're probably reading this on the plane. . .which means you're already miles away from me. I don't have much time. You're in the other room talking with those men again. I just want you to know I love you more than life. . .and even though this whole thing scares me to no end, I'll be praying for you. I know this means a lot to you, helping with. . .well, you know. I'm trying to trust God that you'll be all right, but it's hard. Pray for me as I'm praying for you. I love you so much. Come home to me safely.

Love you forever and always,
Tracy

Her words moved him as he pictured Tracy writing this while he was speaking with Griff and Agent Weston in the kitchen. The image captivated him more than he expected, and he was overwhelmed by what she must be going through. He held his finger in place and closed his eyes, spending several moments praying for God's presence to rest upon Tracy and to comfort her.

Mark felt movement from the aisle, prompting him to open his eyes. It was the Arab man, returning to his seat. He opened the overhead bin, pulled a book from his travel bag, and settled back into his seat by the window. A few minutes later Ross came back through the curtain.

Mark leaned over as he refastened his seat belt. "What'd you see?"

"Not much. He was looking through a stack of magazines in

the galley between business and coach when I got back there. I think he noticed me and headed back up here."

"Was the other Arab back there?"

Ross nodded. "Row thirty-five on the aisle. I don't know if they talked with each other or not."

Mark looked over the seat in front of him, trying to get a feel for the passengers in first class. Funny, before 9/11 he wouldn't have given that a second thought. Now he analyzed his fellow travelers to see what kind of resistance force they could muster if a hijacking was attempted.

Ross, evidently doing the same thing, whispered over to Mark, "I think the guy across the aisle looks like he could take him."

"Yeah," Mark added. "And the two men right behind him look pretty fit."

"Do you want to switch seats?" Ross asked.

"Or are we being paranoid?" Mark returned.

"You started it with all your Sūrahs." Ross leaned back in his seat, picking up his Grisham novel. "But just because we're paranoid doesn't mean they're not really out to get us."

Chapter 11

Wendy walked through the security checkpoint in the lobby of the Old Building. Stepping over the CIA emblem tiled into the floor, she passed the bronze statue of Bill Casey, not giving a second thought to the words adorning the marbled wall: "And Ye Shall Know the Truth, and the Truth Shall Make You Free, John 8:32." It was a quote from the classic King James translation of the Bible.

Minutes later she arrived at her cubicle and turned on the light above her desk. As tired as she was, she couldn't stay away any longer. Sleep had only come in restless fits, and after lying awake for forty-five minutes straight, she finally gave up and got out of bed.

She'd taken the time to shower and down a cup of coffee before driving out the deserted Dolly Madison Parkway to CIA headquarters. She put her purse into the bottom drawer of her desk, then reached up and powered up her computer's monitor, her normal morning ritual. "Match!" It flashed at her within seconds. The search she'd started as she left the night before had come up with something. She pulled up her chair, and her fingers began to fly over the keyboard.

Mark Taylor's name had been matched to a known terrorist. Wendy's head leaned toward her screen, her eyebrows up in anticipation. What had triggered this response? A name appeared in front of her, Abu Zaqi Ressam, matched to Taylor on two occasions. The first, the California State University at Northridge, the place where

116

Mark had completed his degree while working at National Studios. Both had been registered there the fall of 1993 and spring of 1994. Not a big deal in Wendy's mind—thousands of students go through CSU Northridge in a given year. She might have considered it just a coincidence if it hadn't been for the second match. A covert operation performed by a Marine Force Recon unit during the initial stages of Desert Storm—Operation Eagle Lift.

Any information on Eagle Lift was marked restricted access, and she didn't have the needed clearance level. She was only able to access the personnel involved, Sergeant Mark Taylor and a Saudi national named Abu Zaqi Ressam.

Wendy entered Ressam's name, and the screen flashed to what they had on the suspected terrorist. Spent two years in California on a student visa, then returned to Saudi Arabia in 1995. He later went to Afghanistan and joined the civil war on the side of the Taliban, developing a relationship with al-Qaida and Osama bin Laden in the process. After the attacks of 9/11, he hadn't been heard from until his name began popping up in reports on the Jihad al Sharia.

Jack needed this information. She wondered where he was. Picking up the phone and dialing his office, she was shocked when he answered.

"Murphy."

"Jack, it's Wendy."

"I thought I told you to get some sleep." He sounded strained, his voice weak.

"I did; I just got in," Wendy answered quickly.

"Look, I'm sorry I didn't call you about Taylor. I didn't want to wake you. . . ."

"Well, come on," Wendy said impatiently. "Which is it?"

"He's agreed. . .sort of. He has to approve the plan when he hits Paris."

Wendy had wanted to hear those words all night long. It was strange to feel nothing. "I need to see you."

"I thought you'd be excited," Jack commented.

"That's what I need to see you about. I'm on my way up."

Less than a minute later, Wendy entered Jack's office. He looked up at Wendy's worried eyes. "What have you got?"

"Taylor has ties to Jihad al Sharia." Wendy could hear the strain in her own voice.

Jack took in a long breath, then let it out slowly. "Let's hear it."

Wendy quickly briefed him on her search results—and what they knew about Abu Ressam. The adrenaline that had kept Jack hyped up through the night seemed to evaporate. He slumped in his chair, scratching his head with his left hand, wondering how this would alter the plan.

"Is there any evidence that Taylor's a sympathizer?" Jack finally asked.

"None," Wendy answered. "But they obviously know each other."

"Then that's the angle—" Jack thought out loud. "Why Taylor's the one named to do the interview."

"I think so. We need to get clearance on this Operation Eagle Lift."

It appeared Jack wasn't listening. "According to Seth, he doesn't know why he was picked. Could he be working with Sa'id in some way?"

Wendy followed his line of thinking. "Taylor may be in the dark about Ressam. There is no evidence linking Ressam to any terrorist organization until late 1996 when he lived in Afghanistan. The time Taylor spent with him in the Gulf and in California, Ressam may have been clean."

"Taylor asked for a former marine to join him in Turkey, Chuck Fleming."

Wendy looked at the printout she carried of Operation Eagle Lift. "Fleming was there for the same mission, as was Griff Baxter, the CO that met with Taylor last night."

"Makes sense. Baxter got ahold of Fleming in Israel. He's flying to Paris today." Jack rubbed his chin. "I want to meet Taylor. . .see his eyes when I mention Ressam. There's so much riding on his involvement."

Wendy looked at her watch. "You'd have to leave right now to meet him in New York."

"I know." Jack closed his eyes while rubbing at his temples. What he would give to have gone into this operation with a few good nights' sleep. He needed to think clearly—too much was at stake. "But I'm supposed to brief the director this morning."

"He's here now. . .I saw his car when I drove in."

"Great. Let's go."

Wendy gasped. "What do you mean, let's. . . ?"

"Come on, you want clearance for Operation Eagle Lift or not?" Without giving Wendy time to argue, Jack headed out the door and down the hall. She picked up her notes, having no choice but to follow.

The only other time Wendy had been invited into the director's office was when she was first brought into the agency and was given a tour of the building. She'd been in a group of six recent recruits whom the director had used for a photo opportunity. The pride she'd felt that day had been incredible.

Today was different. The past year had brought a hardened reality to the impossible mission the CIA had in dealing with the violent world. Wendy admitted to herself that her thoughts last year had romanticized the whole spy game, thinking by now she'd have been off to exotic lands working undercover. But real life wasn't like a James Bond film. Spying was a lot of painstaking grunt work—much of it relying on the correct analysis of thousands of intercepted E-mails, conversations, and reports from the field.

The reception area was empty, so Jack went directly to the director's door and knocked lightly.

"Come in," they heard through the door.

Tenet sat behind his large oak desk going over his briefing notes. He looked up as the two entered his office.

"Mr. Director, this is Wendy Hamilton. She's the analyst that first spotted the interview with Sa'id."

Tenet stood, acknowledging Wendy's presence. "Good work."

"Thank you, sir," Wendy responded.

"Please, have a seat," Tenet offered. "What gives, Jack?"

"I'm glad you're here so early, sir. . . ."

"Actually didn't go home last night, probably like you."

"Yes, sir. Something's come up, and I want to be in New York when Taylor's flight comes in."

Tenet looked worried. "What's wrong?"

"Nothing yet," Jack tried to reassure his boss. "As I told you last night, we've got Taylor's cooperation. Ruzio is on board, already on his way to JFK. The plan's in place."

"C'mon, Jack," Tenet prompted, irritation slipping into his voice. "You didn't come up here this early to tell me things I already know."

Jack nodded, keeping his voice steady. "There's a tie between Taylor and Jihad al Sharia."

The director quickly looked to Wendy, then back to Jack. "I thought he was clean," he spat out.

"We don't know that he isn't, sir," Jack returned quickly. He proceeded to fill Tenet in on what they'd learned so far. A few questions the director asked, Jack diverted to Wendy. She didn't flinch, providing whatever information she had confidently.

"Can we trust him?" Tenet finally asked Jack.

"That's why I want to be there, to see his face when I mention Ressam," Jack answered.

Tenet nodded once. "I agree. What time does he land?"

"Scheduled to land at 6:12, but it's running late," Wendy answered. "Flight for Paris leaves at 10:30."

"That doesn't give you much time to connect with him."

"We already have a place secured to meet with him," Jack said.

"And my briefing?" Tenet asked.

"Drake and Faxon will be here," Jack confirmed. "Everything's in place."

Tenet thought for a second. "Go—take my jet and get up there. And call me as soon as you've talked to him. I've got to know where we stand before I brief the president."

AMERICAN AIRLINES FLIGHT 10
7:32 A.M.

The chime of the fasten seat-belt sign brought Mark out of his light sleep. He groaned, rubbing at his neck. He looked out his window, seeing the skyline of Manhattan off in the distance illuminated by the rising sun, the twin majestic towers of the World Trade Center conspicuous by their absence. The image hit him hard, opening up a pit in the bottom of his stomach. It was the second time he'd been to New York since 9/11, and he was still deeply affected.

The first time had been six months after the towers had crumbled. He was on assignment in the city and had taken a morning to go down to Ground Zero. He remembered vividly walking around the area that day—there was nothing left. Looking down at the hole that had once been the monolith for the financial community, Mark had been overwhelmed at the massive loss of life, yet at the same time he realized it could have been worse. . .a lot worse.

Ironically, a jet had flown overhead as he was standing there. Looking up to the sky, he had tried to imagine what it would have felt like that fateful day as the first jet hit. Only those who had lived through it would ever really know. He'd looked at the buildings around the area that were still standing, amazed at the collateral damage still evident six months later.

But what had truly grabbed him was the old church and ceme-
tery across the street from Ground Zero. It was surrounded by a
six-foot iron fence that had become an outdoor shrine: flags,
stuffed animals, candles, scarves, grade school banners, posters
signed from people all over the world, and pictures. . .lots of touching pictures of the men and women who had lost their lives that
day. Mark remembered one poem printed on a piece of paper and
hanging next to a picture of a firefighter that had been killed. He'd
written it sometime before the tragedy and left it in his locker. . .to
be found in case he didn't return one day—a touching tribute to
those who lost their lives in the attempt to save others.

The other poster he knew he would never forget was a hand-
written quotation of Psalm 91: "He that dwelleth in the secret
place of the most High shall abide under the shadow of the Almighty. I will say of the Lord, He is my refuge and my fortress; my
God; in him will I trust."

Mark had thought of all the families who had lost their dads,
their moms, their sons and daughters, their brothers and sisters.
Such a horrible waste.

The workers had pulled out three more bodies that day, six
months after September 11.

He turned away from the window, thinking about the four
football stadiums and the three embassies in the Middle East and
all the additional families who had lost their loved ones. Any lack
of resolve to help the CIA get to Sa'id disappeared in that instant.

Mark moved his head around in an attempt to loosen his neck.
It seemed to always end up in some weird position when he slept
on a plane. He moved to the right—catching sight of the Arab man
two seats up looking straight at him. Mark didn't look away, playing a quick game of who'd break eye contact first. Finally the Arab
did, turning around and getting up from his seat. The man concerned Mark. He hoped he'd never see him again after this flight.

Ross was snoring lightly beside him as Mark took a peek at his watch. Hopefully Tracy would be sleeping soundly in their bed, although like him, she didn't sleep well when they were separated. Funny how quickly he'd created new habits after being married for just a year. His body ached to be snuggled next to her. He'd wait until just before boarding the flight to Paris to check on her. . .give her as much time to sleep as possible.

Mark's thoughts were interrupted by the sense of a presence standing over him. He looked up.

It was the Arab.

He held his hand out, offering Mark a small piece of paper folded in half. Mark started to speak, but the man brought his other hand up, palm out, stopping him. He nodded to Ross, evidently not wanting to wake him. Mark took the paper quietly and the Arab returned to his seat.

Mark took a quick glance to make sure Ross was still asleep, then opened the paper.

Meet in Air France Premier Club, terminal 1, near gate 4
Dumbo Drop

He folded the paper and slipped it into his coat pocket, smiling to himself. He'd better sharpen up quick if he was going to make it through this trip. . .worrying last night about this guy, thinking he was a terrorist when he was the CIA. Weston said they'd be watched along the way. He should have remembered that. Mark chuckled.

"What?" he heard Ross ask beside him.

Mark turned to him. "Nothing, just thinking. Did you sleep well?"

Ross slid up in his seat, rubbing his neck. "No! I hate trying to sleep on planes."

"Better enjoy it; we've got a long way to go."

"Ladies and gentlemen, this is the captain." The public address came to life. "We've been asked to circle in a holding pattern. It seems with our delay in leaving Los Angeles, we've hit a traffic snag. It shouldn't be long. We'll keep you updated."

"How's our connecting time for the next flight?" Ross asked.

"We're still okay, if they don't keep us up here too long." *But they are taking away my time to meet with the CIA,* Mark thought.

Ross looked up toward the front of the plane. "Anything suspicious from our Arab friend?"

"No." Mark smiled. "He's been quiet."

"Good. I just want to get off this plane and never see him again," Ross said firmly.

Van Nuys, California
5:48 a.m.

Fazul groaned as the *beep-beep-beep* from his watch alarm yanked him from his dream. He reached up with his eyes half-opened in the semidarkness and grabbed his watch from the nightstand, quickly pushing the button to stop the incessant beeping. He rubbed at his eyes, trying to grab hold of his dream. He'd been in some battle, proudly standing against those who were out to destroy him and his fellow believers. He smiled at the thought—honored to fight in defense of Islam.

Too quickly, the details of his dream faded into oblivion, overtaken by the harsh reality of once again waking before sunrise. The predawn light coming through the window reminded him that the sun would be up shortly. He rose from his bed, opening his closet and pulling out his prayer rug. He laid it out over the carpet of his bedroom floor, then headed into the bathroom to begin the ablution of *wuḍū'*, the ceremonial purification before prayers.

In the master bedroom, Fazul's dad heard the running water as he floated in that morning period just between sleep and consciousness. His wife, Johara, awoke to the noise, pulling back some of the covers that her husband had stolen during the night and snuggling under their warmth.

"It seems Fazul has found his place, Ramsi," Johara said with pride.

Ramsi grunted. "Found his place or become obsessed?"

"Aren't you proud that he has become such a devout Muslim?"

"Maybe," he responded, not wanting to be totally honest with Johara or even with himself how it brought such guilt. The Habash family had been in the United States for nearly fifteen years, ever since Fazul was seven years old. They had come from Egypt. Ramsi originally came to study medicine, planning on returning to his homeland as a doctor. But he had come to like America and eventually chose to stay. After completing medical school and his internship, he'd taken a position as a primary care physician for an HMO. He, his wife, son, and daughter had lived the American way of life, gaining their citizenship ten years ago.

What a person that only attended church on Easter and Christmas was to Christianity, Ramsi had settled into with Islam. He would observe Ramadan. . .well, some of it anyway. His visits to the mosque grew more infrequent, and his daily observance of one of the main pillars of Islam—the five daily prayers—had fallen by the wayside.

"It's strange to see Fazul so committed," Ramsi muttered after a moment's reflection.

"I know, but it seems to have focused him. Given him purpose," Johara reminded him. "Just a few months ago, you weren't sure what we were going to do with him."

"That is true, Johara. I'm just not sure what has prompted his newfound devotion."

"Maybe we should consider our commitment. . . ." Johara let the comment hang in the air.

Ramsi said nothing as he rolled over—hoping to catch another hour's sleep before his alarm would bring the start of his day.

By then Fazul had already recited the *Fatīhah,* the opening Sūrah in the Koran, and had moved on in his early morning ritual. He was standing erect on his prayer rug, facing east toward the *Ka'bah* in Mecca, repeating the words *"Allāhu akbar,"*—God is great. He then moved to prostrate himself upon the prayer rug, repeating the words again and again, *"Allāhu akbar, Allāhu akbar, Allāhu. . ."*

JOHN F. KENNEDY AIRPORT
8:51 A.M.

After over an hour of flying in circles, the passengers were finally stepping off the plane. Mark shivered slightly under his wind-breaker from the chill in the Jetway before the contrasting warmth of the terminal hit him like a furnace seconds later.

Their plane had come into terminal 9, gate D-44. They would have to make their way outside and take a shuttle bus to terminal 1 where they'd pick up their Air France flight.

"Which way?" Ross asked.

Mark saw the sign overhead pointing toward the shuttle. "This way—come on, we don't have much time."

"I hope there's enough time to grab something to eat," Ross mentioned, walking beside him.

Mark silently hoped there was enough time to meet with the CIA.

Twenty minutes later, the bus dropped them off in front of the international terminal, where they had to go through the entire secu-rity procedure again. Afterward, as they walked through the con-course, Mark noticed the Air France Premier Club across from gate 4. Underneath the sign stood an Air France agent dressed in a black sport coat watching the door. Mark wondered if he would need to be an Air France frequent flyer to gain entrance.

They finally made it to their gate with just under an hour left of their scheduled four-hour layover. After checking in, Ross was ready to get some food.

"There's a restaurant two gates up," Ross mentioned.

"You're going to eat airport food when we're about to be served a Concorde meal?"

"Oh, yeah." Ross thought. "How about a cup of coffee? Come on."

"You go ahead. I'll hang out here."

Ross hesitated briefly, his eyes darkening. Mark could tell he didn't want them to separate. Mark tried to laugh it off. "C'mon, Ross, we're not even out of the country yet."

"Sorry." Ross flushed. "I guess that Arab on our flight shook me up more than I thought."

"I understand."

"I'll be right back," Ross said as he turned and walked down the concourse.

Mark forced himself to wait until Ross was out of sight before he got up and headed in the opposite direction.

The attendant in the black jacket was still standing by the door when Mark walked up. He smiled politely and opened the door. It appeared that having to show your frequent flyer ID wasn't necessary. As soon as Mark stepped inside, the agent pulled out a "CLOSED" sign and hung it on the doorknob before closing it behind him.

Inside the otherwise empty lounge stood three men. The Arab man that had been on Mark's flight from L.A. and two others, the younger one dressed in casual Dockers and a short-sleeved polo shirt, the older one dressed in a dark business suit. That was the one who approached Mark.

"Mr. Taylor." He extended his right hand. "I'm Jack Murphy, assistant director of Central Intelligence for the Middle East."

Mark accepted the firm handshake as Jack continued, "This is

Vince Ruzio, the best field officer we have, and you flew in with Joseph. He's from our L.A. office."

Mark shook hands with the other two, smiling at Joseph. "We pegged you as a terrorist, not a CIA agent."

"He's technically not an agent," Jack said with a smile. "We don't use that term."

"Really?" Mark was surprised.

"Really." Joseph laughed. "Only in the movies."

"We use officer or operative when we contract with foreign nationals," Jack explained. "Agents are like FBI, Secret Service. . . law enforcement."

"I'll remember that."

"Your friend looked pretty shook-up back on the plane," Joseph added.

"When you boarded late, walking onto the plane with the guy in the turban, well. . ."

"I wondered about the other guy myself. That's why I went back into coach early in the flight—to make sure he wasn't up to anything."

"Was he?"

"Not that I could see," Joseph answered.

"So what's the plan?" Mark asked.

"First, there's something I have to discuss with you," Jack said.

Mark caught the tone in his voice. Mark shifted his gaze from each man before looking back at Jack. "What?"

Jack watched Mark's face intently. "Your relationship with Abu Ressam."

Mark blinked, his forehead creased as his eyebrows lowered. "I don't understand. What does he have to do with any of this?"

"That's what we'd like you to explain." Jack glared at him.

Mark felt as if the temperature of the room had increased several degrees. He wiped away the line of perspiration that suddenly appeared on his forehead, ducking his head to give him time to think. Why did he feel like he was guilty of something? He'd done nothing wrong.

"I haven't talked with Abu in years." Mark looked up, meeting Jack's gaze head-on. "Why the question. . .and why the attitude?"

Jack didn't back down. "He's tied to the Jihad al Sharia."

"Excuse me?" Mark burst out, the tension swiftly converted to anger. "Are you out of your mind?"

"You admit you know Abu Ressam, then."

"Yes, but he's no terrorist," Mark said indignantly. "Where did you get his name?"

"From our files, Mr. Taylor." Jack backed off slightly. "We have been tracking his moves for a few years now. You admit there is a relationship?"

"Abu saved my life," Mark answered passionately. "I guess you could call that a relationship."

CHAPTER 12

Sergeant Mark Taylor stopped dead in his tracks when the marine in front of him held up his arm, fist clenched. Mark pressed his body tightly against the stone wall of the building, taking in quick breaths. The rest of his unit did the same—standing quietly in the darkened alley. Sweat dripped down from under Mark's helmet in spite of the brisk Iraqi winter. Lieutenant Griff Baxter stood in front, peeking around the corner of the building; a quarter moon cast just enough light so that he didn't need his night vision goggles. But what should have been an empty street at two o'clock in the morning was anything but.

Mark's unit had been dropped off two hours before, far enough into the desert from the town of Al Najaf that they didn't alert the Iraqi troops. Two helicopters had skirted the desert terrain in the dead of night, an AH-1W Cobra gunship to provide cover and an MH 53J Pave Low holding the six-member Marine Force Recon team. The mission: Extract two American pilots whose F/A-18D Hornet had been shot down by Iraqi surface-to-air missiles while returning from a raid over Baghdad. The two pilots now stood along the wall with the marines; actually, one of them crumpled against it. He'd taken some extensive damage to his right leg when their aircraft had been hit.

The first part of their mission had been executed flawlessly. The team had hiked to the small town undetected and located the building where the pilots were being held. Each of the Iraqi soldiers guarding the downed pilots had been taken care of quietly. It was when they exited the building that the mission got complicated.

The team had been given the all-clear sign over their earpieces from Miguel, the sniper who had taken a position on a roof across the street. But just as they stepped out, two Iraqi soldiers emerged from the building underneath Miguel. Gunfire erupted, and the two Iraqi soldiers were killed instantly with silenced shots from the marines' MP-5s, but not before one Iraqi soldier got off a burst from his AK-47. Tony Angelo, who'd been right beside Mark, grunted as he collapsed to the dirt.

"Tony!" Mark reached down, relieved to see Tony's face grimacing in pain as he gasped for breath. He wasn't dead. Two slugs had hit his Kevlar vest, only knocking the breath out of him, but one bullet had torn through his upper arm. It was painful and bloody, but not life threatening.

"How's Angelo?" Mark had heard the lieutenant's voice over his earpiece.

"Let's move," Tony said, catching his breath. Mark helped him up by his good arm as the lieutenant led the unit into the alleyway across the street.

The main problem had been the noise. Every Iraqi soldier in the town was now searching for them. The lieutenant peeked out from the alleyway and looked up the street. There were three Iraqi soldiers yelling to an older gentleman coming out of a door fifteen feet away—with more soldiers coming up from behind them.

"Men coming up on your flank," each member of the unit heard Miguel's warning radioed to their ears. They were trapped.

Without a word, Griff turned to Mark and motioned with his head to the wooden door across the alley from where they stood. Mark responded instantly, rushing the few feet to the door. It was locked. He held on to the doorknob as he crushed his shoulder against the door, trying to knock it in with as little noise as possible.

The second attempt sent splinters of wood flying from the door-frame, but Mark kept hold so that the door wouldn't slam into the room. Instantly, Chuck Fleming burst through the door beside Mark, moving his MP-5 across the empty space. The team followed behind, piling into the room. It was a relief to get out of the biting, sand-whipped wind, but there was no time to savor the warmth.

"Chuck, Mick. . .check the front rooms," the lieutenant whispered his orders into the small microphone that jutted out from his earpiece. "Mark, give a look upstairs."

The three men moved forward instantly. As they separated, the commanding officer took a second to look over Tony.

"It's okay," he whispered through gritted teeth. "I'll make it."

"You make sure you do." Baxter smiled at him as he tore off a section of his shirt and started making a tourniquet. He looked at the navy pilots. "You guys okay?"

"He's lost a lot of blood," one pilot said. "But he's hanging on."

"Our ride's just around the corner," Baxter said, then pulled his 9mm from its holster and handed it to the pilot. "Watch the door, Lieutenant."

Mark made his way up the stairs, stepping lightly to lessen any creaking from the old wood. When he reached the top, he leaned out, checking down the hallway. All clear. There were two rooms; one had the door slightly ajar. Mark pushed it farther open with the barrel of his rifle. Empty.

He stepped over to the other door, grabbed the doorknob, and jerked it open quickly, stepping inside with his gun held in firing position. In the center of the room was a man in a gray robe and white turban, bent over kneeling. A single candle burned in front of him, lighting the room. He looked up surprised, staring down the barrel of Mark's MP-5. It wasn't a man, but a teenager, maybe seventeen, eighteen at the most. Mark brought his left hand up, aiming his index finger perpendicular to his lips.

The young man nodded. Mark kept the gun trained on him as

he checked out the rest of the room. Empty.

"I am alone," the man whispered in broken English.

"Anybody else in the building?" Mark demanded.

He shook his head. But would this boy tell him the truth? Mark stepped around behind the Arab, whispering for him to raise his arms. After Mark made sure there were no weapons hidden under the loose clothing, he came back around to the front.

"The shooting," the Arab whispered. "The soldiers looking for you?"

"Me and a few others," Mark responded quietly.

"They will search every building until they find you."

"Tell me something I don't know," Mark mumbled.

"I can help."

Mark looked at the stranger, studying his eyes. He didn't see any hint of deception. "How?"

"There is an access to the roof." The boy motioned with his head above the room. "From there you can cross over several buildings."

Mark thought it over for a brief moment. They were pinned down. As soon as the soldiers from both streets got together and talked, they'd start a room-to-room search. They couldn't hold out in here long before they'd be discovered—ensuring a bloodbath.

"Lieutenant." Mark keyed the switch that activated his mike while keeping his eyes pinned on the young Arab. "Need you up here."

A few seconds later Baxter stood behind him, eyeing Mark's captive.

"What have you got?"

"He speaks English," Mark informed him, then pointed to the hatch in the ceiling. "He says we can access the roof through there, get down the street on top of the buildings."

The lieutenant nodded, contemplating his options. "What's your name, son?"

"Abu Ressam," the teenager answered.

"Well, Abu," Baxter wondered aloud, "why would you be willing to help us?"

Voices yelling in Arabic could be heard outside the small window in the corner. They were running out of time.

"I'm not Iraqi," Abu answered calmly. "I'm Saudi. I'm just here to study."

The lieutenant weighed the boy's words against the noise drawing closer. His decision was made quickly as Miguel's voice came through his earpiece. "Iraqis heading into your alley."

"Get it opened," Baxter said as he turned and headed down the stairs.

Abu got up from his knees and pulled a chair from the corner. He set it in the middle of the room under the square hatch in the ceiling. Standing on the chair, he pushed the square section of the ceiling out of the way. He jumped up and pulled down a rope ladder attached to something unseen on the top of the roof.

By that time, the rest of Mark's squad and the downed pilots had arrived in the hallway. They could hear the sounds of the Iraqi soldiers yelling in the streets.

Abu looked up at Mark with lines of worry drawn across his brow. "They're going to search the buildings. You must hurry."

Baxter eyed Mark and motioned with his head toward the ladder.

Mark slung his rifle over his shoulder and grabbed the sides of the rope as he made his way up. He heard the lieutenant's voice in his ear telling their sniper across the street to make sure their rooftop was clear.

Mark shimmied up the ladder quickly, pausing at the top as he scanned the roofline. Nobody in sight.

He pulled his full body onto the roof, then once again keyed his mike to the unit. "Roof's clear. . .let's roll!"

The marines quickly exited the room, starting with the rescued pilots, then Tony, followed by Mick, Abu, and the lieutenant. Chuck hadn't cleared the room yet. They could hear men yelling and pounding on the front door below. Then a soldier yelled something in Arabic from the alleyway.

"They discovered a broken door," Abu whispered.

"Let's go!" the lieutenant ordered. The next few moments seemed to happen in slow motion as Mark led the unit away from the Iraqi troops. A loud crash was heard below them as the enemy soldiers broke through the front door and entered from the alleyway with guns blazing. A few seconds later, Chuck finally emerged through the access panel, taking three giant leaps before the room below him exploded in a huge fireball. He lunged forward, barely making it to the next section of the roof just as the one he'd been standing on collapsed on the Iraqi troops.

"Move it! Move it!" Baxter kept repeating into Mark's ear. There was confusion and yelling coming from the street below them. Nobody had caught sight of the team escaping along the roof.

Mark stopped at the end of the building, noticing their sniper working his way down from across the street. There was a metal ladder connected to the side which Mark quickly grabbed hold of, leading the team back down to ground level.

The street was full of Iraqi soldiers, but their focus was on the burning building the marines had left behind. Mark held his hand up palm out, holding the unit behind him as a couple of soldiers walked toward them. They turned toward a door fifty feet from Mark, breaking it down and storming in. Mark immediately stepped into the street with gun drawn and waved his unit forward.

"*Go!*" Baxter's voice cut through to each of his men's earpieces. Abu followed after the last marine; then Mark sprinted across as Chuck covered him at the other corner.

They repeated that pattern across several streets until they reached the outskirts of town. Twice they'd come in contact with patrolling Iraqi soldiers—but the silenced MP-5s kept them undetected.

The lieutenant ordered Mick, their communications specialist, to bring the choppers in while the rest of the unit secured the perimeter. With all the commotion, the extraction could be a problem, but they couldn't risk hiking back out in the desert with the wounded pilot.

In minutes, the men ducked their heads as the approaching MH-53 helicopter kicked up the sand around them, pricking their skin like hundreds of tiny needles.

The main part of the group ran toward the chopper while Chuck and Mick stayed prone in the sand, their weapons trained toward the town behind them. Mark helped the wounded navy officer into the chopper as gunfire erupted. The Iraqis had found them.

"Let's go!" Mark yelled to Tony—getting him into the chopper next. Bullets sprayed around them as Mark turned and fired off a burst toward the approaching attack. He saw two soldiers go down; others scrambled to the dirt. Then the comforting noise of their Cobra gunship swooping over the MH-53 brought a smile to Mark's face as the 20mm cannon quickly extinguished the threat.

Chuck and Mick turned and ran toward the MH-53 as Mark kept his gun trained behind them. After they had jumped into the helicopter, Mark turned to thank the Arab.

Abu's eyes were wide with shock. His hand was placed over his side, dark red blood seeping through his fingers. Mark grabbed hold of the teen, helping him to remain standing. He keyed in his mike. "Lieutenant, the Arab's been hit."

"Take me with you," Abu pleaded in his heavily-accented English over the noise of the rotors. "Leave me behind; they will kill me for helping you."

Baxter appeared over Mark's shoulder. "How bad?"

"Don't know. He wants to go with us."

The lieutenant paused for a second, looking around as the Cobra sprayed another barrage of gunfire toward the Iraqi soldiers. Any time wasted arguing only endangered his men that much longer. Baxter nudged his head toward the aircraft. "Well, we can't leave him here to die. Get him in."

Mark saw a smile creep onto Abu's face through his pain. He led him into the chopper, keeping his rifle trained on the area behind them as the pilot lifted off in a billow of sand.

They wouldn't be out of danger until they landed back at base camp, but being back inside the marine helicopter was the next best thing. The relief was expressed differently on each of the faces inside the chopper. The American pilots were all smiles, even the injured one, having spent the last six hours wondering if they'd ever see another sunrise. Chuck sat expressionless, intently looking toward the ground for any signs of danger. Mick bowed his head quietly and completed the sign of the cross over his chest. Lieutenant Baxter attended to the injured marine, while Mark kept watch out the side of the helicopter, letting his shoulders sag slightly, thanking God he was still alive.

AIR FRANCE PREMIER CLUB, JFK AIRPORT, NEW YORK
9:32 A.M.

Mark brought his focus back to the senior intelligence officer. "That's how I met Abu Ressam."

Jack kept his posture, watching every nonverbal clue he could gather from the journalist.

"The last time I saw him had to be around '95 when he went back to Saudi Arabia. All I can say is that he certainly wasn't a terrorist then." Mark heard a hard edge come to his voice. "What evidence do you have that he's involved with Jihad al Sharia?"

"That would take too much time to go into, and some of it is still classified," Jack answered. "But his name is directly linked to two cells in this country that helped plan the Sunday Massacre."

"That's impossible," Mark argued heatedly. "I know Abu—he couldn't be involved."

"Calm down, Mr. Taylor," Jack spoke evenly, trying to defuse the situation. "How did your relationship develop with Ressam after Operation Eagle Lift?"

Mark flinched at the use of the code name. They seemed to know everything. "After we returned from the mission, I spent some time with him in the infirmary after they pulled the slug out of his side."

Mark paced away from Jack, then turned back forcefully. "Look, he saved eight American lives that night, including mine. If being friends with Abu is enough for you to pull the plug on Operation Dumbo Drop, then do it."

Mark paused, studying the reactions of the three men around him. "But if you want to go through with this, then you'd better give me an idea of what you're planning before that flight leaves, or I'll shut your precious mission down right here, right now!"

He looked at his watch, then pointed toward the door. "My plane is taking off in twenty minutes. Ross is probably already freaking out wondering what happened to me. Now what's it gonna be?"

Jack was convinced. "All right, here's the plan. . ."

Mark interrupted. "What about Chuck Fleming?"

"Baxter got through to him last night in Tel Aviv. He'll meet you in Paris; we've got him on your connecting flights from there."

"Great." Mark released a tense breath of air. It was the first good news he'd had since landing. "He needs a cover story, has to be some kind of radio newsman or print journalist. . . ."

Jack reached into a folder and pulled out a piece of paper and handed it to Mark. At the top was the name Chad Moreland— *Newsweek,* followed by a complete biography, including the titles of several recent articles he'd written that had been printed in the weekly magazine.

"Is there really a Chad Moreland?"

"Yes, there's even a slight resemblance between the two."

"Is there any chance the real one's anywhere near the Middle East?"

"None. He's on vacation for the next ten days in Hawaii. You'll be in and out before he's back on the mainland," Jack answered. He motioned to Vince beside him. "As I said before, there's nobody better than this man in the field. We're going to insert him as your cameraman. You won't see him again until Istanbul."

"Will Mclintock know?"

"No," Jack answered flatly. "Whoever Mclintock has hired will turn up sick at the last minute. . .Vince will replace him."

"And what is Vince's mission?" Mark asked.

Vince took a step closer to Mark. "To electronically mark Sa'id's location for a surgical air strike as soon as we're safely out of the area."

"Your electronics won't be detected by Sa'id's men?"

"We have satellite devices so sophisticated, their little bug detectors won't even blip," Vince said with conviction.

"We don't have time to explain it all, Mark," Jack said. "I'll have another man meet you in Paris when there's time to explain the electronics and the rest of the plan to you and Fleming in detail."

Mark turned to Vince. "How are you getting to Istanbul?"

"Military transport as soon as we're done here."

Mark looked back to Jack, approaching his next comment seriously. "The agreement I had with Agent Weston was that I'd have access to a secure phone and speak with my wife before I agree to anything."

"Yes, that was conveyed to me," Jack acknowledged. "We'll honor that agreement. Joseph will be covering you until you get to Paris."

Mark looked briefly at the Arab, then back to Jack. "You're putting Joseph on the Concorde with us? Ross is going to have a fit."

"I don't care. You'll have somebody watching you every step of the way, Taylor. You're very important to us right now."

For some reason that bit of information didn't comfort Mark. "I have one last question, and I want an honest answer."

"What is it?" Jack asked.

"Is Vince cleared for a direct attempt on Sa'id?"

"No," Jack replied almost too quickly, then cleared his throat, keeping his eyes locked on Mark. "Only the president can authorize that, Mark."

"Besides," Vince added with a smile, "I'm not into suicide missions."

Chapter 13

Tracy could hear the radio kick in from the bedroom. It was time to get up. Little did the alarm clock know she'd been up for the past hour, racing three times to the bathroom. What was it people said—a bad case of morning sickness means you'll have a healthy baby? If that was the case, they were going to have an Olympic athlete.

The wave of nausea seemed to pass as Tracy held a damp washcloth to her forehead. She didn't think there could be anything left in her stomach by now anyway. She got up from the cold linoleum floor and cautiously headed back toward her bed. Reaching over to turn off the alarm, she was startled when the phone rang.

She picked it up, hoping she'd hear Mark's voice.

"Hi, Trace, it's me."

"Mark." She closed her eyes, comforted by his image in her mind. "I was hoping it was you."

"We're in New York, but our flight was delayed. I've only got a second to get on the one to Paris, but I wanted to make sure you were okay."

Considering that I'm pregnant, throwing up, and my husband is off on some spy mission, things are just peachy, thank you very much. "Everything's fine," she replied.

"You sure? You seem. . .down."

"No," Tracy brightened her voice. "I just woke up, that's all."

"I'm sorry to wake you, but this is the last chance before getting

141

on the next flight."

"You sound out of breath. What's going on?"

"I'm hurrying to the gate; I had to meet. . ." Mark caught himself, remembering the instructions from Agent Weston. "I ran into some friends from Washington and kind of lost track of the time."

"Was it good to see them?" Tracy caught on, trying to get any information out of him that she could.

"Yeah, things are going well," Mark answered. "Oh, honey, there's Ross up ahead, and it looks like the flight's already boarding. I've got to go."

"So quick?" Tracy asked.

"Yeah. I'll call you as soon as we land in Paris, okay? Sorry, but I've got to go."

"Okay, I love you."

"I love you too," she heard; then Mark was off the line. She hung up the phone and lay back on the bed, taking a pillow and pulling it into her stomach and chest, cuddling around it. She started crying, for no apparent reason except that she had never felt so alone.

Tracy knew her hormones were on overdrive—her body was making tremendous adjustments. Which made it difficult to understand her emotions. Was she crying because she was pregnant, and would she react the same way if Mark called to tell her he had to work late? Or were her tears the reaction to the growing fear deep within her that she may never see her husband again?

AIR FRANCE PREMIER CLUB, JFK
9:51 A.M.

"Patch me through to the director, please, Nancy," Jack said to the director's executive secretary. He stood in the Air France lounge with Vince. Joseph had left right after Mark, keeping an eye on him all the way back to the Air France gate.

Jack and Vince had talked at length on their assessment of Mark Taylor. Jack was convinced that Mark had no connection with the terrorist organization. Vince wasn't as sure, but Mark had given him the impression that he could handle himself under stress. He could be an asset on this job—if he was for real.

Jack heard the director's voice come over his phone.

"I think he's clean," Jack offered quickly.

"You're sure?"

"As sure as we can be after one quick meeting," Jack confirmed, then knowing his phone could possibly be compromised, he continued in spy speak. "No contact with questionable target since '95. Claimed at that time target not involved with foreign corporation."

"Understood," replied the director. "Get your package on the way, then come home. We'll talk when I get back from the meeting."

"Will do." Jack punched off the call, then looked up at Vince with a sinister grin. "We're a go. Let's get you on your way to Syria."

JFK TERMINAL ONE
9:55 A.M.

Ross was pacing along the rows of empty seats outside the Air France gate. There were only three people left in line to get on the plane. Mark continued his brisk pace until Ross turned and spotted him; then he slowed as if he were casually strolling through the concourse.

"Where have you been?" Ross asked, his voice etched with tension.

"I decided to take a walk," Mark returned calmly, trying to control his labored breathing.

"They're about ready to close the flight!"

"I'm sorry," Mark said, turning toward the gate. "I guess I lost track of the time."

Ross followed closely beside Mark. "Is everything okay?"

"Yeah," Mark said as he handed his boarding pass to the agent. "Why?"

Ross handed his ticket over and followed him down the Jetway. "You're acting funny. I find it hard to believe you lost track of time."

Mark chuckled. "You're too tense, Ross. We'll have enough of that on the other side of the Atlantic. Live it up for the next three and a half hours. We're flying in luxury."

Mark stepped onto the plane, surprised at how small it felt. The seats were arranged in pairs by each window with a small aisle down the center of the plane.

"Aisle seat or window?" Mark asked.

"You can have the window. I don't really care."

They had to duck getting into their seats or risk bumping their heads on the overhead compartment. The plane felt confining compared to the roomy first class cabin of the Boeing 767 they'd taken from Los Angeles, but once they settled in there was plenty of legroom, and the seats fit like a glove. The excitement of being on the Concorde was lost on Mark as he played back Tracy's voice in his mind. He knew how she sounded just waking up, and that wasn't it. She wasn't doing well and there was nothing he could do about it.

"Look!" Ross's elbow nudged him.

Joseph was coming down the center of the plane. This time, he walked right by and took a seat three rows behind them.

Ross leaned over and spoke in a panicked whisper, "This is too weird. What are the odds of him being on both flights?"

"Pretty good if he's on his way to Paris," Mark tried to reassure him. "Like I said before, Ross, try and relax for the next few hours."

Ross stole a quick glance behind him. "Easy for you to say. That guy's got me spooked."

"He's probably just a wealthy corporate executive on a business trip. You want me to go talk to him?"

"No!" Ross was emphatic. Mark leaned back in his chair and

wondered how Ross would handle himself when this trip really got interesting.

He felt a slight jerk as the slender white aircraft was pushed from the gate. On any other day, he would have been eagerly anticipating the next few hours of his life—breaking the sound barrier, being served a gourmet meal at nearly sixty thousand feet, soaring high enough to see the curvature of the earth. But not today.

Mark closed his eyes a moment, offering up a fervent prayer for Tracy. Then he let his mind settle on Jack Murphy. He seemed competent—not that Mark would know a good CIA officer from a bad one. Murphy had questioned him about Abu almost like it had been a test. Whatever suspicions they had about his friend had overlapped onto him. Evidently he'd said the right thing to keep the mission on track—whether that was a good thing or not remained to be seen.

Abu tied to the Jihad al Sharia. . .Mark couldn't imagine Abu becoming a terrorist. He was one of the most gentle people Mark had ever known, a Muslim intent on peace. It just didn't add up.

Vince had stayed pretty quiet. Mark had the impression that he was a focused individual, and in the world of undercover operations he was sure that was a plus. Mark replayed the answer to his question about Vince having black op clearance. Murphy's answer was too quick, a response without a thought behind it. Mark didn't buy it. His only ace-in-the-hole was having Chuck Fleming on board—then it hit him. He needed to get ahold of Russell and cancel the reporter from the *London Times*. His fists clenched.

Things were moving too quickly.

VAN NUYS, CALIFORNIA
7:21 A.M.

Ramsi Habash sat at his kitchen table, joined by his wife and their nineteen-year-old daughter, Akilah. As the three finished up their breakfast, Fazul came in through the back door after his morning run, sweaty and out of breath. He went directly to the refrigerator for the quart of orange juice.

"So, what is everyone doing today?" Ramsi asked as he cut off a section of his baklava and placed it in his mouth, savoring the delicious blend of walnuts, cinnamon, sugar, and pastry.

"I only have two morning classes today, then some studying in the library. I should be home early, Pappa," Akilah answered. She was a freshman at CSU Northridge, getting her general education out of the way as she tried to settle on a major.

All eyes turned to Fazul, wondering what his answer would be.

"What?" he said, still breathing heavily, gulping down the orange juice. It was the daily question from his father. What was he going to do with his day? Fazul had been thirty credits away from completing his degree in computer science, but he had suddenly lost interest in school and stopped attending classes during the fall semester. More and more, his days were spent hanging with a group of friends, most of whom didn't meet his father's approval.

"What plans do you have, Fazul?" His father repeated the question.

"There's a study at the mosque this afternoon. I'm meeting Sofian there," Fazul answered, hoping to get his father off his back.

"That sounds interesting," his mother chimed in.

"It is, Mom." Then he turned to his father. "You should come, Dad."

Ramsi looked sternly at his son. "You know I can't get away from the medical center."

"Just like you can't make it to the noon prayer at the mosque on Fridays anymore?"

Ramsi shot up from the table, causing Akilah and Johara to flinch back. "You show some respect!"

Fazul stood his ground by the kitchen counter, eyes narrowing in defiance. Ramsi wiped his mouth with his napkin, then threw it onto the table. "I'll see you tonight at supper," he spoke to his wife and daughter, ignoring his son as he grabbed his keys and headed to the garage.

"See you later, Dad," Fazul spoke after the garage door slammed.

"Why can't you two just get along?" Johara shook her head.

"He's impossible," Fazul answered.

"Don't talk about your father that way. He just doesn't want to see you throw your life away."

"But, Mother." Fazul approached the table, sitting down beside her. "For the first time in my life, I feel like I'm not throwing it away."

"But you were so close to graduation. . .being able to make a life for yourself."

"No, Mom," he argued. "Making Dad's life for myself. I was never into the college thing. I was doing it for him. I've found something more important, following the path of Allah. Something Dad used to do."

"He still does, Fazul," Johara corrected her son. "In his own way. . ."

"What kind of Muslim family are we?" Fazul rose from the table and walked the room. "You don't even wear the *hijab* unless you're going to the mosque." Fazul referred to the head covering of a devout Muslim woman. He turned toward his sister. "Nor you. And when was the last time Dad prayed the ṣalāh?"

Johara lowered her head, speaking quietly but with authority. "Don't judge your father, Fazul Habash. He observed the Ramadan fast, didn't he?"

"That's all he does anymore, observe Ramadan, and we don't really know what he eats at work, do we? That's the only time he even visits the mosque anymore." Fazul paused, noticing the pain in his mother's face. "I'm sorry, Mother. I didn't mean. . ."

"I know, son," Johara said as Akilah listened intently. "Just watch how you act around him. One day he will not hold back his temper."

"What is the class you're going to?" Akilah asked her brother.

"Just studying different Sūrahs in the *Qur'ān*," Fazul answered without detail.

"I'd like to come; what time?"

"One o'clock, but it's not for women," Fazul answered flatly.

Akilah picked up her backpack from the corner of the table, then leaned over and kissed her mother good-bye as she headed for the door, muttering, "We'll see about that."

AIR FRANCE, FLIGHT ONE
11:15 A.M.

Mark looked up three rows to the bulkhead in front of him. According to the digital readouts, they were now cruising at fifty-eight thousand feet and traveling at Mach 2. Mark wasn't sure what he'd expected, but nothing dramatic happened when they'd hit Mach 1, breaking the speed of sound. He thought he'd sensed a slight increase in the thrust of the engines, then his ears picked up a difference in the sound around him. It could best be described as a sizzle, as the rushing air going around the plane took on a higher pitch than what was heard in subsonic flight.

He looked out the small window beside him. It didn't look like they were traveling over twelve hundred miles per hour. He got Ross's attention, pointing out the view.

"You can actually see the curvature of the earth," Mark informed him.

"That's incredible." Ross leaned over, trying to see as much as he could from his seat. They were so far above the clouds, they looked like they were settled on the top of the ocean. The 747s from other airlines looked like black specks flying five miles below them.

Mark put his hand up against the window, feeling its warmth. He looked up again at the digital display that recorded the outside temperature as minus fifty-eight degrees centigrade.

"Feel the window, Ross," Mark instructed. "It's warm."

Ross put his fingers against it. "I read somewhere that the air passes so fast against the plane that the friction raises the temperature of the plane a couple of hundred degrees."

The flight attendant handing each of them a menu with an unbelievable selection of French gourmet dishes interrupted their scientific curiosity. Mark chuckled. This definitely beat grabbing a sack lunch from some box in the concourse. If not for the dangerous nature of the trip, Mark would have loved to have Tracy experience it all with him.

He glanced over the possibilities for lunch. Besides having some appetizers he didn't know how to pronounce, he could choose between the feuilleté greedy of duck foie gras, filet of poêlé mullet, râble of stuffed young rabbit, or a couple of other dishes Mark couldn't quite identify. He decided on the duck but wasn't sure why they said it was greedy.

Ross, on the other hand, was pronouncing each French word with gusto, languishing over the exquisite choices and which would go good with white or red wine.

After everyone ordered, the flight attendant started down the aisle passing out glasses of champagne and small dishes of caviar. Something Mark could never get into, he politely passed and pulled out a small bag of mixed nuts to chew on.

"Did you get ahold of Frank about the meeting in Paris?" Mark asked between nibbles.

Ross tasted a small sample of the caviar. "Delicious. You should try some."

"No, thanks just the same."

"I didn't want to wake him. I thought we'd try on the plane."

"Well, it's after eight in L.A. now."

Ross pulled out the air phone from the seat back in front of them and slid his credit card through the side. It took a few seconds for the call to go through.

"Hi, Frank, it's Ross. Yeah, we're on the Concorde now, tasting caviar and sipping champagne."

Ross laughed.

"What did he say?" Mark asked.

Ross cupped the phone. "You don't want to know."

"Have you heard from Khaliq? Uh-huh." Ross listened, showing Mark a thumbs-up sign. "Great, that should give us at least a little more background on Sa'id."

At the mention of Sa'id, several people in the seats around them stopped what they were doing and looked in Ross's direction. Ross felt the eyes on him as he shrank down in the seat. Then to Mark's chagrin, the phone was handed to him. "He wants to talk with you."

"Yeah, Frank," Mark said.

"Have you nailed down your journalist yet? If not, I need to get Baker's travel set up."

"Yeah, it's all set." Mark tried to keep his voice down, hoping everybody in the plane would go back to their own business. "I've got Chad Moreland from *Newsweek* on board. He's going to meet us in Paris tonight."

Ross tossed him an inquisitive look. Mark ignored it.

"How did you get Moreland? That's great."

"You know him?" Mark asked nervously.

"Not personally, but I know the name. That's a good choice to go with you. How do you know him?"

Mark hesitated briefly, then answered, "I met him on one of the trips to New York in our first season."

"Well, that's great. I'll let Baker know we don't need him."

"Thanks."

"Anything else?" Russell asked.

"Not that I can think of."

"Then get back to your caviar, and we'll talk later."

Mark ended the call, placing the phone back in place.

"When did you find time to get a *Newsweek* reporter?" Ross wondered.

"I had a friend working on it last night," Mark answered truthfully. "Chad's going to meet us at the hotel in Paris. What did Russell say about the meeting?"

"Khaliq is a go. Knowing we're there for a quick layover, he agreed to meet us at the hotel tonight around ten."

"Good. I hope we'll be able to get some more details on Sa'id's life." *And maybe I can get some information on Abu Ressam at the same time,* Mark thought. He still couldn't fathom Abu being a terrorist.

MARINE FORCE RECON BASE CAMP, SAUDI ARABIA
1991

Mark sat next to the bed. The patient was resting comfortably in the field hospital set up under a tent in the desert. Abu Ressam's eyes fluttered as he started regaining consciousness. Sergeant Mark Taylor sat quietly, not willing to disturb him. A moment passed; then his eyes opened.

Abu spoke something in Arabic before his eyes focused enough to see Mark sitting by the bed. Then he changed to his accented English, whispering, "Where am I?"

"Back in Saudi Arabia," Mark informed him. "You were hit before we got you on the helicopter."

"I remember," Abu spoke through his dry throat. "Water. . . ," he requested.

Mark stood up, placing a paper cup of water to his lips while lifting his head in support. Abu was able to swallow a couple of sips, then let his head settle back on the pillow.

"Thank you. . . ," Abu said.

"No," Mark interrupted. "Thank you. Your help saved my life and the rest of my unit. We are in your debt."

Just then a navy corpsman came up behind Mark. "I see our patient is up and at 'em."

"Yeah, he just woke up," Mark said.

"Don't let him talk too much," she instructed. "I'll get the doctor."

Over the next few days, Abu progressed quickly back to health. The bullet had punctured his kidney and he'd lost a lot of blood on the flight back to the marine base. Mark would come to visit when he was free from his duties. It was on the third day that Abu was able to really talk.

"So what were you doing in Iraq?" Mark asked.

"I was studying," Abu answered. "The Institute of Al-Kufa is in Al-Najaf as well as the Shrine of Imam Ali."

"In the middle of a war?"

"There was no war when I began my studies; then America started bombing. . . ."

"There would be no *coalition* bombing," Mark stressed the multinational effort, "if Hussein hadn't invaded Kuwait."

The two looked at each other—one of those defining moments when the next comment would either send them down an adversarial path or open up a meaningful dialogue.

"Who was Imam Ali?" Mark changed the subject.

Abu brightened, happy to speak of his studies. "Imam Ali, may peace be upon him, was the fourth caliph of Islam. He was martyred in Al-Najaf, where they have built his shrine."

Mark nodded. Knowing nothing about Islam, he wasn't sure how to react.

Noticing Mark's hesitation, Abu continued, "Imam Ali was the cousin and son-in-law to Muhammad, may peace be upon him. He was the fourth one to lead Islam after the prophet's death. Some say he was the rightful one to take over in the first place, but the prophet did not name a successor."

Abu went on over the days of his recuperation to fill Mark in on the early history of Islam. Mark didn't have to feign interest. He actually found Abu's tales fascinating as he went into lavish detail of the early battles that led to Muhammad's control of Mecca. The two began developing an interesting friendship.

"Why did you help us, Abu?" Mark asked one afternoon.

Abu looked away for a second before turning back to him. "I don't know; it was an impulse, really. You were trapped and I knew a way of escape."

"But you are Muslim. . .helping the enemy of a Muslim."

"True in one sense, but I am not Iraqi," Abu explained. "Islam is about peace, my friend, not war. What Saddam Hussein has done is not ordained by the *Qur'an*. He has political reasons for his actions, not religious ones."

"I think you're right about that one," Mark agreed.

"And you—why are you fighting in this war?"

Mark thought for a second. "Because my country has asked it of me, and I don't believe Iraq has the right to take over Kuwait just because it is weaker."

"But you have the right to intervene just because you are stronger?"

Mark smiled. Abu seemed to have a way of turning a phrase. "We have the moral obligation not to allow evil powers of this world to perform genocide on their own countrymen or overtake sovereign nations at their whim."

"And to keep the precious flow of crude oil from being interrupted."

"Yes, there may be economic reasons for our interest in the Gulf, but there have been very few wars in the history of the world that have been as clear-cut about who the original aggressor was as this conflict."

"That I will give you." Abu smiled.

CIA HEADQUARTERS, LANGLEY, VIRGINIA
12:14 P.M.

"Hi, Wendy," Jack announced his return at Wendy's cubicle. She'd been so engrossed in her research on the computer, she hadn't felt him standing behind her.

"Oh, Jack, hi." She sighed, pulling away from the computer screen. "How did it go in New York?"

"Good," Jack answered, stepping into the room and sitting at Phillip's desk. "He definitely knows Ressam, but I think we can trust him."

"That's great news. The director cleared me for the file on Operation Eagle Flight. Pretty incredible."

"Yeah, I heard it firsthand from Taylor. He definitely was surprised to hear Ressam's name linked to terrorism."

"So the mission is a go?" Wendy asked.

"All the way. I just talked with the director. He briefed the president this morning." Jack paused, deciding Wendy had earned the right to know. "He's authorized this as a black op."

Wendy nodded. "He had to. We may not get another chance like this one."

"Any other news since I was gone?"

"Just one thing," Wendy answered. "I've been going over the tapped phone recordings from Taylor's house, and I think I've turned up something that might complicate things for Mark."

"What?" Jack asked, concerned.

"Mrs. Taylor received a phone call last night from her gynecologist." Wendy glanced up to view her boss's reaction. "I think she's pregnant."

CHAPTER 19

PARIS, FRANCE
9:43 P.M.

The tension that Mark had held at bay through the flight across the Atlantic couldn't be contained any longer. As he walked up to the reception desk at the hotel, he nervously scrutinized every person in the room, trying to spot either CIA personnel or members of the Jihad al Sharia. Maybe he was just tired. He'd gotten a few hours' sleep on the flight from L.A. to New York, but the Concorde flight had been so quick that by the time Ross and Mark had enjoyed their gourmet meals and chatted for awhile, it seemed like they were landing.

"This has been the shortest day of my life," Ross said. "Do you realize the time between the sun rising in New York and setting over the Atlantic was only about five and a half hours long?"

"Yeah," Mark said without conviction. He just wanted to get to his room and call Tracy.

The lobby of the Hyatt Regency at Charles de Gaulle was stunning. The five-story glass windows surrounding them reflected the lights from the outside of the hotel into mysterious pools on the light oak wood floor at their feet. The huge lobby under the open glass had a bar on one side of the room, the front desk on the other side, and an atrium and reflection pool artistically placed in the middle. Mark made his way up to the front desk, slapping the network's credit card on the counter in front of him.

"*Bonsoir*, monsieur," the woman behind the counter offered.

155

"*Bonsoir,* madame," Mark returned automatically, thanks to two years of high school French. "Reservations for Mark Taylor and Ross Berman."

"How long will you be staying with us?" she asked in English.

"One night," Mark answered, relieved she spoke his language.

She set a couple of index-sized cards on the counter. "If you'll just fill these out for us, please, I'll get your keys."

Mark started filling his in as Ross spoke. "Khaliq is supposed to meet us here in fifteen minutes."

"Did Russell say where?"

"No, just at the hotel."

"Well, I want to check in with Tracy. Let's get our stuff to our rooms; then I'll catch up with you back here in the lobby."

"Sounds good, but don't leave me hanging down here."

Mark signed his name on the card, then smiled over at Ross. "Don't worry, I won't."

"Here are your keys, gentlemen," the hotel clerk offered. "You're on the seventh floor, rooms 16 and 18."

"*Merci,*" Ross answered.

"Would you like some assistance with your bags?"

Ross and Mark declined. The clerk directed them to the elevators on the other side of the lobby.

"Are you going to call Tracy on the satellite phone?" Ross asked.

"Do they work inside?" Mark asked as he stepped into the elevator.

"I don't know."

"I'll give it a try and let you know."

The elevator doors opened to the seventh floor, and Mark and Ross made their way to the rooms.

"I'll see you in the lobby," Ross said as he opened his door.

"Okay," Mark said and entered his room.

He flipped on the light switch by the door, illuminating a modern-looking room with a bed against one wall and a dark credenza with a television on the other. There was a sitting area by the window with a small glass-and-chrome table, a matching lamp, and a chair that had a very large man sitting quietly in it. In any other circumstance, Mark would have jumped or confronted the man, but after the initial shock he just stood there quietly.

The stranger in the chair raised a finger in front of his lips to keep Mark silent. He turned on the television with the remote control, waiting for the sound to fill the room before he spoke.

"Dumbo Drop."

Mark stepped into the room, letting the door shut behind him. He analyzed the man—judging from the extension of his legs he was definitely taller than Mark, dressed in dark slacks, white shirt, a tan overcoat, and wearing a hat low over his eyes. He was probably somewhere in his fifties. He could have passed for a business traveler from any of a number of countries, or a spy.

Mark placed his bag beside the bed before he finally spoke. "What are you doing in my room? What if Ross had followed me in here?"

"He didn't." The man spoke evenly, without emotion. "I wanted to sweep your room before you got here, to make sure it's bug free."

"Well, is it?"

"Yes, the TV is just a precaution."

"Good. Now get out."

The man cocked his head, raising one eyebrow at Mark's brashness. "I was told you expected a full briefing on the operation and wanted it upon your arrival."

"That's true. But I don't have time for it right now. There is a contact from the Jihad al Sharia meeting us downstairs in approximately five minutes, and I want to call my wife first."

"We weren't informed about this meeting. Who is it with?"

"Look, it was confirmed while we were in flight. I don't exactly have a direct link to tell you guys everything." Mark was running low on patience.

The man rose from his chair, quicker than Mark could have imagined with his bulk. He stepped right in front of Mark, towering over him by a good four inches. "Look, Mr. Taylor. We appreciate your cooperation, believe me. But this isn't a game. Don't think for an instant that any detail, that every second of your life from now until you make it back to United States soil isn't crucial."

Neither of the two moved. Mark finally lowered his head and stepped toward the bed. He opened his suitcase, pulling out the satellite phone. "You have a funny way of expressing your gratitude."

The CIA man turned slowly in Mark's direction, raising the brim of his hat. "I apologize. It must have given you quite a shock to find me in your room. Let's start over. My name is Patrick Wark."

Mark didn't offer a handshake; instead, he unzipped the carrying case. A folded piece of paper fell out with the phone, another note from Tracy. Mark smiled but chose to read it later. The phone was slightly larger than his own Nokia phone, with one huge difference—a second antenna stretched out from the top of the handset nearly three times as large as the normal cellular antenna.

"You know anything about these things?" Mark asked.

"Looks like a Qualcomm GSP 1600 tri-mode. What do you want to know?"

"Can I use it here in the hotel?"

"Sure. It automatically switches from satellite to cell, depending on where you are and what's available."

"Good." Mark powered on the unit. "Then if you'll excuse me, I have an important call to make."

"I need to know who you're meeting with," Patrick said.

"His name is Abdul Khaliq," Mark answered, punching in the required country code for the United States. "Do you know him?"

The agent nodded. "We've been trying to convince France to arrest him and freeze his company's assets since the Sunday Massacre."

"Well, I'll be happy to fill you in after our meeting. Then you can tell me about your plan. But don't ever show up in my room unannounced again. You want to get me killed?"

Patrick ignored the accusation. "We need to wire you for this. . . ."

Mark heard some noise over his phone as the call was being put through. He walked over to the door and opened it, checking the hallway to see if anybody was in sight. "There's no time. Now get out of here. We'll talk when the meeting is over. Just make sure you're not seen."

Mark motioned to the hallway with his head as he heard Tracy's voice come on the line. "Hi, honey."

Patrick scowled, knowing he'd lost this round. He walked out into the hallway, and Mark closed the door quickly behind him.

"Mark, where are you?" Tracy asked.

"In Paris; we just checked in. Where are you?" Mark heard his own voice echo before Tracy's voice came back. He walked over and turned the television off.

"I'm in the car, I'm on my way to. . .to see the friend that visited last night."

"Good, that's why I was calling." Mark understood her to mean Agent Weston. "I've got a quick meeting; then we should be able to talk."

"I'll be ready. How was the Concorde?"

Oh, how he wished he was just on a business trip and could talk freely. "It was great. I wish you could have been there."

Tracy thought back to her morning in the bathroom. It had taken her until noon to actually feel anything like normal. "I'd rather have you here."

"I know, babe." Mark ached. "I wish I was there."

Silence.

"I found your note with the phone." Mark walked back to the suitcase to pick it up.

"What'd you think?"

He read it quickly, noting her suggestion that since he was unpacking the phone to give her a call.

"I called, didn't I?"

"Funny." Tracy laughed. "Would you have if I hadn't left the note?"

"Of course."

"I bet."

"Look, Trace." Mark looked at his watch. "I've got to get to this meeting. I'll talk to you as soon as I can."

"Okay, honey. I love you."

"I love you, too."

Mark turned off the satellite phone and laid it in his suitcase, then grabbed his briefcase and headed for the lobby.

VAN NUYS, CALIFORNIA
12:54 P.M.

Akilah Habash parked her '94 Celica a block away from the mosque. She reached into the back of her car and grabbed her hijab. Glancing up and down the street to see if anybody could see her, she quickly slipped it over her head before getting out of the car.

She walked casually up to the building, surprised that there wasn't more commotion with a class starting in the next few minutes. She slowed her pace, pausing by an oak tree as she spotted two men up ahead. She could tell by the thin frame and profile that one of them was Fazul. She stayed quiet, watching from a distance as they went around the corner of the building.

She walked quickly up to the corner where the two men had disappeared and peeked around. Nothing. She quickly stepped along the side of the building, down an alley that led to a back parking lot. She paused again, hearing voices coming from around the next corner. Akilah shivered from a chill that wasn't there as she thought about what she was doing. She strained to hear what her brother was saying but couldn't make out any words. Then she heard the car doors slam shut and the engine kick to life. She carefully peeked around the corner and saw her brother in the backseat of an old beat-up Ford. In the front seat was his friend Sofian—and then she saw the face of the driver next to him. She ducked back quickly behind the safety of the building as the car spun its tires and pulled away from her.

Ishmael. The name popped into her mind. She didn't know his last name—wasn't sure anybody did. She did know that her dad had warned her and Fazul that he was not to be trusted and had declared him off-limits.

Paris, France
10:10 p.m.

Ross was sitting at a table beside the reflection pool when Mark walked up to him.

"Any sign of Khaliq?" Mark whispered.

"Not yet." Ross looked at his watch. "It's only ten after, though."

"Maybe he's not going to show," Mark warned.

The two sat in silence, each of them looking through the hotel traffic for any sign of their contact. Before long, one of the hotel employees from the concierge desk walked up to them.

"*Excuse,* Mark Taylor?"

"Yes. . .*oui,*" Mark answered.

He handed Mark a folded piece of paper and quickly walked away. Mark read it quickly before he turned to Ross. "We're supposed to go to the Regency Club Lounge."

"I wonder where that is?"

"I don't know," Mark said, getting out of the chair. "Let's find it."

There was nobody in the convention area of the hotel. Mark and Ross ambled down the large hallway, looking at the signs in French above them. When they turned a corner, they saw two Middle Eastern men wearing robes and turbans standing outside a door. Over their heads the room was labeled Regency Club Lounge.

"I guess we've found it," Ross stated.

"You think?" Mark returned with sarcasm.

They slowly walked up to the men. One of them held out his hand for them to stop. The other one frisked them both, then moved a metal wand around their bodies. It wasn't the kind Mark had seen at airline security checkpoints; he figured it checked for electronic bugs. He quietly thanked God he hadn't been talked into wearing a wire. His briefcase was also searched, then the two Arabs opened the door.

It was a beautifully decorated room with windows overlooking the busy airport, and a circular staircase led up to a balcony. In the center sat a short, stout man dressed in a gray gambaz and white turban speaking with two larger men that Mark was sure were bodyguards. He made no effort to rise from his seat when Mark and Ross walked up to his table, but the other men quietly moved off to the side.

"Mr. Khaliq." Mark bowed slightly.

"At your service," Khaliq answered in thickly-accented, but understandable, English.

"We appreciate you meeting with us," Ross said as they took seats across the table from him. "I'm Ross Berman and this is Mark Taylor."

"My pleasure," Khaliq responded. "I hope my. . .associates did not disturb you. Necessary precautions."

"Not a problem," Mark answered, opening his briefcase. He pulled out a notepad, then looked at his microcassette recorder.

"Would you mind if I recorded this?"

Khaliq rubbed his nose as he pondered the question, then

slowly shook his head. "I would prefer that you did not."

"All right." Mark pulled the pen from his pocket. "Shall we get started?"

"Before you ask me your questions, Mr. Taylor, let me ask you one." Khaliq's dark eyes bored into Mark's. "Would you mind telling me what the federal agents were doing at your house last night?"

VAN NUYS, CALIFORNIA
1:18 P.M.

Fazul followed Sofian into Ishmael's apartment, his eyes wide with delight at the table full of the latest high-tech computer equipment.

"Wow!" Fazul exclaimed. "You've got some great stuff here."

"Yeah." Ishmael smiled. "It keeps me up to speed on what's really going on in the world."

Fazul slipped into a chair in front of one of the monitors, looking around at the different pieces of hardware with envy.

"So you can author DVDs?" Fazul asked.

"Sure can. That's how we're sending some of our training materials nowadays," Ishmael answered.

Ishmael had first approached Fazul and Sofian four months ago. It was after the Friday prayer at the mosque. Ishmael had walked over and started up a conversation with them. Fazul and Ishmael had struck up a quick friendship, unified in their dedication to the tenets of Islam. It had also given Fazul a sympathetic ear for his frustrations with his family. Ishmael had shown him how the apostasy and decadence of the American culture had softened them and stripped his father away from the true faith. He started inviting Fazul to some of the meetings at the mosque that weren't publicized, held late at night and attended by mostly young, single Arabic men. The teachings had struck a strong chord with Fazul, showing him avenues to live out his newfound devotion to Islam in much more concrete ways than just his own personal faith.

There was a lot to Ishmael that Fazul still did not know. What he did to make a living was one of them. It seemed like Ishmael was available all hours of the day and night for Fazul to get together with and talk about Islam, to study some of the wonderful Sūrahs that he would never hear spoken in the normal mosque services. Each day Fazul felt like he was gaining more and more of Ishmael's trust, as proven by this first visit to his apartment. It sent a rush through Fazul, knowing his day would soon come when he could serve Allah in some way beyond the daily prayers.

"Do you have any plans for Sunday?" Ishmael asked casually.

"Nothing special. Why?" Fazul returned.

Ishmael just winked, a sly grin spreading across his face. "I might have something for you to do."

CHAPTER 15

Mark felt not only Khaliq's eyes boring in on him, but his producer's as well. Mark didn't flinch—he stared directly back at the Arab in front of him. So much for the CIA's assessment that Mark's house wasn't being watched.

"They asked me to lead them to Sa'id." Mark chose to be direct with his denial. "I did not agree to help them."

Ross tried to mask his shock but didn't quite manage it.

Khaliq shrugged. "Why should we believe you?"

"You don't have to," Mark answered firmly. "But I'm an American journalist. We are not agents of our government. I didn't ask for this assignment; Ahmad Sa'id requested I travel to Turkey. If he wants to call it off, that's fine with me." He almost wished the Arab would get up from his chair and walk out of the room, ending the whole episode right then and there. Ross and Mark could take a return flight to the States in the morning and get back to normal. . .or however close to normal things could be since 9/11 and the Sunday Massacre.

"Don't assume that you are dealing with idiots, Mr. Taylor," Khaliq warned. "It was not wise for you to speak with them."

"They knew about the interview." Mark tried to defuse the situation. "Was I supposed to turn them away?"

"So you let them in twice?"

"They didn't like my answer."

There was no doubt they had somebody watching his house. Mark's first thought was for Tracy. . .and how far away he was from her.

Khaliq seemed to be considering Mark's words as the tension nearly smothered the two Americans. Ross shifted in his chair, making the only noise in the room. Mark studied the smaller man sitting across the table from him. He was pudgy, obviously out of shape. It wouldn't take Mark more than a few seconds to disable him, even kill him if Mark desired. But there were the two body-guards. Probably one snap of this man's fingers and Mark and Ross would be dead. Not to mention the tentacles of the organization that stretched all the way to Studio City. . .and Tracy. He had to play this out carefully.

"What's your relationship with Sa'id?" Mark eventually broke the silence.

Khaliq sighed, evidently deciding to continue. "I have no rela-tionship with Ahmad Sa'id. I run a charity that provides for orphan children in Islamic countries, Mr. Taylor."

"Okay," Mark said. "Then I guess we were wrong to assume you might be able to give us some information on him."

"I didn't say that." For the first time, the short man smiled thinly. "I only said, for the record, that I am not connected to Sa'id."

"This charity—aren't the orphans really the families of suicide bombers?"

Khaliq lowered his head slightly in reverence. "There is no bet-ter charity than to offer financial aid for the family of a martyr."

Mark's face darkened. He couldn't understand that kind of mis-guided loyalty.

"What can you tell us?" Ross cut in, surprising everyone that he spoke.

"You Americans," Khaliq said with a chuckle. "So impatient."

After a dramatic pause he sat up, leaning forward on the table as his voice filled the room with passion. "Ahmad Hani Sa'id is an amazing man. He has united factions of Muslims that have fought each other for centuries. Not since the time of the first caliphs have so many followers of Allah been united."

Khaliq looked deep into Mark's eyes as he continued. "Your country has vilified him, called him a terrorist, and claimed he has done these awful deeds, but it is all lies. He is a man of peace, called by Allah to unify Islam."

"If he is such a man of peace, why is he hiding?"

"Just because he chooses to seclude himself from the West, it does not necessarily follow that he's hiding."

"Mr. Khaliq," Ross interjected, "with all due respect, if he wasn't hiding, there would be pictures of him, stories on his exploits, videos of him spreading his message. We have none of that available to us."

"He has chosen a more difficult path, to unify Islam from within." Khaliq seemed to swell with arrogance. "Spreading his message to the West would have been a waste of his time."

"Until now?" Mark asked.

"I don't know why he has decided to speak with you at this time. His wisdom transcends my feeble understanding of world events."

Mark could see this interview was going nowhere if he allowed Khaliq to continue his diatribe. "Mr. Khaliq, can you tell us anything about Sa'id? What was he doing during the time he was unaccounted for?"

"Ah, you are curious?" Khaliq's eyes looked above Mark, roving the ceiling as his voice took on a deep reverence. "The lost years have made him quite a legend, have they not?" Khaliq smiled brightly.

"Can you tell us what he was doing during that time, where he was, what name he went by. . . ?" With each pause, the Arab remained silent. "Anything that will help us paint an accurate picture of the man."

"I can only tell you this, Mr. Taylor." Khaliq spoke slowly, almost as if what he was about to say had been rehearsed. "The prophet Isa. . .as you say, Jesus, may peace be upon Him, did not reveal details about His younger life, yet you would not say you cannot paint an accurate picture of that man, no? Ahmad Sa'id will reveal all that needs to be revealed at the appointed time."

Mark answered slowly, focused on pronunciation to hold back the boiling rage seething inside. "Is the appointed time when I meet with him and do the interview?"

"Possibly," Khaliq returned. "No one knows the mind of Sa'id but Allah. His plans are holy, ordained by the one true God."

Mark chose to sit quietly, coming to the realization that they had wasted their time with this man.

"You must know how blessed you are to be granted an audience with Caliph Sa'id, Mr. Taylor. When you are with him, I believe all that you need to know will be available to you."

"Why did he choose me?" Mark asked.

"Patience, Mr. Taylor; you will find that out as well. You Americans have no sense of drama." Khaliq chuckled.

"Does it have anything to do with Abu Ressam?" Mark asked, watching the face of Khaliq for any recognition. There was none.

"I do not know that name. Who is he?"

"Never mind." Mark shrugged. "How will we even know it's Sa'id?"

Khaliq filled the room with laughter. "You will have no doubt, Mr. Taylor. No doubt at all."

FEDERAL BUILDING, LOS ANGELES, CALIFORNIA
1:42 P.M.

Tracy placed her purse on the conveyer belt, then stepped quickly through the metal detector in the lobby of the Federal Building on Wilshire Boulevard. She wasn't sure what time Mark would call, but sitting in bumper-to-bumper traffic in the middle of the afternoon trying to get over the Sepulveda Pass on the 405 freeway had nearly pushed her over the edge.

Scanning the area, it looked more like the security stations at the airport. It seemed the price of freedom kept going up. The inflation of terrorism.

The FBI occupied floors nine through seventeen. She had been instructed to go to the seventeenth floor and check in at the FBI lobby. After a quiet ride on an elevator full of people, the doors opened.

Tracy felt a bit uncomfortable checking in with a receptionist sitting behind a bulletproof glass shield. She was issued a visitor's badge and asked to take a seat. She was alone with her thoughts for a few minutes until Agent Weston approached her.

"Mrs. Taylor, welcome to the FBI." Weston smiled warmly.

Tracy stood and accepted his outstretched hand. "Agent Weston."

"If you'll follow me, we're expecting the call any minute." Weston led her back to the elevator and they went down one floor, using his security card to access the sixteenth floor. He took her to one of the offices along the outside wall, equipped with an oak wood desk, a nice leather couch, a western view where she could see the Pacific Ocean on the other side of Santa Monica, and a television tuned to the Fox News Channel.

"I've got access to this office until the call comes through. I thought this would be more comfortable for you."

"Thank you," Tracy said, placing her purse down on the couch.

"Can I get you anything, some water, a soft drink, or coffee?"

"No, thank you," Tracy declined. "Have you heard anything from Paris yet?"

"We know that Mark checked in, but our meeting with him was delayed. He evidently had something else set up that we weren't aware of."

"Oh." Tracy wondered what that could have been. "Mark mentioned a meeting when he called me briefly not long ago. I assumed it was the one with the CIA."

"Well, evidently the studio set up something with a financial front man for Sa'id's organization. We'll know more when he checks in."

"All right."

"Here's what's going to happen, Tracy. Mark is going to be briefed in Paris. In a few minutes, a representative from the CIA will come in here and give you the same briefing. That way, when you and Mark are on the phone, you don't have to talk about specifics. Even though it's a secure line, we want to be careful."

"I understand."

"If you have any questions at all, feel free to ask them."

"All right."

"I'll be back shortly."

Weston closed the door, leaving Tracy alone with Neil Cavuto and some financial analyst arguing over the current stock market drop. She wished it were time for *Hannity & Colmes* or *The O'Reilly Factor*, something that held her interest. She picked up the remote lying next to the phone and muted the sound.

She looked around the empty office, taking in a deep breath. It seemed symbolic of her life. With Mark gone on such a dangerous trip, she'd found it impossible to get into her classes or to study. The morning sickness didn't help either. She wondered if it had been the right decision not to tell Mark. It had kept her awake for most of the night. She couldn't go through this alone, and although she was a new Christian, she knew she shouldn't try. Mark had conveyed to her that the church should be like family, and she needed somebody. As much as it hurt her for Mark not to be the first one she would tell about having his baby, she grabbed her cell phone out of her purse and dialed.

"Brenda?" Tracy asked when the voice answered the phone. "It's Tracy. I'm doing okay. Listen, I need to see you about something. Are you busy this evening?"

Paris, France
10:51 p.m.

Through a string of expletives, Ross managed to convey his anger as soon as the elevator door closed. "What were you thinking?"

"Don't overreact, Ross," Mark insisted.

"Don't you think you should have told me before you put my life on the line in there?"

Mark stayed silent, watching the numbers change on the panel as the elevator made its way up.

"Well?" Ross opened his hands in frustration.

"Well what?"

"Say something."

"Look, Ross, I'm sorry I didn't tell you, but I didn't want to make a big deal about it."

The doors opened on the seventh floor. The two stepped out of the elevator and walked the empty hallway.

"You made a big deal out of telling me how pampered my life has been." Ross stopped in front of his door and looked squarely at Mark. "Well, I'm here now and we're in this together. I would greatly appreciate it if you treated me accordingly and stopped trying to spare my feelings. My life is on the line every bit as much as yours is. I deserve to know if a couple of Feds visit your home the night we leave, don't you think?"

"You're right, Ross. Forgive me." Mark had a hard time looking him in the eye. "It was kind of a shock and I just wanted to forget it."

"C'mon." Ross opened his door. "Let's talk in my room."

Mark followed Ross into a mirror image of his own room. Ross flopped onto the bed, leaving Mark the chair by the window.

"So, tell me what they said."

Mark went on to relate the conversation from the previous night. He was careful to leave out the discussion with Tracy about

171

going along with the plan. He contemplated telling Ross more—but in reality he hadn't agreed to any plan yet. Besides, they could be listening. The deception weighed heavily on him, both with Ross and with the terrorist contact. Maybe he needed to back out no matter what the CIA plan was.

"Wow," Ross reacted. "I can't believe they'd pressure you like that, even bringing your former marine commander."

Mark forced a smile. "Yeah, they were pulling every string they could. I have to tell you, it made me think."

"Of going along with it?" Ross was shocked. "It'd be your last interview if you did and would probably get us both killed. I'm not so sure we're still not in deep with Khaliq back there."

"Yeah." Mark realized he wouldn't be able to tell Ross. "I think we're okay. Khaliq seemed to accept my answer."

"I hope so."

"I thought the meeting was a waste of time," Mark argued. "I think he only met with us because he knew about the Feds coming to my house. He was checking us out for Sa'id."

"You may be right." Ross leaned back against the wall. "I hope you passed his test."

Mark let out his breath. "Me too, Ross, me too." He stood, walking past the bed toward the door. "We need some rest. I'll see you in the morning."

Ross could feel the hours of travel catching up with him. "You're probably right. One last question. . .why did you ask him about Abu?"

Mark thought quickly. "Just playing a hunch. . .it didn't pan out."

"Like maybe Abu is the connection to bringing you here?"

"He's the only Arab I know from the region." Mark shrugged as if it didn't really matter. "Thought it was worth a try."

"Probably so," Ross conceded. "Good night."

"Good night." Mark opened the door.

"Oh, Mark." Ross stopped him.

"Yeah?"

"I didn't like being in the dark." Ross grinned. "But I thought you handled Khaliq very well."

Mark gave a reassuring smile back to him. "Thanks—let's hope we handle Sa'id better."

CHAPTER 16

PARIS, FRANCE
10:55 P.M.

Mark stepped into his room exhausted and wanting nothing more than to take a quick shower and climb into bed. Unfortunately, he still had to deal with the CIA, and at this moment, Mark didn't know himself what his response would be to their plan. He wasn't in the room more than thirty seconds before his phone rang.

"Hello."

"Mark Taylor?" A familiar voice, but Mark couldn't quite identify it.

"Yes," Mark answered.

"You old dog, you," Chuck Fleming said. "It's Chad Moreland. It's been a long time."

"Yes, it has." Mark grinned at Chuck's use of the cover name. "Are you in Paris?"

"You could say that; I'm downstairs." Chuck laughed.

Mark sighed, thanking God for coming through. Even after the CIA said Chuck was on board, Mark had kept his hopes subdued until he could see his face. "Well, come on up; it's room 718."

"How about you meet me down here and we'll take a walk?"

"I'll be right down."

Two minutes later the two met in the lobby with a friendly handshake, resisting their urge to embrace.

"It's been too long, Mark." Chuck smiled broadly.

"It has, Chad." Mark felt weird calling his old friend by the new name.

"Come, let's take a walk."

Chuck led Mark through the lobby and outside into the cold. It was the only way he knew that they could speak freely.

Although Chuck had left the military, it looked like the military hadn't left him. He looked in great shape, and he kept his brown hair cropped short. He'd left a day's growth on his face, probably to take the military edge off his appearance.

Chuck led them out a side door as they walked around the grand hotel. The cold, damp French weather revitalized Mark as they made their way in silence. The grounds were lonely—nobody out this late at night. Chuck paused at a bench, looked back from where they'd come, then took a seat and pulled a cigar out of his coat pocket.

"Do you mind?" Chuck asked before he lit up.

Mark smiled; it was reminiscent of their days in the marines. After every mission, Chuck would find a place off by himself and puff away on a good cigar. Mark shrugged his approval. "It's not like you to have one before an operation."

"Times they are a-changing." Chuck grinned. "So tell me what you've gotten us into."

Mark joined him on the bench, speaking quietly. "How much did Griff tell you?"

"Enough for me to know you need somebody watching your back," Chuck said.

"I do need that. . .and things just got a little stickier," Mark said, then proceeded to catch him up on the meeting with Khaliq.

"Leave it to the Feds to screw it up from the beginning. I can't believe they didn't make sure you weren't under surveillance before approaching you."

"Well, they thought they had."

"You think the Arab bought your story?"

Mark shook his head. "I have no idea. This whole thing is so mysterious. Why did they want me in the first place? Why am I being watched? Each step just seems like I know less about what's going on and I'm that much closer to danger."

"Well, you're not alone now," Chuck said.

"I'm glad you're here."

"Me too."

Mark patted his friend on the back, then rose. "I need to get back to the room. The CIA will be making contact again. Come on, let's go."

"You want me with you?"

"From now until this is over," Mark said.

"Okay, but we'll never know who's watching us and when. I'm Chad Moreland. Don't slip up."

"I won't. Let's go."

While walking through the lobby, Mark spotted Patrick Wark sipping a drink at the bar. He ignored Mark and Chuck walking by but casually laid some euros on the counter and followed in their direction toward the elevators.

Patrick smoothly slipped a piece of paper into Mark's pocket, with just enough pressure to ensure that Mark would notice but so quickly the naked eye would miss it. He continued walking right past the pair and down the hallway as the elevator opened before them.

Mark stepped in, pressed seven, and moved to the back corner. Chuck stood beside him as they quietly waited for the doors to close. No one else entered and they were on their way. Mark casually pulled out the piece of paper and looked at what Patrick had written: "Room 1212." He showed it to Chuck, then punched the button for the twelfth floor.

The elevator stopped at seven, the doors opening to an empty hallway. Mark punched the "close door" button three times before it responded. The twelfth floor had a French couple waiting to go down, but it was empty otherwise. Mark led Chuck down the hallway searching for room 12. They found a locked door, but within moments Patrick was walking quietly toward them. No words were spoken until they were inside the room behind the closed door. Mark started to speak, but Patrick raised his hands while forming his lips in a shush. He turned on the television set, raised the volume a few notches, then went into the corner and pulled a small black object from his suitcase. He set it on the counter and turned it on.

"White noise generator," Patrick explained. "It'll block any attempt at eavesdropping. We're not taking any chances from here on out."

"They knew about the meeting in L.A." Mark sat on the edge of his bed.

"I know," Patrick said. "I heard everything."

"How. . . ?"

"It doesn't matter," Patrick said. "Remember, we have our eyes on you everywhere you go. I'm Patrick Wark." He offered to Chuck.

"Chad Moreland." Chuck chose to use his cover name as he half-sat on the dresser.

Patrick smiled. "Good. I take it you've got all your papers: passport, press credentials?"

"Yeah, your boys gave me everything before I flew out of Israel."

"Do you guys have a handle on this whole thing?" Mark was still steaming from the realization his house had been watched. "How could they have known. . . ?"

"Yeah, I'll admit that surprised me," Patrick stated.

"Surprised you?" Chuck jumped in. "How stupid can you Feds be?"

"Look, L.A. wasn't an agency operation," Patrick explained. "FBI handled that, and, yeah, they screwed up."

"What about my wife? How do I know she's safe?"

"She's waiting at the L.A. Bureau right now to talk with you," Patrick reminded him. "Calm down; nothing's blown here. Khaliq bought your explanation."

"I wouldn't have agreed to this if I knew Tracy would be in any danger."

"She isn't. They'll put an FBI team on her immediately. We can put her in a safe house until this is over if you want."

Mark buried his face in his hands, breathing slowly several times as he thought it through. Tracy would freak out if she knew the house had been watched, but he couldn't leave her unprotected. There was no telling what kind of resources the Jihad al Sharia had in America. . .California. . .Studio City. What events had put him in the middle of it all? *Could it be Abu? Is he really connected in some way to all this?* Mark still had a hard time accepting that. But the biggest question in Mark's mind at that moment: *Is it too late to turn back?*

"Here's what we're planning, Mark, Chad." Patrick pulled the chair away from the window and set it next to Mark on the bed. "You've met Vince Ruzio. He is the best. If there's somebody you can have complete trust with in the field, it's Vince."

Mark looked at Chuck. "He was at the airport in New York. Looked capable enough."

"Oh, believe me, he's capable."

"The James Bond of the CIA?" Chuck asked.

"Without the good looks." Patrick grinned. "Anyway, all he has to do is get one of these—" he held up a flat black disk no larger than a dime "—at Sa'id's location or, if possible, on his person."

Mark reached out and grabbed hold of the disk. It didn't seem like much. It was more dense than a dime and slightly thicker, no marks on it, just a flat black surface. "What is it?"

"It's classified. But let's just say that when this is activated, we can drop a laser-guided smart bomb within twelve inches of it."

"And how do you expect to get this on Sa'id?"

"There are several options Vince will have. We know you'll be searched, so we'll have these hidden in the camera equipment where they won't detect them. They don't produce a signal until activated, so nothing Sa'id's people have will detect them."

"Metal detectors, debugging devices?"

Patrick shook his head. "Nope, even an X-ray won't spot this thing."

Chuck reached over and took it. "That's pretty impressive."

"Obviously," Patrick said as he looked directly at Mark, "this can never be reported."

"I understand," Mark answered.

"Vince will also have one of these implanted under his skin." Patrick held out a smaller silver pellet. "They allow us to monitor everything being said around you guys through untraceable satellite links, as well as keep a satellite fix on your position within a foot. So we'll know what's going on at all times."

"Do you want us to have one of those as well?" Mark asked.

Patrick shook his head. "We recommend against it. That way if anything goes wrong, you have deniability. Vince will be the only link."

"What do you mean?"

"Remember, you two are journalists, not CIA," Patrick answered solemnly. "If for whatever reason this thing turns sour, act shocked. You didn't know Vince was anything but a camera operator. He'll be coming in at the last second with no connection to either of you. They might suspect you but have no proof. You won't be wired, no disks on your person. Nothing. Just play dumb."

"I see what you mean," Mark said. "But I'm not sure it'll be enough if something goes wrong."

Patrick continued without comment. "Now, the black disks are activated two ways. One is by a remote control from Vince. It looks like a wireless microphone pack, standard gear with a camera package, but it will actually send a signal to the disk to begin transmission. If all goes as planned, after the interview and you three are safely out of the area, Vince can activate the signal. Once we receive it, the president can order a launch immediately. We'll have fighters in Turkey ready to go."

"And the other option?" Mark asked.

"In the event that Vince is compromised and the disk is somehow discovered, it'll automatically activate if tampered with. If somebody tries to open it, smash it, even burn it, the signal is turned on."

Mark thought about that one for a second. "So you're telling us that if it is activated automatically, you could strike while we're still there."

Patrick lowered his head. "Yes, but that's only if you've been compromised. And in our estimation already dead."

Silence echoed for several seconds before Chuck spoke. "Thanks for bringing me in on this, partner."

Mark glanced over to him. "What are old friends for?"

"Look, these things are so high-tech, there's no way Sa'id's men will be able to discover them. We're pretty confident that everything will go according to plan and you will be out safely before we strike. Your code name is Dumbo, Mark. Chad is the Circus Mouse."

Mark and Chuck glanced at each other. Neither saw the levity in the situation.

"Vince and anybody else from the agency or military will be designated as Black Crow, Sa'id's the Ringmaster, and any terrorists around him are Clowns. The air force plane standing by is the Stork," Patrick continued. "The CIA's witty way of bringing Sa'id's present to him."

"Why all the names?"

"Standard spook speak," Patrick answered. "That way, if there are any intercepted communications, it makes it harder for the enemy to add things up. Besides, it looks great on the classified reports after it's all over. So, are you in?"

Mark looked at Chuck. "What do you think?"

"It's a different operation than anything we did in Desert Storm," Chuck offered. "We'll be going in unarmed, totally reliant on this technology to pull off the mission. If these little bugs do everything he says, it just might work. If there's a chance to get Sa'id before he can set off his next attack, I'm all for it."

"So you're willing to go along?" Mark asked.

"If you're in," Chuck answered solemnly, "I'll back you up."

Mark, who had been pleading with God in the back of his mind all through the discussion, paused a second to see if he could sense what God wanted him to do. His bravado was telling him he couldn't back down now. . .how could he look himself in the mirror when the next wave of terrorism hit his country if he had this opportunity and backed away from it? Could God be speaking through those emotions, or could they actually be what was blocking His voice? Would he really be jeopardizing the pool of reporters around the world as Russell had claimed? Mark felt like he was facing an impossible decision.

"I need to speak with Tracy."

"Okay, give me a second and I'll set it up."

Patrick went back toward his suitcase, and Chuck stepped over and sat on the bed next to Mark.

"I wish we knew why they picked you."

"I know," Mark answered. "It seemed like Khaliq knew something about that. Almost like he was teasing me."

"Oh, he definitely was," Patrick said, coming back to the bed with a briefcase. "That reference at the end of being patient. . . there's a reason they picked you, but I don't think we'll know what it is until you get there."

"Comforting. The only thing that makes any sense is if it's somehow connected to Abu," Mark said. "If he really is working with the terrorists."

Patrick set the briefcase in front of Mark and opened it. Inside was a keyboard connected to a phone. He raised up the internal antenna, then picked up the receiver.

"Now your wife has had the same briefing that I just gave you,"

Patrick informed Mark.

"The exact same one?"

"Well, I'm pretty sure they would have left out the backup plan." Patrick smiled and dialed a number he had memorized.

"It's Black Crow Two—you secure there?" Patrick waited for the response. "Okay, put her on."

Patrick handed the phone to Mark. "Don't speak about any specific details that we mentioned."

"Can I use her name?"

Patrick nodded.

"Tracy, hi, honey."

Patrick and Chuck politely stepped over by the door, giving Mark at least a sense of privacy. He knew Tracy wouldn't be alone either.

"Hi, Mark. I was getting worried."

"Sorry, I've been kind of busy."

"So what do you think?" Tracy asked gently.

Mark gulped. "I'm impressed. I'm not involved at all except getting to the interview and doing my job. It'll be up to them to make it work after Chuck and I are out of there."

"That's what it sounds like to me. But what if something goes wrong?"

"We just have to pray that it doesn't."

"Oh, Mark." Tracy sighed. "I'm not sure I can go through with this."

"What do you want me to do?"

"Whatever you think is right."

"I. . ." Mark paused. This was the point of no return. *God, shut my mouth if this is a big mistake,* he prayed. *I want to do what You're calling me to.* "I guess I think we should do it."

There, it was out. His career was on the line and most definitely with it his life. Tracy didn't respond, but he could hear sniffling over the phone. He was sure she was fighting to keep her emotions under control.

"I'm sorry, Tracy," Mark whispered. "I wish this were happening to somebody else, I really do."

"I understand, honey." Tracy's voice broke. "Don't worry about me; just come home to us safe."

"I will. . . ." Mark couldn't believe the empty pit he felt in the middle of his gut. "Listen, maybe you should consider staying with a friend for a few days, until I'm on my way home."

"Why do you say that?" Tracy asked.

"I. . ." Mark couldn't tell her. "I just don't think you should be alone. Maybe you should call Brenda."

"You might be right." She surprised him. "I actually called her today. We're getting together later."

"Good. I'm sure they'll let you stay there. Please, Tracy. I'd feel better."

"Okay," Tracy finally answered.

"Keep your cell phone with you," Mark instructed. "I'll call you when I can, but remember, we can't say anything about the mission, just normal husband and wife stuff."

"I understand," Tracy said. Her voice had gained some strength back.

"I love you, Tracy. Pray for me."

"Every minute. I love you, too."

"I'll speak with you sometime tomorrow."

"All right. Sleep well."

"You too, Trace." Mark put his hand over the phone. "Patrick."

Patrick stepped back near the bed, taking the phone. "She's going to stay at a friend's house. I want her watched like a hawk, but discreetly."

Tracy sat on the couch, staring off toward the horizon. He was going through with it. It wasn't like she was shocked. She'd known when he left that's what he was going to do. Now that the decision had been made, she felt numb.

"Can I get you anything, Mrs. Taylor?" Weston's voice interrupted her thoughts.

"Some water, please."

Weston nodded, stepping outside the room for a moment before returning with a bottle of Evian.

"Thank you," Tracy said, unscrewing the cap and taking a long drink.

The CIA representative who had answered the phone when Mark called in sat on the couch beside her, speaking quietly to somebody else.

"Yes, sir, I'll put her on," Tracy heard him say; then he turned to her. "Mrs. Taylor, the assistant director over Middle Eastern intelligence would like to speak with you."

Tracy put the bottle down on the coffee table and took the handset.

"Hello, this is Tracy Taylor."

"Mrs. Taylor, this is Jack Murphy. I had the pleasure of meeting your husband this morning in New York between planes."

"Oh," Tracy said. "How did he seem to you?"

"I think he's handling himself very well. I went there to introduce him to the man we're sending into Syria with him," Jack explained.

"I appreciate you telling me."

"I want you to know we've sent our best field agent to go in with Mark. Between the two of them, I think the plan's going to work." Jack spoke compassionately, knowing he was about to trample on dangerous ground. "Which leads me to one other thing."

"Yes. . . ?"

"Please understand that I hesitate to pry into your personal life, but since I'm in charge of this mission, any information about you and Mark—anything—can be important."

"I can understand that," Tracy said cautiously.

"Then I'll just ask it right out," Jack said. "Mrs. Taylor, does your husband know that you're pregnant?"

Tracy nearly dropped the phone. How could he know? Only Tracy and her doctor's office knew.

"How. . . ?" Tracy heard her voice coming out.

"I'm sorry for what seems like an invasion of your privacy," Jack tried to explain.

"What *seems* like?" Tracy interrupted, her voice rising. "I would say you've crossed way over the line of what seems like, Mr. Murphy." Tracy felt the eyes of Weston and the other man on her. She palmed the phone. "Could you excuse me for a minute, please?"

The men graciously left Tracy alone.

"Please, Mrs. Taylor," Jack pleaded. "Don't be upset. Everything we're doing is designed to bring your husband back safely. The more we know, the better we can do our job."

As Tracy listened, an overwhelming feeling of violation flooded her. It reminded her of the night she had come home to her apartment and found the door broken in. All of her cash, jewelry, television, VCR, and stereo system had been taken. But somehow this felt worse. She wondered what else they might know about her.

"I understand all that, but why are you asking me this question?"

"To make sure we know your husband's state of mind. We're asking a lot of him, and of you, Mrs. Taylor." Jack paused a second, letting his words sink in. "I know you just found out yourself. Did you decide to tell him before he left or keep it to yourself?"

Tracy took in a deep breath and let it out as she thought. She closed her eyes. "I didn't tell him."

"That must have been hard. Probably wise, though." Jack kept his voice soft.

"I'd planned to, until he told me about the interview first. Then things just moved so fast. . .there was never the right time."

"I understand. Thank you for being honest with me, Mrs. Taylor."

Tracy didn't feel like saying you're welcome. "Is that all?"

"Yes, it is, except I think you did the right thing. He's going to be thrilled when he returns and you share the good news with him."

If he returns, the thought hit Tracy before she could reject it.

Jack wished he could offer her more. "Look, I'm in charge of this mission, and I promise to keep you informed personally. Let me give you my office number, and you can call with any questions. That way we'll leave out the middleman."

Tracy liked the idea of having direct access to the CIA. "I'd appreciate that." She jotted the number on a pad next to the phone. "Thank you, Mr. Murphy."

"Now when we talk, if I ever use the code word 'pickle,' I'll want you to get in touch with Agent Weston and get to a secure phone. It'll mean I have information on Mark that I can't say over an unscrambled line."

"Pickle, got it," Tracy responded.

"Perfect. Thanks for making this decision with your husband, Mrs. Taylor. We could be saving thousands of Americans' lives if we're successful."

"I certainly hope that will be the case, Mr. Murphy, but to tell you the truth, I'm most concerned about one life—Mark's."

CIA HEADQUARTERS, LANGLEY, VIRGINIA
5:52 P.M.

"So she didn't tell him?" Wendy asked after Jack hung up the phone.

"No, thank God, he doesn't know," Jack answered, letting a tense breath out as he lowered his head and rubbed at his temples. "Sometimes, this job makes me feel so. . ."

"Proud?" Wendy offered with a sarcastic smile.

Jack let his glasses hang on the end of his nose as he looked up at her from above the lenses. "Yeah, right. The phrase I was thinking about was something closer to hard-hearted. Being thrilled that Tracy didn't tell her husband—who she might never see again— that she's carrying his baby just so it won't distract him or make him back out of working with us just doesn't sit well with me."

"That's our job."

"Well, we don't have to like it," Jack returned.

"I know," Wendy acknowledged. "Let's just do everything we can to get Mark back to her. As soon as Sa'id is dead."

CHAPTER 17

With the events of the past few hours added to his jet leg, Mark's exhaustion went all the way to the bone. He swiped his key card in the electronic lock of his room, then opened the door when the green light flashed. He was relieved to see that this time the room was empty. He put the DO NOT DISTURB sign on the handle, then closed the door behind him. He reached up and added the security bolt.

Stepping into the room, Mark started taking off the clothes that he'd worn since. . .man, it seemed like a month since Tracy had pinned him under the covers of their bed. He spotted another note from her in his toiletry bag. He sat down and read the quick message, smiling at the thought of her writing it. This one said, "Thinking about you and missing you. Come home soon. Love, Tracy."

Moments later he was standing under the spray of a hot shower, slowly increasing the temperature until it was just below scalding. The intensity felt good as he let the water wash over the top of his head, breathing through the steam around his face. He closed his eyes, attempting to shut out the barrage of thoughts that wouldn't slow down. Images of Arabs and secret agents, of Chuck and Griff, of Khaliq and his henchmen, but mainly of Tracy—and somebody watching their house.

He tilted his head up, taking the spray straight into his face, even opening his mouth and letting the water flood in and wash back out. His hands went up, bracing against the tile above the showerhead before he lowered his head and let the beating water attack the back of his neck.

Mark began to focus his mind, silently speaking the name of Jesus. Images began to blur, faces fading away until all that remained was the picture of Tracy as Mark's thoughts gave way to prayer, not the kind of prepared oratory heard in a church, but a simple pleading from son to Father for His protection and comfort to be with the one he loved.

Tracy often joked that God spoke to Mark in the shower. If they were struggling with something in their lives, sometimes Mark would spend time in a hot shower and come out of it with some thought that would lead them forward. Mark brought his head back up, smiling at the thought. Now would be a great time to hear something.

He turned around, letting the water pelt his back, bringing up large splotches of red on his skin before he grabbed the soap and lathered up. Patrick had warned them before they left his room that this was the last time to speak about the mission. Vince would join them as planned in Istanbul, acting as the last-minute replacement for the camera operator. With Mclintock joining them from the network and Ross always around, their orders were to concentrate solely on the interview. That sounded good in theory, but Mark and Chuck had never been behind enemy lines acting out a part. They'd always been armed to the teeth, using every means at their disposal to complete the assignment. It was hard to separate Mark the special ops marine from Mark the journalist in this situation. He'd feel more comfortable sitting in front of Sa'id with his hand on the trigger of his old MP-5 than holding a notepad and pen.

The heat and steam in the bathroom were beginning to suffocate Mark. He reached out and turned the shower knob to the right, sending a refreshing blast of cool water over his half-baked body. He soaked his hair for a few seconds, feeling a chill run from the top of his head straight down through his body. Then he turned off the water and grabbed a towel. He stepped out of the shower and onto the mat. The bathroom was fogged with steam like a sauna.

He dried his hair and face, rubbing hard with the towel, scratching his scalp. As he flipped the towel over his shoulders, his eyes focused on the mirror for the first time and it stopped him dead in his tracks. The mirror was completely fogged up except for a string of letters staring Mark right in the face. The top characters were in Arabic and unreadable to him, but underneath, he surmised, was the English translation.

We are watching you. There is no god but Allah.

Did the hotel just give out keys to my room? Mark thought. *Had the terrorists heard the conversation with Patrick? Are they watching right now?*

Mark spun around the small bathroom area, looking for a camera hiding somewhere. His mind pictured what the terrorists could do to him once he was in their control, and it wasn't pretty.

He grabbed a hand towel from off the countertop and wiped violently at the mirror. He quoted a verse that popped into his mind as the letters quickly blurred into oblivion. "Greater is he that is in me than he that is in the world."

Mark stopped and stepped back, studying his fuzzy image in the mirrored surface. Then the room seemed to flash, either that or something in Mark's brain switched as the reflection changed. Mark saw himself again, but this time he was clothed in full marine battle gear standing face-to-face with the head of the Jihad al Sharia. Mark was holding him at gunpoint and could clearly see Sa'id's face—defiant and fearless, with fire in his eyes as he looked down the barrel of Mark's MP-5. Mark blinked as a second flash appeared and the image morphed. The two again stood face-to-face, but this time Sa'id was totally intimidated as he backed away from Mark in abject fear, his shoulders slumped. . .his eyes lifeless. The MP-5 had disappeared; instead, Mark was now holding his Bible.

Another flash and Mark was standing alone, looking at his shocked reflection through the droplets of moisture on the mirror. What he'd been seeking in the shower now settled over him like a blanket as Mark sensed God's presence. A smile spread across his lips as Mark finished drying off. He began to sing a worship chorus that popped into his mind as he walked into the other room, and he pulled out his Bible before slipping into bed. Not a pretty sound and certainly off-key a bit, but part of Mark hoped they were listening—give the Muslims a chance to hear praises to the real living God.

VAN NUYS, CALIFORNIA
6:18 P.M.

Akilah had gone to her room to study after another meal with her family, or at least her mom and dad. Once again, Fazul was out somewhere, and her dad muttered about it all through dinner.

She heard the front door open, followed by some yelling before she heard Fazul tromp down the hallway and slam the door to his room. Akilah sighed, put her portable PC to sleep, and went to his room.

"Fazul?" She tapped lightly on his door. "Can I speak with you?"

A moment passed; then the door opened in front of her. She stepped in and he quickly closed the door behind her.

"What do you want?"

"I saw you. . . ," she said as he flopped onto his bed. "Today, at the mosque."

Fazul's eyes darkened, his face scowling. "What were you doing there?" he demanded.

"I wanted to see if I could come to your class," she explained. "But there was no class."

"I told you they wouldn't allow women."

"No, Fazul. There was no class at all. I saw you. I saw you and Sofian. With Ishmael."

Fazul's face flushed red. "You did not. . .and what were you doing spying on me anyway? Are you crazy?"

"Not crazy, just wondering what you're doing."

"It's none of your business what I'm doing. Don't you get it? You sound like Dad."

Akilah inched nearer her brother. "Fazul, come on, we used to be tight. What's up?"

"Nothing. You should just stay out of it."

"Ishmael's trouble, Fazul. You can't trust him."

"He knows things, Akilah. And he's committed to fulfilling the will of Allah. He puts our family to shame," Fazul argued.

Akilah said nothing, but the look in her eyes made Fazul realize he'd confirmed her suspicion. But he didn't care; it actually felt good to have somebody in the family to talk to.

"All we do is study, Akilah. What is wrong with that?"

"Nothing, I guess," she said, confused. "Papa said he's a radical tied into some terrorist group or something."

Fazul laughed. "No, Ishmael's just serious about his faith. Dad wouldn't understand that. He's shown me tapes of conferences all over the country. . .Dallas, Chicago, Denver, Charlotte, Atlanta, New York, right here in L.A.; our Muslim brothers are rising up, Akilah. They're following the commands of the *Qur'an.*"

"You're scaring me, Fazul."

"You should be scared. Our parents have left Islam, Akilah. They're not following Allah anymore. America has softened them, perverted them. Don't let it happen to you, little sister."

Akilah shook her head, not sure what to do. "Are you sure you know what you're doing, Fazul? You were so close to finishing college, starting a career—getting out of this house."

"That's the only part I'm regretting. I need to find a place of my own."

"And that takes money."

"Right," Fazul agreed dejectedly.

"What's gotten into you?"

"Faith," Fazul declared. "I want to do more with my life than what I see in Dad. I want be like those people in the videos; I want to serve Allah."

He sat up in the bed, pleading with his sister. "We've become like the Americans, Akilah. We've lost our heritage, our passion."

"We are Americans, Fazul. This is our country."

"No! We're Muslims living in this land of *dār al-ḥarb.*"

NORTHRIDGE, CALIFORNIA
7:39 P.M.

After fighting the late afternoon traffic out of Los Angeles, Tracy had gone back to her house to pick up Shandy and pack up some things for the next few nights at her friend's house. She'd called Brenda again from her cell phone during the drive and asked if she could spend the night. Brenda seemed excited about the idea and was sure that her husband wouldn't mind.

She had met Brenda and Tom Stafford at a Bible study they'd hosted back when Mark and Tracy were dating. They all attended the Church of the Cross, an independent congregation in Van Nuys. Now, two years later, the four had become great friends. Brenda had actually been the one to inspire Tracy to go to law school.

She wove her way through the hills on the northern side of the San Fernando Valley. There were some beautiful homes on this side of Northridge, and on a clear day a person could see over the entire valley; although sometimes Tracy wondered why anyone would want to see the many millions of people crammed into this basin. Maybe the smog that hung around most days hiding the sea of humanity was in some way a perverse blessing.

Tracy knew the route by heart, having been at Tom and Brenda's house nearly every Sunday night, but she intentionally passed Brenda's street, pulling into a small cul-de-sac to see if the car behind her was following her. She kept her eyes glued to the rearview mirror, watching the dark sedan pause at the entrance to the cul-de-sac, then pull ahead slowly. The move didn't confirm or belie Tracy's suspicion. Maybe all this spy stuff was making her see things that weren't really there. She put the car in drive and did a quick U-turn in the street and went back to Brenda's house. She looked up and down the street before getting out, trying to spot any vehicle that looked like the dark sedan. Nothing matched.

"Tracy! Hi, Shandy." Brenda met them at the door; then she noticed the shadow hanging over Tracy's face. "Are you doing okay?"

The overnight bag Tracy had been holding dropped to the tiled entryway as she reached both arms around her friend and lost it. The emotions Tracy had kept in check throughout the day escaped in a flood of tears.

"It's all right, Tracy." Brenda held her tight for a moment. "Come on, let's get you inside."

She kept one arm around Tracy while grabbing her bag with the other and led her into the house, Shandy following closely behind them. She closed the door behind her and instinctively locked the dead bolt.

"I'm sorry," Tracy managed through the tears. "I didn't mean to break down like that."

"It's okay; don't worry about it. What's going on? Did you and Mark have a fight or something?"

Brenda took her to the living room couch, gently getting her settled before sitting next to her.

"No, we didn't have a fight," Tracy said, trying to get herself under control while thinking about how much she should tell her friend. "Where's Tom?"

"He's at a men's meeting at the church. He won't be home 'til late. We have the whole evening to ourselves; so tell me what's going on."

Tracy pulled a tissue out of her purse and wiped her nose, gaining some time to think while Brenda patiently waited.

"Mark is out of the country on an assignment," Tracy began.

"Where did he go?" Brenda asked.

"I. . ." Tracy hesitated. "I really shouldn't tell you, but it's dangerous. I'm really fighting the feeling that he's never coming back." Tracy's breath started coming in quick gasps as she fought to keep control. "And I just found out yesterday that I'm pregnant." The expression of concern on Brenda's face slowly changed as her eyes opened wide and her mouth broke into a joyous grin. "Tracy, that's wonderful."

Brenda reached forward and once again hugged her friend. "I can't believe it."

"Me either." Relief spread through Tracy at finally sharing the moment with somebody she loved, even if it wasn't Mark. For a second, the joy overshadowed the fear as she broke into a smile. "I'm going to be a mother."

"Congratulations," Brenda said as she pulled back. "How did Mark react to the news?"

Tracy shook her head. "I couldn't tell him." She went on to tell Brenda the romantic dinner she'd planned to spring the news before Mark shared his surprise

"I'm so sorry," Brenda said. "I can understand why you didn't tell him."

"I just didn't want to say anything that would distract him."

"Well, I'm glad you called. You just take over our guest room until he comes back." Brenda took Tracy's hands in hers. "And,

Tracy, he is coming back. I don't know what he's gotten himself into, but I know that God has His hands on Mark's life and on yours."

A light gleamed in Tracy's eyes as the comforting words soaked in. Tracy nodded, a smile creasing her lips. "Thanks for being here. I wasn't sure what I was going to do."

"You're welcome. I'm glad you didn't try and walk through this alone. C'mon, let's get ourselves a cup of coffee; then I think we should spend some time praying together."

 CHAPTER 18

The view out the window of the Air France Airbus 320 over the sprawling city of Istanbul was quite a sight. Settled in between the Black Sea and the Sea of Marmara, the clear winter day gave wonderful views of the deep blue water on either side of the ancient, hilled city. Mark could make out some of the landmarks as they flew toward the airport—the great Sultanahmet Camii, or Blue Mosque, with its six tall minarets surrounding the domed center, the Bosphorus Bridge joining the two continents of Asia and Europe, and the Palace Dolmabahçe Museum. Once more he wished this were merely a vacation.

Turkey held a strong fascination for him. Some of the greatest stories from Scripture had occurred within its ancient borders. Ephesus, Galatia, and the rest of the seven churches mentioned in Revelation were all in the western and southern regions of Turkey, as well as the Euphrates and Tigris rivers, Mount Ararat along the eastern border near Iran, and the land of Haran where Abraham settled before going south the three hundred miles to Canaan. Mark had studied his maps on the flight and realized that they possibly could travel through Haran to get to Syria.

The irony of connecting through Istanbul wasn't lost on Mark. On May 11, A.D. 330, Constantine the Great declared what was then called Byzantium to be his capital and dubbed it the New

Rome. The city soon came to be known as Constantinople and was the most important city in the world for a thousand years. Then on May 29, 1453, the city fell to the Turks under Sultan Mehmed II, who rode through the city that afternoon and into the greatest church in Christendom at that time, Hagia Sophia, and declared it a mosque, now known as Aya Sofia. He announced the city should be named Islamboul, the "city of Islam." Istanbul then became the capital of the great Ottoman Turk Empire. This one city, the battleground between the forces of Christianity and Islam centuries ago—was now the gateway for Mark as he began his journey into the heart of the Muslims.

The morning had been uneventful, meeting Ross downstairs in the lobby of the hotel and introducing Chuck to him as Chad Moreland, which seemed a little weird. Ross had quite a few questions about working at *Newsweek,* but Chuck handled them well. It was a quick ride from the hotel back to the airport terminal, where they went through the French security procedure without much of a hassle.

Their plane was a few minutes late, which didn't matter to the three travelers. They had nearly a four-hour layover to make the connection on Turkish Airlines to Diyarbakir. Mark hadn't been able to spot the CIA on board the flight, which both comforted and worried him.

Chuck had climbed right into the role of Chad Moreland, offering heroic tales to Ross of his exploits throughout the region writing for *Newsweek*. He was lucky Ross was a *Time* reader. By the end of the flight, it started feeling natural to call him Chad. Mark prayed he wouldn't slip.

"Couldn't ask for a prettier day," Ross mentioned to Mark as the jet taxied toward Atatürk Airport's new international terminal.

"It is gorgeous," Mark affirmed. "The pilot said it was eleven degrees centigrade; what's that in Fahrenheit?"

"Fifty-two degrees," Chuck calculated from across the aisle.

"That's warmer than I thought it would be," Ross said.

"The days here are fairly nice," Chuck continued. "When the sun goes down, it'll get colder. Not quite freezing, but it'll be chilly."

The plane came to rest at their gate, and before the seat belt sign went off many passengers rose to gather up their belongings. Ross led the three of them off the plane and down the ramp.

"Where is Mclintock going to meet us?" Mark said, coming up beside Ross as they hit the terminal.

"I don't know, either outside customs or in the domestic terminal."

They walked the long concourse until they came to immigration. After showing their passports and turning in their paperwork from the flight, the three were allowed into the international baggage claim area. None of them were stopped to have their bags searched, and they made their way outside the terminal. Mark wondered how different it would have been if he'd told the customs agent that they were in the country to cross the border illegally into Syria so they could meet with Ahmad Sa'id.

"Welcome to Turkey, gentlemen," a voice called out to them a dozen feet away on the sidewalk. Dressed in khaki pants and a safari-type multipocket shirt, the National News Middle Eastern bureau chief approached.

"Josh Mclintock, I presume," Mark said, holding out his hand.

"Correct." Josh grasped his hand. "Welcome to Turkey, Mark, Ross," he continued, shaking hands. "And you must be Chad Moreland; it's a pleasure."

"I really appreciate this opportunity," Chuck responded.

"It's one for all of us," Josh answered, his teeth slightly clenched. "Well, how was the trip?"

"Exhausting," Mark answered. "Everything's happened so fast, it's hard to believe we're here."

"Yeah, I find it hard to believe myself." Josh didn't attempt to hide his displeasure at Mark's arrival. "We have about three hours left before the next flight. I thought we'd get something to eat here—they have a pretty good restaurant upstairs—then we'll head over to the domestic terminal. Everybody okay with the bags?"

The trio nodded. "What about the camera crew?" Mark asked.

"It's a one-man operation, actually. Our network guy came down ill this morning. His replacement had to take a later flight. He'll meet us at the gate for the connecting flight. It'll be interesting to see how he reacts when I tell him what the assignment is."

"You didn't tell him?" Ross asked.

"Didn't want to take the chance until he's committed," Josh answered with a devilish grin.

The group made their way back into the terminal and up to the second floor. The Divan Pub wasn't crowded this time of the day, and the four were seated right away. Mark looked over the combination of Turkish and international foods, finally deciding he might as well experience the culture and try the special, *pastrimale ispanak sugato* with *tavukgogsu*. It turned out to be a spinach and pastrami goulash with chicken bread pudding. Palatable, but a cheeseburger and fries would have been more to his liking. Halfway through the meal, the small talk got more specific.

"So, pretty big opportunity for you, huh, Mark?" Josh said with a hard edge to his voice.

"I want to make sure you understand one thing, Josh." Mark kept his voice warm, attempting to get through to the bureau chief, not further inflame the situation. "I didn't ask for this assignment. I don't know why my name was brought up. And I want you to know I suggested to the network that somebody already assigned to the Middle East do this—" Mark glanced around to see who might overhear "—assignment. So if there's any animosity directed toward me, you're aiming at the wrong target."

The directness of Mark's response took Josh by surprise. After a moment's hesitation, he nodded and smiled thinly. "Since we're being candid with each other, let me make one thing clear to you. I know this group, Mark. They're dangerous. They don't play games." He leaned closer to the table, keeping his voice just loud enough to be heard over the noise of the restaurant, but soft enough that nearby waiters and busboys wouldn't overhear. "There must be some reason Sa'id demanded you come here. If you don't know what it is, then that makes this even more dangerous for you. For us."

"How could they even know who Mark Taylor is?" Ross asked.

"You'd be surprised," Josh answered. "They have a network of connections in the United States. Maybe something Mark reported has made him a cult hero within one or two of the cells. Perhaps Mark's befriended one of them without even knowing it. Or with Sa'id's satellite technology he's taken a personal interest in Mark's show. There are a number of possibilities."

Josh's speculation prompted Mark to give more credence to what Jack Murphy had said about Abu. At this point there really wasn't any other explanation. He wished he could discuss this with Chuck. He was the only one in the group who knew Abu, but that wasn't possible. At least not now.

"Well, Khaliq said I'd find the answer in Syria. I guess we'll just have to wait until then," Mark stated evenly before turning to Josh. "Have they told you how we get to Sa'id?"

"Nothing new." Josh dabbed at his mouth with a napkin. "We're to rent a four-wheel-drive vehicle at the airport and get to the hotel in Diyarbakir. We'll be contacted there."

"You haven't been told anything more since the first contact?"

"No," Josh answered.

Ross looked troubled. "How do we know the interview is still on?"

"It's still on," Mark answered the question. "They left me a message last night at the hotel." He went on to relay the story of the Arabic writing on his bathroom mirror. He left out the part about the visions.

"Why didn't you say something sooner?" Chuck asked.

"I'm not sure," Mark confessed, now realizing he needed to inform the CIA when he got the chance. "I actually kind of forgot about it."

The other three found that hard to believe.

NORTHRIDGE, CALIFORNIA
7:10 A.M.

Tracy walked into the kitchen still dressed in her robe, with Shandy following closely behind her. Brenda and Tom were sitting at their dinette table, Tom reading the newspaper while Brenda sipped her morning coffee. Tracy went to the back door and let Shandy outside.

"How are you feeling this morning?" Brenda asked.

Tracy just raised her eyebrows and rolled her eyes.

"How about some toast?" Brenda offered, getting up from the table. "And the coffee's decaf."

Tracy nodded as she took the seat next to Tom and buried her head in her arms on top of the table. "I never imagined morning sickness would be like this."

Tom placed his arm on her shoulder. "It seems rough, Tracy, but well worth it."

Tracy lifted her head up slightly, letting her eyes roll, "Spoken like a true man."

Brenda giggled as she dropped a couple pieces of bread into the toaster. "Tom has to be babied around here when he has the flu. I'd hate to see how he'd react to a pregnancy."

"God's wisdom," Tom argued. "He knew men could not handle it."

"Right now I'm not sure I can either," Tracy groaned.

"You going to class?" Brenda asked, pouring the coffee into a mug.

"I have to; I can't afford to miss another day."

"Maybe this will help." Brenda placed the coffee in front of her.

"Smells good—I hope it agrees with me."

"You might want to wait for the toast," Brenda cautioned.

"Was it like this with you?" Tracy asked.

Brenda and Tom had raised three children, all grown and out of the house. "I had a hard time with Beth; the other two were easier."

"That's comforting, if I get through this one."

Tom folded the newspaper and placed the front page in front of Tracy. She took a small sip from the coffee, still too hot to drink, as her eyes drifted to the headlines. "FBI Raises Alarm, Terrorist Alert Nationwide." Her shoulders sagged further, the reminder of Mark's journey bearing down on her. Tom noticed, reaching his hand out and resting it over hers.

"Worried about Mark?"

Tracy nodded.

"Brenda filled me in. How long will he be gone?"

"Hopefully he'll have his assignment wrapped up this weekend and be home early next week."

"The time will go quickly, Tracy," Brenda said as the toast popped up and she reached for the butter. "We'll have fun."

"I don't want to be a bother."

"You're not." Tom stood. "I've got to get to the office."

Brenda looked at her watch. "I'm going to have to head in pretty soon too."

"You guys do whatever you need. I'll make myself at home."

"We hope you will," Tom stated. "I don't have any plans to-night. What say I take you two out to dinner?"

Brenda brightened. "You'd better say yes, Tracy; I don't get that offer very often."

"I'd enjoy that." Tracy smiled, then felt the knot in her belly turn a notch. "My stomach should be settled by then."

"Good, it's a date."

VAN NUYS, CALIFORNIA
7:24 A.M.

"The holy *Qur'an* calls for struggle, a holy struggle, jihad, jihad, jihad." The speaker raised his voice with each repetition. "Make war upon such of those to whom the Scriptures have been given as believe not in God!"

Fazul looked around the group of Arabs gathered in the basement underneath the main dome of the mosque. They were focused, following the cadence of the imam as if he had them hypnotized.

Smiling, Fazul looked back at the speaker in front of them. He felt at home, finally belonging to a group that believed and acted as he did. He laughed to himself. America—the decadent, the ungodly lifestyles of drunkenness and indulgence, powerless to stop the rising swell of Islam. What other country would allow the free meetings of groups like theirs, intent on that country's destruction, raising up fighters from within for the jihad to come? America—the weak.

"I will cast a dread into the hearts of the infidels. Strike off their heads, then, strike off from them every fingertip. This because they have opposed God and his apostle."

The small crowd stood, a cheer rising from their throats. *"Allāhu akbar! Allāhu akbar! Allāhu akbar!"*

Fazul shouted the words, clapping his hands together above his head at each phrase. *"Allāhu akbar! Allāhu akbar! Allāhu akbar!"*

Across the room, Fazul didn't notice the eyes of Ishmael on him. He bowed slightly, a wicked smile creasing his lips. Ishmael Basra was pleased. The time was right; Fazul was ready. Sunday would be a glorious day for Islam.

CHAPTER 19

Arriving at the domestic terminal, Mark caught sight of Vince Ruzio standing with several cases of equipment in line at the Turkish Airlines counter. Mark's gaze casually swept the rest of the terminal, looking for any hint of the Jihad al Sharia. It was an impossible task. The people walking around the airport represented nearly every culture that Mark could imagine. Many of the Turkish men wore baggy pants called *sherwal,* with different-colored suit coats over long-sleeved, open shirts. Some had the Turkish-style cap on their heads; many did not. The Turkish women wore mostly Western-style clothing, although Mark noticed several women pass by wearing scarves that covered their heads. A few of them were quite fancy and brightly colorful.

"That looks like our technician," Josh said as they stopped at the end of the line. "I'll go check."

Josh worked his way toward the counter, making his introduction with Vince.

"This is incredible," Ross said, looking around the airport.

"Enjoying the journey?" Mark asked.

"So far." Ross smiled, taking another step forward as the line shifted ahead. "Did you notice the women wearing the scarves?"

"Yeah," Mark said. "Some of them are quite beautiful."

"The women or the scarves?" Ross joked. "I found an article on the Internet about it in my research."

"About the scarves?"

"Yeah, there's a big controversy about wearing them in public. The universities have banned them from the campuses. Even the Turkish driver's license and passports don't allow women to have their head covered."

"That's incredible." Mark was surprised. "I wouldn't expect that from a predominately Muslim country."

"Ninety-nine percent Muslim," Ross added. "But I read that only 25 percent are devout, praying the obligatory five times a day, and just half observe Ramadan. Still, the Turkish people have deep roots in Islam."

Mark grinned at his producer. Evidently he'd sparked some interest from their discussion. Mark inched his suitcase forward as the line moved again.

"At the founding of the republic in 1923, President Mustafa Kemal Atatürk made some sweeping changes. Islam ceased to be the state religion and the traditional Islamic headwear was banned. But there's been a resurgence in fundamentalism recently, and therefore the controversy."

"Interesting, Ross, for somebody who did not think there was much of a difference between Muslims and Christians a few days ago."

"I think this assignment has sparked a new interest."

"I guess it did. But this scarf thing is ironic. Muslims have more freedom to dress according to their religious beliefs in our country than here where they outnumber any other religion a hundred to one."

"I'll bet outside Istanbul you'll find women with *hijabs* everywhere," Chuck said, then glanced over at the man Josh was talking to. "So that's the fourth member of our team?"

Mark caught the implication. "Yeah, that's him."

"I hope he knows what he's doing." Chuck accented his statement with raised eyebrows.

"He's just rolling tape," Ross said. "Besides, you're writing this story; what do you care?"

Chuck shrugged. "Just want to make sure we're all successful here, Ross. Your tape will be the proof of my story."

Mark chuckled, enjoying the banter. "We're a team, Ross, and that man over there will be walking into that desert with us."

"Don't remind me." Ross shrugged.

Josh approached the group with Vince beside him. "Everybody, I'd like you to meet Vince Carusso."

Mark felt a small measure of relief. Using his real first name would make it easier. The group exchanged greetings before Josh continued. "We're lucky to have him. Our normal field operator came down with the flu this morning. We found Vince just in time."

"Happy to be with you." Vince smiled at the group.

"I hope you feel the same way when we reach our destination," Josh said.

"Whatever it is," Vince laughed, "I'm sure it will be an adventure."

CIA HEADQUARTERS, SITUATION ROOM
10:41 A.M.

One and a half seconds later, after bouncing off a satellite in geosynchronous orbit above the earth, the words of Vince Ruzio were amplified through the Bose speakers to the control center of Operation Dumbo Drop in the situation room at Langley.

"It's a good signal," Jack commented to Brad Faxon, the electronic surveillance specialist. "We going to have this kind of clarity through the whole mission?"

"Depends on what kind of building he goes into or how they're traveling," Faxon answered. "Hopefully we'll be tracking him every step of the way."

"Incredible," Jack said. "Just from that small cylinder implanted in his arm?"

Faxon nodded with a smile. "We're going to be using these a lot in future ops."

"Any problems getting Ruzio to replace the network's cameraman?" Dean asked.

"None." Jack smiled. "He came down sick just before leaving for the airport out of Damascus. Ruzio had it timed perfectly." Then Jack turned to Seth. "What do we know about the security breaches in L.A.?"

"The neighbors across the street from Taylor," Seth said as he looked down at his notes, "the Frosts, were found in their house this morning, dead. Stabbed and left lying in their living room. Retired couple in their seventies." Seth let the words settle over the assembled group—two more innocent casualties. "Time of death was early Wednesday afternoon. Obviously somebody was inside the house when Weston approached Taylor."

"What do we know about who did it?" Jack asked.

"Nothing," Seth admitted. "No one in the neighborhood saw him."

"I thought your agents did a sweep before entering Mark's house?" Dean questioned.

Seth nodded, answering defensively, "They did, but they blew it. I'm sorry. They were looking for somebody on the street. No one assumed they'd have already planted themselves inside one of the neighbors' houses."

"That assumption could have gotten Taylor killed," Dean argued.

"Yeah, we know," Seth said.

"It's history," Jack stated. "Let's not dwell on it. What's the latest from the FBI on this security alert?"

"It appears credible," Seth answered. "Heightened activity on E-mails and the Internet specify some kind of action this weekend,

Saturday or Sunday, but no specific targets have been mentioned."

"Any ideas?" Dean asked.

"Just speculation. Besides class one security alerts at all the airports and government offices, we've added agents to all nuclear power plants and water depositories. This one feels legitimate, but we don't know what to guard. We've considered asking governors to activate the National Guard in certain states, but we just don't know where to send them."

"We need some kind of intelligence breakthrough," Jack thought out loud. "Wendy, anything new coming in from overseas?"

"Our whole department is double-checking every piece of intelligence," Wendy answered, then shook her head. "Nothing so far."

Jack turned back to the FBI agent, frustrated. "Is it time to bust down a few doors and ask some questions?"

"Possibly," Seth answered. "It just might be."

VAN NUYS, CALIFORNIA
8:07 A.M.

Most of the men who attended the early morning meeting in the basement of the mosque had left and headed off to work, school, or their homes. The main service would be at the noon prayer time, when Muslims were obligated to pray with their fellow Muslims. In Islamic countries, stores, shops, and even some restaurants closed for the day, although it wasn't required according to the Koran. . . . "And when the prayer is ended, then disperse in the land and seek of Allah's bounty."

Fridays were their Sabbath, but not necessarily a day of rest. In America, Muslims didn't have the luxury of not having to work on Fridays, so most devout followers of Islam used their lunch hour to join the congregational prayer.

Fazul hung around in the basement after Sofian had left. It

wasn't long before Ishmael came up to him.

"Did you give some thought to my question about Sunday?" he asked quietly.

"Yeah," Fazul answered. "I'm with you."

"Good, Allah will be pleased." Ishmael nodded, placing an arm around Fazul. "There's somebody that wants to meet you. Come on."

Fazul followed Ishmael outside the meeting hall and up to the courtyard area. Several men were still talking in small groups, some in English, many in Arabic. Ishmael didn't stop but continued walking toward the back of the mosque.

"His name is Yusef; I've done some. . .projects for him. He wants to meet you," Ishmael said as Fazul spotted a lone figure leaning up against the wall separating the mosque from the back parking lot. Yusef took a final drag off a cigarette, then dropped it, stamping it out with his foot as the two approached.

"Is he in?" Yusef asked.

Ishmael nodded. "He's in." The two spoke as if Fazul weren't standing right in front of them.

Yusef looked Fazul up and down for the first time. "What do you know about explosives?"

Fazul gulped. *They must be planning something big.* He didn't want to appear stupid. "I don't know very much, but I'm a fast learner."

"I hope you are. We've only got two days. Follow me," Yusef ordered as he turned and headed toward the parking lot.

Ishmael immediately fell in step behind him, leaving Fazul with only an instant to consider what he was doing. He hesitated. His next step was the point of no return. This was his opportunity to do something for the cause of Islam, however dangerous it might be. But was he really willing to make the sacrifice. . .to follow the excitement of his newfound purpose? Or turn away, back to the meaningless path of his father?

Ishmael paused at the gate, glancing back through dark eyes.

Fazul lowered his head, averting his gaze, then stepped toward the parking lot.

NORTHRIDGE, CALIFORNIA
8:15 A.M.

After Tom and Brenda left the house, Tracy showered, got dressed, and took Shandy for her morning walk. The toast had helped settle her stomach some, and she hoped it would be enough to make it through class. She put Shandy in the backyard, making sure there was a bowl of fresh water for the day, then picked up her purse when her cell phone rang.

"Good morning," she heard Mark's voice say.

"Mark, how are you?" She forced herself to sound excited.

"I'm fine, just getting tired of traveling. Did you spend the night with the Staffords?"

"Yeah, they've been great."

"Good, I'm glad you're not alone. Shandy do okay?"

"A little nervous last night, but she's adjusting. Where are you?"

"In Istanbul. We're about to get on the flight to Diyarbakir."

"Everything going as planned so far?"

"Right on schedule." Mark wished he could speak freely. "We hooked up with Josh Mclintock, the network's chief out here. And our cameraman just joined us as well."

Tracy knew Mark was referring to the man the CIA had sent. Her lips pressed together, not sure if his presence meant protection or danger—thinking it was probably the latter.

"How do you like Turkey?"

"Istanbul was beautiful from the air. I wish I had the time to visit some of the sights."

"Don't even think about it," Tracy half-joked. "Just get back home as quick as you can."

"I will. But I didn't realize how much biblical history is here. Maybe we can visit together sometime."

"Maybe." Tracy refused to commit. "I don't feel too adventurous right now."

Mark didn't know what to say. He was frustrated trying to talk in circles around what was really happening. He could feel the strain in Tracy's voice, yet there wasn't anything he could do, or was there. . . ?

"I think the Lord showed me something after my shower last night."

For the first time, a smile broke out on Tracy's face. "I hope it was a vision of you stepping off the plane back here in L.A."

"No, but it was a vision of sorts." Mark grinned as he heard a spark of life pop back into her voice. The sea of people walking through the concourse around him seemed to blur away as he focused on communicating what happened to him without any mention of Sa'id. "I was standing in the bathroom. The mirror was all fogged up after my shower, and looking into it I see this image of myself in full marine gear standing over Satan—holding him at gunpoint."

"That's supposed to make me feel better?" Tracy asked.

"Hold on, it will. The devil," Mark paused at the name, hoping Tracy would make the correct connection, "is standing there, not intimidated at all, arrogantly threatening me. Then as I realize what's going on, the vision changes, and instead of holding my MP-5, I'm now holding a Bible, and what was so cool was the devil's reaction. Instead of arrogance and pride, he was backing away in total fear."

Tracy didn't say anything, attempting to visualize Mark's story.

"It shocked me," Mark continued, "and confirmed to me the fight is not against flesh and blood, but against the spiritual forces of this dark world. I've realized that the Word of God and the power of God is what will bring Satan down. Do you know what I mean?"

"Yeah, I think I do," Tracy said.

"God must be orchestrating this whole thing. After the shower I spent some time praying, then read our Scripture in First John and really felt a peace about it. I'm praying God will speak to you as well."

"I'm trying, honey, I really am," Tracy admitted. "I had a good talk and prayer time with Brenda last night. But I'm still scared."

"I know, I know." Mark sighed. "I'm so glad you're with Brenda. Tell her to have the home group pray for both of us."

"I will."

"Good. Look, our flight is about to leave. You going to class?"

"Yeah, I need to leave pretty quick."

"Okay, I'll give you a call later. I love you."

"Love you too."

ISTANBUL, TURKEY
6:35 P.M.

Mark looked up the aisle of the crowded Turkish airliner. He squirmed, knocking his knees against the seat in front of him. The comfort and room from the first class seats aboard American and Air France were behind him, replaced by an airbus with only coach. For the first time since landing in Turkey, the smells were beginning to get to him. Maybe it was the enclosed plane, or possibly it was the fact that this was the first time Mark had sat quietly and taken in his surroundings, but the air around him was unsettling.

Ross was nervously checking out the people up and down the aisle. Mark whispered over softly, "Got a few more terrorist possibilities, Ross?"

Ross's eyes conveyed the fact that he wasn't amused. He leaned in toward Mark. "You know, I've been thinking."

213

"Yeah, what is it?"

Ross looked across the aisle at their traveling companions, then back to Mark. "We need to talk later," he whispered. "But let's just say I'm having my doubts about your answer to the CIA."

Ross settled back in his seat, looking straight to the front of the cabin. Mark looked out the window, disturbed. Somehow Ross was suspicious. What would Mark say if he was asked point-blank if he was cooperating with the CIA? His decision had put Ross's life in as much danger as his own. Was that fair? Could Mark, in good conscience, lie to his coworker and friend for the sake of the mission? He'd have the duration of the flight to decide what to do. He was sure Ross would corner him about it as soon as the opportunity presented itself. Mark had better be ready.

He reached into his briefcase and pulled out his Bible, deciding to read through Tracy's Scripture now; he didn't know what tonight would hold. He turned to 1 John, chapter 3.

"How great is the love the Father has lavished on us, that we should be called children of God!" was the first verse he read. Before moving on to verse two, Mark paused to soak in the words. In all his studies of Islam and his discussions with Ross, even after reading through the entire Koran, Mark realized that this verse pointed out the great difference between the god of Islam and the God of the Bible. Nowhere in the Koran was there a mention of a father/child relationship between Allah and a Muslim. In Islam, God was to be feared, obeyed, submitted to, but never described as a loving father.

Mark closed his eyes, trying to imagine what life would be like as a Muslim. What did they feel when they prayed? Since Muhammad was the last prophet, he didn't think they had any expectation that Allah would speak personally to them.

How sad, praying out of obligation, not relationship, he thought. *Most of the one billion Muslims in the world don't even understand the Arabic words they are required to use when they pray.*

What a burden, serving a God that was all-powerful yet not

full of grace, compassion, or mercy—and who evidently didn't understand more than one language. It all seemed so foreign to him. The more he studied Islam, the more Mark appreciated the path laid down by Jesus, and the personal relationship he now had with the Christ.

He kept his eyes closed and prayed, with more compassion than he'd ever felt before for those trapped in the lie of Islam. He pictured Abu, praying that if he'd become this terrorist the CIA understood him to be, that Jesus would reveal Himself to Abu. Mark also found himself praying for Sa'id, that whatever evil had gripped this man would be broken, and that the love of God would penetrate his heart.

That prayer surprised him.

 Chapter 20

Yusef had driven through the valley crossing under the Freeway 101 on Coldwater Canyon before turning right on Ventura Boulevard. The traffic was heavy this time of the morning; the 101 looked like a parking lot above them as they drove underneath. Fazul sat silently in back, fidgeting with the ashtray in the seat's armrest. Yusef drove a rickety, old, white Chevy van. The seat behind Fazul had been torn out. In its place, stacked on top of the scattered trash from various fast-food restaurants, were large bags of fertilizer.

The van pulled off Ventura Boulevard and headed up into the hills that separated the San Fernando Valley from the Los Angeles basin. Yusef eventually turned down a street lined by eucalyptus trees and pulled into an alleyway between two older-looking homes.

"Start unloading the bags," Yusef ordered before he got out and headed to the house on his right.

Fazul pulled the handle of the side door and stepped outside. The house had been white at one point in its life but was now a blend of chipped graying paint and aged wood. The yard was a mess, full of weeds and a dying lawn without a sign of a slide or playhouse or any other kind of child's toy. They seemed to be alone on the hill; no voices could be heard over the sound of traffic driving by.

Yusef pulled a key out of his pocket and opened the side door to the house. Ishmael had already opened the back of the van and was lifting one of the bags of fertilizer. Fazul grabbed a bag and followed Ishmael.

The inside of the house didn't look any better than the outside. The family room, if you could call it that, was empty with the exception of a table set in the middle—no carpet, just a dirty concrete floor. The kitchen was a mess. Old dishes stacked in the sink were covered with mold, and the refrigerator's door hung half open, releasing a foul stench.

"Put the bags by the table," Yusef ordered.

"Don't worry." Ishmael smiled at Fazul as he set his down. "We won't be in here long."

Fazul nodded, setting his bag down carefully. Yusef went into the kitchen and brought out some pans and a couple of knives.

"Here." He set them down on the table and tore open one of the bags. "Put the fertilizer in the pan; then start crushing the pellets with the side of the knife like this."

Fazul watched carefully, looking at the label on the bag below him—ammonium nitrate. "What are we going to do with it?"

"You'll see." Ishmael smiled as he put a handful into the pan and started smashing.

CIA HEADQUARTERS, LANGLEY, VIRGINIA
12:15 P.M.

Wendy rubbed at her eyes, trying to clear her vision. Going through every report that had come in from the Middle East from the past several days was getting to her. She couldn't find anything to specify a target planned by the Jihad al Sharia. Leaning back in the chair, she wanted to scream at the top of her lungs. There had to be some reference in the communiqués they'd intercepted to give the FBI some kind of lead.

It couldn't happen again. Wendy didn't want to live through

one more massacre—there had to be a way to stop it.

"Anything?" Jack's voice came from her doorway.

"There's got to be a clue," she snapped.

Jack stepped into the office and sat against her desk. "You're pushing too hard, Wendy. You need to take a break."

"A break?" Wendy shook her head. "No, we've got. . ."

"Wendy," Jack interrupted. "Get yourself some lunch. Get away from all this for a minute. There may not be an answer this time. Or if there is one, you'll be too burned-out to see it."

Wendy set the stack of reports on the desk next to Jack. "Maybe you're right."

"You know I am." Jack smiled. "You're going to have to learn how to pace yourself if you ever want to get out in the field."

Wendy brightened at the comment, looking up at her boss. "I guess I learned too much from you."

"Touché. Come on, let's get something to eat. Taylor and Ruzio land in less than an hour."

The commissary at Langley wouldn't rank in the five-star category, but it got the job done. Jack decided on the special for the day, a grilled chicken breast with rice and steamed vegetables; Wendy opted for the salad bar.

The two ate in silence for a moment before Wendy spoke. "What do you think they'd try and hit this time?"

"I don't know," Jack muttered after he swallowed a bite of the chicken. "I don't think Sa'id would repeat hitting major sporting events, like hockey or basketball."

Wendy picked at her salad. "Me either. They always try something we're not expecting."

"Which would be what?"

"I think it'll be something unprotected, like some of the megamalls, movie theaters, or kids' soccer matches. . .wherever large crowds get together on weekends—maybe even churches."

"Why do you say that?" Jack asked.

"They're trying to upset every aspect of American life," Wendy explained. "They struck at the financial and military centers first. We heighten security at our airports and government buildings; then they hit the football stadiums. We put our attention there; they attack overseas at our embassies. Each new wave hits us at an area we're not expecting and makes a political point in Sa'id's twisted mind. We're expecting something at sporting events, our water reserves, nuclear plants, government buildings, airports. . .but we can't watch every church."

"Or every mall," Jack agreed.

"So that leaves it up to our intel," Wendy reasoned. "Which is why I've got to get back to work."

"Not until you finish that salad," Jack ordered. "I'll pass your thoughts along, though; it might give the FBI a new angle to consider."

Diyarbakir, Turkey
8:52 p.m.

The two days of travel were finally over as Mark stood at the top of the stairs and looked out over the Diyarbakir airport. Flying in, Mark had wished their arrival had been in daylight so he could have gotten a feel for the terrain from the air. Diyarbakir sat in a plain nestled along the banks of the Tigris River far enough upstream so that it wasn't very large but still useful for irrigation. It was famous for the wall that surrounded the old city. Made of basalt and built by the Romans around A.D. 349, the black wall gave the city a touch of foreboding. It had been kept up over the centuries and was the second largest in the world, aside from the Great Wall of China. Mark hoped he'd get a chance to see it.

Since the airport was not large enough for Jetways, Mark followed Ross down the steps before walking along the tarmac toward the terminal. It was dark and cold, and Mark tucked one hand in his lightweight jacket pocket while the other was left out in the chill as he held onto his briefcase.

"I guess it won't be long now," Ross said as they stepped inside the terminal.

"Probably not," Mark agreed, once again finding himself analyzing everyone around him.

Vince walked alongside Josh. "When are you going to tell me what the assignment is. . . ?"

"When we reach the hotel," Josh answered.

"That way I don't have my own transportation back to the airport?"

"Oh, you'll want to stay." Josh smiled. He spotted the rental car area up ahead. "You guys go ahead and get your bags. I'll check on the van and meet you there."

Mark, Ross, Chuck, and Vince continued toward the baggage claim quietly. When they arrived, they stood away from the crowd, waiting for the baggage handlers to bring out the luggage.

Mark looked over at Vince. "You got everything you need?"

He tilted his head toward the bag draped over his shoulder. "It's all here and in the camera cases."

"Good."

"You all right?" Vince asked.

"Yeah," Mark answered without conviction.

It took over half an hour for Josh to get the four-wheel-drive Nissan up to the baggage claim area before they could squeeze in the camera gear and their suitcases. Josh drove out of the airport and onto a road marked E-99 heading east into the city. Before they had driven three kilometers, the group was stopped by a military checkpoint.

"Oh, this is good," Ross said from the back, looking out through the window at the armed soldiers approaching the vehicle. Along the side of the road were two Turkish armored trucks.

Josh rolled down the window as the first soldier said something in Turkish.

"*Türkçe bilmiyorum,*" Josh replied in one of the few phrases he knew. "I don't speak Turkish. Do you speak English?"

The soldier turned and yelled something to one of the men by the armored vehicle. He made his way over to them.

"Your papers," he said in broken English.

Josh handed over his passport.

"What is reason for. . .visit in Turkey?"

Josh answered slowly, "We are a news crew with American television."

"CNN?" The soldier grinned.

Josh shook his head. "No, National News."

The soldier lost his smile quickly. He'd never heard of it. "We search. Everybody out."

Josh did as he was told. Mark wondered if it would take some money changing hands to get them back on the road. Vince pulled his equipment out of the Pathfinder and began opening cases for the soldiers.

"Do you need to offer some cash?" Mark whispered to Josh.

"In a second," Josh answered.

The one who spoke English walked back up to Josh with another soldier holding his rifle at the ready. "You need permit."

"I'm sorry," Josh answered. "I didn't know one was required." He reached to his back pocket and grabbed his wallet, pulling out a hundred-dollar bill. "Will this cover it?"

The soldier shook his head. "*Yok.*"

Josh pulled out one more and handed him the two bills.

"*Iyi.*" He smiled. "You free to go."

"Not exactly free to go," Mark said when Josh pulled back onto the road. "Why the heavy military presence?"

"The Kurds," Josh answered. "This is their capital, in a way. Used to be called Amida, and some still call it that. There's been a lot of struggle between the government and the PKK, the Kurdistan Workers' Party. You'll see a lot of the military around Diyarbakir. I'm not worried about them. When we head for Syria, it'll be the Kurds I'll be concerned about."

Mark was pleasantly surprised when the Dedeman Diyarbakir Hotel came into view fifteen minutes later. It stood out as the largest building in the area, twelve stories tall. When they entered the lobby, any thought of being outside civilization vanished. They walked along a high-gloss floor of diamond patterns of gold and white surrounded by beautiful black marble. A string of arches adorned with palm trees separated the hallway from the front desk on one side and the convention rooms on the other.

The sounds of music and laughter could be heard echoing through the lobby. Mark glanced through the open doorway into a convention room—a wedding reception was being held. There was a group in the center of the room lively dancing to the sounds of music created by a man playing a *daval*—a large drum—and another playing a *zurma*—an instrument similar to an oboe. The Americans paused for a moment, watching with fascination the centuries-old celebration before them.

Checking in at the front desk, Josh asked if there were any messages for them. There were none.

"Well, I guess we just wait," he said to Mark as he gave him his room key. "We're all on the tenth floor. Let's put our stuff in the rooms then meet back down here in, say," Josh looked at his watch, "fifteen minutes."

They rode the elevator in silence, exhausted from the trip. When Mark reached his room, Ross paused by his door. "I want to talk. I'll come back in a second."

Mark walked into his room and put his bag next to the bed. Not bad for this out-of-the-way city—very clean, with all the modern conveniences, including hair dryer and satellite television. He opened his suitcase and pulled out his toiletry bag, heading for the bathroom. There was a knock on his door.

He opened it and Ross stepped in. Mark walked over to the desk, picked up the pen, and began writing on the small pad featuring the hotel's logo.

"I want to pick up where we left off on the plane," Ross said.

Mark held up his scribbled message: *The room is probably bugged!*

"Good," Mark said. "We need to go over the list of questions we want to ask Sa'id."

Ross looked at Mark, confused for a second. Mark had to give him a meaningful look and point to the note to get him to read it.

"I'm thinking. . ." Mark continued talking, trying to cover the time it took Ross to comprehend what was going on. "The best thing that can happen is for him to confess to the bombings."

"Yeah," Ross said hesitantly as he scribbled a message back to Mark. *I still want to talk—when?*

"The other thing that would be terrific," Mark said as he read Ross's note, "is if we could get the history on Sa'id during the unknown years."

"Then we could lay out his whole story when this interview airs," Ross said, getting used to the subterfuge.

"Look, I'd like to call Tracy before we eat. After dinner, if it's not too cold, let's take a walk. We can talk more then."

"Okay," Ross reluctantly agreed. "I'll meet you downstairs."

Mark led him to the door, mouthing the words "thank you." Ross just shook his head. Mark went back inside the room and pulled out the satellite phone, punching in the numbers to Tracy's cell phone, but the call didn't go through.

He looked toward the drapes and the window beyond, noticing that there was a balcony on the other side of the glass. He walked over, unlocked the sliding glass door, and stepped outside. He tried the call once again; this time it worked, but all he got was her voice mail.

Mark left a quick message that they were in Diyarbakir and he missed her; then he decided to try their home number in case she'd returned there. After two rings, he heard the home answering machine kick in. Knowing that meant there were messages, he punched in the code to retrieve them. There were two. The first was from an insurance salesman. Mark quickly skipped ahead to the next one. It got his undivided attention.

"Mrs. Taylor, this is Veronica at Dr. Hoyt's office again." Mark recognized Tracy's gynecologist's name. "The doctor wanted me to check back with you and see when you could schedule that ultrasound with your husband. Give us a call when it's convenient."

Mark nearly dropped the satellite phone over the railing as he stood and stared off into the dark night over Diyarbakir in a daze. Why would Tracy be scheduling an ultrasound? Either there was something wrong with her, in which case he was going to kill her for not telling him, or else. . .

She was pregnant.

That had to be it! Why else would she have prepared the candle-light dinner and dressed in that wonderful black dress? He was such an idiot! She said she had some news—something important to tell him. Tracy had a fun and romantic side, but a dinner that elaborate definitely had a reason, and Mark scolded himself for being so self-absorbed about the trip he didn't stop to listen to what Tracy had to say.

He stepped off the balcony and sat on the bed, letting the phone fall from his grasp. He flopped back against the pillows and placed his arms behind his head. Tracy pregnant? Could it really be? He pictured how it could have been, coming home after work to the romantic dinner, Tracy watching him eat a few bites before reaching out and taking his hand in hers, looking up at him with a wonderful smile across her lips, then quietly telling him that they were going to have a baby. Except for the fact that Sa'id had picked him to travel halfway around the world on the same day, that's how it could have been. The happiest moment of his life robbed.

Now here he was, attempting to help the CIA take out the most dangerous man on the planet. *God, what are You doing?* The roller-coaster ride of emotions was nearly too much. The thrill of the realization that he would become a dad gave way to the fear that he might not return from Syria at all. . .and leave Tracy a single parent to raise their child alone.

But what if he were wrong? Could Tracy be facing a tumor or some kind of cancer and have kept him in the dark? Mark wanted to be with her. Suddenly the opportunity of a lifetime meant nothing to him—all he wanted was to be back home, facing whatever it was—joy or sorrow—with her.

UCLA LAW SCHOOL
11:56 A.M.

Tracy stepped out of the law building, heading toward the student center. She had an hour to kill before her next class. She pulled her cell phone out of her purse and took it out of the silent mode. Noticing that she'd missed a call, she went to the menu to see what the number was. It just said out of area, but then the phone flashed, letting her know that she had a message. She stopped walking and selected the check messages button and soon heard Mark's voice. Instantly tears welled up in her eyes. She smiled when he said he missed her, then punched the correct number to save the message. She would savor it later.

She was about to put the phone back in her purse when it rang.

"Hello," she answered quickly, hoping it was Mark again.

"Mrs. Taylor," the voice spoke. "It's Jack. I wanted to let you know that our package has arrived safely."

"I know. He left a message that they were there." Tracy kept walking. "Has contact been made?"

"No, not yet," Jack answered. "I'll be in touch."

And he was gone. Tracy pulled the phone away from her ear and looked at it as if she could somehow pull more information out of it. She was growing weary talking in codes, but at least she hadn't heard the word "pickle." She had to keep in mind that no news would be good news for the next several hours.

DIYARBAKIR, TURKEY
10:00 P.M.

Mark looked at his watch. He was supposed to be downstairs already, but he wanted to try Tracy's cell phone again. He needed to talk to her. He grabbed it off the floor, taking a step to the balcony, when there was a knock on his door. *Must be Ross again,* he thought.

"You go on down. . ." Mark stopped in midsentence when he opened the door and saw the figure standing before him. Dressed nearly the same way Mark had seen him for the first time thirteen years before, with a gray robe over a pair of baggy pants accompanied by a white turban, was Abu Zaqi Ressam.

"Mark, you are looking well." Abu bowed slightly.

Mark didn't respond at first, taken aback by the sudden appearance of his friend. Once again, conflicting emotions nearly overwhelmed him; the joy at seeing Abu was overshadowed by the fact that his appearance confirmed the CIA's suspicions.

"Abu." Mark broke through the paralysis and reached out, giving the young Arab a hug. Abu was uncomfortable at first, then accepted the embrace, patting Mark on the back warmly.

"Come in, old friend." Mark stepped back into the hotel room. "What are you doing here?"

Abu walked through the doorway and into the room. "May I sit?"

Mark closed the door behind him. "Please." He offered Abu the hardbacked chair near the desk and then took the edge of the bed for himself.

Abu glanced down at the floor briefly, then looked up into Mark's grim face as he said, "I'm the contact from the Jihad al Sharia."

Chapter 21

The FBI's Hostage and Rescue Team (HRT) had quietly surrounded the building. They preferred the stealth advantage of performing raids in the dark, but the director had decided the threat of an impending attack did not allow for the luxury of waiting. They needed information, and that was the main reason the HRT unit had been deployed. No one was better at keeping hostages or criminals alive while bringing to bear the latest and most deadly firepower available.

Dressed in his black Nomex flight suit and Kevlar vest, Special Agent John Poindexter sat in the front of a Suburban parked a block away from the target with the rest of Omega Team. Delta Team would be in position waiting to turn into the alley behind the building. A sniper team had been in place on the roof across the street for the past half hour. Poindexter radioed in on his microphone to the Tactical Operations Center (TOC) that they were at yellow, the last position of concealment, and requesting permission to move to green. TOC's voice came back over their earpieces, telling them to wait. Seconds later they gave the command.

"Omega one, Delta one, you are clear to green."

Poindexter nodded to his driver, and the van moved slowly down the street toward the target, an old warehouse off Canal Street on the east side of Manhattan, believed to be the base of operations for a cell linked to the Jihad al Sharia. In the alley, Delta Team's Suburban

228

moved slowly toward the back of the building from the other direction. The HRT mission was to take alive every captive possible while securing all computer and communication equipment.

Poindexter keyed his mike a few seconds later. "Omega Team is at green, standing by." The radio squelched and an instant later TOC's voice returned.

"Copy, Omega one, stand by."

Delta Team reported in immediately after and got the same reply. The agents in the back and by the doors of the Suburban had their hands on the handles, ready to spring out. Poindexter made sure the magazine from his MP-5 was in place, the safety still on as he waited. He placed his hand over the top of his Springfield Armory 45-caliber semiautomatic and gave it a quick pat, his ritual that always preceded a raid. Seconds later the TOC issued the command. The agents poured out of the two vans and headed toward the building.

DIYARBAKIR, TURKEY
10:04 P.M.

Although Mark had been warned about Abu's connection to the Jihad al Sharia, it still felt like a kick to his stomach to hear it directly out of his mouth.

"What do you mean, you're the contact?"

Abu smiled. "Didn't you wonder why you were notified to meet with Sa'id?"

Mark nodded.

"It's because of me. I wanted you to come."

"You're telling me that you're part of the Jihad al Sharia?"

"Yes," Abu acknowledged.

"Abu, how?" Mark stopped acting. "You and I discussed Islam for hours upon hours. What could possibly have turned you from a man of peace to a terrorist?"

"I did not say I was a terrorist," Abu corrected. "I simply said I was part of the Jihad al Sharia."

"And the difference would be. . ."

"Do not believe the lies of your government, Mark. Please accept this assignment with an open mind. All will be revealed to you."

"You deny that the Jihad al Sharia was responsible for the attacks on our embassies and the bombings of our stadiums?"

Abu held Mark's stare. "I simply state that all will be revealed to you with time."

"Abu," Mark's voice grew in intensity, "what's going on? How did you get involved with this group? And why did you bring me out here?"

"I guess I owe you that much." Abu smiled thinly. "I have always been involved, as you say. You see, Ahmad Hani Sa'id is my uncle."

"You're kidding," Mark said without thinking. Abu kept a straight face, his eyes determined. "Of course you're not kidding. I'm sorry; I'm having a hard time accepting all of this."

Abu leaned forward, putting his face inches away from Mark's. "It is this way, my dear friend. Your president is about to turn the might of the United States military against my uncle. I convinced him it was time to tell his side of the story, but he doesn't trust the American press. He believes them to be controlled by the government to spread its filthy lies."

"He's wrong."

"In either case," Abu continued, "I told him there was one journalist whom we could trust. One reporter who would listen to him and be honorable enough to make sure the truth is told." Abu welled up with pride. "I told him that man was Mark Taylor."

Mark sighed, lowering his head into his hands and muttering to himself, "That explains it."

"You have been chosen, Mark," Abu concluded with a smile.

NEW YORK CITY
3:07 P.M.

"Omega Team secure," Poindexter spoke into his mike. "Need ambulance ASAP."

He stood over two groaning Arab men, their deep red blood pooling on the concrete floor, while two of his team kept the barrels of their MP-5s aimed at three others lying facedown with their hands on the back of their heads. Omega and Delta teams had crashed through the front and back doors at exactly the same time, catching most of the men inside totally by surprise.

Poindexter had dropped one of them himself when the terrorist had pulled up a weapon in response to the raid. Rather than using a laser sight that pinpointed the target by projecting a red dot—in too many cases warning the bad guys of their presence—the HRT team had a special scope on top of their MP-5s called the "aim point" that had a florescent red dot floating inside. The unit allowed for the agent to visualize the dot on the target even though it didn't project outside the sight. It was deadly accurate. Poindexter had taken the terrorist out with a quick burst directly into his right shoulder and arm before he could get a shot off.

"Johnson," Poindexter barked. Almost instantly, Agent Johnson appeared by his side. "Take a look at the computers. Make sure they aren't booby-trapped."

Brad Johnson nodded and headed toward a bank of tables crammed with electronic equipment against the wall. Poindexter held his gun on the wounded terrorists while he took a quick glance at the table in the center of the room, which was filled with chemical bottles, wires, fuses, and timers. It was obvious that the warehouse was being used to construct bombs. The million-dollar question: to blow up what?

DIYARBAKIR, TURKEY
10:15 P.M.

"Right now, Abu, I honestly wished you had picked somebody else." Mark's brow creased.

"I am sorry you feel that way." Abu sat back in his chair. "But Allah has willed it."

"Just like Allah willed the slaughter of over twelve thousand innocent civilians in the United States?"

Silence.

"Abu, what happened to the man who saved my life, the peaceful soul who was studying Islam in Al Najaf, the college student I'd spend hours with discussing the tenets of Islam in California?"

"I am he," Abu answered coldly and turned away. "You don't understand."

"You're right, I don't understand."

Abu sighed, and a look of frustration mapped his face as he turned back to Mark. Whatever Abu was going to say was interrupted by the hotel phone. Mark crawled over to the head of the bed and picked it up.

"Hello."

"Everything okay up there?" It was Chuck. "I was getting kinda worried."

"I'm fine," Mark answered, looking over at Abu. "I've been contacted; he's here right now."

"I'll be right up."

"No," Mark said. "It's all right. Give me a few moments alone with him. Go ahead and order me something. I'll join you guys as soon as I can."

Mark hung up the phone. Abu stayed silent for a moment, then stood, pacing the length of the room to the sliding glass door. "When we first met, I was on a spiritual journey, searching the lives of the early caliphs. That's why I was at the shrine of Ali."

"I remember," Mark stated evenly.

"Later, partly because of our relationship, my search took me to your country." Abu's voice became more passionate. He walked back to the chair, sitting on the edge and facing Mark, then placing his hands in front of his face and slowly interlocking his fingers. His dark eyes became intense. "Not to just go to university like you thought, but to see how Islam and the West could be intertwined."

Abu separated his hands quickly. "They can't. With all the freedoms you Americans claim make you the leader of the world, it will be your undoing."

Mark chose not to respond.

"Your society is corrupt," Abu continued, his eyes flashing, "a wasteland of sensuality; your people are selfish. You export your evil across the world through your television shows and movies. Pornography, drunkenness, and violent crimes are your bill of rights. You use your military power to support terrorist regimes— ruthless dictators, allowing the Jews to control one of our holy cities while oppressing and terrorizing the rightful landowners."

With his head lowered, Mark looked at the stranger before him. How could he get through to the real Abu and get past the rhetoric?

"Abu," Mark spoke softly. "I will grant you that in our society there are abuses, even things that I detest. But we have choices. I don't choose to watch that stuff or get drunk; our freedom allows me to go to the church of my choice, to speak out on issues that concern me, to marry the woman I love. To start a family. . ." Mark lost his train of thought as the picture of Tracy holding a newborn child flashed across his mind.

"Morality cannot be legislated," he continued. "It's been tried and has always failed. Can you name me one Islamic country that works? That doesn't stamp out civil rights and put women back into seventh-century slavery?"

"That's the point!" Abu flared. "None of them are perfect. There shouldn't even be Islamic nations, just the united ummah of

Islam. My uncle has the power, the authority of Allah, to unify the Muslim world."

"And he thinks he can do that by destroying America?"

"Those who deny Allah. . .the infidels, have to be taken down," Abu answered coldly. "We are not the aggressor here; we are defending Islam."

"Are you talking about me?" Mark asked slowly. "Am I an infidel? Are you saying I need to be killed in order for your pure Islamic ummah to take over the world?"

Abu shook his head. "No, I choose you to be here because you are different. I wish you could understand."

"I'm trying, Abu; help me out here," Mark said.

"You are a person of the book. The holy *Qur'an* says you are to be respected."

Mark moved down the bed, closer to Abu's chair. "And tell me, Abu, how does that respect live out in Islam? Like the Iranians who imprison and kill 'people of the book'? Or the Saudis? How about Iraq? The life of a Christian isn't worth the same as a Muslim in Pakistan. I can't think of one Islamic nation that gives Christians and Jews equal rights, the freedom to practice their religion and to share their faith openly. What kind of respect will your uncle show us?"

"Whatever the *Qur'an* dictates, Mark. He is a holy man. That's why I wanted to bring you here to meet him."

"The Koran would dictate that I have my fingers cut off along with my head—Sūrah eight," Mark exclaimed. "Unless I convert, observe your prayers, and pay the obligatory alms, and then Allah is merciful. What kind of respect is that?"

Abu slid back slightly in the chair. "You have a deeper understanding of the *Qur'an* than the last time we talked, but you still do not understand Islam."

"I understand I have committed *shirk* according to your faith."

Abu sat stunned at Mark's confession.

"I have been on my own spiritual journey, Abu," Mark

continued warmly. "When I met you, and even when we were in school together, I was not living a Christian life. I believed in God but hadn't committed totally to Him. That changed several years ago, and since 9/11 I've done a lot of studying on Islam. I wish I'd known back then what I do now. I might have had the words to reach you."

"I'm on the path of truth, Mark."

"No, Abu, you're not. God loves you, more than you could ever know."

"I know Allah wants me to submit and obey."

"Not Allah—God," Mark said passionately. "They aren't the same. God desires for you to know Him personally, to have a relationship with you as intimate as a father would have with his son. To speak to you."

Abu recoiled. "You speak blasphemy."

"No, Abu, I speak the truth. That's why Jesus came to earth, to sacrifice His life in order for us to have a relationship with God. He loves you and wants you to know Him." Mark reached into his briefcase and pulled out his Bible. "This Book that you're supposed to respect says that when we accept what Jesus did, we become the children of God. Children, Abu. God is the loving, heavenly Father over us, not the vengeful, sword-wielding Allah. God loves you. He wants to let you know that."

"Allah does not speak to us." Abu was shaking his head. "He gave us his will in the *Qur'an*, spoken through the final prophet Muhammad, may peace be upon him." Then he looked intently into Mark's eyes, his expression dark, his tone condescending. "You think you are good enough to hear from God?"

"No, I know that I'm not, Abu." Mark set the Bible on the bed, then returned Abu's stare with soft eyes and a heartfelt compassion. "The question isn't, Am I good enough to hear God's voice. The question is, Is God big enough. . .is He all-powerful enough to break through my faults and my inadequacies so that I can hear His voice?"

Abu's expression softened. Mark smiled warmly and continued.

"If I'm sincerely asking for Him to speak to me, then yes! He is big enough, and He wants me to hear His voice. Abu, He desires to speak to you as well."

Abu grimaced. "You must not talk of this—my uncle, he will. . ."

"It's okay, Abu." Mark put his hand on Abu's shoulder. "I don't plan to talk like this with your uncle. We are friends and I care about you. I want you to know the truth."

Abu looked up at Mark, his brow creased. "I have spent my lifetime searching for the truth. It lies in the *Qur'an!*"

Mark sighed, wishing he could get through. His next thought was interrupted by a knock on the door. Abu glanced that direction, then back to Mark.

"Do you want me to answer it?" Mark asked.

Abu nodded, relieved by the interruption. Mark walked to the door and looked through the peephole, spotting Chuck standing in the hallway.

Mark opened the door.

"I got worried," Chuck whispered.

"Come on in." Mark led him into the room. "Abu, I'd like you to meet Chad Moreland. He's with *Newsweek* magazine. Chad, this is Abu Ressam."

Abu stood, bowing slightly, then shook Chuck's outstretched hand before he turned to Mark. "What is he doing here?"

"I was getting to that." Then it hit Mark. Chuck and Abu had met before on Operation Eagle Lift. Abu might recognize him. Mark could see Chuck out of the corner of his eye lowering his head slightly. He must have had the same thought. It had been thirteen years, and Mark had been the only one to befriend Abu after the mission. With the gunfire and action of that night, it would be hard for Abu to remember the faces of the five other marines. At least Mark hoped that would be the case. The silence was too long.

"A reporter never goes into a situation like this, interviewing

a. . ." Mark searched for another word besides *terrorist*, ". . .foreign statesman without a witness from another news organization going along to verify."

"The caliph only wants you there," Abu said.

"Then you have to convince him it's in his best interests. Without a corroborating journalist at the interview, the world will not accept that I was with Sa'id."

"I do not think he will allow it."

"He's right," Chuck said. "That's why Mark asked me to come along. Without corroboration, Sa'id would be wasting his time."

Abu looked at Chuck, then back to Mark, analyzing his options. "I will have to check on that."

"Where are we meeting him?" Mark asked.

"I can't tell you."

"What guarantee is there for our safety?"

"You have my word, Mark," Abu stated firmly. "I didn't bring you all the way out here to see you harmed."

"Maybe not," Mark returned. "But I'm assuming we're heading into Syria. . .right through the heart of the PKK. My safety may not be under your control."

"Everything is prepared. Trust me."

Mark glanced over at Chuck, looking for consensus. "I guess we have to take his word for it."

"Sounds like it."

Mark turned back to Abu. "Is there anything you can tell us?"

"I can give you one piece of information you may transmit back to your network in preparation for the interview."

Mark tensed, wondering what was coming.

"Ronald March."

Mark and Chuck exchanged confused looks before Abu continued. "Check out his transcripts from Stanford University, 1978 through 1982."

"And what will we find?" Mark asked.

237

"The beginning of the lost years of Ahmad Hani Sa'id." Abu grinned, then turned toward the door before Mark could ask any more questions. "A storm is coming; the meeting has to be tonight. Your team is to be in your vehicle at midnight. Wait in the back part of the parking lot. You'll be contacted there and told what to do."

CIA Headquarters, Langley, Virginia
3:15 p.m.

"What's going on?" Jack asked as he and Wendy stepped into the situation room.

"Taylor's been contacted by Sa'id's people, but Vince isn't with him," Faxon answered. "Just small talk at dinner right now. Vince, Mclintock, and Berman are there."

Jack took his place at the table facing the wall of screens. Wendy sat beside him. Since their connection was just audio, the massive plasmas were dark, with the exception of the main screen that displayed a beeping red dot on top of a map of eastern Turkey.

"I wish Taylor was wired," Jack said. "I'd love to hear what's going on. Where's Fleming?"

"He was at the table with them a few minutes ago," Faxon answered. "He called up to Taylor's room and found out that contact had been made. He just got antsy and headed up there."

The group sat quietly in the darkened room, listening to the innocuous conversation at the hotel restaurant. Jack picked up the phone in front of him and dialed the director's exchange. "Contact's been made," he reported.

Diyarbakir, Turkey
10:22 p.m.

Mark and Chuck made their way past the empty tables until they reached their group. The restaurant had officially closed twenty-two minutes ago, but they had allowed the Americans to order. Mark found a plate filled with rice and small pieces of chicken that had been skewered on a stick. He sat down but didn't feel especially hungry.

"Well, what do you know?" Josh asked.

Mark released his silverware from the napkin, then placed it on his lap. "We have an hour and a half to be loaded and ready to go. They'll meet us in the parking lot."

"Wow," Josh said. "They're not wasting any time."

"No, they're not."

"Any other details?" Vince asked.

"A couple. The contact was an old friend of mine, Abu Ressam."

Vince masked any knowledge of the name, but Ross looked up. "That's the guy you met during the Gulf War. He is connected?"

"Yes," Mark confirmed. "It turns out Sa'id's his uncle."

Mark could see the whites of every eye at the table staring at him. "You're telling us that the guy who saved your life over ten years ago is Sa'id's nephew?" Ross asked.

"Yes."

"Well, that explains why they demanded you do the interview," Josh commented.

"Yeah, it's hard to believe he's one of them."

"How well did you know him?" Chuck asked.

"Evidently not well enough," Mark answered. "I didn't think he had the capacity to hurt anyone before tonight. But he's changed. . .he's much harder than he used to be—angry."

"Ahh, terrorist life. . .it'll make a man out of you," scoffed Ross.

"I can't figure it out. He's definitely not the same guy who saved my life," Mark said. "Oh, and there's one more thing."

Everybody at the table seemed to lean toward him expectantly. Mark turned toward Vince, hoping his electronic bug would pick up the next comment for Langley to hear. "He gave us the alias

Sa'id lived under, at least for the start of his missing years. He attended Stanford, under the name of Ronald March, 1978."

Josh was the first to react, rising from the table. "I'll call New York, get somebody researching right away."

"I'll need to give *Newsweek* the heads up. . . ." Chuck played along with what he thought a reporter would do, rising from the table.

"Hold on that." Josh stopped and turned around. "We'll give you any information we dig up after our interview airs, but until then I don't want you contacting your magazine. This information is exclusive to National News."

"I understand," Chuck said and sat back down.

Ross stood from the table. "I think we need to contact L.A. as well. Let's take a walk, Mark."

Mark put his napkin back on the table, rising with Ross. "I wasn't really hungry anyway."

"Okay, here's the plan," Josh ordered. "We'll all meet in the lobby at quarter to twelve. Ross and Mark, you contact your people in L.A.; I'll talk to the news chief in New York. That way we'll have both coasts digging up what they can on Sa'id. Vince, make sure all your gear is ready to go. If you need a hand, Chad can help you."

Chuck nodded his agreement. "Good," Josh continued. "Then I suggest we all get our hiking boots on, and we'll see you in a little over an hour."

CIA HEADQUARTERS, LANGLEY, VIRGINIA
3:27 P.M.

Wendy was already out of her chair and moving toward the door as Jack bellowed to the CIA team, "I want to know everything there is to know about Ronald March, and I want it an hour ago."

"I'm on it!" Wendy called back as she exited the room.

Jack picked up the phone in front of him to contact the CIA director as the FBI and Homeland Security agents followed suit to contact their chiefs. Within seconds, the entire force of the American intelligence community was digging into the history of one Ronald March.

CHAPTER 22

Instead of heading upstairs to one of their rooms, Ross led Mark outside into the cold Turkish night. They walked away from the hotel and down one of the side streets. The darkness was broken every thirty feet by a pool of light under a streetlamp. Other than an occasional stray car passing by, the two were alone.

"Don't you want to get Russell the information on Sa'id?" Mark asked.

Ross shook his head. "It's time to level with me, Mark."

"What do you mean?"

"Things aren't really what they seem, are they?" Ross stopped, meeting his reporter eye-to-eye.

Mark stood next to him in the shadows; then he looked up and down the street to see if anybody was around. "What do you want to know?"

"What did you really say to the CIA?" Ross asked.

Mark didn't respond right away. He struggled, trying to weigh the lesser of two evils: lying to Ross or jeopardizing the mission.

"Come on, Mark," Ross pleaded. "My life is on the line here too. Level with me."

In spite of the cold, Mark could feel the perspiration dripping down from under his arms and along his side. He sighed, making his decision. "You're right. I owe you that, but first you have to promise me one thing."

"What?"

Mark glanced around one last time, then looked back at Ross. "You can't repeat this to anyone ever, without my permission. . . agreed?"

"Well, that depends on what you tell me. . . ."

"No, it doesn't," Mark cut in coldly. "Look, Ross, if you don't like what's going on, then you can stay back at the hotel. You'll be safe here and out of danger. I'm not so sure you shouldn't stay behind anyway the way this thing is going."

"I'm not coming this far just to stop now," Ross argued.

"Just hear me out. If you decide not to go, I want you to promise me you'll guard what I tell you with your life."

Mark paused, waiting for Ross's response. The heaviness in Mark's eyes finally brought Ross around. "Okay. I promise. Now what's going on?"

Mark heard some noise and noticed a group of teenage boys coming toward them from a block away. He didn't want to meet them out here this late at night, so he started walking back toward the hotel, Ross stepping alongside him.

"At first I didn't agree to what the CIA wanted, but after listening to their plan and talking it over with Tracy, I agreed to let one of them come along as part of the team."

Ross stopped dead in his tracks. "You what?"

"Keep walking," Mark commanded as he turned and walked along the main street in front of the hotel. "And keep your voice down."

"How could you?" Ross switched to an urgent whisper.

"How couldn't I? Think about it, Ross. What if we went in there and got our great scoop, then two weeks later Sa'id hits again and thousands more Americans die? How would you feel then?"

Ross shook his head. "I wouldn't feel. If Sa'id is planning more attacks, our being here won't change that. . . ."

"It would if we stopped him."

"You're crazy. We're journalists, not commandos." Ross kicked at a small rock in front of him, sending it flying down the sidewalk.

"It's not we," Mark added. "I'm not supposed to do anything except get the interview. It's up to them."

"So who is the secret agent?" Ross asked. "Chad or Vince?"

"Do you really want to know?"

Ross stopped walking again. "Why wouldn't I?"

"Your protection," Mark answered. "The less you know. . ."

Ross uttered a couple of choice phrases that both interrupted and offended Mark. "Get off your moral high horse and quit making decisions that could get me killed. You had no right to put me in this situation."

Mark glanced down. "I know and I'm sorry." He brought his head up. "If there were any other way. . ."

"Of course there was another way; you could have said no!"

"No, Ross," Mark answered. "I don't think I could have."

Ross shook his head, pausing a moment before speaking again. "Well, what's the plan?"

Mark's eyebrows rose but he didn't answer.

"Oh, right. I'm on a need-to-know basis," Ross snapped.

"I think it might be best if you stayed behind at the hotel."

The anger flared. "There you go making decisions for me again."

Mark's shoulders dropped as he shuddered from the cold; the wind seemed to be picking up. A group of teenage boys approached, so he waited before responding to Ross's comment. Mark tensed as they walked by until a couple of them spoke. *"İyi akşamlar."*

Mark nodded, repeating the phrase back to them. As they continued walking, Ross looked over at Mark. "What did they say?"

"I think it was good evening," Mark answered. The two continued slowly making their way toward the hotel in silence.

"Look, Ross, if I could stay behind and send the CIA off without me, I'd do it in a heartbeat." Mark paused, weighing his next words. "I called home and checked messages. It looks like Tracy is pregnant."

The shock was apparent in Ross's eyes even in the darkness. "Then what are you doing here?"

"Evidently my job," Mark answered.

"But how can you bring the CIA in on this, putting your life at risk knowing that Tracy's pregnant?"

Mark shook his head. "I didn't know until just a few minutes ago. I'm still not even sure. I think Tracy was going to tell me Wednesday night, but she decided not to when I told her about the trip."

"Wow."

"Yeah." Mark lowered his head. "If I were still in the States, I don't think I'd make the same decision."

"Then don't. Tell the CIA to get lost!"

"It's too late. The ball's in motion. Besides. . ."

"Don't tell me you still think you need to go through with this?"

"Ross, please," Mark pleaded. "I did what I thought was the right thing to do."

Ross let out a long sigh. "The right thing to do was to tell the CIA to take a flying leap."

"Yeah, well, it's a little late for that now," Mark said. "Look, Ross, I'm sorry for the deception, but I'm not sorry for the decision. I want Sa'id taken out. I hope this does it."

"Well, whether it does or not," Ross looked at him coldly, "you've certainly killed your career."

CIA HEADQUARTERS, LANGLEY, VIRGINIA
3:52 P.M.

Wendy had been working with her counterparts in the FBI looking for anything they could get their hands on concerning Ronald March. On her computer screen were two pictures, one of Sa'id at the age of eighteen taken in Saudi Arabia before he disappeared and one from the California Department of Motor Vehicles taken off a license issued in 1978. The two matched. The Saudi picture showed a serious-looking young man with a scraggly beard and his head covered by a turban. The California license showed a clean-shaven, dark-complexioned man with jet-black hair hanging down below his shoulders, accented by thick eyebrows over dark eyes. Those eyes. . . that's how Wendy knew she was looking at the same man. The old saying that the eyes were a window to a man's soul was true. No matter which picture Wendy stared at, she could see the same darkness and evil that lurked within. She sat back in her chair and sighed, amazed that Sa'id would pick such a European-sounding name.

There was no record of a Ronald March or an Ahmad Hani Sa'id entering the country from Saudi Arabia that year, so he evidently had entered the country illegally and assumed this identity. She wondered what he thought the advantage was of abandoning his name in coming to America to go to college. Thousands of Arabs had attended universities over the years in America on student visas. Why did he feel the need to change his identity? Her thoughts were interrupted by the chime on her computer that told her E-mail had been received and the shrill ring of the phone sitting atop her desk nearly in unison.

"Hamilton," she answered as she switched the computer over to her E-mail program.

"Wendy, it's Seth," FBI Agent Maxwell answered. "We've got the transcripts from Stanford. I wanted you to have them right away."

Wendy noticed that the E-mail was from Maxwell. "I'm opening it now."

She clicked on the attachment button and within seconds she was staring at the four-year records from Stanford. The first couple of years looked like the standard transcript of undergraduate requirements. His final two years were crammed with courses, double majoring in business and computer sciences.

"He was quite busy." Seth waited a beat for Wendy to view the attachment.

"Yes, he was." Wendy's trained eye picked up several classes that had nothing to do with either major. "What was a business major doing taking three upper-level courses in chemistry?"

"Preparing for life as a terrorist, I would assume." Seth had noticed the same thing.

"Do we have any leads on what happened to him after Stanford?"

"Chicago," Seth answered. "If it's the same Ronald March, some graduate courses at Northwestern. We've got a team researching that as we speak."

"Any ideas why he needed the new identity?"

"Beats me."

"I wonder," Wendy thought out loud, "if it started as a security measure, with him coming from such a rich family."

"That could be," Seth returned. "Perhaps the family didn't want to risk having some kind of kidnapper trying to get at their millions."

"But it took some doing to slip him into the country and create a new identity for him, and all this was back in the seventies."

"Yeah, I've got people talking to the INS now. If he was planning to be a terrorist back then, he was way ahead of his time."

"Makes you think, doesn't it?" Wendy asked. "Have you seen the California ID?"

"Yeah, he looks like any other American, doesn't he?"

Wendy didn't agree. "Until you look into his eyes. You can't hide that kind of evil."

DIYARBAKIR, TURKEY
11:12 P.M.

Mark and Ross separated when they reached the tenth floor. Mark stopped at his room while Ross continued down the hallway. They had decided that Ross would be the one to check in with Russell in L.A.

Opening his door, Mark was happy to see that the room was empty. The main thought on his mind was Tracy. He desperately wanted to connect with her before they left the hotel. He just hoped Ross would keep his promise not to mention the CIA in his phone call with Russell, but it wasn't something he was going to worry about. It was out of his hands.

He picked up the satellite phone and opened the sliding glass door to the balcony. The drapes flowed into the room as a gust of wind whipped around him. He punched in the numbers and stepped outside, feeling the cold wind whip around him while praying she'd answer the phone.

After four rings, Mark heard the familiar greeting of Tracy's voice mail. He sighed deeply, trying to think of what he should say.

"Tracy. . . ," he stammered. "It's me. I, ah, man, I wish you'd answered. We're here in Diyarbakir and we've been contacted. It was my friend I got to know in the Gulf War. . .then at school; you know who I'm talking about. . . ." Mark's mind was spinning, trying to edit his words as they came out. He didn't want to say anything over the sat phone that could be intercepted, and he still hadn't decided if he wanted to let on that he knew about the gynecologist. If he paused too long, the recording would stop. . .he had to keep speaking.

"Anyway, we're going tonight in a few minutes, and I'm not sure when I'll be able to check back in. Hopefully when I do this will all be over, and I'll be on my way home. I love you, Tracy. . . ." This was it—the last chance to mention the pregnancy. "I. . .I'll be home soon."

He turned the phone off and leaned over the balcony, looking out over the darkness. *Where are you, Tracy?* He subtracted the ten hours he was ahead of the West Coast, estimating that it was after one in the afternoon. She'd be in class, required to have her phone silent, and she wouldn't get out for another ninety minutes. He stared off into the distance and started praying.

NEW YORK CITY
4:27 P.M.

After looking over the stash of chemicals and wiring in the blood-stained room, Keith Chapman, assistant special agent in charge of New York's Counterterrorism Unit of the FBI, moved his attention to the papers around the computers. It was his job to put the pieces together and come up with what the Jihad al Sharia was planning to attack on Saturday or Sunday, and it could take days to break through the security systems in the computers.

"Look at this, Chap." Keith's partner handed him a long cardboard tube, the kind used by architects to hold their drawings.

Keith took the tube and pulled off the cap at one end. He tilted it and allowed the papers inside to pour out, then spread them out on the table over the tops of the computer keyboards.

"Blueprints," his partner said.

"Yeah, but of what. . . ?"

There were a dozen different blueprints from three different buildings. Keith flipped from one to the other, keeping his eyes glued to the top corner of each sheet, reading the descriptions: St. Patrick's Cathedral, Times Square Church, the Brooklyn Tabernacle. . .all large churches in the New York area, buildings that held thousands of people when services were in attendance.

"Oh, no!" Keith muttered.

DIYARBAKIR, TURKEY
11:48 P.M.

Mark had changed into a comfortable pair of black Levis, a black pullover sweater, and hiking boots before he made his way down to the lobby of the hotel. He'd tried Tracy's phone one last time, but she still hadn't answered. He carried the satellite phone in his travel bag just in case he had the opportunity to try again, but he didn't have much hope.

Josh and Chuck were standing near the front desk. Josh saw Mark and approached him. "Where's Ross?"

"I don't know," Mark answered. "I thought he'd be down here already." Mark hoped he'd taken his advice and decided not to show up. "What about Vince?"

"He's already with the car."

"Did you get through to New York?"

"Yeah," Josh answered. "They've got the entire news division looking through March's history with a fine-tooth comb."

Mark nodded. "Good. I hope Ross got through to L.A."

"I did," Ross said behind him. "Russell's excited. He's got everybody on the staff who's available working on Sa'id's background. He thinks this is going to be huge, bigger than anything National's ever done."

Mark closed his eyes briefly, wishing he shared Russell's enthusiasm. "I'll just bet he does."

"We'd better get outside," Josh warned. "I'm sure they won't want to wait for us."

"Are you ready, Ross?" Mark asked, looking intently into his producer's eyes.

Ross stared back, keeping their gazes locked for a moment before he nodded slowly and a smile creased his lips. "I'm with you all the way, partner."

"Okay." Mark returned the nod. "Let's hit it."

The four of them stepped outside the hotel, walking into a brisk and biting wind. It seemed like the temperature had dropped ten degrees since Mark and Ross had taken their walk. Sand whipped through the air, stinging their faces and hands.

"Seems like a great night for a midnight drive, doesn't it?" Mark yelled over the noise of the wind.

"Wouldn't have it any other way." Chuck laughed.

They made their way to the back corner of the parking lot where Vince was waiting with the Pathfinder. It was a tight fit the first time from the airport. Mark wondered how long they'd be in the vehicle tonight.

"I'm all set," Vince told the group as they approached. Mark felt like Vince's line was intended for him and had nothing to do with the video equipment.

"Okay, then," Josh said, speaking to the group. "I asked my contact the first night he brought this whole thing up if we could bring along an armed escort, and he flatly refused. They're calling the shots on this; we don't have any choice. These guys are serious, but they've been honorable in their dealings with me. Still, if any of you have second thoughts, now's the time to speak up. There's no turning back after we leave this hotel."

The somber message hung over the group, but from Mark's point of view it seemed to settle directly on him. Without his presence, there would be no interview, yet he had the greatest reason to take Josh's words to heart and turn back now. It wasn't about saving his own skin; it was about Tracy and how she needed him.

"Ain't no stopping this train." Chuck laughed bravely.

"I'm a journalist," Ross managed as he looked toward the darkness beyond the hotel. "And there's a story out there."

Vince chuckled at the attempted bravado. "I'm just hired to shoot. Point me in the right direction."

Mark grinned at Vince's hidden meaning. "For some reason, my presence is required. I guess I don't have a choice."

As if cued by Mark's stage manager back in Los Angeles, a black Toyota pickup came barreling through the parking lot, stopping right beside the group. Abu got out of the passenger seat and walked over to Mark.

"The other journalist will be allowed to join you," he stated flatly.

"Thank you," Mark responded. "Guys, this is Abu. I think he'll be our tour guide tonight."

The driver of the pickup had gotten out and now stood alongside Abu. They stood in contrast to the Western group, the driver dressed in military apparel, including an ammo belt slung over his shoulder and a pistol holstered at his side. He wore a simple black turban on his head. Abu, on the other hand, was dressed in baggy wool pants and a loose-fitting white shirt underneath his heavy, dark coat. On top of his head was the traditional checkered headpiece worn by many Turkish nationals.

Abu addressed the group. "One of you will ride with Mustafa. I'll drive your vehicle."

Josh inched closer to the Pathfinder. The presence of Mustafa had unnerved him. He didn't want to be the one who would have to ride with him.

"You will stay here." Mustafa stopped Josh in his tracks.

"What do you mean. . . ?" Josh started to protest but was silenced when Mustafa suddenly stuck his pistol in his face. Perhaps staying behind at the hotel would be a wise thing.

"Here's the plan," Abu ordered, pointing at Chuck. "You will ride in the pickup. Leave sat phones or any other communication devices here."

Abu waited a moment for the order to be obeyed as phones were given to Josh, then said, "Let's go!"

Ross quickly loaded into the Pathfinder. Chuck paused a moment, making eye contact with Mark, not wanting them to separate. Mark nodded quickly, a silent order to go along with the plan. Chuck sighed and made his way to the Toyota with Mustafa while Mark jumped into the Pathfinder with Ross, Vince, and Abu.

"When will you bring them back?" Josh asked Mustafa.

"Soon enough. You just stay put," Mustafa ordered.

Within seconds the two vehicles sped off into the night, leaving a shocked and very chilled cable news division chief standing out in the cold.

As expected, they weaved through Diyarbakir, heading south toward Syria. Abu kept his focus on the roads before him, leading the way with Mustafa driving closely behind them. The streets were quiet at this hour; they rarely passed another vehicle. No one spoke.

The night grew darker as they made their way through the southern section of town. The streetlights quickly faded away, and soon they were on a deserted highway leading toward Mardin and the Syrian border. A few kilometers later Abu pulled off onto a dirt road where three other vehicles waited in the blowing sand. One was an old-model Chevy van. The other two were pickups like the one Mustafa was driving—with one exception: Both had machine guns mounted in the bed of the truck, manned by serious-looking Arabs in battle fatigues.

Abu put the Pathfinder in park and looked over his shoulder at the passengers in back as another man approached Abu's door. "I want Mark to come with me. The rest of you stay here."

Mark didn't like what was shaping up, but for the life of him didn't know what he could do about it. He gave a questioning shrug to Ross and Vince behind him, then opened his door. A terrorist was there, pushing him toward the van before stepping into the Pathfinder and taking his place. Another Arab slipped in the Pathfinder's driver's position and closed the door.

When Mark got to the van, he saw that Chuck was being shoved right behind him. They were forced into the backseat and the door was closed. Abu quickly jumped into the driver's seat and put the van in drive.

They pulled out. One of the military pickups took the lead position, followed by the rented Pathfinder, Mustafa's pickup, Abu's van, and, finally, the other armed truck.

"What's the plan, Abu?" Mark asked. "Why are we being separated?"

"Don't ask questions," Abu ordered. "Just sit tight; we're right on schedule." The caravan continued south.

The map of southeastern Turkey filled the image of the large plasma in the center of the situation room wall. The little red dot blinked ominously along the road between Diyarbakir and Mardin, inching closer to the Syrian border. Except for the sounds of breathing and a cough now and then, the audio signal had been silent since the changing of the passengers.

"How much longer until the Syrian border?" Vince's voice broke the quiet in the room.

Jack and the others seemed to lean forward in their seats, waiting for the terrorist's reply. No answer came.

"Do you speak English?" Vince asked their new driver. "Why did you put Mark and Chad in the van following us?"

"Shut up!" the driver ordered with a heavy Arab accent.

Silence once again filled the CIA room. Jack rubbed his eyes, then looked at the staff assembled in the room. "What do you think it means?"

"I don't know, but I bet it's not good. Vince wants to make sure we know they've been separated but are still heading in the same direction."

"I hope they stay together," Faxon commented, "or we'll have no way of monitoring Taylor."

"Yeah, let's hope," Jack answered softly.

CHAPTER 23

Tracy sat in her car listening to Mark's message, furious with herself that she'd missed another of his calls and probably the last one he could make.

She heard Mark's final words, "I'll be home soon." Something in Mark's tone scared her. His pauses weren't natural, as if there was something more he wanted to say but couldn't. Maybe somebody had been in the room with him. That must have been it, either one of the network people or perhaps the terrorist. Tracy shuddered. The fact that Mark was in their hands unnerved her to no end.

The mention of his friend from the Gulf War had surprised her. He must have been referring to the Arab Mark had mentioned in his war stories. . .what was his name? She couldn't recall, but she did remember that he'd saved Mark's life once. Shouldn't that make her feel better?

It didn't. Her mind struggled with the fear, as if she stood at the top of an enormous cliff being mystically drawn into the great chasm, knowing it was certain death if she lost her balance, but some mysterious force was tugging at her to jump. She knew as a Christian her trust should be in God, but God seemed to be standing on the other side of the canyon, separated from her by her fear of never seeing Mark again.

She closed her eyes, trying to fight it, but she realized it was a losing battle. She prayed, feeling nothing at first, but at least she'd made the first step. She heard the sounds of students walking around her, getting into their cars or striking up conversations, but she blocked them out, focusing totally on God.

The thought came to her mind of Mark's vision after the shower in Paris, of Sa'id recoiling in fear from the Bible. She prayed that God's Word would be alive, through Mark and in her. The fear didn't immediately vanish, but the desire to give into it was gone, replaced by an emerging sense of peace, not necessarily with the full assurance that Mark would return safely, but with the knowledge that God was doing something. And that she could live with. For now.

SOUTHEASTERN TURKEY
1:17 A.M.

Mark looked at his watch, breaking up the monotony of looking at the desert highway. The wind had steadily increased, at times strong enough to make Abu have to adjust his steering to keep the van on the road. He calculated Tracy would be out of class by now.

"Abu," Mark broke the silence in the van, "any chance you could let me contact my wife?"

Abu laughed. "You never cease to amaze me, Mark Taylor."

"Then it's okay?"

"No." Abu shook his head. "No communication until you're back at the hotel."

Mark glanced at his old friend. "Please, there's something I need to talk with her about, before we get. . ."

"No!" Abu shouted. "If you want to see her again, you'd better start following orders without question. Our friendship will only keep you alive if you do what you're told."

"What about the others?" Mark turned toward him. "Why did you separate us from the rest of the group?"

"Just following orders."

"Come on, Abu," Mark pleaded. "It's just us—none of your buddies can hear us. What's going on?"

"Nothing." Abu's voice grew irritated. "Just relax. We're almost there."

The caravan passed through Mardin without event. Coming up on a small town called Kiziltepe, Mark could feel Abu beginning to tense. His face grew more determined as he studied the road, and his knuckles showed flashes of paleness as he held the steering wheel in a viselike grip.

Mark looked up ahead. They were coming to an intersection with a road marked E-90. The vehicles up front drove straight through—heading toward the Syrian border. Abu slowed abruptly and turned the wheel to the left, taking E-90 to the east. The armored truck following them made the same turn.

"Abu, what are you doing?"

"We don't need them," Abu said coldly.

"You can't separate us," Mark pleaded, looking outside the window at the other three vehicles continuing on the other road. "Ross, our cameraman, the equipment. What's going on?"

Vince noticed the headlights behind him make the turn onto the other highway.

"Hey, the other van turned left. . . ."

His statement was interrupted by the man in the passenger seat turning around and aiming a 9mm at him.

"You silent," the man ordered.

Ross fought back his panic, seeing the gun drawn and aimed at the cameraman.

"I'm supposed to be recording the interview; you can't. . ."

He fired, the sound deafening in the small four-wheel-drive Nissan. Ross screamed, but Vince was still beside him unharmed, although there was a hole in the roof above them.

"We meet them soon. Now shut up," the terrorist ordered.

He didn't have to tell Ross twice, but Vince's eyes hardened, staring at the terrorist before he turned and looked out the window as Mark's van continued pulling away.

CIA HEADQUARTERS, LANGLEY, VIRGINIA
4:18 P.M.

"What was that?" Jack asked as the speakers in the conference room spat out a loud, distorted grumble. The sound from the gunshot had overdriven the sound system. There was a tense silence in the room, everyone fearing the worst until the terrorist's voice came through ordering them to shut up.

Jack let out a relieved breath, knowing that Vince was at least alive for the moment. Then he looked up and stated the obvious to the people assembled before him. "They've separated Taylor. We have no way to track him."

"We've still got our satellite coverage," Faxon stated.

Jack grabbed the phone in front of him. "Get me somebody at Chantilly." He was referring to Chantilly, Virginia, the headquarters for the National Reconnaissance Office, the agency that runs the spy satellites.

"We might be able to get a visual on Mark's vehicle depending on cloud cover," Jack muttered.

"Vince said the van turned left. That means they're heading further east, still in Turkey," Faxon said. "The other voice said they'd meet up soon."

"Don't hold your breath," Jack said as the phone in front of him rang. "Murphy."

It was the NRO.

"Are you guys tracking Vince?" he asked.

"Yeah. . .they're just about to the border."

"Taylor's been separated. He's heading east, still in Turkey. You got any satellites overhead?"

"Yeah, we do, but there's a storm front coming through. I'm not sure how long we can keep our eyes on him."

"Do your best, and patch over the bird, will ya?"

"Right away."

A few moments later and, with a touch of Faxon's hand, the thermal image filled a monitor on their wall. The heat signature from the Chevy van and the pickup behind it could be seen as little blurbs moving across the screen, at times hidden by cloud cover, then reappearing again.

"Please don't lose them," Jack whispered.

SOUTHEASTERN TURKEY
1:19 A.M.

All the preparation, the electronic wizardry, the wonderful CIA plan. . .destroyed. All Mark had left was Chuck, riding off to who knew where.

Abu continued along at a good rate of speed, running parallel to the Syrian border. Then as he came around a blind turn he was forced to slam on the brakes before crashing into an old Jeep parked across the road, surrounded by men brandishing automatic weapons. The pickup behind them pulled up alongside, the terrorist standing ready behind the machine gun.

"What's going on?" Mark asked.

"The Kurds," Abu answered. "Just stay calm."

He rolled down his window, shouting in Kurdish to the armed men. Whatever he said got their attention. One of them came up slowly to the window with an AK-47 across his chest at the ready.

He shouted a question back to Abu, which Abu apparently answered to his satisfaction. The man waved his arm and they were allowed to continue.

"What was that all about?" Mark asked, watching the men glare at him through the window as they drove by.

"PKK," Abu answered. "Militant group. Freedom fighters really, seeking their independence from the Turks."

"Are they part of your uncle's coalition?"

"He's been known to help out with their cause from time to time. Having bases in the northern part of Syria makes it in our best interest to understand the plight of the Kurds."

They rode in silence for the next ten minutes before they took a side road off to the left and drove out into the night.

SYRIAN BORDER
1:31 A.M.

Ross and Vince were told to keep quiet as the driver in the lead truck spoke to the guards at the Syrian border. Ross looked out at the billboard dimly lit on the other side of the guard gates, proclaiming their welcome to Assad's Syria in Arabic, accompanied by a huge image of President Bashar al-Assad. After the discussion went back and forth like a tennis match, the vehicles were finally waved through.

Riding into Syria separated from Mark brought a deep sense of heaviness over Ross. For the first time since the trip began, Ross began to wonder if he were going to make it home—and to think he could have stayed in the hotel. The question burning through his mind—was Vince or the journalist supposedly from *Newsweek* from the CIA? The way things were developing, Ross had mixed emotions about whether he wanted it to be Vince or not.

Once they were past the border, the terrorist in the passenger seat threw a couple of black hoods into the backseat and ordered Ross and Vince to put them over their heads.

The vehicles headed through the border town of Darbasiyah, then turned off the main road and drove several kilometers into the desert. They finally came to a stop outside what looked like a quasi-military compound comprised of three buildings and a couple of tents. The driver of their Pathfinder backed the vehicle up against one of the buildings.

"Take the hoods off. Get out!" the guy riding shotgun ordered. Ross and Vince did as they were told and were led to the back of the four-by-four.

"Put equipment in there and open up every case," they were instructed. "We'll check it, then you can set up."

Vince nodded, surprised that the mission might still be a go. Perhaps they'd separated the group to allow the camera gear to be ready when Sa'id and Mark arrived here.

"You heard the man," Vince spoke to Ross. "Help me get this stuff in there. We've got an interview to get ready for."

SOUTHEASTERN TURKEY
1:32 A.M.

Abu drove down the dirt road of a small village as a light rain started to fall. No streetlights, no signs of electricity anywhere—just a couple of oil lamps visible in a window here and there. Some buildings were doorless—just shacks open to the elements. They passed several before Abu turned one last time and parked next to a large field tent.

They got out of the van and followed Abu into the tent where, illuminated by a single lantern, there was a bench with two white robes next to a man in military garb. Two pairs of sandals rested on the dirt in front of the bench.

"Take off your clothes," the soldier ordered.

When Mark and Chuck didn't move right away, Abu jumped

in. "You need to do what he says."

Mark started first, taking off his jacket, then the shirt below it. Before long, Mark was down to his underwear and reaching for one of the robes.

"No!" the soldier ordered, motioning to his briefs.

Mark eyed him intently, then bent down and did as he was ordered. Then they were put through the indignity of a body cavity search and stripped of their watches and rings before being allowed to don the robes and sandals. A man walked into the tent, scooped up their belongings, and walked out.

"Where's he going with those?" Mark asked.

"He's searching them for any satellite tracking or listening devices," Abu answered.

"You really think I'd have the nerve to bring in something like that?" Mark asked, relieved that the plan called for him and Chuck to be clean.

"You never know," Abu answered. "You were visited by your government, were you not?"

"Yes," Mark answered. "But journalists in my country are free—independent of the government. I'm here for the story." He thought a little self-righteous indignation was called for.

The man in the military fatigues grunted his lack of belief. "You will wait here until we're sure you brought nothing with you." Then he stepped out of the room.

Mark took a seat on the bench, trying to resist the urge to scratch where the robe's wool had started to irritate certain parts of his body. "Where is our cameraman and my producer, Abu?"

"They are safe," he answered.

"I'm tired of hearing that. Where are they?"

"They'll be detained for a while, then taken back to the hotel. Don't worry about them."

"Then how are we supposed to videotape this interview you so badly want me to do?"

Abu turned and opened the partition behind him. Stepping through to the other side, Mark was surprised to see a Sony digital camcorder on top of a tripod sitting next to a couple of stand lights. A few feet beyond the equipment sat two metal chairs facing each other.

"You see, Mark." Abu smiled. "You won't be needing your camera gear."

"Where are you going to get the electricity to run this stuff?" Chuck asked.

"There is a generator behind the tent."

"Why didn't you leave Vince and Ross back at the hotel then?" Mark questioned.

"They, like you, are being searched. If they are clean, then they will be returned."

"Does your uncle have a problem with paranoia?" Mark asked.

Abu smiled. "Let's just say he's a careful man."

Chuck opened his arms. "I'm a print journalist and I don't have my notebook."

"We'll supply you with something, Mr. Moreland," Abu promised.

"Abu." Mark turned to his old friend. "Is this life really better than the one you had in America?"

"My time in your country darkened my spirit. Here, the dirt only soils my skin. Sacrifices have to be made if the world is to progress." Abu was interrupted by one of his men on the other side of the partition. "You'll have to excuse me, old friend; I'll be back."

Abu bent down and exited through the tent flap.

"This isn't what we expected," Chuck whispered to Mark.

"I know," Mark returned. "I hope Ross and Vince are okay."

"Me too. So what's the plan now?"

Mark pointed to his ear, implying that they could be listening in. "I guess we do the interview with their lovely camera gear and then go home."

CHAPTER 24

Ross felt violated. After helping Vince unload the Pathfinder, he was put in a small room and commanded to strip down—totally. He was then put through the most humiliating moment of his life as his guard completed his search. Then another man came in and waved a metal wand around him, like the kind at an airport security checkpoint. Next he was thrown a gray wool garment and told to dress while the guards walked away with his clothes.

He slipped the robe over his head, putting his arms through the holes. It loosely draped over him, stopping just short of the dirt floor. He felt helpless. They had taken everything, including his wallet and passport.

He stepped out of the small room and saw three of the terrorists ransacking their equipment. Each of the containers was opened and whatever cables or pieces of electronics that Vince had brought along for the job were scattered about the room. One man was tearing into Vince's camera with a screwdriver. They had no intention of letting them interview Sa'id. A fourth terrorist stood next to Vince, keeping an Uzi trained on him.

"What's going on?" Ross demanded.

"Keep quiet!" Vince ordered.

The terrorist holding the Uzi shoved Ross over to a metal folding chair along the side wall and made him sit. Ross studied the pile of rubble in front of him, wondering how many thousands of dollars the camera had been worth.

They led Vince into the small room. He knew what was expected of him and began to undress. After being thoroughly searched as Ross had been, another terrorist came in with the electronic wand. Vince kept his eyes on the Arab throughout the whole process, wondering if their wand would discover the new technology from Langley. Standing naked, Vince was told to raise his arms. He complied and the wand ran down one arm, then the other. It passed over a red welt on the inside of Vince's armpit, but nothing seemed to register; at least he didn't hear a beep. The guard stopped and pointed at the welt.

"What's that?" he asked.

Vince smirked. "I have a wild girlfriend."

The guard laughed, pleased with Vince's answer. Vince played along, laughing as well.

A few moments later, Vince joined Ross on a second metal chair, wearing a duplicate gray robe.

"They treat you okay?" Ross asked.

"I would have preferred dinner and a movie first. Just stay quiet and do whatever it is they say, and we might just make it out of here."

"What about your gear?"

"It's all replaceable," Vince answered coldly.

CIA HEADQUARTERS, LANGLEY, VIRGINIA
6:35 P.M.

"Now there's no chance they'll put Vince in the same location with Sa'id," Jack said as his pencil slammed into the opposite wall from where he was seated.

The rest of the people remained silent. Every contingency they'd planned for didn't include Vince being separated from Taylor before Sa'id even showed up. Add to that the cloud cover obscuring any chance of continued satellite surveillance on Taylor, and the operation was over before it had even begun.

Jack turned to their communications expert, Faxon. "Any chance they'll find the disks in Vince's gear?"

"I don't think so, sir," Faxon answered. "The most detectable object was the cylinder in his armpit, and they missed that one."

"I hope you're right. Vince's life won't be worth a plug nickel if they find something." Jack looked over at his assistant. "I need to speak with the director. Get him on the line."

"Yes, sir," she answered. "He's monitoring the feed over at the White House."

SOUTHEASTERN TURKEY
3:15 A.M.

Mark was pacing back and forth in the tent, wondering what was taking so long. They hadn't heard a thing since Abu had been pulled away. The silence was broken by the noise of the generator firing up.

"It is time," Abu said as he entered the tent a moment later. "He'll be here shortly."

"Who do you have to run this gear?" Mark asked.

"Nobody," Abu answered. "You may set it up how you wish."

Mark sighed, then looked over at Chuck. "Give me a hand here."

Mark looked over his possibilities. He had two lights; he hoped both would work. He plugged in the first one and turned it on. It seemed blinding after their eyes had adjusted to the light from one oil lamp. He plugged in the second light and made sure it worked as well.

He decided to light Sa'id from the sides, using one lamp to key one side of Sa'id's face and the other to fill the shadows on the opposite side. Without a third fixture, he couldn't give Sa'id a backlight.

He wished they'd let him use Vince's light kit with some frost and scrims, allowing him to model the lighting better. But then he remembered whom it was they were shooting. It would probably be more fitting to place both lights on the floor of the tent and shine them directly up into his face, giving him a ghoulish image.

Next he started working with the camera. He flipped the power switch on, then opened the tape compartment to make sure there was a tape in it and it was rewound to the beginning. It had one of those flip-out panels that showed the image in color, so Mark had Chuck sit in the chair and see how it all looked. Not too bad for a reporter.

"Now what about audio?" Mark asked.

"What do you mean?" Abu returned.

"Microphones. Do you have a microphone for Sa'id?"

Abu looked around the room with a shrug. "Doesn't the camera have one?"

"Well, yeah." Mark shook his head. "But it won't pick up Sa'id's voice very well. We need to put a microphone on him."

Abu's blank stare told Mark he was barking up the wrong tree. He grabbed the camera and tripod and placed it as close to the chair Sa'id would be sitting in as possible. It wouldn't be great, but it would have to do.

"I guess we're ready," Mark finally said.

"Good. I'll go get him," Abu stated and left the tent.

Mark looked over at Chuck, who gave him a weak smile. "This should be interesting."

"Yeah, not exactly what we expected," Chuck agreed.

Mark fidgeted with the camera, snapping his fingers a couple of times in front of it and looking for some kind of audio meter. "I hope this thing picks him up okay."

"Are you really worried about the sound?"

Mark stopped what he was doing and looked at his friend. "No, I'm really worried about Ross, but there's nothing we can do for him."

At that moment, the tent flap opened and two men holding AK-47s walked in and stood on either side of the opening. Then Ahmad Hani Sa'id stepped in, covered in a white robe with a gold sash tied around the middle. His head was covered with a matching turban adorned by a gold rope band that circled it. All he needed was a scruffy beard and he could have been cast in any church's passion play. But he was clean-shaven, with what looked like short-cropped hair underneath the headpiece.

But dark, empty eyes overshadowed Sa'id's striking outward appearance. Just looking at them sent shivers down Mark's spine. Without realizing it, Mark had begun praying in his mind as he faced the terrorist. The men in the room stood silent in his presence until Abu entered behind him and made the introductions.

"Caliph," Abu used the historical term of the early Islam leaders to refer to his uncle, "I present to you Mark Taylor from the National Network in America, and Chad Moreland from *Newsweek* magazine."

Sa'id bowed ever so slightly, glancing quickly at Chuck, then looking directly at Mark, his eyes seeming to strip beyond the surface and gaze deep into his soul.

Mark bowed slightly in return, attempting to not let Sa'id's presence intimidate him. He remembered the verse he'd uttered in the hotel in Paris and mentally repeated it: *Greater is He that is in me. . . .*

Then in clear, standard English without any hint of an accent, Sa'id spoke. "It's a pleasure to meet you, Mr. Taylor. Thank you for coming so far."

Mark raised an eyebrow. "Thank you. I'm honored to be here, although it was quite a surprise to be asked."

Sa'id smiled warmly. "You have my nephew to thank for that. Something about you has touched his heart. He believes you are different from many of those in your country. I hope he is right."

Mark didn't quite know how to respond. He knew the kind,

gentle-sounding man before him wasn't real; he was an actor portraying a part. Get him offstage and out of the limelight, and the real personality would be revealed. He could see it in his eyes. Mark had to keep reminding himself of the thousands of innocent lives lost because of the orders of the man in front of him.

"Abu and I have shared some interesting moments together."

"Yes, you have." Sa'id nodded, then turned to Chuck. "And you, Mr. Moreland; it's a pleasure to have you join us in this endeavor."

"I'm honored," Chuck replied with a hint of a bow.

"Now, where do you want me?"

Mark took a step back, opening the way for Sa'id to get in front of the camera. "This chair right here. How would you like me to address you. . .Mr. Sa'id, Caliph, Imam. . . ?"

"Please call me Ahmad," Sa'id said as he stepped toward the chair, adding, "But when the camera's rolling, it might be better to use the more formal title of Caliph Sa'id."

"All right, Ahmad," Mark said. "Please, have a seat."

Sa'id did as he was instructed, adjusting the robe to flow comfortably around him.

Mark sat in the chair opposite him, trying to ignore the itching caused by the wool against his skin. Sa'id was going to be a tough interview. Having to forget about the CIA's plan, Mark faced the assignment at hand—getting the real Sa'id to appear on tape. He reached over and put the camera into record mode, then looked back at the terrorist in front of him. Mark knew it wouldn't be easy, but glancing at the two armed thugs at the door, it clearly was the only mission he had left.

CIA HEADQUARTERS, LANGLEY, VIRGINIA
8:20 P.M.

Wendy walked back into the situation room, noting the despair etched on the faces of the CIA staff seated around the table. The preliminary report she'd scrambled to compile on Ronald March suddenly seemed unimportant. She set the papers on the table and looked at Jack.

"What's going on?"

"We've lost Taylor," he answered dejectedly.

"How?" she asked, slumping into a chair. "What about Vince?"

Jack quickly updated her on the situation as the static from Vince's signal occasionally sent a pop through the room's speakers.

"What are Vince's options?" Wendy asked.

"I don't know of any," Jack answered. "He's not within the vicinity of Sa'id, so anything he does would just put him in jeopardy without any hope of completing the mission. For now, he's got to just play this out and see how it all develops."

Wendy slowly settled into the chair next to her boss, her hopes shattered. Nothing had mattered in her life since her brother's death—no, her brother's murder. Any chance of getting her life back hinged on seeing Sa'id dead—or at least that's what she thought. She and her brother had been so close.

The static coming in from Syria suddenly came to life as voices could be heard speaking excitedly in Arabic.

"What are they saying?" Jack asked Wendy.

She leaned her head toward the speakers, listening intently before she spoke. "They've found something inside the camera."

The noise rose in volume as the terrorist walked closer to Vince screaming in anger.

"He's in trouble."

NORTHERN SYRIA
3:20 A.M.

"What is this?" The accented voice began to speak in English as

270

the one called Mustafa approached Vince. He was holding up a black disk.

"I don't know." Vince's reply sounded unconcerned. "Must be part of the camera."

The backhanded slap came quickly. Vince could have deflected it, but he resisted his years of training, allowing the blow to strike, nearly knocking him off the metal chair.

"You lie! This is some kind of homing device," the terrorist spat out.

Vince settled himself back in the chair, then looked up, his lip starting to bleed. "I'm just a camera operator; I don't understand all the electronics. If there's something in there that doesn't belong, I didn't put it there."

Ross watched the events unfold before him in disbelief. The terrorist shouted something in Arabic, and suddenly there were two other men around them and Ross's arms were being tied behind his back.

Vince quickly calculated his options and decided to act before he was restrained. His foot shot up and connected with Mustafa's groin at the same instant he jerked his head back and slammed the back of it into the face of the terrorist who had leaned in behind him to tie his hands. Moving more quickly than Ross thought possible, Vince then grabbed the neck of the man whose nose he'd just smashed and flipped him over his head squarely on top of Mustafa. He followed the move with an expert knuckle punch into the terrorist's throat, sealing his windpipe as well as his fate. He snatched up Mustafa's Uzi, then turned to the last terrorist still standing.

The Arab had stopped trying to tie Ross's hands and was going for his pistol. So far, there hadn't been enough noise to alert the terrorists outside. If Vince had to fire. . .

CIA HEADQUARTERS, LANGLEY, VIRGINIA
8:25 P.M.

The men and women gathered in the situation room held their collective breaths, listening to the scuffling sounds coming from halfway around the world. How many men would Vince be up against? Would the noise alert others? The worst sound any of them could imagine hearing would be a gunshot.

"Can't we send in help?" Wendy asked.

"We've got a special ops unit standing by in Turkey, but by the time somebody gets there," Jack motioned to the map on the wall in front of him, "Vince will either be dead or have the situation under control. It's up to him."

Wendy had never been this close to a mission before—to hear it in real-time was incredible. And she felt helpless.

Then Vince's voice cut through the scuffling. "Drop it."

Wendy tensed, waiting anxiously for the next sound.

CHAPTER 25

"Caliph Sa'id," Mark addressed the terrorist from beside the camera, "I thought before we got started, there might be something that you'd like to say. Perhaps you can help the American people understand how you view the recent tragedies."

Sa'id eyed Mark and nodded slightly before turning to look directly into the lens of the camera. His countenance changed from that of a friendly, smiling host to that of a very somber and concerned man.

"I am saddened by world events. The suffering that has been forced upon the American people is a terrible, terrible thing. My heart cries with the families who have lost loved ones, especially the children who will never see their parents again. I join with all Muslims in praying for the victims of these. . .tragedies. May Allah be merciful on their souls. Perhaps comfort can be taken from the words of Sūrah thirty-nine: 'Those who are mindful of their duty to their Lord will be driven in groups to Paradise till they reach it and its gates are opened, and its keepers say to them: Peace be upon you; you are the joyous; So enter here to live forever.' "

Mark watched Sa'id's eyes carefully. They never strayed from the camera lens. Having interviewed hundreds of people over the years, he knew it was something that took a good deal of training. The natural instinct was for the eyes to dart around, a reflection of how nervous an amateur can be when speaking to an inanimate object that records every imperfection. But Sa'id spoke with passion, never letting his eyes wander, almost as if he were on the campaign trail of a national election and as comfortable speaking into a cold glass lens as he would be with his best friend.

Mark also sensed Sa'id was lying through his teeth. Everything within him cringed at Sa'id's attempt to comfort those Americans who had lost loved ones. The audacity of this man, the one who had orchestrated the suicide bombing attacks, to sit piously in front of Mark and speak words of comfort to the grieving was beyond Mark's comprehension. It was as if he were watching Adolf Hitler eulogize a Jewish victim of Auschwitz. It was sickening. Mark struggled to keep his focus on the job at hand.

Sa'id lowered his head slightly, as if drawing from emotions deep within himself. "The senseless violence disturbs me greatly, and I want the American people to know that it cannot be attributed to a follower of Allah. Islam is peace, the surrender to Allah's will."

Then Sa'id spoke in a few sentences of Arabic before translating his recitation into English. "The holy *Qur'an* says, 'For whoever kills an innocent life, it shall be like killing all humanity, and whoever saves a life, saves the entire human race,' Sūrah five, ayat thirty-two. A true believer in the ways of Allah would not have committed these acts."

Mark opened his mouth to begin his interview, thinking Sa'id was finished, but he didn't stop. His statement continued in a flawless performance of innocence. "For the leaders of the American government to spread lies to the world that this evil was perpetrated by Muslims is inconceivable to me. Jihad al Sharia is the struggle for Islamic law and peace; it is not about death and destruction. Muhammad himself, may peace be upon him, said that the most excellent jihad is that for the conquest of self. Our jihad is the struggle within. We are not terrorists. . .our purpose is to unify Islam under one ummah, not to murder innocent people. Whatever it is your president thinks we have done, he is mistaken. Or he is intentionally attempting to mislead the world. He has no proof and his crusade is an attempt to turn the West against our peaceful mission. The jihad is originating from the American military toward peaceful Muslims, on the orders of your president."

NORTHERN SYRIA
3:31 A.M.

The Arab stood with his hand on his holster, itching to grab the handgun. Vince could see the hesitation in his eyes; perhaps this one wasn't ready to meet Allah. Vince took a step toward him, and the Arab raised his hands in submission. Not wasting any time, Vince turned the Uzi around and crashed the back end of it against the terrorist's jaw, dropping him instantly. He then spun around and pointed the gun at Mustafa, who had managed to escape from under the weight of the Arab fighting in vain to suck in a life-saving breath.

Mustafa moaned loudly, holding his crotch as he lay on the floor. He looked up into the barrel of his own Uzi and groaned. "You can't get away." His dark eyes told Vince that Mustafa wouldn't hesitate to kill him if given the slightest chance.

"Maybe not," Vince said coldly. "But you won't be alive to worry about it long. You've got three seconds to tell me where Sa'id is."

Mustafa spat at Vince, missing him by inches.

Undaunted, Vince began counting, "One. . .two. . ."

"I'll see you burn in hell, infidel." Mustafa prepared himself for paradise.

Vince stepped toward him and kicked him across the chin. "I don't have time for this."

Ross surveyed the room—two unconscious terrorists and one dead without a shot fired—in less than fifteen seconds. Any doubts about who was the CIA on this mission were instantly erased.

"Let's get out of here." Vince stepped behind Ross and untied his hands. "Check the room we changed in. See if any of our stuff is still there."

Ross remained fixed to his chair.

"C'mon, move it, we don't have much time," Vince ordered.

Ross finally moved toward the small room. Vince grabbed the black disk out of Mustafa's hand, then walked over to the mess of electronic equipment left over from the terrorist's search. He found the remote-control device designed as an RF microphone pack, leaving the second disk hidden in the back of a light fixture. Once they got out of here, he'd activate the signal. Then Langley could decide if they wanted to level the terrorists' camp or not. He hoped they would.

Ross came back into the room, shaking his head. "Nothing there."

Vince nodded. That left them without passports or IDs. He walked back over to Mustafa and searched the body. He found the keys to the Toyota pickup, then added the terrorist's Glock 9mm automatic handguns and another Uzi to the one he already possessed. Just to be sure, Vince grabbed an extra magazine of ammunition as well.

"Do you know how to use one of these?" he asked Ross.

Ross shook his head.

"You'd better take the pistol then. Just release the safety here, then point and shoot."

"I can't. . .I'm a j–j–journalist," Ross stammered.

Vince grabbed him by the fabric of his robe and looked him square in the eyes. "You're nothing to these people except a pawn in their war against the West. Does the name Daniel Pearl mean anything to you? Now do what I say, and we just might live through the next few minutes."

Ross took the weapon nervously but didn't argue. Then Vince reached down and took Mustafa's turban and expertly wrapped it around his own head. He grabbed the headwear off another terrorist and wrapped it around Ross's head.

"Now follow me and don't say a word," Vince ordered.

Without questioning, Ross obeyed.

SOUTHEASTERN TURKEY
3:34 A.M.

"That is an amazing accusation, Caliph," Mark said when Sa'id finally paused. "How can you claim the jihad is emanating from my government when your network planned the attacks at our football stadiums and on our embassies?"

For the first time since he had begun speaking, Sa'id turned his gaze toward Mark, tilting his head slightly. "Answer me this, Mr. Taylor. As an experienced journalist, would you not seek out independent confirmation of what a source has told you before reporting a story?"

"Whenever possible, yes," Mark agreed.

"Yet you do not corroborate your government's propaganda that these acts were orchestrated by my followers, and we're to believe that your press is indeed independent?"

"That's a creative way of dodging the question with a question," Mark began. "But it doesn't take into account the mounds of evidence surrounding the attacks that killed thousands of Americans. Can you explain to me the arrests of dozens of Arabs that are part of Jihad al Sharia cells in Saudi Arabia, Kuwait, Egypt, and not just within my own country?"

"Fabrications," came the reply. "Lies, planted documents. Have you seen this evidence? Have you interviewed these so-called Muslim extremists that are linked to my cause? Or are they tucked away in Cuba or some secret location, kept hidden for reasons of national security while your president prepares his military campaign against the next Islamic country? There are millions of Arabs around us, Mark, who do not believe Muslims committed these acts or the hijackings of 9/11."

"That doesn't make it true. At least bin Laden had the courage to admit his accountability in the destruction of the World Trade Center."

"I am not Osama bin Laden." The first crack in Sa'id's armor appeared as he expressed an instant flash of anger. But he recovered so quickly, Mark wasn't even sure the camera had captured it. "I don't have political ambitions as he did. My desire is for the soul of the world. My plan is for a peaceful revolution to Islam."

"A peaceful revolution wouldn't require military training camps, an arsenal to rival many armies of the world, instruction in explosives. . . ."

"We are peaceful, but not foolish," Sa'id returned. "My people remember all too well the Crusades and the atrocities committed by the West centuries ago and that have now been repeated in Iraq and Afghanistan, as well as Palestine. We have to be able to defend ourselves. That is all we are doing."

NORTHERN SYRIA
3:35 A.M.

Vince cracked the back door open, peering out into the night. It had been raining steadily, and the dirt around the building had already started to puddle, which also meant no one was hanging around outside. He closed the door and looked back toward Ross, coming face-to-face with the barrel end of Ross's 9mm. Vince shook his head and gently moved the gun away from his face. Ross shrugged an apology as Vince handed him the keys to the Toyota.

"We're going to try and sneak around the back of this building and make it to the pickup. We need to put some distance between us and this camp before they find out we're gone."

Ross shook his head, his lips pursed nervously. Vince didn't wait for further confirmation that Ross would follow. He turned and opened the door, stepping into the night. The wind whipped around them as the rain came down in sheets. Their gray robes weren't dark enough to give them cover if they were seen, but with the turbans on their heads, they at least resembled the terrorists.

As Ross stepped to the side of the building, his sandals at times stuck in the mud, the cold mixture of rain and dirt oozing through his toes. He stuck as close to Vince as he could, pausing at the corner while Vince surveyed the scene before them.

The vehicles were guarded by a pair of terrorists, one standing near the back end of Mustafa's pickup, the other sitting in the Pathfinder, a faint red glow from the burning end of his cigarette giving away his location.

"Stay here," Vince whispered to Ross. "I'll take care of the one in the SUV first, but when you see the one by the pickup go down, run to it and get ready to drive. Don't wait for me; I'll jump in the back as you're heading out."

Ross took in a deep breath, then nodded. He was as ready as he would ever be.

Vince ducked down and made his way toward their Nissan by keeping his body lower than the front of the pickup. The terrorist standing out in the rain had his back to him as if he were guarding against somebody attacking the camp from the outside, not the Americans they had contained within. If Vince could take the first one out quietly, there would be a good chance he could also get the second one.

Vince could see the face of the terrorist through the side mirror of the Pathfinder as he came around the vehicle, which also meant the terrorist would see his approach.

To Ross's shock, Vince stood up and walked directly up to the side of the Nissan.

Coming up by the door, he kept his head down as if he was ducking the rain and tapped the window with his hand. The terrorist inside took a drag off the cigarette, then opened the door. In a flash, Vince yanked the door fully open and slammed his fist across the man's jaw. He was stunned but not unconscious, but one more quick hit did the trick, and the terrorist slumped over in the seat.

The other guard turned as the noise interrupted the sound of the raindrops hitting the vehicles. He yelled something in Arabic in Vince's direction.

Keeping his head hidden, Vince yelled back in perfect Arabic, walking toward the back of the pickup. When the second terrorist walked up to him, Vince lashed out with the barrel of his rifle, striking the Arab's skull and dropping him to the ground.

Ross hesitated a second until Vince caught his attention and waved him forward. Ross headed for the pickup. He had just opened the door and started to climb in when he heard yelling coming from inside the building they'd just left. His hand shook as he tried to put the key in the ignition, taking two attempts to slide it in place. He turned the key—not realizing the pickup had a manual transmission—and it lurched forward, nearly striking the building. He put his left foot on the clutch and slammed it to the floor, turning the key again. The pickup roared to life just as the door in front of him opened.

Ross had lost sight of Vince and was sure he was about to die. He slammed the gearshift into reverse and popped the clutch, jerking the pickup backward. Through the blur of the wet windshield, Ross could see two Arabs coming out of the building, their guns drawn and pointed right at him. The sound of automatic gunfire erupted, but instead of bullets crashing through the windshield, Ross was amazed to see the terrorists slammed back against the building as their blood splattered the white wall.

With eyes wide, Ross hit the brakes, surprised he remembered to push in the clutch. He'd never seen somebody hit by gunfire.

The gory scene viewed through the rain-soaked windshield was forever embedded into his mind, but he couldn't dwell on it now.

He grabbed the gearshift and shoved it into first, turning the wheel away from the encampment. Shouts in Arabic could be heard as armed men dressed in a mixture of military fatigues and robes began to exit the other buildings. Ross jumped nervously when he felt the pickup bounce as somebody jumped into the back. He looked behind him, relieved to see Vince aiming his gun behind them. Ross pushed the accelerator to the floor with his right foot while popping the clutch, and the pickup lurched forward.

Bursts of light reflected in his rearview mirror just before the back window shattered and the sound of gunfire again filled the night air. Ross swore as he ducked, a shower of broken glass spraying around him.

Vince returned fire, sending a deadly arc of bullets back and forth toward the terrorists behind them. Two of them went down, but there were plenty left. Vince ducked down in the back of the pickup, pulling his spent magazine out of the Uzi and slamming in the spare one. The headlights of the pickup that had the machine gun mounted in the back flared to life as it lurched forward in pursuit.

SOUTHEASTERN TURKEY
3:38 A.M.

"Let's talk about your Jihad al Sharia," Mark said, taking a quick glance at the colored flip-out screen from the camera, making sure it was still recording. "If it's not a terrorist organization, then what is it?"

Sa'id smiled. "Terrorism is not what we're about, Mr. Taylor. The Jihad al Sharia is committed to ushering in the golden age of Islam, when the world will be at peace. As I stated before, jihad is an internal struggle, as we submit to the will of Allah. To help you better understand, think of it resembling what Christians call dying to self."

Mark doubted that very much. Keeping his eyes glued to Sa'id's, he challenged the caliph. "Since you bring it up, the process in Christianity of dying to one's self refers to the joy of becoming like Christ Jesus, putting away our sinful nature and living our lives in an attitude of love, first to God, then to one another." Mark noticed Sa'id flinch when he mentioned Jesus. He was sure his words were blasphemous to the Muslim; still he continued.

"In fact, I can't recall ever hearing of a Christian suicide bomber, or a Buddhist suicide bomber, or even a Jewish suicide bomber—only Muslim. In Christianity there is no interpretation of dying to self that would encourage suicide bombings or declaring war on those of differing beliefs as the world has come to understand holy jihad."

"I believe the more accurate word for what you describe would be crusade," Sa'id argued with a cold stare. "You must understand in Islam there is no belief in what you Christians call original sin; there was no fall of man. We are born innocent and good, and it is through Islam that we return. But we are not here for a theological discussion. . . ."

"Why are we here then?" Mark asked, but before the answer could come, three men rushed into the room with automatic rifles, shouting excitedly in Arabic. Mark looked behind him, his surprise quickly giving way to fear as one of them stopped with his gun pointed right at Chuck and the other two pointed theirs in his face.

Mark slowly raised his hands into the air, and out of the corner of his eye he could see Chuck doing the same. Sa'id carefully rose from his chair and approached the two men, speaking in Arabic. They answered his questions with raised voices, heightened by excitement. Mark couldn't understand the words, but the emotions were clear. Something had happened, and it wasn't good.

Sa'id turned from his men, staring down at Mark with evil intent in his eyes. He lashed out, slapping Mark across the face, sending him off his chair and knocking over the camera. Abu stepped toward his friend but was held at bay by an angry look from his uncle.

"You said he could be trusted!" Sa'id yelled to Abu.

"He can be. . . ," Abu answered.

Mark managed to lean on one elbow as he wiped at the blood forming on his lip. "What's happened?"

"Your friends," Sa'id informed him through clenched teeth as his anger seethed. "Spies! They were caught with some kind of bug, probably trying to track my location so that your military can murder me."

Mark shook his head, as if he were shocked. "That's impossible. . . ." Sa'id's foot slammed into Mark's stomach, knocking the breath out of him. "You lie, infidel. You will die for this, as they have!"

Mark wasn't sure he'd heard right, struggling to suck in his next breath. Finally it came in gasps, as did the significance of Sa'id's words. *Ross and Vince, dead?*

Orders were shouted in Arabic, and Mark found himself dragged to his feet, a black hood forced over his head, and his hands bound behind his back. He was dragged to the van, punched once in the kidneys for good measure, then thrown into the backseat next to Chuck. Immediately the door closed and the vehicle sped away.

NORTHERN SYRIA
3:46 A.M.

"Take the next right!" Vince yelled through the broken glass into the cab. "When you hit the main road, turn left. That will take us toward the border."

"Whatever you say!" Ross screamed back. He had no idea where Vince was taking them, having been blinded by the black hood when they drove in. He hoped the hotshot secret agent knew what he was talking about.

Suddenly their pickup was hammered by large-caliber bullets coming from the machine gun mounted in the back of the pursuing pickup. Ross heard Vince's Uzi returning fire with a long burst. In the rearview mirror, Ross could see the pickup abruptly veer to the left, then swerve back to the right before the driver lost control altogether and the vehicle rolled. The gunman in the back was thrown into the air as the pickup flipped over twice. A second vehicle, some kind of van that had been following closely behind the pickup, couldn't stop in time and crashed into the rolling truck, bursting into flames.

"Great shot! You got 'em," Ross cried as he continued as fast as he could down the muddied road. Thirty seconds later, he came upon a paved road, turning left as instructed. He slowed down enough to make sure the pickup would negotiate the turn, taking a quick second to glance in the back. Vince was lying down, not moving. Ross pulled over to the side of the road and jumped into the back. Vince's gray robe was soaked from the rain, but two dark stains of blood were evident from his left shoulder and stomach area. Ross reached down to him, calling out his name. He tore off part of his robe and held the cloth to Vince's wounds, pressing firmly.

Vince's eyes flickered, then opened halfway as he winced in pain. "Any. . .body. . .following?"

Ross looked back the way he'd come. No headlights. "Not yet."

"Must keep moving. . . ," Vince whispered.

"I have no idea where to go," Ross explained.

"Don't head toward border. . .turn around. . .go east into desert."

"You're delirious," Ross said. "We can't survive in the desert. We need to get help."

Vince struggled, gasping in pain as he tried to sit up.

"Don't move; you'll make it worse."

He didn't listen and instead reached for the electronic box. A wicked grin spread across his face as he flipped a switch, activating the black disk back at the terrorist camp. Then he grabbed a piece of glass from the shattered windshield, rolled up the sleeve by his right arm, and began digging into his skin.

"What are you doing?" Ross asked in disbelief.

Vince grunted as he fought the pain but eventually pulled his hand away, holding a tiny bloodied cylinder. "They'll come for us. . .for you. CIA. . .can hear you. . . ."

Vince fell back onto the pickup bed, unconscious. Ross took the cylinder from his hand, inspecting it closely. Could this be a listening device? Could they find them through it? Ross didn't know, but it was probably their only chance for survival. He quickly tied some pieces of his robe around Vince's stomach, holding the fabric in place around the wounds. Feeling like that was all he could do for now, he jumped back into the front of the truck.

He whipped the pickup into a quick U-turn, heading. . .he had no idea which way he was heading. But wherever it was, he was traveling fast. He held up the messy cylinder and started talking, hoping his voice was getting through somewhere. "If this is the CIA, we're in trouble. I'm driving somewhere in Syria. Your agent's been hit, twice. I'm not even sure if he's still alive." Ross's voice started shaking, followed by the rest of his body as he fought to keep himself under control. "We need your help. Oh, please send someone."

SOUTHEASTERN TURKEY
3:48 A.M.

Staying on top of the bench seat proved to be difficult with Mark's hands tied behind his back as the van bumped along the old Turkish dirt road. The jarring ride increased the pain in Mark's body from where he'd been punched and kicked.

He tried to focus on where they were headed. With the hood covering his vision, he had to rely on his other senses to get a feel for direction. He could hear the rain pelting the top of the van and the windshield wipers slapping the moisture off the window. The two terrorists up front spoke occasionally in stunted Arabic. All he could tell by that was that Abu was not with them.

He fought to keep his hopes alive, struggling with the image of Daniel Pearl's kidnapping and subsequent murder. Being blinded and tied up made it hard for Mark not to visualize the same fate for himself and Chuck. Mark prayed, a combination of pleading for his safety and quoting Scriptures from memory, promises of God's protection and His presence. The Twenty-third Psalm poured through his mind: *"Yea, though I walk through the valley of the shadow of death, I will fear no evil: for thou art with me."*

The van drove over a large pothole, causing Mark to groan as the pain from the kidney punch flared.

"You all right, partner?" Chuck whispered to him.

"Yeah, how about you?" Mark returned, wondering what images Chuck was dealing with. Before he could answer, the guard in the front passenger seat screamed at them to shut up.

The pounding of the rain settled back over the van as they drove in silence into the night.

CHATSWORTH, CALIFORNIA
5:57 P.M.

Tracy entered the Olive Garden a few minutes early and found Brenda and Tom already seated at a table by the window. She weaved her way through the tables and waiters, smiling at the sight of her friends.

"How was your day at school?" Brenda asked.

"Hard to concentrate," Tracy said as she took the seat next to her. "My notes are probably worthless, have been for two days."

Brenda gave a reassuring smile. "Don't worry; you'll catch up."

"Did you hear from Mark?" Tom asked.

"He called right after you both left this morning. . . ."

"Everything all right?" Brenda interrupted.

"At that point, yeah." Tracy sighed, weighing how much she could tell her friends. Feeling so alone, she chose to speak out. "He had some kind of a vision last night." Tracy went on to recount Mark's story of stepping out of the shower and seeing the image of Satan in his hotel bathroom. She finished just as a waitress delivered hot garlic breadsticks to their table.

Each of them grabbed one and then ordered their meals.

"Tracy," Brenda leaned in close to her friend, "Mark isn't meeting with Ahmad Sa'id, is he?"

Tracy took a bite of the breadstick as she stalled, enjoying the soft, warm bread, always one of her favorite parts about coming to the restaurant.

Brenda could see her wrestling with the question. "Don't answer that; it wasn't fair."

Tracy smiled warmly, appreciating the gesture.

Brenda placed her hand over Tracy's, the silence all the answer she needed. "I called the prayer chain earlier. They should all be praying by now."

"Good," Tracy responded. "Mark called back this afternoon, but I missed him. He left a message that they'd been contacted and he was on his way to the meeting."

"How long ago was that?" Tom asked.

Tracy tried to figure out the time difference. "That was nearly four hours ago. . . ."

"You should be hearing from him soon," Brenda finished her sentence for her.

"You'd think. . ."

"Depending on how far they were taking him," Tom added.

"What do you mean?" Tracy asked.

Tom picked up his water glass, holding it in front of him as he spoke. "It might be awhile. You don't know how far they're taking him before the interview happens. They could be traveling most of the night, or hold him for a day before he's done." He took a quick sip of water. "I just don't want you to worry unnecessarily. It could be a while."

Tracy sucked in a deep breath and sighed heavily. "I hope not. I don't know how long I can hold out waiting for his next call."

NORTHERN SYRIA
3:59 A.M.

Ross had driven on the main road for a few kilometers when a pair of headlights appeared in his rearview mirror. He panicked. This late at night there wasn't any reason for other vehicles to be out in the rainstorm. He pushed the Toyota pickup as fast as it could go, but the headlights continued to loom larger.

"If anybody's out there," he spoke into the cylinder, his voice shaking, "I think they've found us again."

Pushing the small pickup to the limits didn't seem to be enough; the headlights kept growing larger and larger. Ross's hands gripped the steering wheel tighter in a psychological attempt to push the truck faster. His concentration was shattered by the sound of machine-gun fire behind him and the clang of bullets connecting with the metal around him. He ducked down at the waist, keeping his right foot glued to the floorboard.

Another spray of gunfire erupted, causing Ross to turn the wheel back and forth in an attempt to make his truck a more difficult target. It was dangerous, nearly causing him to flip the vehicle, but Ross didn't have a choice. The headlights were right behind him when he felt a vibration go through the truck, and a loud rumble overtook the sound of machine-gun fire. The noise was followed by a blinding light above him. The shock nearly made Ross run the pickup off the road.

The next few moments happened in a blur. The sound of another gun blast echoed in the night, this one heavier, larger-caliber, more rounds per second. Ross realized that it was a helicopter. The terrorists must have brought in air support. He was dead for sure.

Before that thought could really take hold, the truck behind him exploded in a massive fireball. Ross slowly brought himself upright behind the wheel as the night once again grew quiet around him. The peaceful sound of rain splattering against his windshield came back to his ears. He looked through the rearview mirror. The truck that had pursued him sat burning brightly in the middle of the road. No other headlights appeared. He slowed down, looking up into the rain trying to spot the attack helicopter.

Within seconds it appeared again, hovering fifty feet in front of him. Ross brought the pickup to a stop. The chopper dropped slowly. Marines jumped out the sides before the chopper could touch the road. They approached with guns ready on either side of the truck. Ross raised his hands in the air.

"Are you hurt?" the first marine to reach the truck asked.

"I don't think so," Ross responded. "There's an injured man in the back."

A second marine jumped into the pickup's bed, quickly checking over Vince. "He's still alive," he called out.

Ross's door swung open. "Get into the chopper. You're going home!"

He didn't have to be told twice. Ross headed for the helicopter on rubbery legs as the two marines grabbed Vince and quickly followed Ross. As soon as they had all jumped aboard, the chopper lifted off.

It felt like it was the first time he'd breathed since starting the pickup. Ross slumped against the back wall of the helicopter, his body shaking as he looked out at the burning tomb of the terrorists who had sought to kill him. As the pilot turned the chopper around and headed toward safety, the flames faded quickly away, but the memories would stay for a lifetime.

He had never faced death before—and hoped it would be a very long time before he would have to do so again. He glanced over, trying to get a look at Vince as a navy corpsman worked frantically to stop the bleeding. Would he live? Ross sincerely hoped so. He looked around at the young men sitting in the chopper, having risked their lives to save his. He'd never been a fan of the military— it just didn't fit in with his politics. Until now.

Ross looked over at the young marine across from him and their eyes met. He mouthed the words "thank you," then closed his eyes, fighting back the emotions, not wanting to break down and bawl like a baby.

CIA Headquarters, Langley, Virginia
9:00 p.m.

A cheer rose from around the table at the sound of the helicopter taking off, until Jack's stern face brought the people back under control. The map of the region from the center screen illuminated their faces. Vince's last action resulted in a second dot on the map, this one blinking orange with the location of the terrorist camp that had held him and Ross.

"We've still got two of our people out there, everyone. Now how are we going to locate Taylor?"

Silence. The satellite contact was gone; southeastern Turkey was covered by a storm front. Without carrying any of the fancy electronic devices that Vince had taken across the border, there was no way to track Mark. In all respects, they had lost Mark Taylor.

Jack knew why nobody spoke. He didn't expect an answer because there wasn't one. It now became a waiting game. What would the terrorists do? Would there be any clues left as to where they had taken Mark when the storm passed?

"I want every training camp, every location that we know about with any connection to Sa'id under the eyes of our satellites," Jack instructed the quiet group. "There has to be something that will tip us off where they're holding Mark."

He let his words sink in, then turned to his assistant sitting next to him. "Get me the White House." This was one report he'd give anything not to make. In seconds, she handed him the phone.

"We've lost Taylor, sir."

CHAPTER 27

TURKISH MILITARY BASE, DIYARBAKIR, TURKEY
4:25 A.M.

The helicopter came in fast, landing hard next to a waiting ambulance. Two marines ran up to the side of the craft, quickly pulling Vince out and taking him to the waiting vehicle. Ross watched the activity, hoping the man who had saved his life would survive. The grim expression on the navy corpsman told Ross that Vince's hopes were slim.

"Ross Berman?" A man stepped up to the side of the chopper.

"Yes, that's right."

"I'm Patrick Wark, State Department." The man extended his hand. Ross took it and stepped out of the helicopter.

"I'd like you to come with me, sir," Patrick said, leading Ross to a waiting military Jeep as the ambulance sped away.

"I'd like to contact my network," Ross asked.

"All in good time, but first let's get you cleaned up. I'd like to hear what happened out there."

NORTHRIDGE, CALIFORNIA
9:21 P.M.

With each passing hour, the fear and tension grew within Tracy. Adding in the ten-hour time difference, it would be after seven in the morning in Turkey. Why hadn't Mark called? Could the meeting

292

with Sa'id still be going on? What could possibly be taking all night long?

She lay on top of her friend's guest bed with Shandy curled up beside her. Tracy's open Bible lay on top of her stomach. She kept trying to read 1 John, chapter 3, to keep their schedule, but she was just staring at words. Besides, there was no way Mark had read it yet with the way his day had gone.

Tracy closed her eyes, picturing Mark's face as she rubbed behind Shandy's ear. He would be okay, she tried to convince herself. They just hadn't gotten back to the hotel yet.

Her cell phone beside the bed rang and she leaped at it, causing Shandy to jump up and growl at her sudden movement.

"Hello."

"Tracy, it's Jack Murphy," she heard on the other end.

"Oh, hello." Her voice dropped.

"Sorry, I know you were hoping to hear from someone else. He hasn't called then, I take it?"

"No, he hasn't." Tracy's concern grew. *Why would he be asking me if I've had a call; wouldn't he know that?* "What's going on, Jack?"

"I'll be honest with you, Tracy, as I promised. We've lost contact."

Time stood still. The empty hole in the pit of her stomach burned like fire. Shock, fear, anger, rage, confusion, and loneliness seemed to pass through her simultaneously.

"Tracy, are you still there?" She nearly dropped the phone when Jack spoke again.

"What do you mean, you've lost contact?" Tracy finally managed to get out.

"I can't really explain over an unsecured line. . . ."

"You'd better explain. I don't care what phone I'm on!" Tracy demanded.

"The contact was made at midnight as planned," Jack spoke slowly and softly, trying to calm her. "But at the Syrian border, they split the group. The cameraman and your husband's producer were in one vehicle that entered Syria. Mark and the other reporter were kept in Turkey. We assume they went on to meet up with. . ."

"I know. . . ," Tracy interrupted. "Just go on."

"Well, once they were separated, we had no way to keep tabs on Mark."

"What's happened with the other two?"

"You'll have to get to a secure phone for the details. All I can say is they're in our hands."

"And you don't know anything about Mark?"

"That's correct. I wanted to tell you what we do know at this point, but I don't want you to panic. We are hoping that the interview went on as scheduled and that we'll hear from him shortly."

Tracy thought about what she'd heard. "But something happened with Ross's group for them to return. . .so things haven't gone according to plan."

"No, they haven't," Jack admitted. "But I can't tell you anything more at this time."

"Get my husband out of there!" Tracy yelled.

"We are doing everything within our control to make that happen, Tracy. You have to hold on. Don't give up hope."

"I'm not giving up; I just can't believe you lost him. He should have never agreed to this; he should never. . ."

There was a knock at her door. "Tracy, are you all right?" Brenda opened the door and stuck her head in. Tracy waved her inside the room.

"If you'd like, Tracy," Jack continued, "we can have you picked up and taken to the FBI office and briefed further."

"Would it help?"

Jack thought about telling her about Vince being shot. "Probably not."

"Then just keep me posted. I want to hear the minute you know where Mark is."

"Agreed, and call me if you hear from him as well."

"Of course I will."

"And, Tracy, I'm sorry. We'll get him out. I won't leave him behind."

"You see to that," Tracy said as she punched off the call.

Tracy set the phone back on the nightstand, then looked at Brenda standing near the doorway. "Mark is missing. . . ," she whispered before bursting into tears.

"Oh, Tracy," Brenda said as she sat next to her on the bed. Tracy leaned over and held onto her friend tightly and sobbed. Shandy whined and crawled up next to her.

"It's okay; he'll come back," Brenda tried to console her, but in the back of her mind she didn't know if her words were true or not. She immediately began praying for both Tracy and Mark.

Tracy just continued to cry, facing head-on the fears she'd kept at bay since the night Mark left. No words could help. . .but at least for the moment she had someone to cling to.

CIA HEADQUARTERS, LANGLEY, VIRGINIA
12:30 A.M.

Jack placed the phone down in his office. His heart broke for Tracy. The plan had seemed perfect; Vince was one of their best. How could he have known that the terrorists would separate Vince from Mark? The president was livid; the director was in the hot seat, but no one was suffering more than Tracy. . .not knowing was the worst.

He slammed his fist down on top of the desk. Sa'id was making him crazy. He had to be stopped. He struggled to convince himself that what the CIA tried to do was the right thing. He was too emotional about this, losing his objectivity. He was too tired. He had to stay professional and get the job done. He had to get Mark back alive.

"You okay?" Wendy asked from the open doorway.

Jack looked up. "No, I just got off the phone with Mrs. Taylor."

Wendy sighed, stepping into the room. "That must have been hard."

"Extremely. I can't believe this one went bad. I really thought we had it covered."

Wendy nodded. "Me too. Any word from Turkey?"

"Last I heard Vince was still critical and Ross was in debrief. But I don't think we'll learn any more than what we heard through the satellite connection."

"Are we going to strike the compound where they held Vince?" With one word from the president, the terrorists' camp in northern Syria could be obliterated.

"No," Jack answered. "It's not worth it. It would put Taylor in more danger. Besides, we know Sa'id's not there."

"It's not over yet," Wendy cautioned. "We still have two ex-marines somewhere in Sa'id's camp."

"What are you saying?"

"I don't know," Wendy confessed. "But as I've gotten to know Mark Taylor through my research. . .well, I just don't think this game is over."

Jack looked up and eyed his young analyst standing over him with determination in her eyes. "I hope you're right, Wendy."

Jack's phone buzzed; he looked at the caller ID. "It's the director."

"I'll leave. . . ."

"No, stay," Jack offered, then picked up the phone. "Yes, sir?"

"What are we going to do with Ross Berman?" the director asked. "The president wants a recommendation."

"That's a tricky one," Jack admitted. "If the marines keep him confined too long, we run the risk of a scandal. If we set him free and he talks about the CIA connection, we definitely have a scandal and put Mark's life in further danger."

"That's what I've been mulling over," the director said. "I want you to go see him, see if he'll play ball for awhile, at least until Taylor is free."

"Are you sure you want me to go, sir? We're right in the middle of this whole thing."

"You met with Taylor; you know how he struggled with what we asked him to do. Maybe you'll be able to reach Berman. We need his help to keep a lid on this."

Jack nodded. "There's one more thing we haven't covered."

"What's that?"

"The ex-marine that we sent in with Taylor. If Sa'id turns this into a kidnapping, how will he react when he finds out he doesn't have Chad Moreland from *Newsweek*?"

"Let me think about that one." The director paused for a second, probably scribbling some note on the legal pad he always kept by the phone. "In the meantime, there's an air force jet waiting for you at Andrews."

Jack hung up the phone slowly, looking up at Wendy. "I guess I'm flying to Turkey."

"I figured." Wendy smiled. "Maybe it's for the best to have you on-site."

Jack stood up, gathering paperwork into his briefcase. "Get the team together. I've got some details I want covered before I leave."

TURKISH MILITARY BASE, DIYARBAKIR, TURKEY
7:32 A.M.

"Look, I've told you all I can remember; now get me to a phone," Ross pleaded. "I need to talk with my executive producer."

CIA officer Patrick Wark looked across the table at the young producer now dressed in borrowed marine fatigues. Ross had been allowed to shower and change before the briefing that had begun several hours ago. "I'll have to get clearance for that."

"What do you mean, clearance? What am I, a prisoner?"

"No," Patrick assured Ross. "You're our guest."

Ross's forehead creased. "I want to talk with L.A."

"And you will, soon. Look, Ross, this is a delicate situation. As long as Mr. Taylor is unaccounted for, we have to be careful. One miscue on our end could put his life in greater danger."

"Oh, you mean like sending in the CIA in place of a cameraman?" Ross replied sarcastically.

Patrick's face darkened, but he didn't answer.

"By the way," Ross's voice softened, "is Vince going to make it?"

"The next few hours will be critical. We just don't know."

Ross shook his head. "I'm not sure whether I should be grateful the guy saved my life or furious that he put it in jeopardy in the first place."

"You ought to be very thankful he was there," Patrick answered coldly. "If you only knew what Vince has accomplished undercover these past few years. . .well, let's just say you should have been honored to be alongside him."

Ross thought for a second, not sure how to respond. "What did you think you guys were going to accomplish?"

Patrick once again didn't respond but got up and walked toward the door. "You have to be patient, Ross. We'll let you call your producer when the time is right." He motioned toward the cot with a pillow and blanket on top of it in the corner. "For now, why don't you try and get some rest?"

Van Nuys, California
11:42 p.m.

Fazul sat on the passenger side of the flatbed truck, slumped down in the seat in hopes that anybody who passed by wouldn't see him. He glanced nervously at Ishmael, who sat behind the steering wheel calmly smoking a cigarette.

"Why can't we just go to a gas station?" Fazul asked in a whisper.

"Because we need the barrels."

"How much longer are we going to wait?"

"Just a few more minutes," Ishmael answered. "Yusef said there would be a security check just before midnight. We'll wait for that."

"What is he planning on doing?"

"That's not for you to know yet, my young friend." Ishmael smiled. "You just be ready to go Sunday morning."

They were parked on Dulheny Street in the industrial section of Van Nuys, just down the street from a farming supply house. After spending hours crushing the fertilizer at that run-down house in the hills, Yusef had given the pair an additional assignment. He needed barrels of diesel fuel.

Fazul sat quietly, struggling with what he was about to do. He'd never broken the law. The excitement he'd felt at the mosque, the sense of commitment to the cause of Allah, was now being tested. Would he be able to go through with it?

Looking over at Ishmael, Fazul felt the weight of his actions settle over him. He didn't want to get caught trying to steal diesel fuel and embarrass his family. He had to complete whatever task Yusef had set up for them so that Fazul's family would be honored, and they would know that he had accomplished something great for Allah. Looking back to the front of the farm supply store as a security patrol car slowly drove by, he wondered just what that was going to be.

NORTHRIDGE, CALIFORNIA
MIDNIGHT

Tracy lay wide awake, watching the green digital alarm clock numbers change over to the new day. Sleep wouldn't come. She wondered when it would again. Her mind raced with thoughts of what could be happening to Mark. Was he all right? Being tortured?

Already dead? She couldn't accept that. He had to still be alive. She would know if he were dead, wouldn't she?

She did know that he was in trouble. Her spirit was restless, urging her to pray for him. She pleaded for God to intervene on her husband's behalf, rescue him from the evil one, and bring him back to her safely. And soon. She struggled for the right words, wanting to pray with faith and strength, battling the fear that simmered inside.

After the phone call from the CIA, Brenda had stayed with Tracy for quite awhile, providing both comfort and a prayer partner, although for Tracy the prayers were laborious, the words difficult to express.

It wasn't her faith in God that was shaken. At least she hoped it wasn't. She wasn't sure how she would react if she were told that Mark was dead—that thought would have to wait. At this point, it was her mistaken belief that bad things didn't happen to good people that was shaken. How could God allow Mark to be caught up in the middle of this, his life now hanging in the balance? But wasn't that the question asked by thousands of families who lost loved ones during the Sunday Massacre and 9/11?

The nation had covered this topic from every angle, but nothing philosophical or intellectual seemed to make a bit of difference in the pain stabbing at her heart.

Her eyes spotted the Bible tossed to the side of the bed, still opened to 1 John, chapter 3. She pulled it close to her and looked at the first verse: "How great is the love the Father has lavished on us, that we should be called children of God! And that is what we are! The reason the world does not know us is that it did not know him."

Tracy sighed, closing her eyes and letting the words sink in. What she needed now more than ever was to crawl up into the lap of her heavenly Father. She didn't even know what that would feel like in the earthly sense, much less with the Creator of the universe, but she knew that's what she needed. Her eyes stayed shut as she prayed. The dam that seemed to hold back the words earlier when Brenda was with her broke free as Tracy poured her heart out to God. Letting first her anger pour forth, followed quickly by her fear, Tracy pleaded for God's hand to be on Mark's life, her life, and especially on the baby's.

There wasn't just a release of the words bottled up within her but of the emotions as well. Tracy cried until there were no tears left to fall. Yet within that spent moment, in the lingering just before sleep mercifully swept her away, she felt a presence envelop her as invisible arms seemed to cradle her in a gentle, loving hug.

CHAPTER 28

At first there was nothing, a void to be embraced.

Then flashes of green light darted across Mark Taylor's vision, appearing like fireflies dancing in the blackness of a moonless Tennessee night. Next came the pain. . .terrifying waves of agony. He fought desperately to keep hold of the darkness.

Through the mental fog his first thought took shape. . .not about himself, where he was, or how many bones might be broken, but a hazy impression of his wife, Tracy. The image lured him toward consciousness. His eyes blinked open, the light immediately piercing through his head. He winced and shut them in a vain attempt to block out the pain.

After a moment he tried again, slowly this time. Before he could orient himself, he heard footsteps. Holding the image of the stark room and dirt floor around him in his mind, Mark gently closed his eyes and lay still.

There were voices now, but he couldn't make out the words. Arabic? It sounded like it. The noises combined with the pain began to clear his head.

He remembered where he was—somewhere in the Middle East—Turkey, possibly Syria. And as the thought took shape, so did the realization that he was in desperate trouble.

Lying on his side, Mark was curled up in a fetal position on the hard surface. There was no way to tell how long he'd been unconscious. As the voices approached, he remained motionless, taking in short, shallow breaths.

Suddenly a shower of foul-smelling liquid drenched him. His attempt to feign unconsciousness shattered as he gagged and coughed. The pain throughout his body was nearly unbearable.

"I trust you've had a pleasant nap," a voice spoke above him in near-perfect English.

Spitting away the putrid water and wiping at his eyes, Mark looked up. Surrounded by three men brandishing AK-47s stood Ahmad Hani Sa'id, the infamous leader of the Jihad al Sharia terrorist network.

"Now, Mr. Taylor," Sa'id continued calmly, "I think it's time you and I had another little chat."

CIA HEADQUARTERS, LANGLEY, VIRGINIA
9:16 A.M.

Jack's team gathered in the situation room in the Old Building of CIA headquarters. Jack had flown overnight to an American base in England and had taken a moment to check in with his staff before taking the next military transport on to Turkey.

"So what do we know?" Jack's voice boomed through the speakers around the room.

"Nothing new out of Syria or Turkey," Wendy began.

"Clouds still covering the area?"

"Negative, sir," Ryan Drake responded. "The storm front passed through around noon, Syrian time. But the NRO has not been able to spot the vehicle they were riding in."

"So we don't know if Mark's in Turkey or if they took him into Syria."

"Correct," Wendy confirmed. "We've got five possible locations where they could have taken Taylor, all of them in Syria. We can't imagine they'd have the support to hold Mark in Turkey. We're watching all of them like a hawk, but nothing suspicious yet."

"Don't leave out the Kurds. The terrorists were willing to drive Taylor's team right through their territory."

"Understood," Drake answered.

"Options?" Jack's voice asked through the speakers.

"We're monitoring all communications in both areas," Wendy reported. "Plus we've got electronic surveillance covering every move Josh Mclintock makes at the hotel in Diyarbakir. If he's contacted again, we'll know it."

Across the Atlantic, Jack's face turned grim. "So all we can do is wait?"

"When daylight hits," Wendy continued, "we might be able to get a horizon shot at it—try face recognition at the terrorists' camps." She referred to the technique of utilizing a satellite closer to the horizon instead of one directly overhead, effectively giving them a picture that would appear closer to ground level. With the amazing clarity of the images obtained by the NRO, they could actually recognize faces. But that would have to wait until after sunrise.

"Sir." The voice of Kristen, Jack's assistant, cut into the speakerphone. "There's a call coming in I think you should take—Seth Maxwell from the FBI's Counterterrorism Division."

"Go ahead and patch him in. Are you there, Seth?"

"Hi, Jack."

"We've got you on a speaker at Langley; what've you got?"

"We've got an intelligence situation we think you all need to be aware of. We busted in on a New York cell of the Jihad al Sharia. It looks like they were planning to bomb a church or two in Manhattan."

Wendy wished she could see Jack's face respond to the news.

"What did you find?"

"Explosives, detonators, and blueprints for several prominent churches in the area. We don't know which one the target was. . .

maybe all of them. But it looks like this is tied to the alert we received about this weekend."

"Do you think it's contained to just New York?"

"We don't know. We're trying to break through the security codes in their computer equipment. Maybe that will tell us."

"Okay, Seth, thanks," Jack responded. "Please keep us informed if you find anything else."

The FBI agent disconnected.

"It can't be the only attack," Wendy stated sharply. "Sa'id doesn't plan things one at a time. I would guess that we're dealing with multiple plans to bomb churches across the nation."

Jack's voice cut through the heaviness in the room. "I think you're right, but how will we know where?"

"We won't if the FBI can't break their codes," Wendy concluded.

"Then we need to find the information some other way," Jack ordered. "I want to double our efforts. I want to know what cities are targeted by the time I land in Turkey. And we've got to somehow locate Taylor. Let's move it, people; we're running out of time."

NORTHERN SYRIAN DESERT
4:16 P.M.

"How long. . . ?" Mark tried to speak, but his mouth was too dry. He realized his clothes were gone, and instead he was wearing a robelike garment with nothing on underneath, the top part of it soaked in the foul-smelling water. He vaguely recalled the night before, the separation of Ross and Vince from his group, the body search along with the change of clothes, then the hasty interruption to the interview and their subsequent drive through the desert with a hood over his head. Through the fog, he wondered where Chuck was. . . .

"That's not important," Sa'id said as he knelt next to him. "What is important is why you brought a spy into my camp!"

The words sank in slowly, but evidently Mark didn't respond quickly enough as a boot from one of the men with Sa'id came crashing into his ribs. Instantly Mark's breath was gone. He struggled to suck in some air; his eyes watered as pain racked his entire body. Thinking back on the night before, he couldn't remember much of anything once their drive through the desert ended. All that came back to him were flashes of pain when the terrorists had beaten him until he was unconscious. The next thing he remembered was waking up on the floor where he was now.

When he was finally able to take a breath, Mark looked up at Sa'id and grimaced through the pain. "I don't know what you're talking about."

Sa'id flashed Mark a smile similar to the one that had been so charismatic on camera, but the eyes remained dark, foreboding. "Now, now, Mark. There's no sense in lying to me. When we found one of your miniature GPS bugs in the camera equipment, your CIA agent attempted to escape."

Mark remembered hearing something about that when the terrorists had stormed in, interrupting the interview.

"What do you mean, CIA?" Mark dropped his head and coughed, the pain stabbing at his chest. He placed his hand there, wondering if they might have broken a rib or two. "Josh hired him. I had nothing to do with it."

"Like you didn't have a meeting with your government the night you left?"

"I told your man in Paris, they came to my door; I turned them down."

Sa'id leaned in closer to Mark's face. "You lie."

Mark looked up, meeting the man's stare, thinking, *Yes, but I'll never admit it.* "If you thought I'd agreed to help the CIA, then why did you go ahead with the interview?" Waiting for his answer, Mark looked over Sa'id's shoulder. In the background stood Abu, anxiously watching the confrontation, concern etched on his face.

"My nephew said I could trust you. Evidently he was wrong."

"I thought I could trust you," Mark returned defiantly. "Evidently I was wrong."

Sa'id's hand moved quickly, slapping Mark's face as he had done the night before. "You will speak with respect!"

Mark kept his head down, waiting for the bright flashes to subside. "What have you done with Ross?"

"He's dead, as is the spy," Sa'id answered proudly.

Mark closed his eyes, rage burning within him. Was it true? Could he have gotten Ross killed? Then a thought pricked at the back of his mind: *Don't believe anything you're told in a captive situation.* In his training with special ops over a decade ago, that had been drilled into him by every instructor. *Never believe the enemy when you're a prisoner of war.* This certainly qualified. The smallest speck of hope kept Mark from being overwhelmed by the news.

"Why Ross? He was simply a journalist."

"So you admit the other was not?"

Sa'id was quick. Mark realized he needed to think carefully about every word he spoke. "I told you I had nothing to do with bringing him along. Josh Mclintock hired him from the Damascus office. I'm just concerned for my friend."

"Touching," Sa'id returned. "But your concern had better be for his soul; may Allah have mercy."

"Uncle, please." Abu stepped toward Mark. "He's telling the truth. I'm sure Mark would not have brought in the CIA."

"Your history with him clouds your judgment, Abu. He's an American, an infidel. He can't be trusted."

It was painful, but Mark sat up, leaning his back against the rough wall behind him. He still couldn't tell where he was or even what kind of building he was in. There was no window to tell him if it was night or day, just the illumination of a bright light at the center of the room. The dirt floor told him he was somewhere far away from civilization.

"What are you planning to do with me?"

"I have not decided," Sa'id informed him.

"My government doesn't negotiate with terrorists."

"It does not matter; you are not my hostage. You are my prisoner. You will be tried under *Islamic Sharia* for attempting to murder me."

"Caliph," Mark said respectfully, thinking it couldn't hurt, "I came to do an interview at your request."

When Sa'id didn't respond, Mark continued. "What happened to the man of peace I first met, filled with compassion for the American families of the tragedies? What did you say in the interview? Whoever kills an innocent life has killed all humanity? Or was that just an act and this is the real face of Islam I'm seeing now?"

Sa'id paused, and a wicked smile crossed his face as he nodded. "Very good, Mark Taylor. But what you don't understand is that they are both Islam. What I said was true; the *Qur'an* does teach that to take an innocent life is like killing all humanity. The important word there is *innocent*. The killing of American infidels hardly applies. You are not innocent!"

"Under your teachings, you have to be at war to allow for the killing. . . ."

"We are at war!" Sa'id shouted. "As long as America is propping up evil regimes in the Middle East, as long as your economic sanctions take away food and medicine from starving Muslim children, as long as the world is perverted by the pornography and filth of your culture, as long as your country allows the children of pigs to survive and inhabit Palestine and your soldiers invade our holy land, then we are at war!"

"And that justifies your terrorism?"

"It is not terrorism when one is defending Allah or fighting for what was stolen from him. Americans are the terrorists!"

"What do you call it when school buses are used as bombs to

kill thousands of innocent people?"

Sa'id smirked. "I call it justice, the hand of Allah!"

"Then your religion is meaningless." Mark braced himself for the next attack. It came with a fury, but at least unconsciousness wasn't far away.

NORTHRIDGE, CALIFORNIA
6:45 A.M.

Shandy jumped up onto the bed, pawing at the blankets covering Tracy. She opened one eye, which was all the encouragement Shandy needed to nuzzle in and give her a quick lick on her nose.

"Oh, you." Tracy reached out and pulled the dog in close to her, hoping she'd lie down and stay still a bit longer. "I'm not ready to face the world yet."

The two lay there for a few moments in silence, but Tracy's mind was off and running. Images flashed through her of Mark being held hostage—confined in some inhuman way, treated to unspeakable acts. She had to get control of her thoughts. This wasn't the way to start the day. She had to stay positive.

She suddenly felt hot. Pushing the covers away, she felt the first wave of nausea roll over her.

"Move over, girl," Tracy said to Shandy as she struggled to get her feet on the floor and head to the bathroom.

Ten minutes later, she sat back on the edge of the bed, trying to decide what her best course of action would be. She reached for her purse and took out the card that the FBI agent had left with her. She dialed his cell phone.

"Agent Weston," Tracy heard as a groggy voice answered the phone.

"This is Tracy Taylor. I'd like to meet you again. I need to speak with Jack Murphy on a secure phone."

Mark opened one eye. He found himself again curled up on the dirt floor, trying to grasp what had happened. It came back faster this time, along with the pain from every bone and muscle in his body.

Had he really told Sa'id that his religion was meaningless? Where had that come from? Mark smiled faintly, getting some satisfaction in condemning Islam in front of the madman. The dried blood on his lip tore apart, sending a new flash of pain into his brain. Maybe it hadn't been worth it.

He tried to slowly lift his upper body against the wall. A pain shot up at him from his ribs, but he fought through it and managed to right himself. He looked around the room; it looked like he hadn't been moved. He wondered how Chuck was doing and where they were keeping him. The situation looked grim, hopeless. Would he see Tracy again? Ever get to know the baby they had created together?

His mind kept fighting the thought of Ross lying dead in the desert somewhere. He knew he needed to move beyond that, follow his training and not believe what Sa'id had said. But if they had found one of Vince's bugs, it would surely follow reason that he and Ross could have quickly been taken out. *Fight it,* he thought. *Don't believe!*

Before the despair could drown him, Mark began to pray, first for Tracy—that God would bring peace to her through this time. He knew God wouldn't forsake her, or him, for that matter. Between the vision, or whatever that had been in the Paris shower, and the little hints along the way, Mark knew those were obvious signs that God was orchestrating events.

It was too early to give up hope. Biblical stories came to mind: Psalms of David pouring his heart out during times of trouble,

Daniel in the lions' den, Paul and Silas in jail singing and praising God. He shook his head lightly, which sent the room spinning. It would be just great with him if God sent an earthquake to release him like He'd done for Peter.

Mark's thoughts drifted back to the poster he'd seen hanging on the church fence next to Ground Zero in New York City. Psalm 91. He remembered a worship chorus that had set those words to music. He didn't have the energy to actually sing it, but in his mind Mark's heart poured forth, *"He that dwelleth in the secret place of the most High shall abide under the shadow of the Almighty. . . ."*

NATIONAL STUDIOS
10:32 A.M.

For a show like *Across the Nation,* Saturday was not a day off. They aired live on Sunday evenings, which meant that Saturday was a catch-up day to make sure the pieces that played into the show were edited and approved. Usually, Frank Russell would show up sometime just after lunch and view all the tapes. His approval meant the producing team could go home early—his rejection usually meant a late night in the edit bay.

Today was different. The entire staff had been brought in early and split into teams to work on Sa'id's lost years. The activity was moving at an accelerated pace as researchers and producers tried to piece together the life of Ronald March, a.k.a. Ahmad Hani Sa'id.

After looking through the notes from his staff and giving direction on how the historical piece should be edited, Russell sat back to clear his mind. He immediately started worrying about not hearing from Mark and Ross. Something must have happened for them not to have checked in by now. He decided he couldn't sit by any longer. He picked up the phone and dialed the satellite number he had written down for Mark. After a few rings, a strange voice came on the line.

"Mark?" Russell asked.

"No, this is Josh; who's this?"

"Josh?" Russell was surprised. "This is Frank Russell in Los Angeles. I'm wondering what's happened to my boys. Why are you answering Mark's phone?"

"I'm wondering the same thing, Frank." Josh's voice seemed hollow through the satellite connection. "They left at midnight last night, and I haven't heard from them."

"You didn't go with them?"

"I was told in no uncertain terms to stay behind."

Russell fumed. He should have been informed. "That's strange." He grabbed a paper clip and started bending it outward. "Is there a way to get ahold of your contact?"

"I've tried. All I can do is leave a message and wait for somebody to get back to me."

"I don't like the sound of this," Russell said.

"I agree. You think I should get back to Damascus?"

"No, you'd better stay put," Russell ordered. "You're our only link at this point."

He put down the phone, shaking his head. He didn't like it, not one bit. They should have been in and out of there within a few hours. Russell did a quick calculation in his head. It'd been nearly twenty hours since the initial meeting.

He looked through his old Rolodex, searching for *Newsweek* magazine. He knew one of the editors in New York; maybe they'd heard from Moreland. There it was, Scott Elliot. Russell looked below the main office number, thankful he had a cell phone number written down.

"Scott," Russell said when the phone was answered. "It's Frank Russell with *Across the Nation.*"

"Frank, it's been a long time. How are you?"

"Doing good, thanks," Russell answered. "Look, I'm sorry to

bother you on a weekend, but I wanted to see if you've heard anything from Chad."

There was a pause before Elliot responded. "Are you talking about Chad Moreland?"

"Yeah, has he checked in? We haven't heard from Mark yet."

"Look, Frank, I'm not sure I'm following you. Chad's on vacation in Hawaii."

Russell switched the phone to his other ear, inching closer to his desk. "Are you sure?"

"Yeah, positive," Elliot answered. "He won't be back on assignment until a week from Monday. What's going on?"

"That's what I would like to know," Russell grumbled.

CHAPTER 29

Mark sat next to Chuck, leaning against the wall of the small room with his hands tied behind his back and his feet bound with fabric. He figured the room to be roughly ten feet by eight feet, just white walls and a dirt floor. No chairs or mats. One bare light fixture hanging from the eight-foot ceiling illuminated the room.

Earlier, some of Sa'id's men had brought Chuck into the room and placed a Syrian newspaper in Mark's hands. The terrorists commanded them to look up as they snapped several Polaroids of the pair. Mark acted quickly and held the newspaper firmly with his left hand, bending the middle fingers of his right hand in toward the palm while extending his thumb, index finger, and pinkie and subtly spreading them out in front of the newspaper.

Now the terrorists had what was called proof of life—Mark and Chuck in a photo with a newspaper where the front page could determine the date the photograph was taken. When they were finished taking the pictures, they left Mark and Chuck alone for the first time.

"How you holding up?" Chuck asked.

"I've had better days; how about you?" It hurt to move his mouth, but Mark fought through it.

"It looks like you've taken the majority of the rough treatment," Chuck responded. "I'm surviving so far."

"Make sure you do." Mark inched away so that his back leaned against the corner wall; that way he could get a better look at his friend. "Sorry I got you into this."

"Don't be; it was my decision."

Mark looked around at the stark white walls. "Do you think we're being watched?"

"I'd be surprised if we weren't."

"You know what that picture is for, don't you?"

"Proof of life. And you know what I'm thinking," Chuck said.

"Yeah, Chad," Mark answered. "Pretty soon your editors at *Newsweek* are going to know you're missing."

Chuck nodded. Mark's use of his fake name told Chuck that they were both thinking it wouldn't be long before Sa'id's men knew he was an impostor. "Things should get pretty interesting when that happens, huh?"

Mark smiled thinly. "Yeah, I can't wait. Sa'id said that Ross and Vince were killed."

"Don't believe him," Chuck cautioned. "You know the drill: Don't believe a word they tell you."

"Yeah, I know. Still it's hard."

The door opened slowly and Abu walked in carrying a bowl of food. Mark looked up at his old friend.

"Mark, how are you feeling?" Abu asked.

"I've been better," Mark answered.

"I'm so sorry. I didn't think it would turn out like this at all," Abu tried to explain. "I brought you some rice."

"How did you think it would turn out? Your uncle is responsible for killing thousands of my countrymen. Do you think he acts rationally, Abu?"

Abu paused, looking away. "This was supposed to be a simple interview. You should have been halfway home by now. But how did you expect him to act when you bring along a CIA agent to assassinate him?"

"He came from Damascus. I didn't hire him." Mark dodged

the accusation.

"He believes you allowed him to come."

"He believes a lot of things that aren't true," Mark stated flatly.

"If you keep antagonizing him, he'll kill you," Abu whispered to him. He dipped a spoon in the rice and brought it to Mark's lips. "Here, take a bite."

Mark did—it was a dry white rice with no flavoring at all, but Mark knew he needed to eat something if he were to keep up any kind of strength. Abu took a second spoon and did the same for Chuck.

Mark swallowed, then stared intently at his friend. "Abu, it doesn't matter what I do or say. Your uncle plans on killing us."

"No, I don't believe that."

"Think about it, Abu," Mark insisted. "He can't let us go. We've seen the real Sa'id—his anger, his abuse, his terrorism. Do you think he wants what we know to make it back to America?"

Abu sat silent.

"He'll let us live for only as long as we are useful to him," Mark continued. "Uncle or not, I don't see how you can follow Sa'id."

"You don't know my uncle," Abu argued. "He's a righteous man. If you had given him a chance, you would have seen how holy he is. He only does these things to fulfill the will of Allah."

"You really believe that killing innocent women and children can be done in the name of Allah? Open your eyes, Abu. When I first met you, you were a sincere and devout Muslim, searching the Koran, looking back through the historical records of early caliphs. You were on a spiritual journey, in search of what? Something beyond yourself. Some kind of life-changing fulfillment, a divine purpose. Did you succeed, Abu? Is this what you expected to find at the end of your journey?"

Abu lowered his head. "You don't understand. How can you? You haven't seen the truth."

Chuck watched the discussion unfolding before him in

stunned silence. Mark seemed to be reaching what Chuck thought to be the unreachable—a fanatical Muslim terrorist.

"I have seen the truth, and you know what it is?" Mark asked. He waited for Abu to look up and for eye contact to be made.

"The truth is that God loves you more than you could possibly know, Abu. Your sincere desire to follow His will and lead a life worthy of Him is noble, but you're on the wrong path. It won't be fulfilled in Islam."

"Do not speak to me of these things," Abu said, then quickly got up, heading for the door.

"I must. If I don't tell you, who will?" Mark's words held Abu at the door. "Look into your heart for what you know is right. Were the attacks on my country the will of Allah? Am I at war with you, Abu? Is your uncle treating my friend and me according to what you know the Koran dictates?"

Abu looked at his old friend. The image pained him. Dark bruises were evident on his arms and legs; his hair was matted where blood had dried; the right side of his face was swollen and several open cuts were visible. Abu's head turned slightly from side to side as Mark's words took hold before he spun around and walked out the door, closing it behind him. The last sound Mark and Chuck heard was the lock clicking into place.

NATIONAL STUDIOS, HOLLYWOOD, CALIFORNIA
11:22 A.M.

"I've got a bad feeling about this," Russell said into his phone. After speaking with the editor at *Newsweek,* he couldn't stop thinking about Mark's situation. It was driving him crazy to be so far away and not be able to offer Mark and Ross any kind of help. It had taken him a while, and he had bothered several people in New York on a Saturday, but he'd finally gotten through to Steve

Thompson, the head of National's cable news.

"I understand, Frank; I'm concerned too. But there's nothing we can do at this point."

"I think we should at least alert the State Department that Mark and Ross are over there, possibly in Syria."

"And what do you think they'd do about it?" Thompson countered. "We've got to wait this out. They could be on their way out now, and you'll still have your story for tomorrow night."

"I'm not worried about the story, Steve. Right now I'm worried about my people, and who it is that went in with them saying he was Chad Moreland."

"I know," Thompson said. "Look, I'll quietly get the word out to all our correspondents in the region. Maybe they can turn up something."

Russell sighed. He didn't know what else could be done. "Okay, but if we haven't heard from them in the next twelve hours, I'm calling the State Department or the FBI. I want somebody looking for them."

"Agreed," Thompson said. "Let's just see how the next few hours go. You never know, Mclintock's connection may get back to him."

"I hope so. Keep me posted." Russell ended the call. He set the phone down, then dropped his head into his hands. There was one more call he knew he had to make, but he wasn't sure if this was the right time or not. Tracy Taylor. Maybe Mark had gotten through to her and she knew something. If not, she deserved to know that Mark had not reported in.

He rubbed his forehead, and the image of Daniel Pearl flashed before his eyes. Had he sent Mark and Ross to the same fate? He hoped not. *Be strong, Tracy,* he thought as he reached for the phone.

He dialed Mark's home number, hearing the phone ring several times before Mark's recorded voice told him to leave a message. A chill went up Russell's back, listening to the voice of his young reporter as he pictured him thousands of miles away.

"Tracy. Hi, it's Frank Russell down at the show. I wondered if you could call me back. You know the number, but let me give you my cell in case I'm not in. . . ."

NORTHERN SYRIA
9:22 P.M.

Abu stood outside the doorway of his uncle's room, hesitant to be seen. Sa'id was dealing with Mustafa, who had returned from the camp where Ross and Vince had been held. Sa'id's shouting could be heard throughout the building, blaming Mustafa for allowing the spies to escape. Abu heard a sharp slap followed by silence; then his uncle dismissed Mustafa.

Abu decided he would speak to him later, but before he could get away from the door, Mustafa came through it, head bowed, with Sa'id right behind him.

"Come in, Abu; join me," Sa'id called out to his nephew in Arabic.

The room was simply furnished—a sleeping mat lay in one corner and a small desk, set against the opposite wall, held a portable computer. Abu nodded in respect and followed his uncle back into the room, taking a position across the desk from him.

"How are the infidels holding up?" Sa'id asked.

"They are surviving," Abu answered slowly.

Sa'id looked up at the troubled expression on Abu's face. "What is on your mind, Abu?"

"Nothing. . . ."

"No, no, you're not going to get away with that." Sa'id laughed, the anger seemingly gone from the meeting with Mustafa. "You are troubled. Is this not a glorious day for Allah? What could be troubling you?"

Abu felt trapped. The last person he wanted to talk with about his feelings was this man.

"He is my friend," Abu said quietly, ducking his head.

Sa'id's laughter stopped instantly. "He cannot be your friend! It is forbidden!"

"He saved my life! That has to count for something."

"Only that Allah had use for him, as I do. You heard what he said to me, 'Islam is meaningless.' I should have killed him right then. That kind of blasphemy will not go unpunished. He is not going to be convinced of our righteous cause as you claimed, nephew!"

Abu lowered his head. "He is not the same man I knew before. He has changed."

"He is what I hate about Americans—the arrogance that they know all truth, yet they live in darkness, fighting the will of Allah. I should not have agreed to this interview. Our mission could have been better served by providing our own videotape directly to Al-Jazeera."

"I'm sorry, Caliph," Abu spoke quietly. "I thought you would be able to persuade him. If the interview had not been interrupted, perhaps. . ."

Sa'id softened his voice, looking at his nephew with compassion. "Abu, I know you and Taylor have a history, but don't let that cloud your judgment. He did not come to hear the truth but to try and kill me."

Abu started to protest, but Sa'id stopped him with a wave of his hand. "We are on the verge of great things. Allah has granted me favor. I can see the unification of Islam just around the corner. We will be able to bring *Sharia* to the world and finally live in peace. Don't let your emotions run away with you because of one insignificant man."

"But he speaks of love, not war. He is not like the Americans we fight."

"He is exactly like the Americans we fight, Abu. They speak

of love, then send their cruise missiles into our cities, killing our children. They don't love; they only destroy. Mark Taylor is no exception."

Sa'id didn't stop but continued berating America in general and Mark Taylor specifically. He thought he was convincing, bringing the arguments to light that would keep Abu focused on the mission at hand. But when confronted with the character of Mark Taylor in contrast to the image his uncle despised, Abu could not reconcile the two. He listened respectfully, while his mind for the first time began to reject his uncle's arguments.

LOS ANGELES, CALIFORNIA
11:30 A.M.

Tracy arrived at the FBI building right on time, making her way through the security screening and taking the elevator to the seventeenth floor. She checked in with the receptionist, then waited for Weston to meet her in the lobby.

Five minutes later, another agent came and escorted her down three floors to Weston's office on fourteen.

Weston looked up from his desk. "Mrs. Taylor."

"Thanks for making the arrangements again, Agent Weston." Tracy smiled uncomfortably. She wasn't sure if he had had to make a special trip into the office on a Saturday morning or not.

"Not a problem. I've been here since six."

"You're kidding. On a Saturday?"

"Yeah." Weston shrugged. "The nature of the beast in these times. We're on a heightened alert this weekend. Please, have a seat."

Tracy entered the small office with a window looking toward downtown Los Angeles and took a seat in front of Weston's desk. Another hazy day of smog in L.A.

"You wanted to speak with Jack Murphy again?"

"Yes. He called me last night and told me all he could without being on a secure line," Tracy said. "After thinking it over, I wanted to get the full story."

"All right," Weston nodded. "Let's see if we can reach him."

It took a few seconds for Weston to make the connection to Langley. When he finally got through, he listened for a second, then cupped the mouthpiece with his right hand and looked up at her.

"They've sent Jack overseas. They're going to patch you through to someone else. Hold on. . . ."

CIA HEADQUARTERS, LANGLEY, VIRGINIA
2:30 P.M.

Across the country, Wendy sat at her desk going over every overnight file that had come in from the Middle East, looking for any hint of the terrorists' plans for Sunday. The phone beside her rang. She picked it up without taking her eyes off the computer screen.

"Hamilton."

"Wendy," Kristen, Jack's assistant, said. "I've got Tracy Taylor calling in looking for Jack. Can you talk with her?"

Wendy lifted her head and looked around the room, almost as if searching for somebody else to take the call.

"I don't know. . . ."

"Please, Wendy," Kristen said. "I know Jack spoke with her late last night and briefed her. She's on a secure phone at the FBI office in L.A. and wanted to talk with Jack about specifics."

Wendy sighed. "All right, put her through."

She heard the connection being made. "Hello, Mrs. Taylor, my name is Wendy Hamilton. I've been working on your husband's. . . mission."

"Yes, hello. Please, call me Tracy."

"All right, Tracy it is." Hearing the voice behind the name

touched Wendy. "And please call me Wendy. Now what can we do for you?"

"Well, I was hoping to speak with Jack Murphy. He called last night. . . ," Tracy fought to keep her voice under control, "and told me about Mark being missing."

Wendy knew this wasn't going to be easy. All the emotions she had forced below the surface since her brother had been killed flooded over her.

"Don't give up hope, Tracy," Wendy encouraged. "They separated Mark's group, and because of that we lost our electronic capability to track him. That doesn't mean anything tragic has happened to him."

"But you don't know where he is."

"Not for certain, no," Wendy spoke gently. "We think he's probably in northern Syria, maybe still in southeastern Turkey."

"What about Ross?"

"He's been flown back to a Turkish air base where our marines have set up their own base."

"That's what Jack couldn't fill me in on last night. How did that come about?"

Wendy paused. "Tracy, the situation is classified. I'm going to have to speak with Jack before I can give you all the details."

"We're talking about my husband's life. . . ."

"I know this must be extremely hard on you. All I can say is that Ross and our man were airlifted out of the area."

"So the terrorists must know that you were tracking them."

"I would assume so, yes."

"Doesn't that leave Mark in a precarious situation?"

Wendy sighed. "We hope not, Tracy. We intentionally made sure there wouldn't be anything on Mark that could raise their suspicions. And don't forget the reason Mark was picked in the first place was because of his relationship with Abu Ressam. We hope that will weigh in his favor."

Tracy paused. It seemed like Wendy was grasping at straws. The name of Abu Ressam struck a chord. That was the name of Mark's friend from Saudi Arabia. "So, Abu Ressam is the reason Mark was invited along, but how is he connected to the Jihad al Sharia?"

"Your husband's friend is Sa'id's nephew."

Tracy didn't know Abu personally, but from what Mark had told her about him, she was stunned.

"Look, Tracy," Wendy broke the silence, "let me give you the number of my direct line. I'll be here if you have any questions until Jack returns."

Tracy wrote the number down and added one last plea before hanging up. "Please, just bring my husband home."

CHAPTER 30

"You seem troubled, Fazul," his mother said. "Everything okay?"

"Yeah, fine." Fazul smiled softly, picking at his plate. "I'm just not hungry."

"You sure came in late last night. What was that about?" Ramsi inquired.

"Just a movie with some friends," Fazul answered his father. "As a matter of fact, we're getting together again at Sofian's house tonight. He's having a special prayer time before sunrise. I thought I might just spend the night over there."

"You sure seem to be spending a lot of time with him lately," Johara warned.

"We've been studying the *Qur'an* together for the classes at the mosque. I've really learned a lot from him."

"Like what?" his dad asked, taking a sip of his tea.

Fazul knew he had to be careful. "Like how important education is in making something of your life as you seek to follow Allah's will."

His dad nodded his head in appreciation, but the look from his sister Akilah nearly ruined the moment. Fazul glared at her to keep silent.

"I think it's great if you find a way to incorporate your Muslim beliefs into a good career," his dad said with a smile.

Like you have? Fazul wanted to ask his father but wisely remained silent.

"So what's going on at his house?" his dad asked.

"I wanted to go over some possible night classes I'm considering." Fazul laid it on thick. "I think I can make up some of those credits this spring, then complete my degree in the fall."

"That'd be great!" Ramsi exclaimed. His mom smiled graciously from the other side of the table.

"Then it's okay if I go?"

"Of course it is, Son."

Fazul smiled at his dad, not daring to glance at the shocked expression on Akilah's face.

TURKEY AIR BASE, DIYARBAKIR, TURKEY
SUNDAY, 6:21 A.M.

Jack was exhausted. Traveling all night in a military transport wasn't exactly the best way to catch up on his sleep. He had his marine escort take him by the hospital where Vince was being treated. He was still critical, but at least he'd made it through the first night. He had yet to regain consciousness. He'd nearly died from the loss of blood, but after six hours of emergency surgery, they'd finally gotten him stabilized.

Jack had to focus on the task at hand to get Vince's life-and-death struggle off his mind. He was sitting in a small office in the barracks where Ross had been held. After a quick tap at the door, Wark brought Ross inside the room.

"Mr. Berman," Jack said, standing and offering his hand. "My name is Jack Murphy."

Ross hesitated before accepting the handshake. "If I have to go through my story one more time. . ."

"That won't be necessary." Jack looked up Wark. "Thank you, Patrick. Can you leave us alone for a few minutes?"

Patrick nodded, moving to the door and closing it behind him.

"I'm the chief of Middle Eastern Intelligence at Langley." Jack waited for his words to sink in.

"CIA," Ross muttered.

"That's correct. I'm here to ask for your help."

Ross shook his head, not believing what he was hearing. "You don't think you've screwed this up enough by asking for Mark's help—now you want mine?"

Jack took a hard look at the young producer before extending his hand toward the chair nearby. "Please, have a seat."

"I want to make sure you understand the situation, Ross." Jack scooted his chair close to him before he sat down. "You don't mind if I call you Ross, do you?"

Ross shrugged. "Whatever you want, man."

"I was monitoring everything that happened to you and Vince. It took a lot of courage to do what you did. You probably saved Vince's life."

Ross said nothing.

"Look, obviously things haven't worked out like we'd hoped," Jack spoke earnestly, trying to break through the resistance. "But I'm here on behalf of the president of the United States to speak with you personally."

Ross held up the palm of his hand toward Jack. "Don't give me your patriotic spiel. I'm tired; I've been through hell, and I just want to get out of here and head home."

Jack paused. This wasn't going to be easy. "Aren't you concerned with what's happened to Mark?"

Ross looked offended. "Of course I'm concerned, but there isn't exactly anything I can do for him now, is there?"

Jack had to force himself not to smile. "Actually, there is." He let the force of his statement sink in a bit before continuing. "We're not going to hold you here any longer, Ross, unless you decide you want to stay and see this thing through on your own. After we've had our talk, you'll be free to go."

That got a faint smile out of Ross. "But?"

"No buts. I just want you to consider what you'll say to your network and to the outside world."

"That I was separated from Mark, searched, and then. . ." Ross suddenly realized where Jack was going.

"You'd be putting Mark's life in greater danger if you confirm that Vince is CIA."

Ross looked away, thinking carefully. "I see what you mean."

"Yeah, it's complicated," Jack agreed. "There's no problem with the first part of the story, that you were indeed separated from Mark, but why didn't you and the cameraman just wait it out until Mark's interview was complete?"

"Because they found the bug. . . ," Ross answered the question. "But we can't say that."

"Exactly." Jack had him. "You need to know one more thing that's sure to come out soon."

"What's that?"

"The other man—he isn't Chad Moreland from *Newsweek*."

"You're kidding." Ross was incensed. "You planted two agents?"

"No, this one was Mark's idea. He's not CIA."

"Then who is he?"

"That information is classified, but if we come to an agreement, I'll share it with you."

Ross lowered his head, trying to put all the pieces together in his mind to make a relatively intelligent decision. After a moment he looked up and spoke. "So what are you suggesting I do?"

"That's up to you. I'm hoping we can come up with a scenario that will give Mark the best shot at coming back alive. If you and I can agree on what that is, then you're on your way back to the States, or, if you prefer, you can stay here on the base and get the latest updates on Mark's situation. You could be the liaison back to your network with up-to-the-minute reports, as long as they're cleared by my people."

Ross leaned back in his chair, taking in a deep breath. This was going to be a tough decision.

CIA HEADQUARTERS, LANGLEY, VIRGINIA
11:30 P.M.

Nothing in the world infuriated a CIA analyst more than seeing something he or she didn't know broadcast by a television network. Such was the case as Wendy worked furiously at her desk late into the night. She'd kept a video window open on her computer's screen of the satellite feed from Al-Jazeera out of Qatar. She kept the sound just loud enough for her to pick up any key words that might float by. She was nearing exhaustion after going over and over the field reports and intelligence gathered from the region. The last three pages she'd looked at hadn't even registered. She leaned against the back of her chair and closed her eyes.

Just a minute's rest, she thought as she took in a deep breath and let it out slowly; then she would get back into it. She was close to submitting totally to the absence of thought gently settling over her when she heard the Arabic voice say "Mark Taylor." *Must be my imagination,* she thought. The exhaustion made her want to continue the slide downward toward sleep, but before she was completely out, one eye opened and Wendy took a glance at the computer screen.

She bolted upright in the chair, leaning in close to the small insert of the television feed as any hint of drowsiness instantly fled. It was a picture of a dreadful-looking Mark sitting next to another man. They were both dressed in loose-fitting robes, and Mark was holding up a newspaper. She grabbed the mouse, desperate to turn up the sound and enlarge the window on the screen.

TURKEY AIR BASE, DIYARBAKIR, TURKEY
6:32 A.M.

A sharp rap at the door interrupted the discussion between Jack and Ross.

"Enter," Jack ordered.

Patrick stepped into the room, moving quickly to a television set sitting on top of a filing cabinet and turning it on. "We just got a call from Langley; you need to see this."

Nearly instantly, they heard the sound of a CNN reporter as the picture faded up on the screen, revealing a shot of Mark and Chuck holding the front page of an Arabic newspaper. "There's been no report of any ransom demands. Instead the Al-Jazeera Satellite News channel is reporting that Mark Taylor of the National Network and Chad Moreland from *Newsweek* magazine are being held captive by the Jihad al Sharia and charged with espionage and attempting to assassinate Ahmad Hani Sa'id. CNN has not been able to confirm their identities or where they are being held. . . ."

Both Ross and Jack stared at the television screen in shock. Mark looked like he'd been through hell. Through the grainy image on the screen, they could make out the bruises and cuts on Mark's face and the dried blood around his mouth and caked in his hair. Jack wondered what injuries weren't visible. Chuck, on the other hand, didn't look as if he'd been treated as roughly. Perhaps that was to their advantage.

Looking at the picture of Mark impacted Ross deeply. After a moment he turned back to Jack. "I'll do whatever you ask, but I want to stay here and be as close to what's going on with Mark as possible."

"Done," Jack agreed as he grabbed his satellite phone.

NATIONAL STUDIOS, HOLLYWOOD, CALIFORNIA
8:30 P.M.

Frank Russell sat at his desk, contemplating his options. Should he call the FBI or the State Department? The twelve hours he'd promised to Thompson in New York were nearly up. It was time to do something.

The light coming from Russell's office was the only one on in the building. Everybody else had left hours before, but Russell felt he needed to stay. Mark had been out of touch too long. . .something must have happened.

The phone beside him rang. Frank looked at it suspiciously, then picked it up.

"Hello."

"Is this *Across the Nation*?" a male voice asked.

"Yes," Russell answered. "Who's this?"

"This is Mike McDermit with CNN in New York. We're breaking a story right now coming out of the Middle East and wanted to get verification of Mark Taylor's identity and if he is currently on assignment in the region."

Frank grabbed his remote control while he listened, turning the television on and clicking in the numbers for CNN. "What's happened?"

"You don't know?" the voice asked. "The Jihad al Sharia is saying they have captured Taylor. He's accused of being a CIA spy."

The television screen flared to life, giving Frank an eyeful of Mark and a man he didn't recognize staring blankly at the camera. Frank swore before he could stop himself.

"Who am I speaking with?" the CNN producer asked.

Frank didn't want to give a competing network anything more to work with; besides, he wasn't sure what to say. "Look, nobody's in the office today. You'll have to try back tomorrow."

He slammed down the phone and turned up the volume on the TV as he dialed Steve Thompson's cell phone number in New York.

STUDIO CITY, CALIFORNIA
9:19 P.M.

Shandy sat in the passenger seat next to Tracy, becoming more energetic as she recognized the area around their house. Tracy had rolled the passenger window down so the dog could stick her nose out of the car and get a whiff of home. Shandy knew every smell along this street from their twice-daily ritual of walking the neighborhood.

But nothing prepared them for what was around the next corner. Shandy immediately started a low growl deep in her throat while Tracy just stared in open-eyed shock. A barrage of media vans was surrounding their house. A quick glance told her that every station in the L.A. market was represented, along with CNN and Fox. Along the street were various reporters and camera crews—all waiting for her.

Tracy put on the brakes and turned into the Collins' driveway three houses away from hers. She jumped when Shandy let out a sharp bark. A couple of the reporters on the outskirts looked in her direction.

"Shandy, shush!" Tracy reached for the dog, trying to keep her quiet as she put the gearshift in reverse. She angled her head away from the onlooking press, hoping they wouldn't get a glimpse of her face as she backed up into the street and drove off in the opposite direction. In her rearview mirror she could see two guys running for their van, so she slammed the accelerator to the floor and spun around the corner and out to the main street. She took a right turn along with the traffic and sped away before the press could catch up to her.

There must have been some news about Mark! That's why they were waiting at the house. Great timing to decide to stop and get a change of clothes and some more dog food.

Tracy turned the radio on and punched through the stations, listening for somebody reporting the news. She finally found it on KNX 1070 but had to wait through two local stories before she heard what she was looking for.

"Repeating our top story, Al-Jazeera is reporting that Mark

Taylor from *Across the Nation* and Chad Moreland from *Newsweek* magazine are being held by the Jihad al Sharia on charges of espionage and an attempt on the life of Ahmad Hani Sa'id, the leader of the terrorist organization. The report made it clear that this was not a kidnapping and there is no ransom demand. Taylor and Moreland will be tried for crimes against Islam. A photograph of the pair appeared on the satellite news network that services the Middle East. . . ."

"Oh, no!" Tracy cried out. Her worst fears were confirmed. Mark wasn't just lost—he was now a captive of the murdering terrorists. She turned her car down a side street and pulled over to the curb, burying her face in her hands and weeping as the voice on the radio continued the report.

"Oh, God, where are You?" she cried through the tears.

VAN NUYS, CALIFORNIA
9:41 P.M.

"Leaving soon?" Akilah stuck her head in her brother's room.

"Yeah," Fazul answered without turning around as he grabbed a shirt from his drawer and stuck it in his backpack.

Akilah walked past him and sat on the edge of the bed. "What's going on, Fazul?"

"What do you mean?"

"Come on; I didn't buy your act at dinner. I bet you're not even going to Sofian's house."

Fazul laughed. "Come on, Akilah, lighten up. You heard Dad tonight; he thinks Sofian's been a good influence on me."

"Only because you lied to him. You didn't mention Ishmael, did you? Now what's really going on?"

Fazul stopped packing his things and looked directly at his sister. "Just leave it alone. I know what I'm doing."

"Do you, Fazul?" Akilah asked, concern in her voice. "You've changed, and it's starting to scare me."

"Of course I've changed, but for the better." Fazul walked over to the bed and sat next to her. "If you could only see how important this is, not just to me, but for Islam."

"What are you talking about?" Akilah's head tilted and a confused look entered her eyes.

Fazul avoided her gaze, dropping his head. "Never mind; you wouldn't understand. Your love for the American ways, the short skirts, the boys, the movies—it has clouded your mind and pulled you away from the truth."

Akilah shook her head, tired of the same old argument. "Fazul, I am still a Muslim and proud to follow Allah. Our religion must adapt; it must be relevant to the times."

"You speak blasphemy!" Fazul jumped off the bed, his anger startling Akilah. "The *Qur'an* leaves no room for the perversions of this country!"

The two didn't speak for a moment, then after a long sigh Fazul looked intently at his sister. "Akilah, if anything should happen to me. . ."

"Fazul, you're scaring me."

Fazul smiled determinedly at her. "If Allah wills, nothing will happen, but if Allah wishes me to join him in paradise, make sure our family knows that I served him willingly."

Akilah shook her head. "Listen to me, Fazul. Whatever it is that Ishmael has talked you into, don't do it. You're not thinking clearly."

"No, Akilah." Fazul stood up and walked over to his closet to collect his prayer mat. "I've never seen things more clearly."

CHAPTER 31

"What have you got?" Keith Chapman finally made it back to the FBI lab where his team of specialists were going over every inch of the computers and paperwork they'd confiscated from the raid on Friday.

"We finally broke through their encryption codes an hour ago," the agent sitting at the computer explained.

Since the raid Friday when Keith had emptied out the tube containing the blueprints of the churches, the NYPD bomb squads had been going through each of the buildings. No explosives had been found inside, so the operating theory was that the terrorists had planned to hit the buildings from the outside.

Keith picked up some of the E-mails that had been printed out. "What's the bottom line?"

"An isolated cell. We can't find information on any other ones. . . ."

"But. . ." Keith could hear the hesitation in his technician's voice.

"There are several E-mails mentioning multiple attacks across the country, planned for—" the agent looked down at his wrist-watch, "—today."

"Churches?"

"I would assume so, sir. This group was supposed to hit all three, St. Patrick's, Brooklyn Tabernacle, and Times Square Church, at 11:30 A.M."

"All three?" Keith was surprised.

"Yeah, it looks like they're going for another simultaneous attack at several locations."

"Unbelievable." Keith sighed. "I've got to get ahold of the director and SIOC. We have to initiate an all-office alert." Keith referred to the Strategic Information Office Center, the twenty-four-hour-a-day command post operating out of the bureau's headquarters in Washington, D.C. "We've got about ten hours to figure out how to protect every church in this nation."

NORTHRIDGE, CALIFORNIA
9:57 P.M.

Tracy had no idea how she'd made it back to Brenda and Tom's house. She'd just driven through the city without thinking and ended up pulling into their driveway. She could have been sitting there for ten minutes or an hour; she wasn't sure since she had flipped through the radio stations, stopping every time somebody mentioned the report on Mark. It wasn't until Brenda had called her cell phone that she snapped out of her shock.

"Where are you, Tracy?" Brenda asked, concerned. "I'll come get you."

"No need," Tracy answered. "I'm in your driveway."

Before Tracy could get out of the car, Brenda was there to meet her with a warming hug. The two embraced for a long moment until Tom interrupted from the front door.

"Here comes the ten o'clock news."

Tracy rushed inside to the television set, drawn by a strong sense of terror, almost like passing an accident on the freeway and anxiously looking to see if anybody was injured. She wondered how the real picture would measure up to her imagination when it finally hit the screen during their lead story.

It was worse.

Not that Mark didn't look awful; in fact, he looked just like the image that had tormented her brain for the past hour. What made it worse was that seeing the picture on television made the events happening to Mark undeniable. He really was in the hands of lunatics.

Tracy reached her hand out to touch the television screen, fighting back the overwhelming sense of dread and the tears that seemed to never stop—when she noticed something in the picture: Mark's hand.

She laughed.

Brenda rushed to Tracy's side, putting her arm around her, sure that she was on the verge of totally breaking down. But Tracy shocked her again when she looked directly at her and smiled.

"Look at his hand," Tracy said, pointing to the picture.

"What is it?" Brenda asked.

"There, look at his right hand, the way he's holding the newspaper."

"What?" Brenda tried to follow her, but she didn't see it.

"Look at his thumb, the index finger, and his pinkie."

Brenda leaned in and could make out his hand through the individual pixels of color coming from the screen. He did seem to be holding the paper strangely, as if either he had tucked in his middle two fingers, or they had been cut off. Brenda's eyes widened in fear. Had they mutilated his hands?

"That's our sign!" Tracy exclaimed. "It's the sign language symbol for 'I love you.' We wave that to each other all the time."

Tracy took her eyes off the TV and looked at Brenda, feeling a spark of hope through her anguish. "He did that deliberately." She turned back to the television screen as her tears fell. "To tell me he's okay."

HOLLYWOOD, CALIFORNIA
10:02 P.M.

Frank drove through the Cahuenga Pass on the 101 Freeway, heading out to his home in Woodland Hills. He had to get out of the office. The phone was ringing constantly, and he didn't want to talk with anybody. He'd gotten through to the news division chief in New York, and they'd gone over their plan. No comment to the other networks. This was National's story; everybody else would just have to speculate.

That was fine for ratings, but all Frank cared about was Mark's safety. What could they do to get him back alive? And what had happened to Ross? And who was the man in that picture with Mark? It certainly wasn't Chad Moreland.

His cell phone rang. He was tempted to let it go to voice mail.

"Russell," he answered.

"Frank, it's Ross."

It was a good thing there wasn't any traffic this time of night, as Russell's car crossed over two lanes before he regained control. "Ross, thank God you're alive. What's going on over there? Are you okay?"

"I'm fine. . . ."

"Where are you? How did you and Mark get separated. . . ?" The questions fired off his tongue.

"Hold on, Frank, and I'll fill you in," Ross interrupted. "I'm at a Turkish military base. . . ." He told Frank the story Jack had concocted, how they had been separated from Mark and Chad, then dropped off miles outside the city of Diyarbakir, and how they were forced to survive through the rainstorm before a marine unit happened upon them and brought them to the base.

"So you don't know where Mark is then?" Frank asked.

"No, we're assuming he was taken into Syria."

"We?"

"I've got a good relationship going with the marine commander here in Diyarbakir. They have a camp set up at the Turkish military base."

"Are they going to look for Mark?"

"If they had any clue where he was, they would already have a rescue squad knocking down tents. The commander knows Mark was a marine. I believe the phrase he used was, 'We don't leave our own behind.' "

"We need to get your story on the air, Ross," Frank said.

"What do you mean?"

"I want you on the air from the military base. See if you can get permission, and I'll have Josh work out the details. If not, we need to get you back to the hotel."

"I'm not a reporter, Frank."

"You are now. We've got to answer Sa'id's charges that Mark is a spy. You are a direct witness of what went on, how they tricked us. And you can say to the world that Mark was not working with or for the CIA. You might be the key to keeping him alive."

"I see your point," Ross said, looking across the table at Jack listening in on another extension. Jack nodded his head, giving him silent approval. "I'll check things out on this end and call you back."

"One more thing," Russell noted. "The man with Mark is not Chad Moreland."

"How do you know that?" Ross asked.

"I called one of their editors. Moreland's on vacation."

Jack motioned with his hand, cutting across his neck. Ross nodded. "I'll have to check on that, Frank, and get back to you."

Ross hung up the phone.

"Good job, Ross," Jack said. "You played it perfect. Getting you on the air to counter Sa'id's propaganda is just what we need."

Ross shook his head. "I can't believe I'm doing this."

"What?" Jack smiled. "Going on the air as a reporter?"

"No," Ross answered grimly. "Working with the CIA."

Halfway around the world, Frank decided he was heading the wrong direction. He turned off the 101 at Barham and headed back over the freeway, then turned left on Ventura Boulevard. With Ross back in the game, he needed to be at his office. He kept his cell phone in his hands and started speed-dialing his staff. Anybody he could reach would be joining him shortly.

CIA HEADQUARTERS, LANGLEY, VIRGINIA
1:14 A.M.

Wendy walked back into her cubicle with another cup of fresh coffee. She couldn't count the number of cups she'd put away throughout the day. It didn't matter at this point; she just wanted to stay sharp.

She sat back in front of her computer, the picture of Mark frozen on the screen. She felt responsible. Would he be in this situation if she hadn't started the ball rolling?

The phone rang. Looking over at the blinking light, she realized it was her direct line. She picked it up. "Hamilton."

"Wendy? It's Tracy Taylor."

The guilt doubled. "Tracy, how are you doing?"

"Not great!" Tracy was irritated. "Jack promised that I would be kept informed. I have to find out my husband is captured by finding the press hounding the doors of my house? Then see his picture on CNN?"

Wendy's stomach dropped. They'd been so busy, she hadn't thought about informing Tracy of what they knew. "I'm sorry, Tracy. It took us all by surprise."

"You didn't know either?" Wendy's apology only served to increase Tracy's fear. What hope did Mark have if the CIA was totally in the dark?

"We didn't know until Al-Jazeera aired the story. We've been doing everything we can to locate Mark, but that's no excuse why somebody didn't call you."

"I want to talk with Jack," Wendy demanded.

"That could be difficult, Tracy, but I'll try. What do you want to know?"

"I've got something he should know," Tracy offered, letting Wendy in on Mark's secret message.

NORTHERN SYRIA
8:21 A.M.

"Get up," the Arab shouted in heavily accented English. "You're coming with me."

With his hands clasped behind his back and his feet tied together, Mark struggled to get his weight over his two feet to be able to stand up. The pain never seemed to end, both from the beatings and now from lying on a hard dirt floor the past thirty hours. Chuck groaned next to him in his attempt to rise when the terrorist stepped over and slammed the butt of an AK-47 in his gut.

"You stay," he ordered, then roughly grabbed ahold of Mark's arm and pulled him to his feet. "Move!"

The only way to comply with the order was to hop, which is what Mark did, grimacing from the pain in his ribs. Fortunately they weren't moving him far.

He was led into the next room and pushed into a small metal folding chair. He was surprised to see a video camera pointed at him and an empty chair sitting next to it, exactly how he'd had things set up when he interviewed Sa'id. Mark squirmed, trying to find a comfortable position for his hands behind him, which was impossible. The rope around his wrists had rubbed his skin away so that his hands had begun to bleed, causing a flash of pain every time he moved them.

At least this room had a window and he could see the daylight outside. . .he guessed it was still morning. Thinking through the events that had led him here, he hoped it was Sunday. If not, then he would have been unconscious a lot longer than he'd thought. He looked through the window, hoping to get some kind of bearing of where they might be, but the view only went far enough to see the outside wall of the stone building next door, maybe five feet away. It didn't tell him anything.

A few moments later, Ahmad Sa'id entered the room clothed in his white robe accented with the gold braiding, followed closely by Abu.

"Ahh, Mr. Taylor," Sa'id said, entering the room. "You're becoming quite the international celebrity. I'll bet your picture is on the front page of every newspaper from here to Los Angeles."

Mark looked up at his captor. "And just where is here?"

He smiled. "Here is my kingdom. That's all you need to know."

Sa'id turned to one of his men, speaking orders in Arabic. The man moved over to the camera and hit the record button. A steady red light glowed over the lens.

"Now, I thought this would be interesting." Sa'id turned back to Mark, taking a seat in the chair by the camera. "We started with you interviewing me; now it's my turn. I want to make sure we get all this on tape so that everyone in your country can see how well you're being treated."

Mark took in a deep breath to try to prepare himself for what was to come, causing another sharp pain in his side. He glanced over at Abu, standing quietly in the corner. Abu quickly looked away, not willing to meet Mark's gaze.

Once again, his marine special ops training came back to him, particularly to the many ways he knew that a man's spirit could be crushed. The last thing he wanted was for a tape of a broken Mark to get back to Tracy. The marine training aside, Mark fervently prayed for God's presence to be with him as it had been for Stephen when he was questioned by the high priest, although he deeply hoped for a more favorable outcome than being stoned to death as Stephen had been.

"Are you willing to answer my questions, Mark?" Sa'id teased.

Mark acknowledged Sa'id with a nod that made him instantly nauseous. "My name is Mark Taylor; I'm an employee of the National Network. I am an investigative journalist on the news-magazine show, *Across the Nation*."

"Ahh, your name, rank, and serial number." Sa'id laughed. "But you are not in the military any longer; you are under arrest for espionage and an attempt to assassinate a Muslim caliph. How do you plead?"

"I'm innocent," Mark answered, deciding to try to engage in the propaganda war. "I was asked here on your behalf to do my job, interviewing you in good faith."

"That is a lie," Sa'id shouted. "Vince Carusso. Does the name sound familiar to you? It didn't to officials in Damascus. He doesn't exist, yet he masqueraded as a cameraman in an attempt to kill me."

"I don't know what you're talking about." Mark struggled. His mouth was dry, and the pain in his body was making it difficult to concentrate.

"Don't insult me! I want the truth." Sa'id's voice rose in irritation. "The world needs to know the truth. How your government engages in acts of war by attempting to murder an innocent holy man!"

Mark shook his head involuntarily. "Innocence by definition would not include ordering the deaths of thousands of American citizens."

"Then you admit your complicity with your government?"

"I admit no such thing." Mark's voice was etched with irritation. "I was simply trying to do my job."

"Your job did not include bringing along a CIA spy complete

with his high-tech electronic bugs."

Mark looked directly at Sa'id. "I told you I had nothing to do with that man, whether he was working for the CIA or not."

Sa'id smiled—an evil, haunting grin, then leaned closer to Mark. "It will go much better for you if you're honest with me, Mr. Taylor. . . ."

Mark chose not to answer. Sa'id nodded to one of his men standing outside of the camera's view.

The punch came without warning, right across Mark's chin. He teetered on the edge of consciousness, the pain coming in waves. When his vision cleared, the dark eyes of Sa'id sparkled with pleasure.

"Now, let's try again, shall we. . . ?"

NORTHRIDGE, CALIFORNIA
10:35 P.M.

Tracy wasn't alone. Brenda had called two other couples from their home group, and they'd come over to the house. The six of them had gathered around Tracy and prayed for Mark. She couldn't recall the words. Her mind just couldn't focus, but the fact that they were there with her meant a lot.

They kept the television on quietly in the background in case there were any new developments. Every time Mark's picture flashed back on the screen and Tracy's eyes caught it, she'd jump back on the emotional roller coaster. The valleys were deep when she focused on the bruises and cuts, the swollen cheeks, or when she thought about never seeing him again. But there was just enough of a crest, his hand formed to communicate "I love you," to know that they hadn't broken his spirit, and it gave her hope to hang on.

Tracy's cell phone interrupted the prayer time. Everyone stopped as she reached into her purse and answered the call.

"Hello."

"Tracy, it's Frank Russell."

Tracy covered the phone, letting her friends know it was Mark's boss.

"Are you doing okay?"

"I'm trying."

"I called the house. It took awhile for us to locate your cell number." Frank tried to ease his conscience. "I'm so sorry about Mark."

Tracy wanted to blast into him for sending her husband in the first place, but she could hear the strain in his voice. . .he was going through his own pain. "I know, Frank," she graciously answered. "I just want him home."

"We all do, Tracy. I've got a little good news. Ross is okay."

"I know," Tracy answered without thinking.

When Frank paused, Tracy realized what she'd said and her head dropped.

"What do you mean you know? How. . . ?"

"I meant since he wasn't in the picture, I figured he hadn't gone on the interview." Tracy scrambled for an answer. "What did you mean?"

"I just spoke with him," Frank said, explaining the conversation he'd had with Ross. Tracy listened, relieved that Frank was talking and not her. "We're going to have Ross do some live cut-ins from Turkey, and I'm assembling the staff right now." Frank paused; Tracy felt as if he were struggling with his next thought.

"Would you consider speaking about Mark on the air?" the question came.

Tracy couldn't believe what she'd heard. It was one thing for the national media to stake out her house, looking for their scoop without any concern for her privacy or what she might be going through, but Frank?

"It's not what you're thinking, Tracy." Frank spoke over her silence.

"Oh, it's not, Frank? You're not trying to scoop the rest of the news world by having an exclusive with the reporter's grieving wife, crying on cue for your cameras?" Tracy was suddenly aware of the people around her and what her outburst must have sounded like.

"I was afraid you'd think that, Tracy." Frank responded as warmly as she'd ever heard him speak. "I want you to do it for Mark. He's being accused of working with the CIA. We're putting together a campaign to fight against Sa'id's propaganda to try and save Mark. Your voice of support and being able to refute Sa'id's story would be powerful."

It would also be a lie. She didn't know if she could pull it off. "I can't believe you're asking me to even consider this."

"I wouldn't be if I didn't think it would help Mark," Frank countered.

"I'll have to think about it," Tracy returned.

"I understand. . . ." The phone stayed silent as Frank paused. "Tracy, I need to ask you one thing. The man in the picture with Mark isn't Chad Moreland from *Newsweek*. Do you know who he really is?"

Tracy froze. If they found out Chuck was a friend from the marines, not a reporter, that's all the proof Sa'id would need to execute Mark. She couldn't tell Frank.

"All I know is that you sent him on this assignment, Frank." She forced an edge into her voice. "I have no idea who went with him other than Ross."

"Okay, I had to ask. Consider what I've said, Tracy. Mark needs all the help he can get. Is there anything we can do for you?"

"Get the press hounds off my front porch."

"I wish I could. Where are you, by the way?"

"With friends." Tracy looked around the room, understanding the word more deeply than ever before as she hung up the phone.

NORTHERN SYRIA
8:37 A.M.

Sa'id kept hammering the same question at Mark, trying to break him. Occasionally he would pause to allow his henchman to inflict more damage to Mark's already bruised body—a rifle butt to the stomach or a strike across his face, a few kidney punches now and then. Mark didn't know how much more he could take, but he knew admitting to being a spy would seal his fate.

Another crushing blow came from the back of the machine gun, this time square against his side. The blinding flash of pain knocked him unconscious for a brief instant. He came to quickly, gasping desperately for his next breath. The relief of being able to finally suck in some oxygen was quickly shattered by the intense agony coming from his rib cage. He silently pleaded for God to be his strength.

"I told you," Mark gasped. "I'm just a reporter."

"How long are we going to do this, Mark?" Sa'id asked.

Mark looked up, glancing quickly at Abu's pained expression before turning back to Sa'id. "I'm willing to stop right now."

"Then in the name of Allah, the merciful, confess!"

"Merciful?" Mark said through clenched teeth, surprised at his outburst. "Is this your idea of mercy? Was 9/11 and the Sunday Massacre in our country acts of Allah's compassion?"

Sa'id sprang up, knocking Mark's chair off its legs, sending him to the floor. Sa'id kicked Mark where he lay and cursed at him in Arabic. "Do not speak the name of Allah; you are not worthy."

Mark struggled to get back on his knees, fighting the overwhelming urge to succumb to the blackness closing in.

"The attacks upon America have been anointed by Allah!" Sa'id continued in a rage. "He has given me the power. I ordered the buses into your precious stadiums. It was at my hand your embassies exploded. Because Allah the almighty has chosen me!"

Mark looked up directly into the enraged face of Sa'id, now towering over him. "You speak as if you know the heart of your god, but you know only your own hatred."

Mark could see the anger flaring in Sa'id's eyes, but he continued, his voice rising in passion. "You say there is one god, and about that you are right, but it's not the one you serve. Allah is no more alive than the idols Muhammad threw out of the Ka'bah!"

"Shut up!" Sa'id screamed, pulling a pistol out from underneath his robe. Suddenly a 9mm barrel was pointed directly between Mark's eyes as Sa'id shook with rage. "I have the power of life and death over you, Taylor! Your blasphemy will send you to hell!"

"You have no power over me," Mark heard himself say, "except what the Son of God, Jesus Christ, allows you to have."

The room was silent, everyone expecting the next sound to come from the gun shaking violently in Sa'id's hand. Sa'id's mixed expression of rage and shock gave Mark the impression that he was as surprised as everyone else in the room that he hadn't fired the gun yet.

As the words came out, Mark fully expected them to be his last. Not that he had a death wish; his greatest desire was to return to Tracy and their baby. But a boldness had settled over him; speaking the name of Jesus had seemed to lift the veil of darkness emanating from Sa'id.

Staring into the empty eyes, feeling the cold steel of the pistol pressed against the bridge of his nose, Mark wasn't sure what would happen next. His mind flashed to the image in the fogged-up mirror in Paris, and he imagined Sa'id holding a copy of the Koran instead of a 9mm gun to his head. *Greater is He who is in me than he who is in the world.*

"If I am to die at your hand," Mark spoke calmly, "it won't be because Allah willed it, but because my heavenly Father is calling me to Him. If that's the case, then I gladly await being in the presence of my Lord. But it's not your decision, Sa'id, and it's certainly not Allah's."

Sa'id's hand shook violently, causing the barrel of the gun to break the skin of Mark's nose, his bright red blood adding to the bizarre scene. Abu watched in horror as his uncle struggled to squeeze the trigger.

"You have committed *shirk,* infidel!" Sa'id's voice trembled. "You deserve to die!"

Abu couldn't contain himself any longer. He lunged toward Sa'id, shouting in Arabic, "No, Uncle, stop!"

He grabbed Sa'id's right hand, pointing the gun away from Mark and toward the floor just as Sa'id's finger unfroze and the gun blasted, sending a round harmlessly into the dirt floor.

Sa'id spun around, throwing Abu across the room in anger. He spat out a long string of Arabic, then stomped out of the room, not giving Mark a second look. The other terrorists grabbed Mark and dragged him back into the next room.

Mark thought the ordeal was finally over, until one of them entered the room with a strand of wire. They wrapped one end around Mark's legs, then brought the other end around his neck with his feet bent back at the knees. They tightened the noose and left the room.

Chuck swore as he realized what they had done to Mark. With the wire wrapped tightly around his neck, to be able to breath Mark had to keep his legs continually bent with his ankles angled up toward his head. If he relaxed, the wire would strangle him.

Mark analyzed the situation, then saw the concern etched on his friend's face. He wheezed through the pain as he struggled to keep his legs curled back. "I think I may have said something they didn't like."

CHAPTER 32

Akilah tapped on her parents' door, then opened it quietly. "Mom, Dad, you guys awake?"

"What is it, dear?" Johara answered, sitting up in the bed.

Her father, who had been snoring, snorted in a breath of air and looked up groggily. "What?"

Akilah stepped into the room and sat on the edge of the bed. Her mother reached over and turned on the lamp on the nightstand.

"Are you okay, Akilah?"

"Yes, I'm fine. It's about Fazul."

Her dad groaned as Johara cocked her head. "What is it, honey?"

"I'm not sure. I think something's going on, that he might be involved in. . ."

"In what?" Johara asked, concerned.

"I don't know."

Ramsi sat up in his bed, looking at his daughter. "What's going on, Akilah?"

Akilah sighed, trying to put her feelings into words. "I went into Fazul's room before he left. He was acting weird. It was like he was saying good-bye. For good."

"That doesn't make any sense," her mother said.

"I think he's planning something," Akilah blurted, trying to find the words to convince her parents. "Something bad."

Ramsi and Johara looked at each other, not sure what to say.

"I swear, he was scaring me, talking about doing the will of Allah. He wanted me to make sure you guys know that if he ended up in paradise, he had been serving Allah willingly."

"Oh, my." Her mom brought her hand up to her chest.

Ramsi tried to comfort Johara. "It's okay, honey. I'm sure Akilah just heard it wrong. Fazul wouldn't be mixed up in something dangerous. . .he's a good kid."

"Dad," Akilah pleaded, "I saw Fazul with Ishmael."

"What do you mean?" Ramsi exclaimed, his face reddening. "When?"

"Fazul's been lying to you, Dad; he has no plans to get back into college. He's involved somehow with Ishmael. I bet he isn't even at Sofian's house."

The words hit Ramsi hard. Whatever his son was planning, if Ishmael was involved, it wasn't good.

"How do you know this?"

"I followed him down to the mosque the other day when he said there was a meeting. But there was nobody there. I saw Fazul and Sofian drive off with Ishmael."

"Why didn't you tell us?"

"Fazul made me promise not to."

"Do you know where he is?"

"No, but he should have his cell phone," Akilah said.

Ramsi reached over to his nightstand and picked up the phone, punching in his son's number. After several rings, he looked up at his family. "He's not answering. Somebody get me Sofian's number."

NORTHERN SYRIA
8:40 A.M.

"You need him." Abu sat alone with Sa'id, pleading with his uncle. "If you kill him he is of no use to you."

"Then you tell your *friend*," Sa'id spat the word out as if it were blasphemous, "to shut his mouth."

Sa'id paused, then grinned slightly. "No, you tell him that unless he confesses to being a spy and proclaims that Allah is God and Muhammad is his messenger, may peace be upon him; then I shall indeed kill him in a very painful way. He must renounce that Jesus is the Son of God in front of me, or he dies."

"Uncle," Abu said, "I cannot believe that Mark is working with the CIA. He is a man of peace."

"As I said, you are blinded."

"That may be, but how can you force him to reject his beliefs? Does not the *Qur'an* say there is no compulsion in religion, and we are to respect the people of the book?"

"Do not quote the holy words to me." Sa'id gritted his teeth. "Taylor does not deserve any considerations. He is an infidel. He has blasphemed our religion and joined other gods with Allah. How can you defend him, nephew?"

"Because I know him." Abu looked down, not able to meet Sa'id's dark gaze.

"You don't know him. . . ." Sa'id voice trembled. He was interrupted by a knock on the door as one of Sa'id's men stuck his head into the room.

"Al-Jazeera is reporting that the man with Taylor is not Chad Moreland."

The cramping in Mark's legs had gone way beyond unbearable. Not being able to simply scratch his cheek or stretch his arms could drive him crazy, but to be forced to keep his legs bent back at such a severe angle or risk choking himself to death was pure torture.

When the terrorists had left the room, Chuck had positioned his body at Mark's feet and leaned his weight against Mark's knees and slightly over onto his shins, allowing Mark to relax his muscles without causing the wire to tighten around his neck. But as time wore on, all Mark could think about was straightening his legs and relieving the cramping.

"Hang in there, buddy," Chuck encouraged. "I know it's tough."

Mark just grunted in return.

Outside the door, they could hear excited voices approaching. Within seconds, the door to their room was unlocked, and four terrorists burst into the room. They kept speaking in Arabic as they roughly pulled Chuck away from Mark, then kicked him in the stomach several times.

"What is your name?" Mark could hear shouted in accented English. "Who are you?"

The questions were useless since they did not allow Chuck to answer as the beating continued.

"Stop!" Mark cried out but was quickly silenced when a boot came his direction. The blow caused Mark to involuntarily straighten his legs, and he immediately felt the wire cutting off his breath. He concentrated and, though it was excruciating, brought his ankles back behind him, sucking in the oxygen as he watched the men drag Chuck out of the room. His heart broke for his friend. What had he gotten him into? First Ross, now Chuck. Mark didn't have the right to put their lives in danger. He was so sure God had intended for him to go along with the CIA's plan. How could it turn out this way? How could he have been so wrong?

TURKEY AIR BASE, DIYARBAKIR, TURKEY
10:00 A.M.

"You haven't come up with anything yet?" Jack asked Wendy over his secure satellite phone. It was frustrating to be so far away and not back at Langley in the middle of the hunt.

"Not yet. Sorry, Jack," Wendy answered. "I think the most likely camp they've taken him to is Tall Hamis in northern Syria, almost equidistant between Turkey and Iraq, up in the northern tip. They could have transferred him over the border during the storm in plenty of time before our eyes were back on them. We've got real-time twenty-four-hour satellite surveillance on that camp and two others, as well as constant sweeps of southern Turkey. If any of those places show a disruption in normal activity, I'll call you immediately."

"Do that."

"Mrs. Taylor wants to speak with you," Wendy said.

"I'll bet she does."

"Seriously, Mark was able to send her a message." Wendy went on to describe what Tracy had told her.

"That's interesting. I'll give her a call when we're through," Jack promised.

"How long are you staying there?"

"I'm not sure. Until I know for sure that we can trust Ross."

"So you got him on board?"

"Yeah, he wasn't sure until the picture of Taylor came over the TV. I think that swayed him."

"I'm glad something did."

"What about the local threat?" Jack asked. "Where does Homeland Security stand?"

"As far as we know, they've issued a red alert, calling it highly likely terrorists will attack on Sunday, but they didn't specify any targets. Or churches," Wendy answered.

Jack was livid. "Are they crazy? Do they just want thousands more Americans to die today?"

"Maybe they thought it would cause too much of a panic or cause violence against Arabs; I don't know. It doesn't make sense to me."

"Idiots—they have to realize Sa'id doesn't act with one target in mind." Jack swore. Sometimes he just couldn't figure out the mind of a bureaucrat. "I need to get the director on this one."

"There's no time left," Wendy added. "It's already three in the morning here. Services begin on the East Coast in five hours."

"Wendy, I hope we're wrong about this one."

"Me too, Jack," Wendy sighed. "Me too."

VAN NUYS, CALIFORNIA
12:14 A.M.

"We have to do something." Johara paced nervously in the bedroom. Ramsi had just gotten off the phone with Sofian's family. He was home, but Fazul wasn't there. Ramsi had pushed hard on the boy, trying to get him to tell him where Ishmael lived. At first the boy swore he didn't know, but when Ramsi demanded his father get on the line with them, Sofian finally came around and gave him directions to an apartment in Reseda.

On top of that, Johara had turned on the television as *Saturday Night Live* was interrupted with a special bulletin about Homeland Security raising the terrorist alert level to red, meaning there was a serious probability of an attack on Sunday.

"What if he's part of that?" Johara pointed to the graphic on the screen.

"I'm going over there," Ramsi announced, pulling himself out of bed. "I can't let him get involved with this."

"Daddy, you can't," Akilah protested. "How are you going to stop them? If what you think about Ishmael is true, don't you think he'll have enough guns to stop you from getting Fazul?"

"She's right, Ramsi," Johara agreed. "Don't go."

"You just said we have to do something. . . ."

"I meant call the police," she said firmly.

"On our own son?" Ramsi questioned. "What chance do you think he'll have of making something of himself if he's arrested for sympathizing with terrorists?"

"And what future do you think he'll have if tomorrow he becomes a suicide bomber?"

"He wouldn't do that!" Ramsi cried.

"Just a few months ago, you didn't think he'd drop out of school and become a fanatic either!" Johara countered. "We can't let him do this!"

Ramsi held eye contact with his wife a few seconds, then glanced over at Akilah. "Do you agree?"

She nodded. "I think he's planning something, tonight."

Ramsi breathed deeply before reaching for the phone and dialing 911.

NORTHRIDGE, CALIFORNIA
12:18 A.M.

Tracy turned the television off; there was nothing new to report. Each station kept repeating the same story over and over—Mark's picture flashed on the screen every time. She had to let it go. Her friends had stayed and prayed with her until midnight, and their comfort had been welcome, but it got to the point where she really wanted to be alone.

She'd talked briefly with Jack Murphy. He'd called and apologized, identifying himself as someone with the State Department, always cautious that somebody could be listening. She told him about Mark's message of "I love you." He thought that was a great sign, showing that Mark was keeping his wits about him. Tracy felt that it was a good thing for Jack to be in Turkey, that much closer to Mark.

Now in Brenda's guest room with Shandy curled up on the bed next to her, *alone* felt very empty. Her mind was restless, alternating between visions of Mark being tortured, flashes of anger directed at God for allowing him to be captured, then brief moments of desperation that she would be raising their child by herself. How could life have changed so drastically in such a short time?

Brenda peeked her head in the doorway. "I saw your light on; you doing okay?"

Tracy looked up. "I don't know. . .I guess."

Brenda entered and sat on the edge of the bed, rubbing Shandy behind the ear. "Have you decided if you're going to go on TV?"

"I don't think so, Brenda," Tracy responded. "I know Frank said it might help Mark, but I don't think I can do it."

"I understand. I don't think I could either. You deserve your privacy."

"Brenda," Tracy said, "it's not just about privacy. I'm not very good at lying."

Brenda's eyes smiled with compassion. "I know."

"You know?"

Brenda nodded. "I wasn't sure until now, but the way you were acting, I kind of figured there was more going on than Mark just doing an interview. He was trying to help the CIA, wasn't he?"

"They came to us the night he was leaving. . . ." The story poured out of Tracy. . .and it felt good.

VAN NUYS, CALIFORNIA
12:20 A.M.

"Here's what we're going to do." Yusef sat on the floor of Ishmael's apartment. In front of him, Fazul and Ishmael listened intently. Yusef had led them through the ritual prayers during 'isha', the hour of darkness. He found it helpful when preparing his followers to come together invoking dua'—Allah's aid. He would also recite selected Surahs that would ignite the passions against the infidels. It set a strong spiritual bond between them. . .ensuring their total commitment. Fazul and Ishmael were primed and ready.

"This morning, what we are about to do will be repeated in major cities all across America. At precisely 8:30 our time, 11:30 in the East, the vengeance of Allah will strike at the very heart of the false religion of the infidels."

Fazul's eyes widened, anticipating Yusef's targets. "What are we going to hit?"

"All in good time." Yusef smiled. He liked his enthusiasm. "First things first. We have some final preparations to make over at the house in Reseda. We'll do our morning prayers there. Let's get moving."

NORTHERN SYRIA
11:21 A.M.

Mark was choking, yet there was no strength left in his legs to bring his ankles up toward his back to allow him to breathe. His thighs burned beyond belief, and the rope around his hands had left his wrists raw. He knew he couldn't hold out much longer. With all the determination he could gather, he drew his ankles back, loosening the noose enough to draw in several quick breaths, not realizing that blood was seeping from his neck where the wire had cut through his skin.

Then his legs gave out.

Once again, his supply of air was cut off. Mark tried not to panic. . .to accept his fate, praying for Christ to receive him.

The door opened. Or at least he thought it had. The room was growing darker. Mark wasn't sure what was happening around him. He perceived a hand on his legs, pulling his ankles up behind his back—loosening the wire, breaking the noose.

Mark coughed, sucking in a lungful of air. His legs straightened, sending a fire of pain from his thighs and calves. He looked up at the face of the man who freed him.

It was Abu.

"Thank God you came. . . ." Mark choked on the words.

Abu couldn't stand to look at his friend. He tried to ignore the image, suppress the compassion welling up inside him. "I have a message."

"Can I. . ." Mark struggled. ". . .water."

Abu nodded and turned away, stepping out of the room briefly before he returned with a small cup of water, pressing it to Mark's lips.

"You have managed to infuriate my uncle, Mark," Abu said. "I told you not to antagonize him."

"He's not an easy man. . .to get along with." The water felt like a taste of heaven. "That's twice you saved my life, Abu. Thank you."

Mark squirmed on the floor, wanting desperately to move his hands and feet freely. He looked up at Abu. "Can you untie my hands?"

"I cannot," Abu returned. "I'm sorry."

Mark nodded. It was worth a try. "What have they done with Chad?"

"What's his real name?" Abu asked.

"That is his real name. What's going on?"

"A report from Al-Jazeera. The *Newsweek* reporter Chad Moreland is on vacation in Hawaii. That man is not who you claimed him to be."

Mark chose not to deny it, praying quickly for God's hand to be on him. "You said you had a message for me from your uncle?"

"You have offended him greatly, my old friend. But he is offering to save your life." Abu studied Mark's face, wanting to analyze his reaction. "You must confess to being with the CIA."

Mark raised his eyebrows slightly. "That was evident the last time I was with him. And what else?"

Abu looked away. "You must also profess the *Shahādah*. Declare there is no god but Allah, and Muhammad is his messenger.

And Jesus was not the Son of God, but only a prophet."

Mark shook his head. *Could things get any worse?* "So in order to save my life, I must become a Muslim. Do you think that I will do this, Abu?"

"My fear is that you won't."

"It's not that I won't." Mark coughed again, the pain in his ribs as sharp as ever. He struggled to breathe; speaking made it worse, but he fought through it. "It's that I can't. Muhammad tried to claim fourteen hundred years ago that Allah was the same god that Abraham, Isaac, Jacob, and Jesus worshipped. But it's just not true. The God I serve is the same yesterday, today, and forever. He is just, but He's also compassionate and defined by love. As I told you before, when we refer to Him as the heavenly Father, that is a true image of the relationship He wants with those who follow Him through His Son. That's the kind of relationship I have with Him."

"I am beginning to understand," Abu said. "I've never seen anybody face death with as much peace as I witnessed with you. In a way, I envy you, Mark Taylor. From what I've seen, you have what I have been searching for all my life."

"You can have it too," Mark pleaded. He didn't know how he was able to continue balancing on the edge of consciousness, but he felt the presence of God infusing him with strength.

"No, I do not think so." Abu looked away. "We have come from different worlds, and we are on different paths. My path is set; I must follow it."

"Abu, Jesus came to show the one path we must all take. It is for you as well. It's even for your uncle if he would choose to follow it."

That startled Abu. "How could you say that, after what my uncle has done to you? If he is wrong, would not your God seek revenge?"

Mark smiled. "No, Abu. Sa'id would be welcomed in my Father's kingdom just as Paul was after killing the Christians of his day. That's where you are wrong about the nature of God. John said for all who receive Him, those who believe in the name of Jesus, they shall have the right to become sons of God. That includes me, you, and even your uncle."

"I can see that you have found your way, Mark." Abu's voice was painted with sadness. "But I'm afraid that path will cause your death."

"Perhaps. . ." Mark said. "But it won't be at the hands of your uncle. He is too late."

Abu was puzzled. "I do not understand."

"I died years ago, when I gave my life to Jesus. Paul said it this way: 'For me to live is Christ, and to die is gain.' "

"You amaze me, Mark Taylor. So there's no way I can convince you to take my uncle's offer?"

"No," Mark said, pausing with the heaviness of the moment. "Could I ask one favor of you?"

"What is that?"

"I would like to write a letter to my wife and have you make sure she gets it."

Abu nodded. "I will try, my friend."

VAN NUYS, CALIFORNIA
4:51 A.M.

Ramsi sat in his car a half-block away from Ishmael's apartment. He couldn't stay at home and wait. After calling 911, the police dispatcher asked him to hold, and he was connected to an FBI agent. He gave the man what little information he had, including the directions to Ishmael's apartment. The agent was gracious, but he wouldn't give Ramsi any clue as to what would be done.

So he sat, minutes away from the morning sun that added a glow to the Valley's haze, wondering if he'd done the right thing. He'd circled the apartment several times, spotting Fazul's car parked on the street around the corner from the apartment.

Then as if a switch had been pulled, the quiet street suddenly filled with life. Two dark vans marked with the letters FBI pulled up to the front of the complex from opposite directions, and the doors opened immediately as armed men dressed in black stormed out with barely a sound. The chaos seemed orchestrated as several held positions along the street while the rest headed inside the complex. Ramsi kept a sharp eye on it all, praying to Allah that Fazul would not be killed in the raid.

But when they got to Ishmael's unit and broke through the door, it was empty.

CHAPTER 33

Tracy lay in bed, her eyes wide open—as they'd been most of the night. Some sleep had come, but only in short, restless waves. Shandy was bugging her to go outside, indicating that it must be time to face the world. She pulled the covers back and dropped her feet onto the carpeted floor. Her stomach rolled but she was able to control it this time.

She slipped her robe on and headed downstairs. Shandy led her all the way to the back door.

"I'm surprised to see you up," Brenda said, standing over the toaster. "Would you like some coffee?"

"Please." Tracy opened the back door and Shandy bounded out, heading for the grass.

Brenda grabbed a mug from the cupboard. "Did you sleep at all?"

Tracy sat at the table, the morning edition of the *Los Angeles Times* spread around it. The headlines caught her attention. A picture of Mark and Chuck split the front page with a bold headline about Homeland Security raising terrorist threats to red alert—attack imminent. She turned her head away from Mark's gruesome picture.

"Not much," Tracy answered. "When I did fall asleep I'd wake up from some terrible dream. This all just seems like a nightmare to me anyway."

Tom walked into the kitchen. "Good morning, Tracy." He grabbed the front page and set it upside down away from her. "Sorry."

"Don't be." Tracy shrugged it off. "Where you going?"

"Church."

"I thought I'd stay home and be with you, Tracy," Brenda said, placing the coffee cup in front of Tracy. "Tom's ushering today."

"Thanks. I didn't even realize it was Sunday," Tracy said, then took a sip. "I think I'd like to go."

Brenda looked at her. "Are you sure?"

"Yeah." Tracy smiled. "I'll go crazy sitting around here."

Brenda nodded. "Then I guess we'll all go."

NORTHERN SYRIA
4:45 P.M.

Mark looked around the stark white room, trying to figure out what day it was. He didn't realize how disorienting it could be to stay in a room without windows for days, not having the sunlight and darkness to orient your internal clock.

He knew his strength was fading. He hadn't had enough rest or nourishment. The only sustenance he'd received was the few bites of rice from Abu, and that had been some time ago.

The lock on the door clicked. Mark looked up to see Sa'id walking through—this time dressed in sand-colored military fatigues.

"I understand you have declined my gracious offer to let you live," he said, walking up and standing over Mark.

Mark's throat was dry; he sensed he was dehydrating. His voice came out scratchy. "I'm sorry to disappoint you."

"No disappointment to me; the *Qur'an* predicts your foolishness. A dark veil covers your heart; your ears cannot hear."

Mark shrugged, then grimaced. Every movement brought pain.

"What have you done with Chad?"

"His death is imminent if he does not confess to being CIA."

"He's not CIA. Neither of us are. You have to believe. . ."

"Lies." Sa'id's brow furrowed. "But you will pay, as your country is about to pay again for its sins."

"What do you mean?" Mark asked.

Sa'id smiled and sat on the floor in front of him. "I guess it won't hurt for you to know. In a matter of hours, thousands more American infidels who believe as you do will die as they worship their false god, then face eternity as they realize their error. It is too late for them. It is not for you."

Mark could see the joy spreading across Sa'id's face as he unveiled his plan. The evil was palpable.

"You're going to kill thousands of Christians?"

"Does that surprise you?" Sa'id smirked. "First the Saturday people, then the Sunday ones."

"What have you done?" Mark looked directly into the black, lifeless eyes.

"What needs to be done to unite Islam."

"America will retaliate."

"I need them to." Sa'id laughed. "It has taken your president longer than I thought. I grow impatient."

"How will the destruction of Syria work to your advantage?"

"By uniting Arabia and eventually every Muslim around the world. Any action your country takes will bring condemnation from around the globe. The Great Satan cannot stand against one billion Muslims. The Christian West will fall."

Mark shook his head. "How can you order the killing of innocent women and children? The Koran. . ."

"Don't speak to me about the *Qur'an*," Sa'id shouted. "Islam is at war—against the children of pigs and the Christian West. You support Israel; you defile our most holy land of Mecca. Americans are not innocent in this. They must be killed to achieve peace."

"God's kingdom isn't about political strength, forcing people into religious obedience and killing those that disagree with you," Mark said softly. "You believe Jesus was a prophet; listen to His words. He said the greatest commandment was to love God with all your heart, then to love others, even your enemies. Not kill them."

"You speak ignorance. You don't understand Islam."

"I understand that this must stop," Mark pleaded. "Killing thousands more Americans will only result in many more thousands of Arabs dying. Doesn't that bother you?"

"Does it bother me when young Palestinians give their lives in their struggle? Will it bother me if more American bombs kill thousands of Arabs because of my plans? Sure!" Sa'id admitted. "But the suicide bombers from Hamas and Hezbollah have achieved the world's sympathy for the Palestinian cause with their sacrifices. The brave Muslims who became martyrs in what you call the Sunday Massacre have brought the Muslim world a step closer together. They will be rewarded for their sacrifice. And when the attack comes from your mighty military—and I'm hoping it will come soon—then we take one more step.

"You see, Taylor, when terrorism is the only weapon we have, it must be used, because it works. The world is responding. I can achieve the will of Allah by using this weapon on a global scale."

Mark started to argue, but Sa'id's hand shot up in front of his face. "With each sacrifice, we are nearing the final goal—the Muslim world uniting, transcending national boundaries, and ushering in *dār al-Islām,* the world at peace."

Mark stared directly at Sa'id. "There will be no peace until the Prince of Peace, Jesus Christ, returns to this earth. Even the Koran speaks about it."

"Silence," Sa'id commanded, rising to his feet. "I will not listen to any more of your lies. You are a pawn in my game of chess, Taylor. When you cease to be useful to me, you will die by my hand."

He bent down, the evil emanating from him as he came within inches of Mark's face. "You claim Allah is dead and not the one true God. I have decided that you must live through this day—not because I don't have the power of death over you—but because I want you to see for yourself that your God will not be able to save those who call upon the name of Jesus. Then you will know the truth before you die, and Allah will be praised!" Sa'id smiled, the darkness in his eyes like a bottomless pit. "The time comes. We'll see who is the one true god!"

He turned and walked out the door, leaving Mark alone with his thoughts.

RESEDA, CALIFORNIA
7:05 A.M.

Even in the cool January morning, the sweat dripped off Fazul's forehead as he watched Yusef work inside the rented panel van. He was attaching the wires from a digital timer he'd placed in the front seat to a blasting cap that was sitting on top of their explosive mixture stored in the barrels.

Fazul had no idea how volatile the mush of crushed-up ammonium nitrate and diesel fuel would be, but watching Yusef work around the barrels made him very nervous.

"Will it be safe to drive?" Fazul asked.

Yusef wrapped the last wire with black electrical tape and backed out of the van. "Nothing will happen until you set the timer. Do not worry."

Fazul nodded. They'd spent the rest of the night mixing the final ingredients of the homemade bombs, then loading four barrels into each of the three rented vans that Yusef had brought to the house. They had stopped to pray in the glow of the predawn light, when Yusef had once again recited heroic passages from the

Qur'an. Fazul still didn't know the full plan, but he had a feeling that was about to change.

"Okay, here's what's going on. We don't have much time, so listen carefully. Each of us has to get to a different part of the city." Yusef handed Fazul and Ishmael each a piece of paper with directions on it.

"Your mission is to drive these vans as close to the buildings as you can. The timers are already set. Make sure you park just before the digital clocks hit twelve."

Fazul's stomach dropped. In his wildest imagination, he didn't think he had agreed to sacrifice his life. Sure, there was the chance that they might get caught—and that was okay; it added to the thrill. But this wasn't Palestine. He wasn't ready for that kind of commitment.

Yusef noticed the look on Fazul's face. "What's wrong, Fazul?"

"I. . ." He didn't know what to say. "I didn't know you were planning suicide missions."

Yusef's eyes widened, then he looked over at Ishmael, and the two started laughing.

"What?" Fazul asked, embarrassed by their reaction.

"We don't want you to die today, Fazul. You're too valuable to the cause. Allah is not asking that of you—yet. But your willingness shows your great devotion."

Relief flooded over Fazul. "Then how. . . ?"

Yusef smiled. "All you have to do is park close to your target. The bomb will do the rest. Just get out of there before the timer hits twelve. You'll be able to get away in all the confusion. Then take a bus back here, and we'll celebrate the victory of Allah!"

"Okay." Fazul laughed with them, relieved. "I can do that."

"We have not been called to the ultimate sacrifice as our Muslim brothers in the Middle East. We need to be able to strike again and again. So be careful. Do not get caught."

Fazul nodded. Ishmael acted like he'd been through this before.

"What are the targets?" Fazul asked.

"Three churches," Yusef informed him. "They're all big. I've got a Catholic one in Burbank, Ishmael has a Presbyterian one in Hollywood, and you've got the Church of the Cross, in Van Nuys. It's time to hit it."

CHURCH OF THE CROSS, VAN NUYS, CALIFORNIA
8:12 A.M.

Tracy sat toward the back in what the Church of the Cross referred to as their East Campus. Over the years, the attendance had risen so that they'd had to purchase a former Baptist church across the street from their original building, and they ran services out of both sanctuaries.

The music touched her deeply. There was something about standing in a gathering of other believers and singing praises to the Lord that could not be duplicated. As the Bible promised, where two or three are gathered together, Jesus would be in their midst. Tracy let loose of the fear and dread for a few minutes as she centered her thoughts on her Savior.

Outside, the streets were calm. A few latecomers were scrambling for parking places down the street and walking briskly up to the sanctuary. Fazul pulled out slowly from the main cross street, passing a few of the stragglers. . .imagining that they would be dead in the next few minutes. It was an eerie feeling. He drove around the block a few times, trying to decide the best location to leave the van to get as close to the building as possible. He decided to use the side street on Rockland, estimating that if he parked along the curb the van would be fifteen feet from the wall of the church. If nobody was watching, he might even jump across the sidewalk and leave the van parked in the flower bed. He went around the block one last time, then parked a block away, waiting for the right time to pull up to the perfect spot.

NORTHERN SYRIA
6:12 P.M.

From the instant Sa'id left the room, Mark spent the time praying earnestly. He couldn't imagine the devastation to his country and the innocent loss of life if they bombed churches across the nation. He thought of his brothers and sisters in Christ worshipping peacefully, only to be torn apart by the explosive evil. The image disturbed him greatly, yet the same types of attacks were happening to Christians around the world. America had just been spared—until now.

God, don't let it happen today.

Abu entered the room, walking quickly up to Mark. There was a different expression on his face; he was tense, nervous. He bent over the back of Mark and started working on the ropes that had kept his hands tied together since his arrival.

"What's going on?"

"You must leave. The attacks are about to begin, and my uncle will be distracted."

"American churches?"

Abu nodded as he pulled the fabric off Mark's legs. "Dozens of them."

From what Sa'id had said, Mark was afraid that was the case. "We've got to stop it, Abu."

"It is too late."

Mark's hands were free. The pain was intense as blood flowed once again through his veins. "You're helping me escape?"

Abu looked at him darkly. "I'm not sure how far you can get, but at least you'll have a better chance of surviving in the desert than here with my uncle."

Abu sat on the floor next to Mark and began taking off his boots. "You'll need these."

"Why are you doing this?" Mark grimaced as he reached for the first boot.

"You are my friend. I could not sit by and watch this happen to you any longer."

"I wish Sa'id felt the same way."

"If he knew you like I have come to, maybe he would." Abu pulled his other boot off, then looked intently into Mark's eyes. "You have touched me beyond measure, Mark. It has made me look at what you believe differently."

The words surprised Mark. "I hope it will lead you to the truth, Abu. . . ."

Abu nodded and a slight smile creased his lips. "We do not have time for another of our discussions. You must go."

"What about Chad?" Mark asked as he struggled to stand. His legs wanted to collapse, but he pushed himself, forcing them to hold his weight as his face turned a bright crimson.

"He is in another room. You must leave while you have the chance."

"I'm not leaving without him."

Abu could see the determination in Mark's eyes. "Then you will get us both killed."

"Tell me where he is, please. You've done more than enough. Just point me in the right direction."

VAN NUYS, CALIFORNIA
8:20 A.M.

Fazul looked at his watch—ten minutes to go. He felt sick to his stomach, and sweat soaked his body. The street had quieted down.

Only a couple of stragglers were left, running into the church building. People were starting to gather across the street on the West Campus in preparation for the second service. Fazul wasn't sure if he could go through with it. He was crossing a line that he had never imagined he would cross.

He began to recite, *"Allāhu akbar! Allāhu akbar! Allāhu akbar!"* hoping to steel his nerves and prepare himself to follow Allah's will.

His cell phone rang and he jumped. He'd forgotten he even had it with him. He pulled the phone out of his pocket and looked at the display—it was from home. He hesitated as it rang again. . . and again until he finally punched "talk."

"Hello."

"Fazul, it's Akilah. . .are you okay?"

"I'm fine." Fazul sighed with relief. He welcomed the diversion, thrilled that it wasn't his dad. "Why are you calling?"

"I was worried about you. You were talking weird last night, and I was afraid you were doing something. . .crazy."

"No." Fazul laughed, sitting there in front of a busy church in a van loaded with explosives. "I'm just hanging out with Sofian."

"I'm glad to hear that. You don't know how you scared me."

"I'm okay. Look, I'm in the middle of something; I've got to go. . . ."

"No, wait," Akilah said urgently. Beside her, the FBI technician was signaling to her with his hand circling, letting her know she needed to keep Fazul talking as they triangulated the cell signal.

"It's about Dad. . ." She thought quickly. "He called Sofian's house last night. . . ."

Fazul's interest was piqued as he stayed on the phone, glancing at the electronic display. He had a few minutes.

NORTHERN SYRIA
6:20 P.M.

Sa'id's top lieutenants were gathered in the building next to the one holding Mark and Chuck, watching the satellite feed from CNN in eager anticipation of the live news coverage from across the world. It worked to Mark's advantage. The hallway was empty as he stumbled along, touching the wall for support.

"Hurry, your friend is in there." Abu pointed to a door across the hall.

"Thank you, Abu, I won't forget this."

"And I won't forget you."

They were interrupted by voices coming around the corner.

"Quick! Inside," Abu ordered. They lunged into Chuck's room. The quick movement sent waves of pain throughout Mark's body, but he ignored it when he saw his friend.

Chuck was unconscious, lying in the corner, his face bloodied and swollen, his hands and feet tied as Mark's had been. They had really worked him over. Mark knelt beside him, first checking for a pulse along his neck; then he gently slapped his face. "Chuck, come on. I need you, buddy."

Abu smiled thinly at Mark. "I knew his name wasn't Chad Moreland."

"It's Chuck Fleming," Mark whispered as Chuck moaned. "He's not CIA, just a friend. He was in my unit at Al Najaf. You saved his life as well as mine."

Abu shook his head. "You continue to amaze me, Mark. I should have recognized him."

Chuck came to slowly. Mark coaxed him along, checking him over to see if he could travel. "Come on, Chuck. We've got one chance to get out of here."

"I'm with you." Chuck's eyes finally focused.

Mark helped Chuck to his feet, then looked around the room.

It was the one they'd brought him to when Sa'id had interrogated him. Still sitting in the corner was the camera they'd used. Mark walked over to it and hit the eject button, smiling when the digital tape popped out.

Mark grabbed it and turned to Abu. "Where are we?"

Abu looked behind him at the closed door, unsure how much he should help his old friend. "We're in Syria, at our northernmost training camp outside Tall Hamis. Al Qamishli is forty kilometers northwest, on the Turkish border. Iraq is thirty kilometers in the opposite direction."

Mark nodded. They were in the middle of nowhere, seriously injured and malnourished. He didn't like their odds, but it was better than staying.

"Which direction is Turkey?"

Abu pointed behind him. "When you leave this building, turn right and you'll be facing west. Head in a northwesterly direction and you'll find the Turkish border."

"Any fence around the compound?" Chuck asked.

Abu shook his head. "There's no reason for it out here."

"Abu, you went with us once. . . ," Mark pleaded. "Come with us again."

"No, my place is here. Perhaps I can reach my uncle."

Mark didn't think that was possible, but he nodded. "I understand. I pray you are successful."

"What day is it?" Chuck asked.

"Sunday, just after nightfall," Abu answered.

"That means back home. . ." Mark realized.

"It's Sunday morning," Abu confirmed. "The attacks have begun."

CHAPTER 39

"All units. . .code four twenty-two." The radio in the police cruiser broke through the peaceful Sunday morning silence as Officers Charlotte McBride and Craig Tenant cruised through the heart of the San Fernando Valley. "Possible terrorist attack, corner of Van Nuys and Rockland. Handle code three."

Officer McBride looked over at her partner. "We're close. Punch it, Craig."

He turned on the lights and siren as he negotiated a tight U-turn in the middle of the street.

She picked up the microphone and keyed the switch. "Nine Adam Eighteen responding, ETA two minutes."

"Roger, Nine Adam Eighteen; be advised FBI has units responding as well. Looking for Arab suspect, name Fazul Habash; photo will be up on computer screen in a second. Be advised target believed to be Church of the Cross."

"Roger that," McBride replied, looking over at Tenant. "Let's roll, partner!"

Less than a mile away, Tracy sat down in the pew, wiping away the tears that had collected in her eyes. The first part of the service had been wonderful, as the music seemed to numb the pain. But as the worship service continued, Tracy began to feel the presence of God settling sweetly over her. The fear for Mark's life was still present—actually, it was more urgent. She lowered her head into her hands, asking again and again for God to protect Mark.

Brenda noticed Tracy beside her and sat down as well, wrapping an arm around her shoulder and praying silently. The songs continued as the two friends prayed and cried together.

NORTHERN SYRIA
SAME TIME

Mark placed his ear to the door, listening for any movement in the hallway.

"Sounds clear." He turned to Abu. "We'll need to get Chuck some boots, and we'll need coats; otherwise we're going to freeze out there."

Abu shook his head. "There's no time. The guards will be back soon; you must leave. . . ."

He was interrupted by voices outside the door speaking Arabic.

"They're looking for me," Abu said.

Mark nodded toward the door with his head. Abu opened it and entered the hallway, answering their call. Mark would have given a month's pay to be able to understand the language behind the door. The words were unintelligible, but the inflection wasn't. Something was wrong; the exchange was heated. Chuck and Mark looked at each other, trying to decide what to do when the door suddenly burst in upon them.

Mark stepped back quickly. Flowing with the momentum of the terrorist rushing in, Mark rolled on his back and flipped the man over. Forcing his body to move through the pain, Mark twisted to his side and drove his elbow deep into the man's throat. A second terrorist came through the door, an AK-47 in his hand, lifting the barrel up toward him. The terrorist didn't see Chuck standing beside the doorway, or the fist that crashed against his temple. The man dropped straight down, unconscious.

Abu entered the room. "You must get out of here—quickly."

"In just a second," Chuck said, unstrapping the boots of the terrorist on the floor next to him. Fortunately the two guards were wearing fatigues, so Mark quickly took the jacket of the one closest to him while Chuck was putting on the boots and collecting the other guard's weapon and ammunition. Mark placed the digital tape in the top pocket, then grabbed the guard's AK-47 and looked up at his friend. "Thanks, Abu. I hope we meet again."

"Me too," Abu said. "Now hit me."

"What?"

"Knock me out. It can't look like I helped you or my uncle will kill me."

"He's right, Mark," Chuck said.

"I don't want to hit him," Mark responded. "You hit him."

VAN NUYS, CALIFORNIA
8:27 A.M.

Fazul waited anxiously, the van still running with the gearshift in park. After getting off the phone with Akilah, he'd struggled with completing his assignment. It wasn't too late to just walk away from the car, but how could he ever return to the mosque? How could he live with himself and continue his commitment to Islam? He tucked the cell phone back in his pocket, grabbing the steering wheel with determination.

He glanced at the digital display of the timer in the passenger seat—three minutes to go. It was time.

He pulled out onto Rockland into the oncoming traffic. A car had to change lanes behind him, honking as it sped by. Fazul kept his eyes on the spot up ahead that he'd picked to park the van when the sound of an approaching siren cut through the early morning quiet.

With lights flashing, the officers approached the church from the north on Van Nuys. Charlotte McBride was looking every direction as they drew near. When the buildings cleared her view of Rockland Street to her right, the sight of a paneled van driving slowly toward the church caught her attention. She reacted instantly.

"Craig," she yelled to her partner, pointing toward the slow-moving vehicle. "The van—get in front of it!"

Craig turned the wheel sharply to the right, putting the patrol car into a skid.

Fazul looked up in shock at the police cruiser aimed directly at him. He panicked and slammed his foot on the accelerator. The van shot forward; Fazul swerved in an attempt to miss the police car, but he couldn't turn in time.

The vehicles met with a devastating impact. Office McBride tried to brace for it as the van crashed into her side of the car. The sound of crunching metal and screeching tires filled the intersection. Then there was a deathly silence.

Officer Tenant opened his door, grabbing hold of McBride and pulling her toward him. She screamed in pain; the impact had broken her right arm and leg. It didn't deter him as he swept her up in his arms and pulled her out of the car, laying her on the pavement before quickly pulling out his gun and taking aim at the unconscious driver slumped over the steering wheel of the van.

"Police!" he yelled, seeing if the suspect would respond. He didn't move, so Tenant approached the van. Keeping his gun ready, he looked inside the window. He nearly fired when the man fell back against the seat, his head hanging limply to the side as a moan escaped his lips. Then Tenant saw it—the timer with the red glowing display flashing—11:59.

He turned and screamed at the top of his lungs, "Bomb! Clear the area!" The sight of the officer pulling out his gun had been enough to keep the concerned people from the church out of the intersection; the word "bomb" made them scatter.

Tenant returned to his partner, scooped her up, and broke into a dead run. They got twenty feet before the van exploded. The shock wave from the blast picked them up off the ground and threw them another ten feet before smacking them to the grass in front of the church.

All the windows in the lobby shattered. Several church members on the corner were slammed hard to the cement, the fireball causing second- and third-degree burns to many of them.

The concussion rocked the building, and the sound of the explosion stopped the service dead in its tracks. The lights went out and the sound system shut down as the associate pastor was giving announcements. There was a moment of stunned silence. Most of the congregation thought they were in the middle of an earthquake. Tracy looked up in shock, not knowing what to do as her prayer time for Mark was shattered. Tom gathered Brenda and Tracy under his arms and pulled them to the floor between the pews as the building continued to shake.

Screams began to cut through the eerie silence outside the church as a hunk of metal that had once been the van burned in the middle of the intersection. The front lobby was destroyed; broken glass and bricks were thrown everywhere. Officer McBride regained consciousness, calling out to her partner to get off her. The pain was excruciating as he lay over her broken leg.

Officer Tenant groaned as he came to, then rolled to the side. They were alive. People began running to the aid of the injured as sirens wailed in the distance.

Fazul was vaporized in the blast; his last conscious thought on this earth was how he'd failed. His next conscious realization was how wrong he'd been—and that the promise of seventy virgins in paradise was a complete lie.

NORTHERN SYRIA
SAME TIME

"Last chance," Mark pleaded with Abu. "You sure you won't come with us? This isn't the life for you."

Abu shook his head, and a determined look came over his face. "It is all I have."

Mark understood.

"Would one of you just get it over with?" Abu urged. "They'll miss the guards soon."

Mark nodded and looked over at Chuck. "Please. . ."

Chuck sighed, then brought his arm back with his fist clenched when the door behind him opened and in walked one of the terrorists. He must have heard their voices, because his gun was already drawn and ready to fire. Mark made a move for his arm just as the 9mm discharged. He could nearly feel the bullet as it passed by, missing him by millimeters. Mark knocked the gun out of the guard's hands, punched him in the stomach, and when he doubled over, followed it with a knee in his face—smashing his nose and dropping him out cold in the doorway. Chuck held the AK-47 he'd taken from the previous guard and looked out into the hallway. Clear for now, but the loud gunshot had suddenly made the terrorists' pursuit that much more imminent.

Then Mark heard the unmistakable sound of a man struggling to breathe while his lungs filled with blood. He'd heard that gurgling noise before. . .and never forgot it. Mark whipped around. Abu had collapsed against the wall; a bright spot of red was growing on the front of his robe.

"No!" Mark exclaimed, kneeling beside his friend. "Abu. . ."

"We've got to go, Mark," Chuck called from the doorway. "Now!"

Mark reached out and held Abu's head off the floor. His eyes were wide in shock, his breathing labored. . .the sound haunted Mark.

"That peace you had. . ." Abu choked, struggling to get the words out, "when facing death. I want that. . . ."

"Mark. . . ," Chuck called. "We don't have time for this."

Mark glanced over his shoulder. "I know, hold on." Then he turned back to Abu. "You know where to find it, Abu. . . ."

Abu coughed, blood dripped out of his mouth, and his eyes were dilating. "I. . .want. . .to. . .believe. . . ."

Mark looked into his eyes, begging God to let him hang on.

"Jesus. . . ," Abu whispered just before his eyes glazed over totally and his final breath wheezed out of him.

Mark fought back the tears. There would be time for that later. He reached out and closed Abu's lifeless eyes, laying Abu's head back on the dirt floor. Mark wouldn't know about Abu for sure until his own death. But he prayed Abu's last breath had saved him and one day they would be reunited.

A loud burst from Chuck's AK-47 snapped Mark back to the present. He'd better move or he'd be joining Abu shortly. Mark got up and rushed to the door.

"How many?"

"I saw two. I think I hit the lead guy. The other one is outside behind the door."

"Okay."

"Decision time." Chuck smiled. "Do we try and take Sa'id out or make a break for it?"

Anger flashed in Mark's eyes. "Right now I'd like to find him and tear his head off—with Abu gone, we're probably as good as dead here anyway."

Chuck didn't question; he just turned toward the door. "Then let's do it."

Mark took one last look at Abu, silently saying good-bye to his friend, wanting to make Sa'id pay for his senseless death. He turned back to Chuck and nodded.

Chuck leaned outside the doorway, spraying a quick burst

where the men had appeared as Mark moved as fast as he could down the hallway in the opposite direction.

VAN NUYS, CALIFORNIA
SAME TIME

Tracy stepped outside the church, amazed at the damage to the building that had been in pristine condition just moments before. The ushers had evacuated the congregation through the back doors, away from the damaged lobby. When she came around the side of the building and saw the devastation and the flaming mass in the middle of the intersection, she gasped in shock. There were two ambulances on-site already, along with an FBI van and a dozen police vehicles. The news vans were just arriving, and overhead three helicopters hovered directly above the church. The scene looked like a scene from Jerusalem after another suicide bomber. . . . It was almost impossible to believe it was here in California.

What a transformation, from peaceful early morning church service to a war zone in a matter of seconds. Tracy closed her eyes in appreciation of God's protection and continued the prayer that He would miraculously take care of Mark as well.

Across the nation, what had been meant to be a catastrophic blow to the country had failed. The FBI had identified hundreds of churches that fit the pattern planned in New York, Los Angeles, San Francisco, Seattle, Chicago, Dallas, Denver, Baltimore, and Philadelphia. Each major city had deployed their entire law enforcement community. Every police officer, sheriff, deputy, and FBI agent was on duty, stationed outside those churches that fit the criteria of a potential target.

Sa'id's plan had also been smaller in scope than feared. The only targeted cities were Los Angeles, New York, Chicago, Washington, D.C., and Atlanta—three churches in each of the cities—in the areas where the Jihad al Sharia had its strongest cells. But because of the dragnet surrounding the high-profile churches, only one van other than the Van Nuys attempt got through—St. Mary's Catholic Church in Washington, D.C. And the explosives in that van were wired by an amateur, causing it to fail to explode when the timer hit twelve. In Atlanta, one van exploded in the street when police shot the driver to keep him from getting close to the church. Knowing what to expect, the officers there escaped with minimal injuries. The terrorist was dead before the van exploded.

In Los Angeles, both Ishmael and Yusef were arrested and their timers deactivated before the explosives went off. The Church of the Cross had not been on the FBI's list of potential targets, which was the reason Fazul got as close as he did.

"I don't believe this," Brenda said, standing beside Tracy as they surveyed the damage.

"There's no way we would have survived if that van had been next to the building," Tom said, looking toward the church and estimating where their seats had been.

Tracy couldn't speak; it was too much to take in. She couldn't fathom the evil and hatred that had to be behind something so heinous. After 9/11 and the Sunday Massacre, it had been a psychological exercise to comprehend such evil; now it grabbed hold of her deepest emotions and threatened to rip her apart. Adding to her terror was the fact that they were the same people in control of her husband's life.

"Are you okay, Tracy?" Tom interrupted her thoughts.

"Yeah. Just trying to understand what kind of sick person could do this kind of thing to innocent men, women, and children."

A group of church members stood along the side of the building and began to pray. In the midst of the sirens and emergency workers attending to the injured, the news crews began feeding live reports back to their studios.

"We'd better get you out of here, Tracy," Tom offered.

The three turned around, heading to the parking lot. They passed a news crew taping reactions of those who had been in the service. Tracy didn't notice the intense stare the female reporter gave her as she walked by.

Christine Jensen, a CNN field reporter, tapped her cameraman's shoulder, effectively cutting off an interview.

"I think Tracy Taylor just walked by," she said quietly, not wanting to alert a rival news station.

"You're kidding. Are you sure?"

"Of course I'm sure. We spent all night outside her house, didn't we? Come on, let's go!" she ordered, taking off after Tracy without a look back.

CHAPTER 35

Flying down the narrow hallway as fast as he could with the burning pain in his legs and side, Mark couldn't see what was around the corner. The hallway came to a T with a door straight ahead that was cracked open slightly. The exit would be to either his right or his left—maybe both. When he was just three strides away from the hallway's end, Mark saw the muzzle of an AK-47 coming around the corner to his right. Without thinking, he sprang into the air, firing a quick burst from his gun as he sailed by the terrorist.

His shoulder crashed into the door, sending it slamming against the wall inside. Mark tucked and rolled into the empty room. He came up with the AK-47 ready to fire as Chuck limped toward him. Mark looked back to where the terrorist had been. The man was lying on the floor, a puddle of blood growing underneath him. An uneasy feeling flooded Mark, but he couldn't dwell on it. He looked beyond the terrorist and saw a door that led outside.

"Let's go," Chuck shouted, arriving next to him.

Mark's head spun for a second from the impact, but he shook it off, getting up to head toward the door when a flash of white next to him caught his attention. He turned and noticed the robe that Sa'id had worn in the first interview along with the gold braided rope lying over a chair next to a desk. On top of the desk was a laptop computer.

"Hold on, Chuck," Mark said, moving quickly. "Cover us

for a few seconds."

"Are you crazy? They're going to have us surrounded!"

Chuck fired a quick burst from his AK-47, hoping to keep the pursuit from down the hallway at bay. Using his bloodied hands, Mark unplugged the cables connected to the back of the PC, then closed it up and placed it in a bag sitting beside the desk. Throwing the bundle over his shoulder, he readied his weapon and stepped back into the hallway.

A head appeared in the window of the outside door, and Mark sent a quick burst of lead in that direction, shattering the glass. They could hear yelling in Arabic from the other side of the door.

"That way!" Mark yelled at Chuck, pointing toward the opposite door, hoping it would free them from the building. Mark fired once more behind them, then turned and ran.

Chuck rushed to the door, pausing just long enough to throw it open and scan the area for guards. Shots rang out as bullets flew around him. Chuck's expert aim hit the two areas where the muzzle flashes had come from, and the immediate threat was eliminated.

They ran out the door into the darkness, hoping they'd get away before they encountered any more terrorists. Running through the empty compound, Mark was thrilled it was dark and was thankful for his marine training as he found somewhere deep within him the will to continue running despite the intense pain that was coursing through his body.

"Keep going!" Mark called out beside Chuck. They were nearing the last building when suddenly the compound was bathed in light, giving them the first look at the terrain immediately around them—desert, sand, and scrub brush. They were spotted and shots rang out, the dirt kicking up around their feet. Both ex-marines shot a burst behind them as they continued running, finally making it behind the last building and out of the floodlights.

Mark yanked his empty clip out of the machine gun as Chuck reloaded his AK-47 and handed Mark a new magazine.

"I don't think we have a chance to get near Sa'id," Chuck gasped through deep breaths.

Mark sent a quick spray of bullets toward their pursuers, hoping to hold them off a minute longer. "I agree. Staying here is a death trap." A couple more shots from his AK-47 and the two turned, running off into the desert toward what looked like rock-infested hills looming in the darkness.

CIA HEADQUARTERS, LANGLEY, VIRGINIA
SAME TIME

Wendy sat in the situation room with the team leaders of Operation Dumbo Drop. On the plasma screens in front of them were real-time satellite images of the three known terrorist training facilities that could possibly be holding Mark and Chuck. The center screen held a full-frame view of the Tall Hamis camp.

The team had been going around the clock since Friday when Mark's team had met with the terrorists. They were punchy, groggy, and had been working straight shifts to keep their eyes glued to that part of the world.

The satellite image on the center screen suddenly brightened. The compound was immersed in light.

"What's going on at Tall Hamis?" Wendy shouted.

"Floodlights," Phillip Nest, her cubicle partner, stated the obvious.

"I saw some flashes just before they came on, but I thought my eyes were playing tricks on me." Wendy stood up, staring at the screen. She turned back to Brad Faxon, their electronics expert, as she picked up her phone. "Brad, get me a playback of the last two minutes of Tall Hamis on screen three; keep the live feed on two. I'm going to get Jack on the phone."

NORTHERN SYRIA
SAME TIME

"Turn out the lights! Are you crazy?" Sa'id screamed in Arabic into his walkie-talkie. This should have been a crowning achievement for the movement, watching in glory the devastation of the West about to appear on his television screen. CNN was just breaking the story of a church bombing in Los Angeles. Sa'id knew there were about to be a dozen more such reports. He wanted to revel with his top lieutenants in the great victory for Allah. Why were his guards screaming and shooting in the compound and firing their weapons? Were they celebrating the victory of Allah? And what idiot turned on the security lights? They might as well have shot off a flare telling the American spy satellites where his camp was!

"Mustafa, get out there and find out what is going on!" Sa'id demanded.

As Mustafa ran from the room, Sa'id turned back to analyze the video from Los Angeles. There was a burned-out car in the middle of the street, not near enough to the church building where the devastation would have been much greater. He swore. This did not look like a great victory. Not enough people killed. He fidgeted in his seat, anxiously waiting for video footage from the other attacks.

The radio crackled back to him. "The prisoners have escaped, Caliph," Mustafa's voice cut into the room.

Sa'id swore. "Well, stop them without the floodlights! Turn them off now!"

The bright glow from outside the window ceased, and they were plunged back into darkness at his command. Bursts of gunfire could be heard coming from farther away as the chase ensued.

"We need to get you out of here immediately," Sa'id's top lieutenant spoke out.

Sa'id looked quickly back at the television set. A graphic crawled across the screen, reporting terrorist attacks across the nation stopped by FBI and police action. Sa'id lowered his head. Failure? Failure. *Failure!* His rage overwhelmed him as he knocked over chairs and kicked at walls.

"Caliph, you must leave, now. Your position is compromised."

Sa'id stood in the center of the room, looking at his subordinate darkly. "Get Abu and let's go."

One of the terrorists stuck his head in the room. "Caliph. . ."

"What?" Sa'id screamed.

"Abu is dead," he said.

"No!" Sa'id dropped to his knees. How was this possible? Abu was like his son. He couldn't lose him. "Kill the infidels! Kill the infidels!" Sa'id screamed over and over. His chief lieutenant came up to him and helped Sa'id to his feet.

"We must leave, Ahmad."

Sa'id stared him down. "Not until I see Abu!"

CIA HEADQUARTERS, LANGLEY, VIRGINIA
SAME TIME

"Jack, we've got a situation here," Wendy informed Jack through his satellite phone.

"I know—the church attacks; we're just getting word over here," Jack answered.

"No, Jack, it's not that. There's some activity at Tall Hamis, northern Syria." Wendy quickly filled Jack in on what they'd seen. "Hold on, Jack, the floodlights just went out."

Wendy looked over at Faxon, placing her hand over the phone. "Get the NRO to change the feed of Tall Hamis back to thermal, now!"

Faxon was already speaking to the National Reconnaissance Office in Chantilly, Virginia, on a direct communications link. He relayed Wendy's order.

"We're switching to thermal, Jack. There's something definitely going on. Floodlights came on for just a minute, then just got shut off again. We replayed the moments right before the lights came on and saw automatic weapons fire. I'd bet my life that's where Mark is. And possibly Sa'id."

"Understood," Jack said. "You may be right, but we need to know for sure. You got thermal yet?"

Wendy had her eye on the center plasma screen. "Hold on."

The middle screen changed from the dark image to a muddy green. "We've got it now, Jack. . .let me try and make sense of this."

She analyzed the screen. There were small green blobs moving about the compound in a frenzied motion. The images were like small, soft, glowing stick figures. The activity seemed to be focused toward the northwest end of the compound. She followed the trail of activity where two of the green blobs were running away.

"Looks to me like there's a pursuit going on. Two figures are escaping, heading in a northwestern direction."

"Any shot at an ID on them?"

"Not until morning."

"Keep tracking; don't lose them. I'm going to get permission to scramble a Force Recon team. And, Wendy?"

"Yes?"

"If any vehicle leaves that compound, don't lose it."

Wendy kept her eyes glued to the screen. Maybe this was their chance. "Understood, sir."

VAN NUYS, CALIFORNIA
SAME TIME

"Mrs. Taylor. . ." Before she could stop herself, Tracy turned around to see who was calling her name. She froze when she stared right into the lens of a camera as a microphone with a CNN logo clipped to it was jammed in front of her.

"Christine Jensen, CNN News," a voice confronted her from beside the camera. Tracy looked over at the young brunette with short-cropped hair and an irritating smile. "Do you have a comment about your husband, Mrs. Taylor? Was he working for the CIA as reported by Al-Jazeera?"

Tracy's eyes darted from Jensen to the camera and back. She was so emotionally upset, her first instinct was to lash out at the woman. People had been injured, an attempt to kill thousands had just been averted, and she wanted to know if Mark was CIA! Her pause allowed Tom to step in between them.

"Please." Tom held up his hand toward the camera. "Respect for Mrs. Taylor's privacy. This has been a nightmare for her. . . ." Tom looked up and saw that another camera crew had taken notice and was heading toward them. He turned around, tossing the keys to Brenda. "Get Tracy in the car, now."

He stood as a barrier on the sidewalk as Tracy and Brenda headed into the parking lot.

"Mrs. Taylor, the nation has a right to know!" Jensen called after her.

Tom continued to try to stay between the camera and Tracy as he glared at the reporter. "You people have no compassion, do you?" Then he turned and ran toward the car, the cameraman following right behind him.

NORTHERN SYRIA
SAME TIME

Mark gasped for breath, his ribs sending waves of pain that with each stride made him want to stop. But he refused, concentrating on just one more step, one more step.

There hadn't been any shots fired at them for a few minutes.

Perhaps they'd lost their pursuers. The terrain was difficult. Running through the dark over unfamiliar ground caused a lot of stumbles, each of which treated Mark's body to a fresh dose of pain.

He hoped Chuck was faring better. Mark wasn't sure what condition he was in after his beating. The moonless sky was their ally, but the blackness of the night made it difficult to navigate the uneven terrain. Up ahead was a rocky hill, but in the darkness they couldn't tell how far away it was. Mark plunged ahead, looking for a place to stop and assess the situation.

He crested a small mound just ahead of Chuck and stopped. "Hold on," Mark wheezed. They both hit the dirt, lying prone and looking back the direction they'd come. Nothing. Yet.

"What do you think we should do?" Mark asked Chuck, gasping for breath.

"Keep moving," Chuck panted. "They'll be coming, I'm sure."

"I agree, but we can't keep up the sprint. We're going to have to pace ourselves."

"What's the matter?" Chuck cracked with a grin. "Do we need to send you back to boot camp?"

"I'm holding my own," Mark responded. "Seriously, how are you feeling?"

"Bad. But I'm not stopping or I know I'll feel worse," Chuck said, taking a quick peek over the mound. "What was so important in that room?"

"Sa'id's computer." Mark smiled at him. "With any luck it will contain the names and locations of Jihad al Sharia cells around the world."

"That gives us another reason to find our way home."

"I'm with you on that."

"We need to find a way to call the cavalry," Chuck said.

Mark had been thinking the same thing. "Yeah, I agree. But first we've got to lose the terrorists."

"Then we'd better change directions."

"You're right." Mark thought for a second. "Abu said Turkey was to the northwest; let's go east for awhile. Might confuse them."

"Sounds good."

They looked at each other, neither knowing which direction that was.

Finally Chuck pointed to their right. "I think it's that way."

"Your guess is as good as mine," Mark said, and he headed in that direction.

VAN NUYS, CALIFORNIA
SAME TIME

By the time Tom got to the car, Brenda and Tracy were already inside and backing out of the parking spot. He jumped into the passenger's seat, and Brenda took off, leaving the cameraman running after them.

Tracy ducked in the back, hiding her face. Tom turned around behind them, spotting the reporter turning her back in disgust as two more camera crews tried to videotape their exit.

"You okay back there?" he asked Tracy.

"Yeah," Tracy returned. "Thanks for jumping in when you did. I almost said something that would not have been appropriate for the six o'clock news."

"I can't believe how cold they can be. . . ," Brenda remarked. "She didn't care a bit about you. Just her story."

"I know." Tracy sighed, but a smile creased her lips. "I'd probably hate all journalists after this if I weren't married to one."

Back near the intersection, Ramsi Habash stood in shock, staring at the devastation before him as his wife and daughter huddled together by his side. When the FBI had pinpointed Fazul's location, he had known he had to come. But never in his wildest imagination could he have believed Fazul would be involved in something like this.

"Could he have gotten away?" Johara asked through her tears.

"I don't know," Ramsi answered quietly. "Stay here."

He walked up to a police officer who was stretching the yellow tape across the intersection to keep control of the crime scene. They spoke for a few seconds. Ramsi came back to his family, shaking his head.

"No!" Fazul's mom cried out, falling to her knees. Akilah knelt down with her, holding her mom.

"How could he have done this?" Ramsi asked, but there was no answer. He shook his head, fighting back his own tears, allowing the anger to take hold instead. His fists clenched in rage. . .he wanted to lash out at someone, something. How could his son be taken away from him?

"He thought it was the will of Allah." Akilah tried to make sense of it all.

"Allah had nothing to do with this," Ramsi spat out.

The family held each other, trying to find comfort where none could be found.

One of the members of the church who had been praying beside the building noticed them. He tapped his wife, pointing to the distraught family huddled across the street. "Let's go see if there's something we can do for them."

They pulled away from the group and headed toward the Habash family.

CHAPTER 36

Sa'id looked down at the lifeless body of his nephew, and a mix of rage and sorrow filled his heart. America would pay for this. First Mark Taylor, then his entire country. He would come up with another plan to kill thousands, more if possible. It was Abu's idea to bring in the journalist, to wage a propaganda war within the United States by using their own media. Now it had brought about his death. How had the journalist gotten free?

The evidence was confusing, but now wasn't the time to figure it out. He reached out and gently placed his palm against Abu's cheek, offering a prayer that he believed would be received in paradise.

"I want the Americans found!" He swore at the men behind him.

"It will be done, Caliph," Mustafa answered.

Sa'id stood and turned away from Abu, thinking of ways to exact his revenge. His glorious hour was destroyed. The new wave of attacks was somehow stopped, the American prisoners were running free, and Abu was dead. They would pay.

"We are ready to leave." His lieutenant spoke.

"Get my computer and let's go!" Sa'id said and walked out of the room.

Mark and Chuck continued through the desert. Their pace slowed somewhat, knowing they'd be on the run for the indefinite future, but they still worked hard to put as much distance between them and the terrorist camp as they could.

Their own labored breathing was all they could hear until the faint sound of motorized vehicles could be heard. They were coming.

"We've got to find a place to hide!" Chuck said, scrambling up another small hill.

"Over there." Mark pointed to his right where a small mound of rocks could provide a hiding spot. Chuck nodded and they kept moving.

Looking out over the landscape, Mark spotted the headlights of the pursuing trucks. He estimated them to be just about where he and Chuck had decided to change course. He prayed they'd continue west and angle away from them.

The vehicles stopped and two beams of light swept over the darkness.

"Go the other way. . . ," Chuck urged them.

Then their engines roared back to life, one of the trucks continuing directly west, but the other vehicle turned and headed right for them.

"We can't outrun that," Mark stated.

"Then we'll have to change tactics," Chuck said as he analyzed the ground around them.

THE WHITE HOUSE, SITUATION ROOM
SAME TIME

With each report that came in from around the country, the spirits in the lower room of the White House complex soared. The Jihad al Sharia had failed, this time. What could have been a disastrous morning—linking this day with the likes of 9/11 and the Sunday Massacre—had been stopped. With the sighs of relief came sincere thanks to God from the Commander-in-Chief. But averting this disaster didn't fool those gathered in the room. This wasn't anything more than one more step in the War on Terror.

Jack's call was routed to the director of the CIA inside the room. "What have you got, Jack?" the director asked. As Jack began to report, the director stopped him. "Hold on, I'm going to put you on speakerphone. I think everyone will want to hear this."

The director punched a button on his phone, then introduced Jack to the group. "Ladies and gentlemen, Jack Murphy is on station in Turkey. You need to hear this. Jack, we're having the satellite feed punched up here as well; please continue."

"Mr. President, ladies and gentleman," Jack's voice cut through the room. "We believe we have a location on Mark Taylor."

"What have you got, Jack?" the president asked.

"If you've got the satellite image up. . ."

"We're seeing it," the CIA director confirmed.

"The thermal image shows two bodies on the run from Sa'id's training camp near Tall Hamis in northern Syria. Minutes ago, the entire camp went on alert. Their floodlights came on, shots were fired, and the two thermal images you now see escaped the area. They headed in a northwestern direction until moments ago when they altered their course to head northeast. We believe the two men are Mark Taylor and Chuck Fleming."

"Any proof?" the CIA director asked.

"This camp was top on our list for where they could have taken Taylor. The timing of their escape coinciding with the attack on our country makes me believe they had enough of a diversion to make a break for it. But it's all conjecture."

"George," the president turned to the CIA director, "what else could it be if not our people?"

"A training exercise, perhaps a trap to get us to invade Syrian airspace in a rescue attempt."

"Opinions?" the president asked the group assembled. Jack listened in as the military and civilian leaders of his country discussed their take on events. At the end of the discussion, it was up to the president to make the call.

"Jack, you still there?" the president asked.

"Yes, sir."

"How sure are you that we're seeing Mark Taylor on this satellite feed?"

Jack didn't hesitate. "One hundred percent, sir."

"Any chance Sa'id is in the same location?"

"I think it's a strong possibility. . .we're tracking every vehicle that leaves that area."

"That's good enough for me," the president responded, turning to his secretary of defense. "Get a rescue operation in there now, and I want attack aircraft in the air as well. I want to be ready to strike as soon as we confirm that those guys are ours."

"Yes, sir."

NORTHERN SYRIA
SAME TIME

Ahmad Sa'id sat in the black Humvee, irritated that he wasn't already on the move. Where was his computer? He had never left any location in his years of hiding without having that computer with him at all times. Finally Mustafa came running up to his side of the vehicle.

"It's not there, Caliph," Mustafa panted.

"What do you mean, it's not there? I left it on top of my desk."

"I looked there," Mustafa answered. "It's missing. They must have taken it."

"On your life. . ." Sa'id pointed at him. "Do not let them escape with that computer."

"It will be as you say; Allah is great!" Mustafa bowed.

"Go!" Sa'id ordered, and the vehicle sped out of the compound.

CIA HEADQUARTERS, LANGLEY, VIRGINIA
SAME TIME

Wendy kept her eyes glued to the image being beamed from halfway around the world. The two escaping figures had separated and stopped. She wasn't sure what they were doing. One of the pursuing vehicles was heading directly for them.

Then her eyes noticed movement lower in the screen, back near the buildings of the training camp. Two vehicles were on the move, heading south. She picked up the phone to alert the NRO.

NORTHERN SYRIA
SAME TIME

Mark sat perfectly still behind the outcroppings of rock, listening for the approaching vehicle. He didn't want to stick his head up in case they had night vision goggles or some type of thermal detection. This had to be a surprise or they were dead.

The noise increased, the engine straining to climb the hill. Mark could see the searchlight's beam hit rocks to his right. It sounded like they would drive past him on his left. Perfect, right between his and Chuck's positions.

A moment later, the Toyota pickup passed by, the terrorists yelling in Arabic at each other. Two were in the back, one flashing the spotlight around the desert, the other manning the submachine gun mounted above the front cab. The truck bounced as it progressed over the rocky terrain. Mark moved the AK-47 up to his shoulder, counting in his head, waiting for just the right moment.

His finger squeezed the trigger, sending a long burst of fire into the back of the pickup. He aimed for the one holding the spotlight first, then went for the gunman. At nearly the same instant, fire from Chuck's position on the other side of the truck slammed into the front cab.

The driver slumped over the wheel, the truck going out of control and smashing into a large rock. The terrorists in back were thrown out of the pickup bed. Mark immediately ran up to them with his AK-47 ready. They didn't move.

Chuck was checking the driver at the same time. "This one's dead. How about you?"

Mark cautiously kept his gun trained on the man nearest him as he prodded him with his boot—nothing. The blood-soaked fatigues let Mark know his bullets had hit the mark, and with the realization came an overwhelming sense of sorrow. Having to kill had affected him during the Gulf War. But he was a soldier then, trained to kill. Now he was a newsman, caught in events over which he had no control. What a waste! Not just for American lives through the terrorists' attacks, but for these young men as well, for people like Abu. Mark wanted to take the time to analyze his feelings, but he couldn't afford to—the other one was moving.

"I've got one alive," Mark called out.

Chuck walked quickly over to the man as Mark kept him dead in his sights. Chuck made sure he didn't have any weapons, then turned him over on his back. The terrorist looked up at Chuck and started screaming in Arabic. Chuck's fist came flying down an instant later, crashing against his chin and knocking him out.

Chuck swore, rubbing at his hand. "How come that didn't hurt when we were marines?"

"It probably did." Mark walked up next to him. "We were just too young to realize it. You think this thing will still drive?"

"No. . .I think we're still on foot."

"Great," Mark said. That hadn't been part of the plan. "It probably won't take them long to realize the other group is out of commission, and they'll know just where to look for us."

"You're right. We need some more ammo. Let's grab whatever's useful and keep moving."

TURKISH MILITARY BASE
SAME TIME

"What's going on?" Ross asked as Jack came out of the building.

Jack paused and smiled. "We're going after Mark."

"You know where he is?"

"We think so. Come on, follow me," Jack said, walking toward the command center the marines had set up. "You've earned this."

Ross followed Jack right into the communications center of the marine operations at the Turkish base.

"Major Smith," Jack said, walking up to the commander.

"Jack." The major smiled. "Looks like you're getting your wish."

"Your orders come in?"

"Just now, but thanks to you, the team was loaded and ready. The chopper's already airborne." Smith glanced over at Ross. "Should he be in here?"

"I think he's earned it," Jack said softly. "But it's up to you."

Major Smith smiled. "Welcome to the command center, Mr. Berman."

"I'm honored, sir," Ross returned honestly. His whole idea of the military had flipped 180 degrees since he'd left Los Angeles.

"All right, people," Major Smith announced. "We've got two ex-marines out there. . .and we always bring our own home. Let's do this one right!"

NORTHERN SYRIA
SAME TIME

Mark thought it would be best to once again change direction since the gunshots had given their location away. So they headed north-west again, keeping an eye out for any sign of the other truck. It didn't take long for Mark to spot it, heading right for them, and another one was coming from the compound.

"We've got company again," Mark said.

"I see them," Chuck responded. "I don't think we can take on two of them. We were lucky the first time."

"I agree." Mark looked around. "But do you see a place to hide?"

Chuck looked over the desert. They were stuck in a flat area; the main hill where they could hide easily was too far away. The vehicles would be on them before they were halfway there.

"This could be a problem." Chuck sighed.

"Maybe they think we'd be crazy to try and hide out in the flat-land and go looking elsewhere."

"We *are* crazy to hide here." Chuck laughed. "We need to figure out how to get help."

Mark looked up into the clear Syrian night. He shivered, realizing how cold he was.

"We need to find the shiniest object we can get our hands on. When the sun comes up, we'll try and get the attention of the satellites that I'm sure are pointed down right at us."

"That's your plan for getting help?"

"You got a better idea?"

"No," Chuck admitted. "Which means we have to survive the night."

"Time to dig in, at least until these goons find somewhere else to look," Mark said, setting his gun down and pulling off the computer bag. Thankful that he'd grabbed a knife off one of the terrorists at their last stop, Mark started working the dirt, grateful to avoid more killing. He glanced up at the approaching vehicles. "We should be all right as long as they don't have thermal capabilities."

TURKISH MILITARY BASE
SAME TIME

"What's the update, Wendy?" Jack asked when he got patched through to Langley on a secure line.

"Two vehicles have left the compound, heading south. Looks like a pickup and a Humvee. If Sa'id was at that camp, I'd bet everything I have he's in the Humvee."

"You're probably right," Jack said.

"Faxon's tracking them. He'll have updated coordinates sent your way every thirty seconds."

"Good. What about the ones on the run?"

"They're holding their own. Looks like they ambushed one of the trucks chasing them. Left three bodies, two cooling off, one still alive but not moving." Wendy referred to the thermal image of a body after it died. Without the blood flow, the extremities cooled off quickly so that the image of hands and feet dropped off the display first. The rest of the reddish blob continued to shrink as the body cooled until it disappeared.

"I guess Taylor knew what he was doing asking for Chuck Fleming, huh?"

"Seems like it."

"What's their situation now?"

"Dangerous," Wendy answered. "They've stopped again, with two units approaching them. It looks like they're going to try another ambush."

She kept her eyes glued to the middle screen. The vehicles were nearly upon Mark's position, but instead of Mark and Chuck's bodies being separated, they seemed to be lying right together, not moving.

"How far away is the Force Recon team, Jack?"

"A few minutes still."

"They're not going to make it," Wendy muttered.

CHAPTER 37

Mark had left a pocket of breathing space just around his mouth as his head lay to the side; otherwise, he was completely covered in the Syrian sand. He remained as motionless as possible, attempting to take in shallow breaths even though his heart pounded in his chest. The trucks were right on them. He could hear one off to his left; the other one he couldn't pinpoint. He hoped they were covered enough to be missed in the darkness.

A worship song came to mind, the melody helping him to remember the words from 2 Corinthians, chapter 4: *"We are hard pressed on every side, but not crushed; perplexed, but not in despair; persecuted, but not abandoned; struck down, but not destroyed."* The song and verses relaxed him and helped to keep his body totally still. The truck to his left was close, just a few feet from him. He could hear the other one now to his right. *Keep driving,* he prayed.

The song continued in his mind. *"Though the sorrow may last for a night, His joy comes with the morning."*

TURKEY MILITARY BASE
SAME TIME

"They're on station, ready to engage. What's the situation there, Wendy?"

"Not yet!" Wendy cried into the phone to Jack. "The terrorists are right on top of Mark's position. Tell them to hold off!"

"Stop them, Major!" Jack yelled to Smith.

Smith gave the order, then looked back at Jack.

"The terrorists are right on top of them," Jack explained. "Hold the Apache back for a second. If they attack now, they'll kill our men."

"Wendy?" Jack asked, wishing desperately they could see the same satellite feed.

"I can't explain it, Jack; there's no ambush this time. The two bodies haven't moved, and the vehicles passed by within feet of their position."

"They dug in," Jack muttered, shaking his head in admiration for the two former marines. "Let me know when the trucks are a safe distance away."

Minutes later, Jack got the word from Wendy. Major Smith gave the order.

NORTHERN SYRIA
SAME TIME

The vehicles never stopped but continued right past the two ex-marines. The noise from the engines began to fade, but still Mark didn't move. He wanted to make sure there was no chance that they'd accidentally be seen. Chuck did the same.

Then another noise could be heard, an unmistakable sound as the ground vibrated and an Apache helicopter flew directly overhead. Mark raised himself out of the dirt, following the sound, but he wasn't able to see the black helicopter until the bright flashes of the hellfire missile launches came from the pods on the side of the chopper. An instant later, the two vehicles exploded 150 yards in front of Mark's position. Chuck sprang up with laughter. "I would know that sound anywhere."

Putting on the finishing touches from the air, the Marine AH-64 Apache helicopter sprayed hundreds of rounds from the 30mm M230 automatic cannon into the flaming wreckage.

Mark gathered his stuff, picking up the computer bag and his borrowed AK-47, and headed off toward the flames.

"Let's go home, Chuck."

CIA HEADQUARTERS, LANGLEY, VIRGINIA
SAME TIME

Wendy watched it all happen in real-time through the green haze of thermal photography. The vehicles passed the two green images only to suddenly burst into balls of flame minutes later. Then the two images moved again, heading toward the wreckage.

A shout went up from her group as they cheered the marine operation. All that was left was to confirm whom they'd saved.

SOUTHERN TURKEY
SAME TIME

Jack waited anxiously, listening for the radio callback from First Base, the call sign of the UH-60 Blackhawk that had flown in with the Apache. The chopper was on the ground collecting the two men. Major Smith had asked for name confirmation as soon as possible from the marine pilot. The entire communication room was deathly silent.

"Home Base, this is First Base. Dumbo is confirmed. Repeat, Dumbo is confirmed and on board along with Circus Mouse!"

Major Smith had handpicked the code words for his base and the Force Recon Marine Unit. Being a baseball fan, he thought it would be ironic to use the code words surrounding his favorite game and America's favorite pastime, a kind of a slap in the face to the terrorists who wanted to destroy their way of life.

"Roger, First Base," Major Smith returned over the cheers in the room. "Can you confirm the Ringmaster?"

"Hold on, Home Base. . . ."

Jack waited breathlessly for the pilot to ask Mark if Sa'id had been at the camp.

"Home Base. . ." The radio cracked back to life. "This is First Base; we have confirmation. . .Ringmaster is still in the stadium, repeat, Ringmaster is still in the stadium."

"Copy that, First Base. Bring the team home. Godspeed."

"Roger, Home Base. First Base out."

Jack blew out a breath of air toward the ceiling. They'd done it. Mark was on his way home. Now only one piece of the mission remained.

The vibrations from the chopper made Mark wince in pain from the broken ribs. He started to take stock of his injuries, then decided it wouldn't be worth it. Instead he looked at the young faces around him. It was hard to imagine he had been that young during Desert Storm.

"There's going to be an attack in America," Mark shouted over the noise of the chopper's engines. "Bombing churches—we've got to alert. . ."

A young sergeant interrupted him. "It's already over. We heard just before we took off. The FBI stopped nearly all of them."

Mark smiled, thanking God that the attempt had failed. If only they'd been able to take Sa'id out.

He turned and looked out over the desert surrounded by the darkness of the Syrian night. He wondered if they could have survived until morning. Thankfully, he didn't have to find out.

One of the men handed Mark his canteen. He thanked him and

took a few small sips, then poured some on the top of his head. He flinched as the water trickled down over the open cuts. He took another swig, his body beginning to relax. He thought of Tracy, of what it would be like when they were reunited. The joy flooded over him, but it was short-lived as his mind settled on the image of Abu, lying on the dirt floor, his lifeless eyes staring at him. What a tragic waste. With Abu's kind heart and desire to please God, he could have done great things for the Kingdom instead of wasting his life on the path of Islam.

Mark relived the ride twelve years ago when Abu rode the chopper out of Iraq with him. His heart longed for that ride to be repeated, rather than leaving his friend behind in the desert.

NORTHERN SYRIA
7:08 P.M.

Stork One and Stork Two, the F-117 stealth fighters, flew in standard formation as they entered Syrian air space. The two had originated at Incirlik NATO airbase in central Turkey. They had taken off soon after the choppers from Diyarbakir had entered Syria, staying in Turkish air space until their mission was approved moments ago.

Flying low across the desert, the Syrian air-defense radar didn't even blip when the black aircraft shot across the border. Coming up on the city of Tall Hamis, the two fighters separated. Captain Bryan Richardson flew toward the terrorist camp; Captain Jerome Jackson followed a vector given to him through his onboard computer toward Sa'id's vehicles heading south.

Minutes later, Captain Jackson smiled as he heard the report from Richardson of mission accomplished. He had seen the explosions off to the side of his aircraft, content in the knowledge that the camp that had once trained terrorists was now an inferno. Then through the clear, dark night, he spotted the headlights of his target—two vehicles traveling along the Syrian highway. He made sure everything was in attack mode and that his special GBU-12, five-hundred-pound laser-guided bomb was armed and ready, the one on which he'd written the name of his cousin, Willie Jackson. Willie had been a great Dallas Cowboys fan. His life had been extinguished in Texas Stadium the day of the Sunday Massacre.

Jackson's attack run lined up with the country road as he brought his visual targeting crosshairs to superimpose directly on the lead vehicle, what looked to him like a Humvee. He didn't know who was in the vehicle, but he had his suspicions, and his hopes. He made sure his microphone wasn't keyed on as he gave the terrorists his final wishes.

Sa'id stared at the road stretched out in front of him, cursing the Americans. With the successes in recent years of his other terrorist activities, failure was inconceivable to him. His stature in the Arab world could be greatly diminished after today. But he would rise again. It was the will of Allah.

His men had to find Taylor; he wanted positive proof of his death—tonight. He also wanted that computer back. His mind replayed the blasphemous statements Taylor had made. It was unimaginable that the infidel had the guts to speak that way directly to his face. He would die. Perhaps his men had already taken care of that.

Sa'id relaxed in the passenger seat, grinning at the image of Taylor's lifeless body shot full of holes, his men standing over him as the American's blood spread over the Arabian desert. Sa'id remembered the last words he'd said to Taylor with a wicked smile: "We'll see who is the one true God."

It was the caliph's last earthly thought.

Captain Jackson kept his eyes on the target until his payload met the earth. The laser-guided bomb hit the Humvee directly at the center of the vehicle, the warhead exploding on target and sending up a huge fireball that totally consumed it and the second vehicle following closely behind. The pilot broke into a smile as he pulled back on the stick, bringing the plane up to cruising altitude, then circling back to catch up with his wingman.

There was one more target to hit, near the Turkish border, strangely illuminated by a GPS electronic signal that he'd never seen before.

TURKISH MILITARY BASE
7:35 P.M.

The Blackhawk landed gently; the Apache touched down seconds later a hundred feet away. Mark looked out, never more thankful to see the men and equipment of the U.S. Marine Corps. He stepped out of the chopper, then helped Chuck do the same. The adrenaline that had driven his body beyond what seemed humanly possible had subsided, now leaving him exhausted and every muscle and bone in his body in agony.

Standing in front of them were Major Smith and Jack Murphy. Mark paused, stood at attention, and saluted the major. Chuck followed suit.

"Welcome home." Major Smith returned the salute happily.

"Thank you, sir," they snapped back in marine fashion.

"We appreciate the ride, Major. Thanks for pulling us out of there," Mark added.

"*Semper fi,*" Smith replied with a smile, quoting the Marine Corps slogan: *Semper Fidelis,* always faithful. "We never leave our own behind."

Mark grinned, ignoring the pain from his mouth, then turned to the CIA officer. "Jack, I've got something for you."

Mark took the bag off his shoulder and handed it to him. "Sa'id's computer. I'm hoping your spooks will be able to break whatever codes he has and get the names and addresses of every member of the Jihad al Sharia cells in America."

Jack reached for the bag, shaking his head and smiling. "You have never ceased to amaze me on this whole venture, Taylor. If you ever want to come to work for us, I could find an opening. You too, Fleming. I think the best idea of this whole operation was bringing you along."

Mark lowered his head. "I'm sorry about Vince. He seemed like a good man."

Jack raised his eyebrows. "He still is. He's going to be fine."

"What do you mean?" Mark's hopes jumped. "We were told he was killed, along with. . ."

"Not me, I hope!" Ross interrupted, stepping up to the group.

"Ross!" Mark exclaimed, reaching forward and embracing his young producer. "You're alive! I can't believe it."

"Believe it." Ross hugged him. "With no thanks to you." He stepped away, grimacing. "Man, you stink!"

Mark laughed, relieved beyond words that the terrorists had lied.

"I told you not to believe anything they said." Chuck smiled.

"How did you guys get free?" Mark asked, but before Ross could respond, he said, "Wait, don't tell me. I want to hear everything, but first. . ." He turned back to Jack. "I want a phone to the States. There's somebody I need to talk with."

Jack nodded. "Understood, but there is probably one more piece of information you'll want to hear."

"I'm listening."

"We got Sa'id." Jack grinned. "Two stealth fighters attacked the compound and two vehicles trying to get away as soon as we picked you up and confirmed that Sa'id had been there."

So it was over. Mark's reaction came as a shock; it wasn't joy over the wonderful taste of revenge, but sadness at the wasted lives, especially the life of one named Abu.

"That's great, Jack," Mark said. "I guess it's really over."

"Yeah, thanks to you."

"Can we get to that phone now?" Mark asked, stepping toward the building, putting his arm around Ross. "Then I want to hear your story, Ross. Every detail."

NORTHRIDGE, CALIFORNIA
9:41 A.M.

Tracy sat in Brenda's living room, glued to the television set, watching the reports from all the cable news channels as they switched from station to station covering the attempted attacks on churches in the five major cities. The reporters didn't quite know how to cover the story. All the up-close-and-personal interviews of those who had survived kept praising their "Lord and Savior Jesus Christ." A conflict for the news directors, but at times like these their personal objections were put aside.

Her cell phone rang. She barely heard it chirping from inside her purse lying near the front door. She ran to it, hoping that maybe the CIA had something to report. She reached it on the third ring, nervously fumbling with it and trying to punch "on" before her voice mail kicked in. She was terrified.

"Hello," she said, slightly out of breath.

"Tracy." It was the voice she feared she would never hear again.

"Mark!" she squealed, bringing Brenda and Tom up off their seats in the living room and Shandy running in from the kitchen barking.

"It's so good to hear your voice," Mark said.

"Thank You, Lord! It's Mark," Tracy yelled to her friends, then spoke back into the phone. "I can't believe it. Is it really you?"

"It's me. I'm all right." Then he remembered his cuts and

bruises. "Well, mostly all right. I'm safe."

"He's okay!" Tracy shouted to her friends as she ran back into the family room. "Where are you?"

"I'm in Turkey. We were just pulled out of Syria a few minutes ago," Mark said, then paused. "Look, I'll give you all the details as soon as I can. Right now I just wanted you to know that I'm okay and that I love you very, very much."

"Oh, Mark. . ." Tracy laughed while at the same time the tears flowed. "I love you too, so much."

"And, Tracy. . . ," Mark added, "I can't wait to feel our baby kick, to hear his heartbeat."

"Mark. . ." Tracy gasped, nearly speechless. "How did you know?"

"I heard the message from your doctor's office Friday night. They want to schedule the ultrasound. I tried to call but never got through to you after that." He paused. "Um, you are pregnant, right?"

"Yes." Mark could sense the smile from thousands of miles away. "We're having a baby."

"I'm so excited. You're going to be a great mother."

"And you a great father."

"That's what you wanted to tell me Wednesday night, wasn't it?"

"Yeah, but things kind of went another direction." Tracy smiled, thinking this moment couldn't be any more perfect.

"I know, and I'm sorry. Light the candles again, honey. I'm on my way home."

TURKEY MILITARY BASE
9:00 P.M.

After having the most refreshing shower of his life and spending nearly an hour being checked over and wrapped up by the navy corpsman, Mark sat in a conference room with Jack Murphy and

Ross Berman. Mark dug into a spaghetti dinner from the mess hall that tasted better than any five-star meal he had ever eaten. It was funny how the simple things in life sparkled since he'd touched death.

"By the way, Mark, I think you hit a gold mine with Sa'id's computer." Jack grinned at him. "We're taking it back to Langley for complete analysis, but from preliminary inspection, we could have the information we've been looking for on cells throughout the world. I think Sa'id never expected us to be able to get our hands on it."

Mark sighed. Next to speaking with Tracy, that was the best news of the day.

"Now concerning your report back to New York tonight, it's a tricky situation, for all of us," Jack continued. "We need some assurances before we beam your story out of here."

"I figured that," Mark said. He turned to Ross. "How much time do we have to prepare, Ross?"

"Five hours. Russell is dying to talk with you."

"I bet. Did the tape I brought out play back okay?"

Ross nodded. "We're ready to uplink it to Los Angeles." Then he looked over at Jack. "Once it's cleared, that is."

"Great." Mark nodded, then looked over at Jack. "Now what can we report?"

"First thing," Jack said evenly, "Vince is off-limits, his being CIA, his infiltration into your team, his injury. As far as you two know, he was just a freelance cameraman that Mclintock hired."

"That's the truth as I knew it." Ross smiled.

"What else?"

"Well, when it comes to Chuck, that's your call, Mark. He was your idea."

Mark nodded. "I understand, but I want to be truthful with Frank Russell about all this. I trust him to keep our confidence. He deserves the truth."

Jack paused a second. "Only if he'll sign a nondisclosure agreement." Mark accepted that.

"Now about Sa'id. It's been decided from the highest sources that you deserve the right to tell the world he's dead, and here's how we would like you to do it. . . ."

NATIONAL STUDIOS, HOLLYWOOD, CALIFORNIA
11:43 A.M.

"Mark, you're okay? It is so good to hear your voice." Russell's relief was evident even through the satellite connection.

"Yeah, it's good to hear yours as well." Mark laughed. "I'll bet you thought I wasn't going to make my deadline tonight, huh?"

"I'll admit you had me worried," Russell returned. "So why am I sitting here with an agent from the FBI talking to you on his satellite phone?"

"Because we had to speak on a secure connection. Some of what I'm about to tell you is classified, restricted for national security reasons. You have to sign a form he'll provide before I can brief you."

Russell looked at the piece of paper placed in front of him by Mike Weston. "Yeah, it's right here."

"Sign it, Frank, then we can talk."

Russell glanced over it quickly. "This had better be good, Taylor." He scribbled his signature. "Done. Now speak to me."

"First of all, Sa'id is dead."

"He's what?" Russell shouted into the phone. Reports had been all over the news about unconfirmed military activity in northern Syria, but no details. A lot of military experts on the cable news channels were guessing at what it could be, but there hadn't even been a hint that Sa'id could have been taken out.

Mark had to repeat what he'd said before the discussion could continue. Russell listened intently as Mark explained everything, vacillating between outright rage at his young reporter for disobeying direct orders to greatly respecting him for putting his life on the line.

"You're making a habit of not following orders, Taylor," Russell said when Mark had finished speaking. "As your boss, I don't like it at all. But I have to say it does remind me a lot of what I was like at your age."

"It all happened so quickly, Frank," Mark explained. "And I knew how you felt about it. I went with my gut."

"And it nearly got you killed," Russell argued.

"True." Mark paused. "But I did what I thought was right."

"I know you did." Russell softened. "I have an idea about your friend who claimed to be Chad Moreland."

"What is it?"

"Tell the truth, or at least most of it. That you decided it would be wise to bring somebody along with you who could be useful in a dangerous situation. Use the State Department as a cover, that you enlisted their help in getting documentation. They're associated with the CIA, aren't they?"

Mark laughed. Russell was coming around. "Yeah, I guess you could say that."

"That way I think I can cover you professionally."

"I think I see what you're saying. Ross said if it ever gets out that I cooperated with the CIA, my career would be over. I'm not so sure that still isn't true."

"Hardly. You're too valuable to me and to this show. Just do it my way, and we'll put this episode behind us. Maybe someday you'll learn how to follow my instructions and save yourself a lot of trouble. Now let's talk about the show tonight. . . ."

CHAPTER 38

Tracy sat next to Frank Russell in the control room of *Across the Nation* with just one minute before they went on the air. Frank grabbed the goosenecked microphone on the IFB panel in front of him and pointed it toward Tracy.

"Say hi to Mark," Frank said, pushing the button that would send Tracy's voice out from the studio, beamed up through a satellite and back to the earth, then through an earpiece to Mark as he stood in front of a camera in Diyarbakir, Turkey.

She looked at Frank wide-eyed at first; then she grinned and spoke softly into the microphone. "I miss you, honey."

"Tracy." Mark's response came a second later through a small speaker in front of her as the shot of him showed a huge smile. "It's great to hear your voice. What are you doing there?"

"Getting a look at the man I love," Tracy said seductively.

"Oh, that's all I need to hear before hitting the air. How do I look?"

Tracy looked intently at the monitor. He'd lost a lot of weight in the past three days; his face looked sunken in, and the swelling and bruises were still visible even through the television makeup. She focused on his eyes, taking her mind off the injuries. "You look great. A lot better than that picture that went all over the world."

Mark laughed. "I hope so. Did you get my message?" He brought his hand up in front of the camera with the same gesture from the picture—thumb, forefinger, and pinkie held out straight with the other fingers bent in toward his palm.

Tracy smiled. "Yeah. . .you don't know what it meant to me to see that."

"That's what I'd hoped."

"I love you, Mark. I'm praying for you," Tracy said.

"Thanks." Mark grinned. "Love you too."

"We're live. . .in ten, nine, eight. . ." the associate director called out in the control room.

Seconds later, the program monitor filled with the opening videotape of *Across the Nation*. Then the studio was live with Tad Forrest hitting the air introducing the momentous broadcast.

"Striking news coming out of the Middle East tonight. We have an exclusive with our own Mark Taylor, who made a daring escape from the Jihad al Sharia hours ago." Forrest kept a somber tone with a hint of a smile as he began the show. "Good evening. I'm Tad Forrest. Tonight we bring you live, from Diyarbakir, Turkey, Mark Taylor on assignment. Mark, the world is thrilled that you are free and alive."

"Thanks, Tad. Believe me, it's great to be joining you from the marine base here in Turkey. It's been an incredible weekend."

"There are more than a few people who are anxious to see you back here, believe me."

"None more than me." Mark smiled warmly. "It's been quite an eventful trip to this land full of history, and for the next hour you're going to see some incredible video from within the terrorists' camps, taped here in Turkey and in Syria, as well as in-depth reports on the latest attack across our nation this morning. We wish to warn our viewers that some of the images will be disturbing, and we advise parental caution in having your young children in the room with you for the next hour."

Mark paused, knowing the impact the first tape playback would have on the nation. He prayed that those watching, like

Hashim Basayav back at the local station in Los Angeles and those of similar political and religious leanings, would see the true evil behind Sa'id, that their lives would be opened to the truth as his broadcast progressed. "We begin tonight with a startling confession. . .not mine, but one from Ahmad Hani Sa'id.

"When presented with this assignment, I had reservations about being the vehicle to allow the terrorists' propaganda to hit our nation's airwaves, but I took the job in hopes of getting Sa'id's admission to the attacks upon our country. I had no idea the path I would have to take to get that confession, but tonight we bring you the leader of the Jihad al Sharia. . . ."

The picture switched to the videotape recorded when Sa'id had questioned Mark. The shot was taken from over Sa'id's shoulder as a beat-up, bleeding Mark Taylor sat listlessly before him. Inside the control room in L.A., Tracy flinched. Seeing how Mark had suffered was difficult to watch. She wasn't alone in that reaction as the rest of the nation watched with her.

"I told you," Mark gasped on the tape. "I'm just a reporter."

"How long are we going to do this, Mark?" Sa'id's voice could be heard off camera.

"I'm willing to stop right now."

"Then in the name of Allah, the merciful, confess!"

"Merciful?" Mark said through clenched teeth. "Is this your idea of mercy? Was 9/11 and the Sunday Massacre in our country acts of Allah's compassion?"

The video showed Sa'id springing up from his chair, blocking the camera for a split second before he lashed out at Mark, knocking him off his metal chair. Then Sa'id reared back and kicked Mark in the stomach, cursing at him in Arabic.

"Do not speak the name of Allah; you are not worthy."

Across the country, Americans were glued to their television sets as they saw Mark struggle to get back on his knees. Sa'id stood beside him in full view of the camera, ranting over Mark. "The attacks upon America have been anointed by Allah! He has given me the power. . .I ordered the buses into your precious stadiums. It was at my hand your embassies exploded. Because Allah the mighty has chosen me!"

Mark looked up directly into the enraged face of Sa'id, the camera capturing perfectly the intensity of the moment. "You speak as if you know the heart of your god, but you know only your own hatred."

The video showed the anger flaring in Sa'id's eyes as well as Mark's resolve, the passion rising in his voice. "You say there is one god, and about that you are right, but it's not the one you serve. Allah is no more alive than the idols Muhammad threw out of the *Ka'bah!*"

"Shut up!" Sa'id screamed, pulling a pistol out from underneath his robe and pointing it directly between Mark's eyes.

Tracy jumped in the control room in Los Angeles, placing her hand over her mouth, holding back her scream. At the same time, millions of people throughout the nation were glued to their television sets, watching Sa'id shake with rage, his voice trembling. "I have the power of life and death over you, Taylor! Your blasphemy will send you to hell!"

The image dissolved, fading back to the live shot of Mark from Turkey. "The Sa'id you just witnessed is quite different from the man I first met when we began the interview. We'll show you exclusive video from that first session, as well as how I got out of the situation you just saw, later in the program.

"All of us here in Turkey and our producers back in Los Angeles thought it was important for you to hear what Sa'id said straight from his own mouth before we reported to you this next piece of incredible news. The State Department is confirming that the man you just saw, the one responsible for the deaths of over twelve thousand American civilians, Ahmad Hani Sa'id, is dead."

The image of Mark was replaced by grainy black-and-white

footage from the gun camera of the F-117, the crosshairs of the targeting system superimposed over a pair of vehicles traveling along a deserted highway at night.

"In this exclusive video supplied by the Department of Defense," Mark's voice commentated, "the lead vehicle carried Sa'id as he was leaving one of the Jihad al Sharia terrorists' camps in northern Syria last night. . . ."

WASHINGTON, D.C.
SAME TIME

Wendy sat in her sister-in-law's living room watching the live report out of Turkey, bouncing her youngest niece on her lap, making sure her face was directed away from the television set. Not very long after she had seen the satellite image of Sa'id's convoy being blown to bits by the F-117's laser-guided bomb, Wendy had left the CIA headquarters, deciding it was time to see her brother's family.

Watching the footage air on the screen from the viewpoint of the F-117 brought bittersweet cheers from her sister-in-law and Wendy's parents.

"That was really him?" Sandi asked Wendy.

"Yeah," Wendy confirmed, now that it was on Mark's television report. "It's over, Sandi."

Sandi blinked away the tears, holding her four-year-old son in her lap and taking a quick glance at her six-year-old daughter playing on the other side of the room. She turned back to Wendy. "No, I've still got to deal with it every day of my life, and these kids will never see their dad again."

"I know," Wendy said warmly. "But this chapter's over. I'm planning on being around a lot more to help you."

Sandi smiled. "We'd love that. The kids have really missed seeing you."

"And I've missed them." Wendy wrapped her arms around little eleven-month-old Jennifer. It was time to start living again. She hadn't realized how her obsession to get Sa'id had stolen from her what made life worth living in the first place.

DIYARBAKIR, TURKEY
FIFTY-THREE MINUTES LATER

The hour was nearly complete. Between the staff in Los Angeles and Mark and Ross in Turkey, it had been a masterful show, bringing the nation some closure on the terrorist tirade of Ahmad Hani Sa'id. Along with a complete history of one Ronald March, Sa'id's alias during the lost years, Mark's report included footage of his first interview with Sa'id, contrasted perfectly with Mark's subsequent interrogation in front of the camera. Sa'id's true evil was broadcast to the world.

The special report had been spellbinding. Millions across the nation hadn't budged from their television sets, calling up their friends as the broadcast progressed, creating the largest audience of any television program in the country's history. Mark had just one final piece to complete the hour.

"Islam and terrorism—they seemed to be intertwined in this modern-day, worldwide struggle. What is it about a religious belief that claims to be about peace, yet is the foundation for the fanatics and the fundamentalists of Islam to create such evil and terror? We plan to bring you a special in the coming weeks to try and answer that question, but I hope some of what you've seen tonight will shed some light on the issue.

"I want to end on a very personal note tonight, and to honor a dear friend of mine. Were it not for his love for me, his bravery, and his willingness to act from his heart, I would not be alive tonight. His name, Abu Zaqi Ressam. His history is very similar to Ahmad

Sa'id, raised in the same city in Saudi Arabia, followed the same reli-gion—Islam. As a matter of fact, he was Sa'id's nephew. But unlike his uncle, Abu was a man of peace. He was the young Arab that stepped into the frame and pulled the arm of Sa'id to the floor before the gun went off. He also came to me later and allowed my escape. He saved my life last night and sacrificed his in doing so."

Mark fought the emotions welling up within him. Willing him-self not to let the tears show, he continued. "He touched my life greatly, and I pray that my life touched his as well.

"His death signifies something very important. He taught me that I can't judge all Muslims by his uncle. And I think I can say that my friendship with Abu taught him that all Americans cannot be judged through the eyes of Ahmad Hani Sa'id. I'm a journalist, not a politician or a theologian, but I think there is a lesson here we all need to learn.

"Reporting from Diyarbakir, Turkey, this is Mark Taylor. Good night."

EPILOGUE

The lone figure prostrated himself on his prayer mat in the middle of what had been the Jihad al Sharia training camp. Something felt right about returning to pay homage for the lives lost here. His prayers were fervent, obsessed with seeking revenge on the infidels who had taken his leader away from him.

Mustafa rose up slowly, his eyes taking in the destruction of the camp in the predawn light. After sending Sa'id away, Mustafa had headed into the desert in search of Mark and the computer. He saw the Apache helicopter and the evil might of the Americans as they murdered his fellow Muslims with their cowardly missiles. He'd watched in rage as the two spies had climbed aboard and flown out of his grasp. Then, within minutes, before he could return to the camp, he saw the total devastation that struck as the bombs leveled the facility in a ball of flames.

The hatred burned within him.

The Americans must pay.

The jihad would continue. . .he would see to it.

It is the will of Allah!

ACKNOWLEDGMENTS

With any book, there are many people behind the scenes who help make the final words come to life. This novel was no exception, and I want to gratefully acknowledge those who shared their life experiences with me to make this story as accurate as possible.

First I wish to thank my wife, Cindy, who is not only my partner in life but has become my collaborator as well. Your valuable insights and ideas were incredible.

To Dan Lovil, who labored through the first draft of this manuscript. Your suggestions were priceless and once again helped me stay on track.

To Frank Augustus, Information Systems Security Representative CIA, now working as Network Security Specialist with First American Corporation. He provided invaluable technical assistance on our nation's security agencies.

And to my new friend within the FBI who asked to remain nameless but gave me great insights into how our country is dealing internally with the threat of terrorism.

Also thanks to Sergeant Kevin Finch of the Los Angeles County Sheriff's Department.

To Melanie Morgan, KSFO Radio talk show host and former ABC News reporter who worked in the Middle East and offered incredible insight into the mind of a journalist—and was kind enough to endorse my book. Thanks also to Angela Hunt and Scott O'Grady for their kind endorsements of this book.

To some very dedicated men in the armed services who gave valuable technical assistance, Lieutenant Commander Kolin Campbell, USN/COMUSNAVCENT–BAHRAIN, Captain Damian Spooner, USMC/COMUSNAVCENT–BAHRAIN, Timothy G. Miller, USMC 1978–1982, 2nd Marine Air Wing, and Dale Steele now with Northrop Grumman in building surveillance aircraft but who, while in the Air Force, served aboard *Air Force One*.

To my new friends, Terry and Mojgon Frazier, who welcomed my wife and me into their home and gave us a crash course in Middle Eastern culture and Islamic beliefs.

To Dr. Craig Johnson, pastor of Bethel Christian Fellowship, Agoura Hills, California, for his insightful knowledge on Islam.

To Cheryl Bock, Director of Intensive Care Nursery, Swedish Hospital, Englewood, Colorado, and my sister-in-law—the best labor and delivery nurse I've ever seen.

To Mike Nappa, my wonderful editor, Jody Brolsma, my editorial consultant, and the great people at Promise Press Fiction. Working with them has been a pleasure.

To Vondia Carusso for her faithful prayers and wonderful words of encouragement, as well as Wade Merganthol for his great help.

And finally, I want to thank my family, my wife and two precious daughters, Sharayah and Shelby, for their love and support and for putting up with the many hours that I was on the computer. I love you all—forever and always.

If you want to dig deeper into the beliefs of Islam and the dangers facing the world from Islamic terrorists, I would highly recommend the following books:

Mark A. Gabriel, Ph.D., *Islam and Terrorism* (Lake Mary, Florida: Charisma House, 2002)

Don McCurry, *Healing the Broken Family of Abraham* (Colorado Springs: Ministries to Muslims, 2001)

Phil Parshall, *New Paths in Muslim Evangelism* (Grand Rapids, Michigan, Baker Book House, 1980)

Peter L. Bergen, *Holy War, Inc.* (New York: The Free Press, A Division of Simon & Schuster, Inc., 2001)

Steven Emerson, *American Jihad* (New York: The Free Press, A Division of Simon & Schuster, Inc., 2001)

 CLAY JACOBSEN is author of the popular Christian suspense novels *Circle of Seven* and *The Lasko Interview*. A twenty-year veteran of the television industry, he's served as director for high-profile shows like *Entertainment Tonight* and The Jerry Lewis MDA Telethon. An expert on media and world affairs, he makes his home in California where he is active in the Hollywood community.

To contact Clay Jacobsen, you can e-mail him at: Clay@clayjacobsen.com.
You can also visit the author's web site at: www.clayjacobsen.com

Would you like to offer feedback on this novel?

Interested in starting a book discussion group?

Check out www.promisepress.com for
a *Reader Survey* and *Book Club Questions*.

ALSO FROM

PROMISE PRESS

An Imprint of Barbour Publishing

Summon the Shadows by Eva Marie Everson and
G. W. Francis Chadwick
ISBN 1-58660-490-2

When expensive gifts arrive at her office, Katie Webster, president and CEO of New York City's five-star hotel The Hamilton Place, believes her missing-and-presumed-dead husband has finally returned. Or perhaps her checkered past is catching up to her. . . .

Time Lottery by Nancy Moser
ISBN 1-58660-587-9

After twenty-two years of scientific research, three lucky individuals will receive the opportunity of a lifetime with The Time Lottery—to relive one decisive moment that could change the course of their lives.

Operation: Firebrand by Jefferson Scott
ISBN 1-58660-586-0

Former Navy SEAL Jason Kromer is appointed leader of Operation: Firebrand, a covert operations team specializing in non-lethal missions of mercy. Its first challenge: a winter rescue of orphaned children made homeless by Russian rebels.

Vancouver Mystery by Rosey Dow
and Andrew Snaden
ISBN 1-58660-589-5

Just days after Beth Martin's long-awaited facelift operation, Beth Martin is found dead—and her cosmetic surgeon, Dr. Dan Foster, finds himself playing amateur detective after being framed for the killing.

Available wherever books are sold.